GIVE ME BACK
MY LEGIONS!

ALSO BY HARRY TURTLEDOVE

Fort Pillow

GIVE ME BACK MY LEGIONS!

HARRY TURTLEDOVE

 ST. MARTIN'S GRIFFIN ⚍ NEW YORK

GIVE ME BACK MY LEGIONS! Copyright © 2009 by Harry Turtledove. All rights reserved. Printed in the United States of America. For information, address St. Martin's Press, 175 Fifth Avenue, New York, N.Y. 10010.

www.stmartins.com

The Library of Congress has catalogued the hardcover edition as follows:

Turtledove, Harry.
    Give me back my legions! / Harry Turtledove. — 1st ed.
        p. cm.
    ISBN 978-0-312-37106-7
    1. Arminius, Prince of the Cherusci—Fiction. 2. Varus, Publius Quintilius—Fiction. 3. Augustus, Emperor of Rome, 63 B.C.–14 A.D.—Fiction. 4. Roman provinces—Germany—Fiction. 5. Germany—History—To 843—Fiction. 6. Teutoburger Wald, Battle of, Germany, 9 A.D.—Fiction. I. Title.

    PS3570.U76G54 2009
    813'.54—dc22

                                                            2008035869

ISBN 978-0-312-60554-4 (trade paperback)

First St. Martin's Griffin Edition: April 2010

10 9 8 7 6 5 4 3 2 1

To Gwyn Morgan, Ron Mellor, and Hal Drake

GIVE ME BACK MY LEGIONS!

 I

Rome brawled around Publius Quinctilius Varus. Half a dozen stalwart *lectiarii* bore his sedan chair through the streets towards Augustus' house on the Palatine hill. The slaves wore matching red tunics. Their smooth, skillful broken step kept him from feeling the bumps in the cobblestoned roadway.

Varus could have lowered the sedan chair's curtains. That would have given him privacy in the midst of untold tens of thousands. But he didn't mind being seen, not today. Anyone could tell at a glance that he was someone important.

A wagon full of sacks of grain drawn by two plodding oxen blocked his path. The ungreased axles squealed and groaned. A man could die of old age stuck behind something like that.

His slaves weren't about to put up with it. One of the *pedisequi* who accompanied the litter—a Roman aristocrat was too special to carry whatever he might need, but had underlings to do it for him—called out in Greek-accented Latin: "Make way, there! Make way for the litter of Publius Quinctilius Varus!"

In narrow, winding streets packed with people on foot, donkeys, carts, and other wagons, making way for anybody wasn't easy. The gray-haired man driving the wagon didn't even try. "To the crows with him, whoever he is," he shouted back. *His* accent said he was a Samnite or Oscan by birth.

" 'Whoever he is'? How dare you, you—peasant, you!" The *pedise-quus* knew no worse abuse. He was as furious as if he'd been insulted himself. The master was the sun; the slave was the moon, and shone by his reflected light. Varus' man went on, "I will have you know he was consul twenty years ago. Consul, I tell you! He is just returned to Rome after governing the province of Syria. *And* he is married to Augustus' grand-niece. Gods help you, wretch, if he has to ask *your* name!"

The wagon driver lashed his oxen. He also flicked the lash at a couple of middle-aged women to make them get out of the way. They screeched abuse at him, but they moved. The wagon slid into the space they'd occupied. The litter and its retinue glided past.

"Nicely done, Aristocles," Varus said. The *pedisequus* thrust out his chin and thrust out his chest and marched along as if he were ten cubits tall and eight cubits wide, not a balding, weedy little Greek. Quinctilius Varus smiled to himself. As with anything else, there were tricks to getting the most out of your slaves. Judicious praise at the right moment could do more good than a denarius.

Aristocles did more shouting as the litter made its way toward the Palatine. Too many people and not enough room for all of them—that was Rome. Musicians strummed citharae or played flutes, hoping passersby would throw them enough coins to keep them fed. Scribes stood at street-corners, ready to write for people who lacked their letters. Hucksters shouted their wares: "Figs candied in honey!" "Beads! Fine glass beads from Egypt!" "Bread and cheese and oil!" "Kohl to make your eyes pretty!" "Roasted songbirds! Who wants roasted songbirds?" "Amulets will give you luck!" "Wine! Genuine Falernian!"

Varus guffawed. So did his bearers. The *pedisequi*, men who made much of their dignity, only shook their heads. No one but a fool would think a scrawny street merchant lugging an amphora had wine fit for Augustus himself. Whatever was in that jug would taste like vinegar—if it didn't taste like piss.

When the litter finally reached the Palatine hill, traffic thinned out. This had been a prosperous part of town for many years. Important people—proper Romans—lived here. You didn't see so many trousered Gauls and swarthy Jews and excitable Numidians on the Palatine. People from all over the Empire swarmed to Rome, hoping to strike it rich. No one had ever found a way to keep them out. *Too bad*, Varus thought.

And the Palatine became all the more exclusive when Augustus, master of the Roman world, took up residence on the hillside. He had dominated the Empire for more than a third of a century now. Senators still pined for the days of the Republic, when they were the biggest fish in the pond. Most people didn't remember those days any more. Most of the ones who did, remembered round after round of civil war. Hardly anyone—except those Senators—would have traded Augustus' peace and prosperity for the chaos it replaced.

Quinctilius Varus knew he wouldn't. He was part of the new order: one of the many who'd risen high by going along with the man who had—who'd won—the power to bind and to loose. He couldn't have done better under the Republic. *Rome* couldn't have done better under the Republic, but Rome mattered less to Varus than Varus did.

His father, Sextus Quinctilius Varus, had thought differently. He'd killed himself at Philippi along with Brutus and Cassius after they lost against Antony and Octavian—who was not yet calling himself Augustus. Almost fifty years ago now; Publius had been a boy. He was lucky the victors hadn't proscribed the losers' families. He nodded solemnly. He was lucky a lot of ways.

Soldiers guarded Augustus' residence. Augustus was no fool—he was about as far from a fool as a man could be. He knew some people still resented his mastery of Rome. Three cohorts of praetorian troops—about 1,500 men—were stationed in the city to protect him. Six more cohorts were based in nearby towns. The armored men in front of the doorway unmistakably separated his house from all the others on the Palatine.

Some of the guards were Italians. Others, tall and fair, had to be Gauls or Germans. In its way, it was a sensible arrangement. Rome as Rome meant nothing to the barbarians. Augustus, as their paymaster and commander, did.

"Who are you? What do you want here?" the biggest and blondest of them asked, his accent guttural, as Varus' litter came up.

Aristocles answered for Varus: "My master is Publius Quinctilius Varus, the ex-consul. He is to meet with Augustus this afternoon." He didn't throw his master's rank in the German's face, as he had with the wagon driver. The praetorian, after all, served a man with a higher rank yet—with the highest rank. But even someone summoned to meet with Augustus was a man of some consequence . . . and his *pedisequus*, therefore, a slave of some consequence.

"You wait here. We check," the guard said. He spoke in his own sonorous tongue. One of the other soldiers ducked inside.

"It will be all right, boys," Varus told the *lectiarii*. "You can put me down now."

Gently, the bearers lowered the sedan chair to the ground. Varus got out and stretched. Unlike his slaves, he wore a toga, not a tunic. He rearranged the drape of the garment. At the same time, not quite accidentally, he flashed the purple stripe that marked his status.

The soldier returned and said something in the Germans' language to the man in charge of the detachment. That worthy inclined his head to Varus. "You may go in now, sir," he said, respect ousting practiced suspicion from his voice.

"Good." Varus left it at that. He never knew how to talk to Augustus' guards. They weren't equals; by the nature of things, they couldn't be equals. But they weren't insignificant people, either. A puzzlement.

As soon as he and his two *pedisequi* went inside, one of Augustus' civilian slaves took charge of them. Varus was sure someone else would bring his bearers into the shade and give them something cool to drink. A great house—and there was none greater—took care of such things as a matter of course.

"I hope you are well, sir," Augustus' slave said politely.

"Yes, thank you." Varus enquired not about the slave's health but about his master's: "I hope Augustus is, too."

With a hint of a smile, the slave answered, "He says a man who gets as old as he is is either well or dead."

That held considerable truth, and truth told with Augustus' usual pith. The ruler of the Roman world was seventy, an age many aspired to and few reached. He'd had several serious illnesses in his earlier days, but recovered from them all. And he'd outlived the younger men he'd expected to succeed him.

Varus, in his early fifties, already felt the first hints that the proud strength of his youth would not last forever—and might not last much longer. And he'd enjoyed good health most of his life, the main exceptions being a couple of bad teeth that finally needed the dentist's forceps. He shuddered and tried to forget those times.

The slave led him and his attendants to a small room on the north side of a courtyard. A roofed colonnade shielded it from direct sun, but the broad doorway still let in plenty of light. The slave darted in ahead of Varus. His voice floated out through the doorway: "Sir, Quinctilius Varus is here to see you."

"Well, bring him in." Augustus' voice was mushy; over the years, he'd had more trouble with his teeth than Varus had.

At the slave's gesture, Varus and his *pedisequi* walked into the room where Augustus waited. Despite his years, the ruler of the Roman world moved very gracefully. He stood so straight, he seemed uncommonly tall, although he wasn't. He wore a toga of solid purple: a luxury he'd reserved for himself alone.

"Good day, sir," Varus said, bowing. His slaves bowed deeper, bending almost double. As he straightened, he went on, "How may I serve you today?"

"We'll get there, don't worry." Augustus turned and waved towards a chair. "In the meantime, sit down. Make yourself at home." Seen full on, his broad face seemed mild and unassuming. In profile, though, the harsh curve of his nose warned there was more to him than first met the eye.

"Thank you, sir," Varus said. The *pedisequi* stood on either side of his chair.

Augustus eased himself down into a larger chair with a cushion on the seat. One of his slaves brought in refreshments: green figs, sardines, and watered wine. He'd always had simple taste in food.

As he and Varus nibbled, he asked, "How is Claudia?"

"She's fine, sir," Varus answered. "She sends her great-uncle her love." If his wife hadn't sent it, Varus would have said she had anyhow.

"That's good." Augustus smiled, showing off his bad teeth. A lock of hair—almost entirely white now—flopped down over his right eye. Varus, whose hairline had retreated farther than Aristocles', was jealous of Augustus'. Smiling still, the older man went on, "She's a pretty girl."

"She is, yes." Varus could say that in all sincerity. His wife was called Claudia Pulchra—Claudia the Good-looking. It made what had been a marriage of convenience more enjoyable.

"How's your son?" Augustus asked.

"He's studying in Athens right now." Varus smiled, too. "Whenever he writes, he wants money."

"What else do children want from their father?" Augustus said with a wry chuckle. "Still, we have to civilize them if we can." He spoke the last sentence in fluent Greek.

"That's the truth," Varus replied in the same language. Dropping back into Latin, he continued, "I couldn't have managed anything in Syria if I didn't know Greek. Only our soldiers there know any Latin—and some of them do better in Greek, too."

Augustus sipped from his wine. It was watered more than Varus enjoyed; Augustus had always been a temperate man. "You did well in Syria," he said as he set down the cup.

"Thank you very much, sir. It's a rich province." Varus had been staggered to discover how rich Syria was. Places like that showed him Italy was only a new land. Rome claimed to have been founded 760 years earlier, but it had been a prominant place for only three centuries. Some of the Syrian towns went back thousands of years—long before the Trojan War. And the wealth they held! Varus went into Syria poor and came out prosperous without being especially corrupt.

"You did so well there, in fact, that I've got another province for you," Augustus said.

"Sir?" Varus leaned forward. He had all he could do not to show too much of his excitement. After you'd been governor of Syria, where could you go? Achaea? It wasn't so rich as Syria, but it held more cachet than any other province. It was under senatorial administration, not formally Augustus' to control, but if he asked the Conscript Fathers to honor his kinsman by marriage, how could they say no?

Or maybe Egypt! Egypt belonged to Augustus—he wouldn't dream of letting the Senators get their hands on the place. Egypt made Syria seem poor by comparison. If you served as Augustal prefect in Egypt, you were set for life, and so were all your heirs.

"Yes." The ruler of the Roman world leaned forward, too. "Germany," he said.

"Germany?" Varus hoped his disappointment didn't show. He'd been thinking of civilized places, comfortable places, places where a man could enjoy himself, could *live*. "It's a long way from . . . well, everywhere, sir." That was as much of a protest as Varus would allow himself.

"I know it is. *And* I know it will be a bit of a shock after Syria." No, Augustus was nobody's fool. When he was very young, Antony made the fatal mistake of underestimating him. Everyone who made that mistake was sorry afterwards, but afterwards was commonly too late. Of course Augustus would have a good idea of what Varus was thinking right now. "I'm sorry," he said. "I *am* sorry, but I need someone I can trust there. It just hasn't shaped up the way I wish it would have."

"I'll do my best, sir, if that's what you want," Varus said. *Gods! How will I tell Claudia?* he wondered. The fit she'd throw would make facing overgrown blond savages seem delightful. It also made him give evasion another try: "Shouldn't you perhaps think of someone with, ah, more military experience?"

"I'd send Tiberius, but he's busy putting down the uprising in Pannonia," Augustus replied. "He's finally getting somewhere, too. Why the Pannonians couldn't see they'd be better off under Roman rule . . . But they couldn't, and so he has to show them."

"I'm glad to hear he's doing well," Varus said. He wished Tiberius were doing better still, so *he* could deal with the Germans. Plainly, though, that wouldn't happen. Which meant Varus was stuck with it. Which meant he had to make the best of it. If there was any best to be made.

"When my father conquered Gaul, he did it in one campaign, and the conquest stuck," Augustus said fretfully. He was Julius Caesar's sister's grandson. But he was also Caesar's heir and adopted son, and he'd taken advantage of that for more than half a century now. The comparison still had to weigh on him, though, for he went on, "I've been sending armies into Germany the past twenty years. They mostly win when they fight the Germans, but the country isn't subdued yet. And it needs to be. A frontier that runs from the Elbe to the Danube is much shorter and easier to garrison and cheaper to maintain than the one we've got now, on the Rhine and the Danube. I could hold it with far fewer soldiers."

"Yes, sir." Varus suspected Augustus had got to the root of things right there. Augustus had been cutting the army down to size ever since winning supreme power. Paying soldiers was the most expensive thing the Roman government did. A shorter frontier would mean he didn't have to pay so many of them.

"Besides," Augustus added, "the Germans are a pack of troublemakers. They sneak over the Rhine and raid Gaul. They helped stir up the Pannonian rebels—they've given them aid and comfort, too. I want them suppressed. It's about time. We've played games with them for too cursed long."

A cold wind seemed to blow through the little room. *You'll answer for it if you don't suppress them.* Augustus didn't say that, but Varus knew he meant it. The ruler of the Roman world rewarded success. He punished failure, failure of every kind. His own daughter Julia had languished on a hot, miserable island for years because of infidelity and vice. No, he didn't fancy people who couldn't live up to what he expected of them.

Licking his lips, Varus asked, "What kind of force will I have to bring the Germans into line?"

"Three legions," Augustus answered. "The XVII, the XVIII, and the XIX. They're all solid outfits. I'd give you even more if Tiberius didn't have a full-sized war on his hands. But three should be plenty for the job. We *have* made progress in Germany. We just haven't made enough."

"Three legions!" Varus echoed. After Augustus' cuts, there were only thirty all through the Empire. Excitement coursed through the younger man. *He* would command close to twenty thousand elite soldiers. Once he pacified Germany, people might not think of him in the same breath as Julius Caesar, but they would remember him. They'd remember him forever. He inclined his head to his wife's great-uncle. "I won't let you down, sir."

"I wouldn't give you the men if I thought you would," Augustus said.

Arminius led half a cohort of German auxiliaries down a trail in western Pannonia. A town called Poetovio lay not far away. The Roman legion to which his Germans were attached had retaken it from the Pannonian rebels a few days before. Deserters from the enemy said the Pannonians wanted to take it back; their warriors still prowled the neighborhood.

"Keep your eyes open!" Arminius called in his own guttural language. "We don't want these barbarians giving us a nasty surprise."

Some of the Germans chuckled. As far as the Romans were concerned, they were even more barbarous than the Pannonians. But they'd taken service with Rome. Why not? Augustus was a good paymaster. The Pannonian rebels weren't, which meant that few Germans had gone over to them.

One of the soldiers said, "Nothing to fear in open woods like these. The rebels couldn't set up a proper ambush even if they wanted to."

"Keep your eyes open anyway," Arminius answered. The other German nodded, but it was the kind of nod a man gave a chief he was humoring. Arminius recognized it; he'd used that kind of nod often enough himself.

And the other warrior had reason enough to use it here. By German standards, these woods *were* open. Pannonia lay south of the Danube and also well to the east of the lands of the Cherusci, Arminius' tribe. It was warmer, drier country than he was used to. Woods here were full of oak and ash and other broad-leafed trees. They were nothing like the dark forests of Germany, with pines and spruces growing close together, with a formidable understory of bushes and ferns, and marshes and swamps and bogs ready to swallow up a traveler unwary enough to wander off the track.

Rome had pushed her border up to the Danube in these parts only a generation earlier: not long after the legions reached the Rhine. Tidy, thrifty Augustus wanted to push east to the Elbe, which would shorten the frontier by hundreds of miles and let him use fewer legions to garrison it. The Pannonians hadn't much minded at first, not till they saw that permanent occupation went hand in hand with higher taxes than they'd ever known—till they discovered they were enslaved, in other words. Then they rose under two men named Bato and a third called Pinnes. They'd put up a good fight, but the Romans were wearing them down at last.

Augustus aimed to enslave Germany, too. The German tribes hadn't yielded as much as the Pannonians had before they rebelled. They loved their freedom, Germans did. Even so, quite a few of them would have welcomed slavery if it came with wine and silver drinking cups and gold coins to make them feel important.

And, obviously, quite a few of them took service in the Roman auxiliaries. Some sought adventure. Some wanted to bring silver back to Germany when they went home. And some didn't aim to go home, but to win Roman citizenship after twenty years of service and to settle inside the Empire.

Most of the Germans with Arminius were dressed Roman-style. He was himself: he wore hobnailed *caligae* on his feet; a jingling mailshirt covered by a knee-length wool cloak; and an iron helmet whose crest, which ran from ear to ear rather than front to back, showed him to be an officer. Which he was, and a chief's son to boot. The troopers he commanded had on cheap bronze versions of the standard legionary helmet. They carried oval shields like his, which covered less of them than the ones the Romans used themselves.

Their weapons, though, were the ones they'd brought from Germany. They all carried spears, longer and stouter than the javelins Roman soldiers used. German spears were good for thrusting as well as throwing. And German swords, made for slashing, were half again as long as the stubby thrusting-swords the legionaries preferred. Since Germans ran at least a palm's breadth taller than Romans and had correspondingly longer arms, they had more reach with their blades than legionaries did.

But Roman soldiers could do wicked work with those *gladii* of theirs. Arminius had seen as much in this campaign against the Pannonian rebels, and before that in clashes with the Romans inside Germany. His own folk, who fought to show off each warrior's individual bravery, often mocked the Romans for slavish obedience to their officers. They were no cowards, though. Arminius had also seen that for himself.

And, because they worked so well together, the Romans could do things in war that his own folk could not. Germans who hadn't come into the Empire had no idea how vast it was or how smoothly it ran. Arminius had signed up as an auxiliary to learn the Romans' tricks of the trade, so to speak, and bring what he could back to Germany. He'd got more of a military education than he'd dreamt of before he left the forests of his homeland, too.

The Pannonians had also learned the Roman style of fighting—they'd made a point of it, in fact. When Arminius and his followers came out of the woods and looked across the rolling meadow beyond, he saw a few scrawny sheep grazing on the lush summer grass and, beyond them, a knot of eighty or a hundred men in chainmail and cloaks and helmets. He peered at them, frowning. Were they legionaries and allies, or Pannonians and enemies? It wasn't easy to tell at first glance.

They seemed in no doubt about his men. They started away from the Germans as fast as they could go. In their commander's *caligae*, Arminius would have done the same thing: his force outnumbered theirs by about two to one.

"After them, boys!" he yelled. "Good fighting, good looting!" The auxiliaries raised a cheer and swarmed across the broad meadow after the Pannonians.

And then, about a quarter of a mile to the south, a force of legionaries about the size of his also emerged from the woods. They were the outliers of the legion to which Arminius' auxiliaries were attached. As soon as the Roman soldiers spotted the Pannonians, they also cheered and began to pursue. One of their officers waved to the Germans, as if to make sure his force and theirs were on the same side.

Arminius waved back, not without resignation. Auxiliaries and legionaries together, they'd make short work of the hapless Pannonians.

But the Germans would have to share whatever loot there was with the Romans, and who'd ever heard of a Roman who wasn't greedy?

An average Pannonian was as quick on his feet as an average German or Roman (even though the Romans had short legs, they were formidable marchers). But that wasn't what a pursuit was about. If the Pannonians wanted to stick together and not get cut down one at a time, they had to move at the pace of their slowest men. The Romans and Germans on their trail steadily chewed up the ground between the forces.

One of the Pannonians shouted something. Arminius heard the words clearly, but couldn't understand them. That proved the enemy *was* the enemy. Like most of the auxiliaries with him, Arminius had grown fluent in Latin. He still sometimes muttered to himself, going through a declension or conjugation, but he made himself understood—and he followed what Romans said to him. Pannonian, on the other hand, was only gibberish to him—and to the Romans as well.

The rebels stopped retreating and formed a battle line. Long odds against them: longer, Arminius thought, than those against throwing a triple six in a dice game. But sometimes long odds were better than sure ruin, and sure ruin faced the Pannonians if they kept trying to run away. Maybe a fierce charge would make their pursuers think twice.

Maybe. But Arminius didn't believe it, not for a moment. "Be ready!" he called to his fellow Germans. "They're going to try to bull through us."

"Let them try," one of the big, fair men said. Several others nodded. Arminius smiled. No, his folk had never been one to back away from a fight.

That officer shouted something. Sure as demons, the Pannonians charged Arminius' band, not the legionaries. The Germans' looks, bronze helmets, and smaller shields all declared them auxiliaries rather than regulars. The enemy officer had to think that made them the easier target. Well, he could think whatever he pleased. Thinking it didn't make it so.

"Sedatus!" the Pannonians yelled, and, "Succellus!" One of those was their fire god; the other was a smith, who carried a hammer. They were using sharper tools now.

They showed almost Roman discipline as they bore down on the Germans. His own men fought with better discipline than they would have back in their native forests. Past that, Arminius indulged in no comparisons. With numbers on their side, and with the legionaries swinging up to help them, it shouldn't matter much.

Of course, even if the Germans and Romans would win in the end, a man still might get killed in the middle of the fight. The Pannonians loosed a volley of javelins at Arminius' auxiliaries. A German screamed when one of the light spears pierced his right arm. Another javelin thudded into Arminius' shield. The Pannonians had copied Roman practice to the extent of using a long shank of soft iron on their javelins. The shank bent when the javelin went home. Arminius couldn't throw it back, and yanking it out of the shield would take time he didn't have. He threw the fouled shield aside. Fighting without one would have bothered a Roman. It left Arminius more vulnerable, but it didn't bother him a bit—he was used to going into battle with no more than spear and sword.

He jabbed at the man in front of him. The Pannonian used *his* big, heavy legionary-style shield well, holding it between Arminius' spear and his vitals. His stabbing sword flicked out like a viper's tongue. But he couldn't reach Arminius with it, not when the German's spear made him keep his distance.

They might have danced like that for some little while, each trying to figure out how to spill the other's blood. They weren't alone on the battlefield, though. Another German threw a fist-sized rock that clanged off the Pannonian's helmet. Without the ironworks on his head, it would have smashed in his skull. As things were, he staggered and lurched like a man who'd just taken a fist to the chin. He dropped his guard, too. Arminius sprang forward and jabbed his spear into the fellow's thigh, just below his iron-studded leather kilt.

The Pannonian howled in pain. He crumpled like a discarded sheet of papyrus—a comparison that never would have occurred to Arminius before joining the auxiliaries. The German chief stabbed again, aiming to finish him. But, even wounded, the Pannonian was wily: He used his shield like a turtle's shell, covering himself with it as best he could. Arminius went on to fight another man. The wounded Pannonian couldn't get away. Once the fight was over, somebody would cut his throat or smash in his head. All the wiliness in the world wouldn't save him then.

Even among Germans, Arminius was a big man. The Pannonian he came up against next was even bigger, and much thicker through the shoulders. The fellow screamed something at him. Since it was in the Pannonian language, Arminius understood not a word of it. Seeing as much, the warrior shouted again, this time in Latin: "Futter your mother!"

"Your mother was a dog, and your father shat in her twat," Arminius retorted. Latin wasn't his language, either, which hadn't kept him from learning to swear in it.

Roaring with rage, the big, burly Pannonian rushed at him. He aimed to knock Arminius down with his heavy shield and then stab him—or, if he was furious enough, kick him to death. What he aimed for wasn't what he got. Arminius sidestepped like a dancer and then used a flick of his spearpoint to tear out the Pannonian's throat. It was as pretty and precise a stroke as he'd ever made. He was proud of it for days afterwards.

Blood fountained from the Pannonian's neck. He clutched at his throat, trying to stem the tide of gore. It was no use—Arminius knew a killing stroke when he gave one. The big man's knees went limp as overcooked cabbage. He fell, and his armor clattered about him.

Romans liked to say things like that. It was a line from a poem, though Arminius thought the poem was in Greek, not Latin. He knew there was such a thing as Greek, and that Romans with a fancy education spoke it, but it remained a closed scroll to him.

And he had no time to worry about poetry anyhow, whether in Greek, Latin, or his own tongue. Another Pannonian was trying to murder him. The man's thrust almost pierced him—the son of a whore even fought like a Roman. The fellow sheltered behind his own big *scutum*. Beating down his guard wouldn't be easy. Arminius' slashes gashed the thick leather facing of the Pannonian's shield, but that didn't harm it and certainly didn't harm him.

Then the legionaries slammed into the rebels' flank. After that, the fight wasn't a fight any more. It was a rout. The Pannonians realized what they should have seen sooner: they were desperately outnumbered, out in the open, and had no hope of reinforcement, nor any strongpoint to which they might escape. They were, in a word, trapped.

Arminius' foe suddenly had to face two other German auxiliaries, as the men they'd been fighting took to their heels. He had no trouble holding off one foe. He couldn't turn enough directions at once to hold off three. One of the other Germans hamstrung him. He went down with a wail. Arminius' stroke across his throat finished him off.

"This is the way it's supposed to work!" said the auxiliary who'd wounded him, wiping blood from his blade on a grassy tussock.

"By the gods, it is," Arminius agreed. "Let's finish the rest of them. The looting should be good."

"So it should. We don't want to let those Roman greedyguts take more than their share, either, the way they like to do," the other man said.

"I was thinking the same thing a little while ago," Arminius replied. "Come on! We don't want to let any of these cursed fools get away."

He loped after the Pannonians, who were frankly fleeing now. The westering sun stretched his shadow out ahead of him. The other Germans followed. War made a grand game—when you were winning.

Quinctilius Varus stepped from the gangplank to the pier with a sigh of relief. He didn't like traveling by ship, which didn't mean he couldn't do it at need. He'd got from Ostia—Rome's port—to Massilia by sea faster than he could have by land. The rest of the journey, up to the legions' base by the Rhine, would have to be by land.

He wished he could just close his eyes and appear there. For that matter, he wished he could close his eyes and have somebody else appear there. But he was the man Augustus wanted in that spot, the man Augustus wanted doing that job. It was an honor. All of his friends said so. They all seemed glad it was an honor he had and they didn't. None of them had shown the slightest desire to accompany him to the frontier.

Neither had his wife. "If my great-uncle said you have to go to Germany, then you do," Claudia Pulchra had said. "He didn't say anything about my going, and I don't intend to." She'd made him very happy in bed till his sailing time came round. He hoped she wasn't making someone else very happy happy in bed right now—or, if she was, he hoped she was discreet about it. If Augustus could send his own daughter to an island for being too open, too shameless, with her adulteries, he wouldn't think twice about banishing a grand-niece.

No matter what Claudia Pulchra was doing, Varus had to make the best of things here. He looked at Massilia from the pier, and found himself pleasantly surprised. "Not *too* bad," he said.

"Not too good, either," Aristocles said darkly. The *pedisequus* liked sailing even less than Varus did—his stomach rebelled on the water. He didn't seem to realize he was on dry land again at last.

But Varus meant what he'd said. Massilia wasn't Rome—no other place came close, not even Alexandria—or Antioch or Athens. But it was a perfectly respectable provincial town. Greeks had settled the southern coast of Gaul somewhere not long after Rome was founded. And Gallia Narbonensis had been a Roman province much longer than the wilder lands farther north. True, Caesar's soldiers had besieged and sacked Massilia a lifetime ago, when it made the mistake of backing Pompey. It had recovered since, though, and was prosperous again. The temple to Apollo near the center of town was particularly fine, dominating the view from the harbor.

"Who will you be, sir?" a dockside lounger asked Varus in Greek-accented Latin. "I can tell you're somebody, and no mistake."

"I am Publius Quinctilius Varus, the new governor of Germany, on my way from Rome to take my post there," Varus answered grandly. He nodded to Aristocles, who flipped the lounger a coin. "Will you be good enough to let the local leaders know I have arrived?"

The man popped the coin into his mouth. Most people carried small change between their cheek and jaw. Varus had himself in his younger days. Aristocles handled mundanities like money now. "I sure will, your honor," the Massiliote said, and hurried away.

If he took the silver and disappeared . . . Well, what could Varus do about it? Nothing much. But the fellow proved as good as his word.

Before long, both of the town's *duumvirs*—its paired executives, as con- suls were the paired executives in Rome as a whole—hurried to the har- bor to greet their distinguished visitor. By their Latin, they were Italians, not Greeks. One was tall and lean, the other short and stocky. Varus for- got their names as soon as he heard them. The tall one sold olive oil all over Gaul; the stocky one sold wine—or maybe it was the other way around.

Each *duumvir* invited him to a feast that evening. By the way they glared at each other, the one whose house he didn't choose would hate him forever after. So he said, "I'll stay a couple of days before going north. Why don't I have my slave toss a coin to see which of you I visit first?"

As he'd hoped, that satisfied them both. "You know how to grease things, don't you, your Excellency?" said the tall one—yes, Quinctilius Varus thought he was the one who sold oil.

"I try," Varus answered.

"Can you grease things up in Germany?" the squat one asked, which confused Varus all over again.

"I intend to try," he said. "Can you gentlemen tell me what it's like up by the Rhine?"

Almost in unison, they shook their heads. They were Italians, sure enough; a Greek would have dipped his to show he meant no. The tall one said, "You wouldn't catch me up there—not unless Augustus ordered me there, I mean." He made a quick recovery. Then he continued, "I'd rather stay here. The weather's better—not so chilly, not so damp. And there aren't any savages around here."

"My job is to turn them into provincials," Varus said.

"Good fortune go with you," the two *duumvirs* said together. It wasn't *Good luck and you'll need it, you poor, sorry son of a whore*, but it might as well have been.

"The Germans do buy wine," the stocky one added. "Not much of a market there for oil, I'm afraid. They use butter instead." He made a face to show what he thought of that. Since Varus thought the same thing, he made a face, too. If butter didn't mark a true barbarian, what did?

"And they drink beer," the tall one said, which answered that question. He went on, "They like wine better, though, when they can get hold of it."

"Who wouldn't?" Varus said. Both *duumvirs* nodded.

"Maybe you can teach them to like olive oil, too," the short one said. "The Gauls use more of it than they did before Caesar conquered them."

"If I can pacify the Germans, they're welcome to keep eating butter, as far as I'm concerned," Varus exclaimed.

"I can see that," the stocky *duumvir* said judiciously. "Maybe you don't have the biggest load on your shoulders this side of Atlas holding up the heavens, but not far from it, eh?"

Varus thought the same thing, though Augustus didn't seem to. He couldn't tell these fellows how he felt, or it might get back to the ruler of the Roman world. Things had an unfortunate way of doing that. He wanted Augustus to go on having confidence in him, which meant he had to act like a man who had confidence in Augustus. He said, "By all the reports that have come down to Rome, there's been real progress the past few years. I've got to put the stopper in the jug and seal it with pitch, that's all."

The *duumvirs* glanced at each other for a moment. Varus had the feeling they didn't like each other much, but they thought the same way. "Good fortune go with you," they chorused again, and he was sure it meant the same thing this time as it had before.

II

Vultures and ravens and carrion crows spiraled down from the sky. The legions and auxiliaries had spread out a feast for the scavengers here near Poetovio. But the birds—and the little foxes that peered out from the edge of the oak woods not far away—couldn't fill their bellies quite yet. Romans and German auxiliaries still strode about the battlefield, plundering corpses and making sure all the Pannonians sprawled there *were* corpses.

Not far from Arminius, another German auxiliary drove his spear into a feebly writhing man's throat. When the man quit wiggling, the German bent and took his helmet. It was a fine piece of ironmongery, far better than the cheap bronze helms the Romans issued to auxiliaries.

The other German set the helm on his own head. Catching Arminius' eye, he grinned. "Fits like it was made for me," he said.

"A god made it so," Arminius said. "May you have better luck with it than the fellow who wore it before."

Something glinted in the late-afternoon sunshine. A dead Pannonian wore a heavy gold ring in his left ear. Stooping, Arminius pulled on the ring till it tore through the flesh of the earlobe. It hardly got any blood on it; the enemy warrior must have died early in the fight. Arminius weighed the bauble in the palm of his hand. It had to be worth a couple of aurei. He stuck it into a belt pouch.

Somebody had driven a spear clean through the dead man's mailshirt. Arminius nodded to himself. That stroke deserved respect. He had no doubt he could have matched it—in his early twenties, he was at the peak of his strength (and also, though he didn't think of it that way, at the peak of his arrogance)—but not many men could have.

A moment later, he nodded again. The way the Pannonians had fought back against the Germans and Romans also deserved respect. The Romans were unlikely to give it. Arminius did. He'd seen, not for the first time, how the Pannonians had imitated Roman fighting methods till they could stand up against the toughest soldiers in the world.

"Do you think we could have fought this well, Chlodovegius?" he asked—he made a point of learning the names of the men he led.

Chlodovegius had taken off his new helmet and was admiring it. He looked up. "That many of us against so many Romans? We'd've licked 'em." He made as if to draw his long, straight sword for a bit of cut and thrust. He was a few years older than Arminius, but he didn't lack for arrogance, either.

Arminius smiled. "Well, maybe we would have." He didn't feel like arguing. But he also didn't believe Chlodovegius. One German had an excellent chance against one Roman. Ten Romans had the edge on ten Germans. A hundred Romans would massacre a hundred Germans.

They would in open country like this, anyhow. In the forests and swamps of Germany, ambushes and harassment came easier. The Romans could send troops through Germany. They'd been doing that since Arminius was a little boy. But they'd never been able to hold down the countryside . . . which didn't mean they didn't keep trying.

"What will we do if the Romans turn our country, our homeland, into one of their provinces?" Arminius wasn't really asking Chlodovegius; he was thinking out loud.

But the other German heard him and, laughing, answered, "What are you worrying about? We're already halfway to turning into Romans. If we serve out our terms in the auxiliaries, they'll make us citizens."

They'd already made Arminius a citizen: he came from a chieftain's family. They'd even made him a member of the Equestrian Order, the social class one rank below the Senators who helped their chieftain, Augustus, rule Rome. While Arminius was tolerably fluent in Latin these days, he'd understood only a few words when he joined the auxiliaries a couple of years earlier.

He was a man with an itch to know. He always had been. He'd joined the auxiliaries to learn how the Romans did things. He'd also learned a lot, not all of it what he'd expected. Roman discipline looked different from the inside. In Germany, he'd always thought Roman soldiers were slaves because of the way they let their superiors order them around. No free German would have put up with that for even a moment.

When Germans went to war, though, they fought as individuals or as members of a little band. They went forward to show off their bravery to their kinsmen and friends. How else would you fight?

How else? The Romans had another way. A man in a legion, or in a troop of auxiliaries, was part of something bigger than himself. He still needed to be brave, but he also needed to remember he was only a part. If all the parts did what they were supposed to do—what their superiors told them to do—the legion or troop was very hard to beat.

They also kept more freedom than they seemed to from the outside. Arminius knew what he'd done in this latest clash with the Pannonians. So did the men around him. But he hadn't done it to prove he was brave. He'd done it to help the larger unit.

The Pannonians fought the same way. They'd learned it from the Romans. Arminius wondered if his folk could, too. He hoped so. If they couldn't, wouldn't they go down the way the Gauls had, the way the Pannonians were now?

A wounded man nearby couldn't hold in a groan. Arminius finished him off, then looked to see if he had anything worth taking. To the German's annoyance, the Pannonian didn't. Had Arminius known that ahead of time, he might have let the foeman lie there and suffer.

But no. Orders were to make sure the wounded died. And Arminius could see the reason for those orders. If legionaries and auxiliaries were parts of something larger than themselves, so were enemy warriors. The Romans didn't just aim to kill individuals. They wanted to kill the very idea of nationhood among their foes.

Here, Arminius thought uneasily, *and back home in Germany*, *too*.

He dogged his men till they finished cleaning up the field and left it to the birds and foxes. Even that thought made him uncomfortable as he marched them back to the encampment they and the legionaries with them had made the night before. *Am I anything but the Romans' dog?* he wondered.

Flavus, his older brother, *was* a Roman dog. Flavus *liked* life in the auxiliaries. He was fighting somewhere else in Pannonia, serving Augustus as best he could. Arminius didn't know just where, and didn't care to find out. He couldn't decide whether Flavus frightened or infuriated him more.

He dismissed his brother from his mind with nothing but relief. Yes, back to the encampment. Only one thing ever changed about Roman fortified camps: the size, which depended on how many men they needed to hold. Otherwise, they were as much alike as two coins. Standardizing things was another idea the Romans had had that was new to the Germans. Arminius could see the advantages: if you always did this and that the same way, you just went ahead and *did* them. You didn't have to wonder whether to do this first or how to take care of that or if you should bother with something else. Again, the Romans made each man one stick in the wattle of a house, so to speak.

A Roman centurion—he showed his rank by the cross-crested helm he still wore—waved to Arminius as the German brought in his warriors. "Your men fought like wolves today," the veteran called.

"My thanks. You Romans were fierce, too," Arminius answered. That wasn't quite the right word. *Capable* came closer, but didn't seem praise enough.

"*Ai!*" The centurion snapped his fingers, reminding himself of something. "There's a fellow from your tribe in camp. He's looking for you."

"Thanks again. Did he say why?" Whatever news the man brought from the land of the Cherusci, Arminius feared it would be bad. Only bad news needed to travel fast. Good news could commonly wait. "Are my father and mother hale?"

"I don't know. Sorry." The Roman spread his hands. "I didn't ask, and your friend doesn't speak a whole lot of Latin anyhow." He never imagined that he might learn the Germans' language.

Well, this was a Roman province, so that wasn't unreasonable. But if the Romans held Germany, wouldn't Latin come to dominate there, too? Arminius pulled his mind back from such things to the business at hand. "Thank you for telling me. I find—I will find—him and see what the news is."

"Hope it's nothing too awful." The centurion's rough sympathy said he knew how these things usually went.

"Thanks," Arminius said once more. He hurried off with his men to the northwest corner of the encampment, where they always pitched their tents. In every Roman camp ever made, auxiliaries were quartered in the northwest and northeast corners. The Romans had done things that way for centuries. They were a tidy folk; everything had its place among them. And, once they found a way of doing things that worked, they stuck with it.

He found his man there—or rather, his man found him. "Arminius!" someone called.

"Hail, Chariomerus," Arminius answered, recognizing him at once. He hurried up and clasped the other man's hand. "Why have you come? Are Mother and Father all right?"

"As far as I know," Chariomerus answered. He and Arminius weren't close kin, though they'd grown up in the same little village. "They were when I set out, anyhow."

"Well, that's the biggest load off my mind," Arminius said. "Come on with me and get some supper—you'll be hungry after so long on the road."

"You're right about that, by the gods." Chariomerus and Arminius got bowls of barley porridge and cups of wine from the cooks. Chariomerus wolfed his down. "I'm still hungry," he said when it was gone. "I want some boiled meat, to let my stomach know it's got something in there." He drank. "Wine's not bad, though."

"No, it isn't," Arminius said. "The Romans think eating a lot of meat makes you slow. Maybe they're even right—I don't know. Going without doesn't bother me the way it did: I know that. I've got used to doing things Roman-style."

"I suppose you have to, but. . . ." Chariomerus let his voice trail away, then resumed: "Better you than me."

"I'm not Flavus," Arminius snapped. "I'm——" He shook his head like a man bedeviled by gnats. There were times when he didn't know what he was. "Give me your news. It's not my parents, and I thank the gods for that. So what did bring you from home?"

Chariomerus drained the cup. He looked as if he wanted more wine, too, to help grease his tongue. At last, with a sigh, he said, "Well, it has to do with Segestes."

Arminius grunted. Segestes was another chief among the Cherusci. He liked and trusted the Romans more than Arminius did. More to the point, he was also Arminius' fiancée's father. "What about him?" Arminius demanded. "Is *he* well?"

"He was when I left," Chariomerus said, as he had when talking about Arminius' mother and father. The newcomer didn't seem eager to go on.

After silence stretched, Arminius said, "If you keep me waiting any more, you'll make me angry. You didn't come all this way *not* to tell me something."

"You're right." Chariomerus sighed. He still hesitated. At last, he brought the words out in a rush: "He's gone and betrothed Thusnelda to somebody else."

People said you didn't always feel it right away when you got wounded. Arminius hadn't found that to be true. Every time a sword cut him or an arrow pierced his flesh, it hurt like fire. But now he just stared, his mouth foolishly gaping. He'd heard the words, but they didn't want to make sense inside his head.

"Who? Who?" he asked, sounding like an owl. An owl in daylight was the worst of omens—everybody knew that. What kind of omen was it, though, when someone took your woman away from you?

"Tudrus," Chariomerus said.

The grinding noise Arminius heard was his own teeth clashing to-gether like millstones. He needed a distinct effort of will to make himself stop. Tudrus was a man of about Segestes' age. He was also friendly to the Romans. All the same . . . "Why?" Arminius seemed to have trouble coming out with more than one word at a time.

"I don't know for sure. He doesn't tell me his reasons," Chariomerus replied. "My best guess is, he doesn't think you'll come back from this war. He wants Thusnelda to give him some grandchildren . . . and Tudrus has been one of his sworn companions for years."

"He should never have promised her to me, then," Arminius said. "Does he think I have no honor, to take an insult like this lying down?"

"What will you do?" Chariomerus sounded apprehensive.

"Go home and set things right, of course," Arminius answered. "What do you expect me to do when you bring me news like that? Just stand here and thank you for it and go about my business?" He looked around and dropped his voice. "Do you take me for a Roman?"

"No, of course not." Had Chariomerus said anything else, Arminius would have killed him. The newsbringer also lowered his voice: "Is it true what they say about Roman women?"

"Not enough Roman women up here for me to know one way or the other. The stories are pretty juicy, but stories usually are." Arminius set a hand on his fellow tribesman's shoulder. "Now I have to tell the Romans I am leaving. They will not be happy to hear it, but"—he shrugged—"what can you do?"

The senior Roman officer with this detachment was a military tribune named Titus Minucius Basilus. He was short and lean and bald, with pinched features, a blade of a nose, and eyes cold as a blizzard. Arminius interrupted him at supper, which did nothing to improve his mood. He redeemed some of his bad temper with reckless bravery.

"You have to go, you say?" he growled when Arminius finished. "Just like that? In the middle of a campaign?"

"I am sorry . . . sir." Arminius could use Roman notions of politeness and subordination, even though he scorned them. "It touches my honor. What would you do if your betrothed's father gave her to another man?" He knew he was making a hash of his subjunctives, and hoped Minucius could follow him.

"I'd start a lawsuit against the double-dealing wretch," Minucius answered. "He'd be sorry by the time I got through with him, too."

His supper companions nodded. Arminius had only a vague notion of what a lawsuit was: a battle with words instead of swords was as close as he could come. He didn't see the point. "We have not got this in my country," he said.

"No, I suppose not." The Roman eyed Arminius as he sipped from a silver winecup. Whatever else he was, he was sharp. "If I tell you you can't go, you'll up and leave anyway, won't you?"

"It is my honor . . . sir," Arminius repeated. Talking to a different officer, he might have asked if the fellow understood the word. Something told him that would be a very bad idea with Titus Minucius Basilus. He would make a dangerous enemy, dangerous as a viper underfoot. Picking his words with care, Arminius went on, "How can I fight as well as I should, sir, when all I think about what this man does—uh, has done—to me?"

"You wouldn't be the first man in that kind of mess—or the last." The military tribune drank more wine. At last, still without warming up, he brusquely dipped his head. "Go on. Go home. If we can't whip the Pannonians because we're short one auxiliary officer, we don't deserve to win, by Jupiter. Straighten out your woman troubles and then come back to us. They've already made you a Roman citizen, but we'll make you a real Roman."

He meant it for a compliment. Arminius reminded himself of that. He also reminded himself he'd got what he wanted—and more easily than he'd expected, too. Minucius was right: he would have deserted had he heard no rather than yes. Since he'd heard yes. . . .

He bowed, red-gold locks spilling down off his shoulders as he bent forward. "My thanks, sir. My many thanks, sir. I am in your debt."

"Maybe you will pay it one day—if not to me, then to Rome," Minucius said.

"Maybe I will." Arminius bowed again. "Please excuse me. I will not interrupt your supper any more." He turned and hurried off, conscious as he went of Minucius' eyes boring into his back.

"Well?" Chariomerus said when Arminius got back to the auxiliaries' tents.

"It is very well, in fact," Arminius said. "He will let me go. He saw I would go whether he let me or not. Sometimes it is easier to lean in the direction the wind is already blowing."

Chariomerus smiled in glad surprise. "I did not think it would be so simple."

"Neither did I. Some god must be looking kindly on me," Arminius answered. "And that can only mean the god is scowling at Segestes. How could it be otherwise? He has broken faith. But he won't get away with it."

"Thusnelda will be glad to have you instead of Tudrus," Chariomerus said. "He is an old man—he has to be forty-five if he's a day."

"So she will." Arminius didn't love Thusnelda. Love, as far as he could see, was something the Romans had invented to give themselves an excuse for infidelity. But he'd known her since they were children. He liked her, and thought she liked him. Segestes had no right to rob him of her. No right at all.

When Varus governed Syria, the immemorial antiquity of the countryside impressed him. As he'd thought while conferring with Augustus, it made Italy, where even the oldest towns had but a few centuries on them, seem downright juvenile by comparison. As he traveled north to the Rhine frontier to take up his new province, he thought about that often. He didn't know whether to laugh or to cry.

Oh, Gaul had had towns before the Roman conquest. But they hadn't been towns with civilized amenities. No theaters for plays. No amphitheaters for spectacles, gladiators, and beast shows. No public baths. No proper law courts. No colonnaded and porticoed public squares. And, of course, the barbarians had gabbled away at one another in their own incomprehensible language, not in Latin—to say nothing of Greek.

More than half a century of Roman rule had brought some changes. A few of the locals had forsaken tunic and trousers for the toga. Here and there, a proper Roman building—stone with a tile roof—sprouted amidst

timber and wattle-and-daub and thatch. But it would be a long time before this country grew civilized, if it ever did.

Vetera, on the west bank of the Rhine, had more than enough Romans to make a good-sized town. It was the headquarters of Legions
XVII, XVIII, and XIX. But legionaries, however necessary they were in
the grand scheme of things, weren't . . . interesting people.

Varus had been used to gossip about matters of state, gossip about
Augustus' family (his own family, thanks to the marriage connection—
not that Claudia Pulchra was daft enough to come up to the edge of the
world, though she'd gone with him to Syria), and gossip about the other
great and powerful men—and women—of Rome.

In Vetera, he got gossip about an ambitious military tribune jockey-
ing for promotion, gossip about a centurion's drunken German mistress,
gossip about what happened when a prefect's Gallic mistress found out
about his German mistress, gossip about the outrageous way a wine merchant overcharged for the swill he swore was Falernian (no, some things
didn't change from Rome to Vetera, not even a little bit).

Power. Sex. Money. What else was there to gossip about? But when
the power was minuscule, when the sex was with women whose fair
tresses reminded Varus that whores in Rome were required by law to
wear blond wigs, when the money was chicken feed, how were you supposed to get excited about any of it?

People in Vetera did. Varus imagined that people in any provincial
town had their tiny squabbles and feuds and scandals and triumphs. The
trouble was, the Roman officers in Vetera expected Varus to be interested
in theirs. And so he had to be, or at least to pretend to be. Hypocrisy
wasn't the least important art a high-ranking Roman needed to cultivate.

In Syria, soldiers always worried about Parthia. If Rome had a real ri-
val, the successor to the Persian Empire was it. Roman armies had come to
grief against Parthia. Back around the time Varus was born, Crassus got his
force annihilated at Carrhae, and even lost legionary eagles—what greater
and more humiliating disgrace was possible? And the Parthian Kings of
Kings weren't afraid to invade the Roman East when they thought they
could get away with it.

In Vetera, soldiers—and no one else there mattered—worried about Germany instead. Varus did not find that an improvement. Parthia was a more or less cultured country. The King of Kings and his nobles spoke Greek as a matter of course. They had elegant manners they'd learned from Alexander the Great's successors while they were beating them. (If the Macedonians had learned *their* manners from the Persians while they were beating them, Varus didn't dwell on that.)

Hearing that two German tribes were threatening to go to war with each other over some stolen pigs was not edifying. Neither was the news that some petty German noble—as if there were any other kind!—was raising a row in his tribe by giving a girl previously promised to one suitor to another instead. And that was the kind of thing Varus had to listen to day after day.

He didn't take long to tire of it. He summoned a meeting of the leading soldiers in Legions XVII, XVIII, and XIX and spoke without pre-amble: "You already know Augustus sent me here to bring Germany all the way into the Empire. I aim to do that as fast as I can." *Then I'll go back to Rome and let somebody else take charge of the miserable place.*

The assembled officers nodded. Vala Numonius, the cavalry com-mander, said, "It shouldn't be too hard, sir. By what I've heard since I got here, we've softened up the Germans a lot. They're getting used to our ways. Plenty of their nobles already see lining up with us is the smart way to go. All they need is a show of force, and they'll roll onto their backs and show their bellies like whipped dogs."

"Does anyone disagree?" Varus put the question for form's sake. He'd said what he intended to do, and one of his principal subordinates had declared that the assembled legions could do it. What more did any-one want?

But, to his surprise, an officer named Lucius Eggius said, "I do, sir. The Germans just aren't that easy. Whenever we cross the Rhine, we own the land where we march and the land where we camp. The rest still belongs to the barbarians."

"It's not so bad as that," Numonius said.

Lucius Eggius set his chin. Even when Varus said, "I should hope not," Eggius still looked discontented. Varus wondered if the soldier found himself in this gods-forsaken spot because of an unfortunate habit of speaking his mind regardless of whether anybody else wanted to listen to him.

"I think you're right, sir," said yet another officer, a prefect named Ceionius. Unlike Lucius Eggius, he knew the words a governor liked to hear. Better yet, he came up with good reasons why Varus was right: "Quite a few of the Germans are learning Latin——"

"The better to spy on us," Eggius broke in.

"Oh, nonsense," Ceionius said. "They're using our coins, too. They buy wine and pottery and jewelry with them, and they spend them among themselves. Little by little, they're turning into provincials. Once we finish the occupation, give them twenty years and you won't be able to tell them from Gauls."

Eggius sent Varus what the governor supposed was meant to be a look of appeal. Somehow, it only made the man seem more stubborn than ever. "Don't listen to him, sir," Eggius said earnestly. "If these savages were going to lay down for us——"

"Lie down, you mean." Now Ceionius interrupted, to point out the other soldier's bad grammar. Varus, of course, had noticed it on his own. If an officer couldn't express himself correctly, how were his superiors supposed to take seriously anything he said?

"If they were going to lay down for us," Lucius Eggius repeated, his chin jutting forward even farther than before, "they would have done it twenty years ago. They're rough customers—that's all there is to it. And there are swarms of them in those little villages. Sometimes we beat 'em when we fight. Sometimes they lick us. If they didn't, the country on the far side of the Rhine would've made a proper province a long time ago."

Several officers drew away from him, as if he carried something catching. And so he did: tactlessness could kill off even a promising career. Varus almost dismissed him from the council. At the last instant, though, he held back, remembering how Augustus had voiced some of the same worries.

"Anyone can do an easy job," Varus said. "You need uncommon men to handle a harder one. Augustus has decided that we are the men he needs for this particular job. To my way of thinking, that's a compliment to every one of us and to every single soldier in Legions XVII, XVIII, and XIX. Will anyone tell me I'm wrong there?"

He waited. No one said a word, not even the obstinate Lucius Eggius. Varus had expected nothing different. A bold man could quarrel with a provincial governor. No one had quarreled with Augustus in any serious way for more than thirty years. If you quarreled with Augustus, you lost. Rome had learned that lesson well.

"Since Augustus gave us this job, we'll find a way to do it," Varus continued. Nobody disagreed with that, either.

The track wound through the woods. Arminius' boots squelched in the mud. He slipped and almost fell. He'd traded his Roman *caligae*—his hobnailed marching sandals—to a farmer for the boots and a meal and a bed. The *caligae* didn't fit the farmer very well, but the iron hobnails made them valuable.

Even if Arminius got less traction on bad ground, he preferred his native footgear. He preferred the soft dirt track to a paved Roman highway, too. March on stone from sunup to sundown and your legs felt like stone themselves when you finally stopped for the night.

Arminius also preferred the way the track followed the contours of the land. Roman roads ran straight as stretched strings. If the straight route was bad, the Romans built it up with stones or dug away hillsides. They were as arrogant in their engineering as they were everywhere else.

He tried to explain that to Chariomerus. The other German didn't get it. "What's wrong with taking the short way if you can?" he asked.

"How can the gods love anyone who tears up the landscape the way the Romans do?" Arminius returned.

He got only a stare and a shrug from his traveling companion, who said, "If the gods don't love the Romans, how come they're so stinking strong?"

That question was good enough to keep Arminius walking in silence for some little while. At last, he said, "To give us foes worth fighting. That must be it. If our enemies were weaklings, what kind of glory would we win by beating them? Not much. They have to be strong, or they wouldn't make proper enemies."

Chariomerus grunted. "But what happens if they're *too* strong?" he asked. "What happens if they beat us?"

"Then we turn into slaves," Arminius answered. "So do our mothers and our sisters and our daughters and our sweethearts."

That made Chariomerus shudder. Arminius had known it would. His folk had a greater horror of slavery for its women than for its men. German minstrels sang of battles that had turned when the women on the side that was losing bared their breasts and warned their men they were about to be enslaved, inspiring the warriors to fight with desperate ferocity. A tribe that could claim hostages from among its neighbors' noblewomen held those neighbors in a grip stronger than iron.

"We mustn't lose, then," Chariomerus said.

"And we won't." But Arminius sounded more confident than he felt. Roman influence seemed stronger in Germany than it had when he went off to learn how the legions fought. It was much stronger than it had been when he was a boy. People passed coins—Roman coins—back and forth without even thinking about what they were doing. In his younger days, barter had been king of all. He'd gotten better wine from some of the nobles who had him as a guest than he had as a Roman auxiliary. When people found out he'd fought for the Romans, they wanted to try out bits of Latin on him. If those weren't the early marks of slavery, what would be?

Dogs barked up ahead. "There's your father's steading," Chariomerus said.

"It's been a long road," Arminius replied. "My father's steading—at last. Here I will stay till I can see my way to avenging the insult Segestes has given me."

When he and Chariomerus came out into the open, four or five dogs rushed toward them. The big, rough-coated, wolfish beasts growled and snarled and bared their formidable fangs. The Romans had dogs like that.

What herdsman or farmer would want any other kind? But the Romans also had small, fluffy, mild-mannered dogs to keep women and children company. They turned good working dogs into toys. They would do the same with—to—Arminius' folk if they got the chance.

He shouted at the dogs. He didn't know if that would prove enough—he'd been away a long time. His hand fell to the hilt of his sword. If they kept coming, he would do what he had to do to keep them from biting him. Chariomerus, perhaps less sure of the animals' temper, drew his blade and widened his stance so he was ready to strike.

But shouting sufficed. The dogs skidded to a stop. A couple of them—beasts Arminius recognized—cocked their heads to one side. He had to laugh at their expressions: they looked like men trying to remember something. Did they know his voice? His scent?

Something a Roman had told him floated up into his thoughts. There was a Greek poem that had an old dog remembering its master in it. He came home after years and years away adventuring, and the dog died after it realized who he was.

Arminius didn't know much about the Greeks. He gathered that the Romans thought them very clever. Since Germans thought the same about Romans, that made these Greeks clever indeed . . . didn't it? If they *were* so clever, why didn't they run things instead of the Romans?

"Hail, Lance. Hail, Speedy," he said gravely, and scratched the dogs he knew behind the ears. They let him do it, where they would have snapped at a stranger. The other dogs—young ones that had grown up or been born after he went away—eyed Speedy and Lance as if wondering why they would betray a trust like that.

Some Germans were friendly to the Romans. Arminius' brother was one. And Segestes was another. He always had been. He thought Germany stood to gain more than it lost by coming under the Roman eagle. Arminius had thought he was wrong before. Now the younger man despised any opinion of Segestes' just because his betrayed fiancée's father held it.

The commotion from the dogs brought a gray-haired man carrying an axe out to see what caused it. A gray-haired man . . . "Father!" Arminius shouted, and ran to him.

"Arminius!" His father's name was Sigimerus. He definitely hadn't been so gray when Arminius went off to learn what he could of Roman fighting. He hadn't been so stooped, either. He wasn't an old man, not yet, but the years had a grip on him.

As they embraced, Arminius forgot all about that. "It's good to see you. It's good to be home," he said, and kissed Sigimerus on both cheeks and then on the mouth.

"How is Flavus?" his father asked.

Arminius' mouth tightened. "The last I heard, he was hale," he said carefully. "That was . . . let me think . . . two months ago, or maybe a little more."

"The Romans are fools not to put two brothers in the same band, where you could spur each other on," Sigimerus said.

"The Romans are fools," Arminius agreed. But he found he couldn't leave it there: "They don't care so much about men spurring each other on. They want men who do as they're told." He grimaced again. "Flavus has always been good at that."

His father coughed. "Sometimes obeying is good. I walloped you a lot more than I hit your brother."

"Yes, I know." This time, Arminius did leave it there. Taking it any further would have started a quarrel, which he didn't want. He did say, "Flavus likes fighting for the Romans."

As far as Arminius could tell, Flavus wished he'd been born a Roman himself. If anything, Flavus was even more pro-Roman than Segestes. Arminius respected the Romans, not least for their ruthlessness. That didn't mean he wanted to be like them. If anything, it made him more determined to go on being what he was already.

His father heard the edge in his voice. "I know you two don't see eye to eye. You're both still my boys."

"Yes, Father." Arminius didn't suppose Sigimerus could say anything else. Despite their disagreements, Arminius didn't dislike Flavus, either. But he also didn't trust him. Had Flavus known how deeply Arminius despised, resented, and feared the Romans, they would have found out about it in short order. And, in that case, Titus Minucius Basilus might not have been so willing to let him go back to Germany.

"And since you're home," Sigimerus went on, "come into the house and drink some wine with me to gladden your heart." He nodded to Arminius' companion. "You, too, Chariomerus, of course. I am in your debt for finding my son and bringing him back to Germany."

"I was glad to do it." Chariomerus stayed polite, but he didn't deny that Sigimerus did indeed owe him something. One of these days, he would call in the debt, either from Sigimerus or from Arminius.

The farmhouse was a wooden building, about forty cubits long and fifteen wide. Four posts running down the centerline supported a steeply pitched thatched roof that shed rain and snow. Stalls for the family's cattle and horses and pigs and sheep adjoined the eastern wall; the hearth was against the western wall, under a window, so in good weather a lot of the smoke escaped. On freezing winter nights the window was shuttered and the animals came inside with the people. It made the place crowded and smoky and smelly, but that was better than losing livestock.

Sigimerus pulled the rawhide latch cord and shoved the door open. "Veleda!" he called. "Look who's here at last!"

Arminius' mother was spinning wool into thread. She sprang off the wooden stool where she sat—a Roman luxury, bought from a trader—and hurried over to hug and kiss him. "So good to see you home!" she said between kisses.

"It's good to be home, too," Arminius answered. "I only wish I didn't have to come back for a reason like this."

His father, who was pouring the wine, growled down deep in his throat like an angry hunting hound. "Segestes didn't just insult you when he took Thusnelda away and swore her to this wretch of a Tudrus," he said. "He put the whole family in the shade, and everyone who follows us. Whatever you want to do to pay him back, you'll have plenty of men behind you."

"I've told him the same thing," Chariomerus said.

"I would have known it even if you didn't say a word," Arminius replied. "I've been thinking about things all the way back from Pannonia. . . . Ah, thank you, Father." He took an earthenware cup from Sigimerus. A German potter had made the cup; the sweet-smelling red wine inside came from some land the Romans ruled.

"Your health," Sigimerus said, lifting his own cup in salute.

"Yours." Arminius copied the gesture. So did his mother and Chariomerus. He drank. He'd tasted better wine, but also plenty worse. He nodded appreciatively.

"You've been thinking about what to do. . . ." Sigimerus prompted. He fiddled with the brooch that held his cloak closed. Because he was wealthy, the brooch was gold, and decorated with garnets red as the wine. An ordinary farmer would have closed his cloak with a bronze pin; a poor man would have made do with a thorn. "If you go after Segestes or Tudrus, we'll back you."

He tensed as he said the words; Arminius could see as much. But he said them anyhow, and didn't hesitate over them. Arminius loved him for that. "I don't want to start a bloody feud with Segestes, Father," he said. "We shouldn't fight one another now. We should all march side by side to fight the Romans."

"You say this, and I think you speak wisely," Sigimerus said. "Not everyone will, though. Segestes won't. He'd sooner march with the Romans than against them. I hear that's part of why he took Thusnelda away from you and gave her to Tudrus. Tudrus loves the Romans, too."

"Loves to lick their backsides, you mean," Chariomerus said.

"Some of them would like it if he did," Arminius said. Chariomerus and Sigimerus both made horrible faces. So did Veleda. Men who wanted to use other men as if they were women did what they did in secret among the Germans. You heard whispers about such things, but that was all. Anyone caught doing them died slowly and painfully.

The Romans didn't just talk openly about such things. Those who wanted to do them . . . did them. Arminius had got one of his many shocks inside the Empire when he learned that. He'd got another shock when he discovered it didn't make them effeminate—not even the ones who were pierced rather than piercing. They fought the Pannonian rebels as bravely as anyone else. He wouldn't have believed it if he hadn't seen it, but he had.

"If you don't aim to start a feud with Segestes and his retainers, what *will* you do to regain your honor?" His father brought the talk back to the business at hand—and steered it away from what he didn't care to think about. No flies on Sigimerus.

"Well, that depends," Arminius answered. "Is Thusnelda wed to Tudrus, or is she only promised to him?"

"She is promised," Veleda said. "She still lives in Segestes' steading."

Arminius breathed a sigh of relief. "That makes things easier." Even killing Tudrus wouldn't necessarily have got him Thusnelda if she'd already married Segestes' comrade. Widows often stayed single the rest of their days. With one as young and pretty as Thusnelda, that would have been a dreadful waste, which didn't mean it couldn't happen.

Sigimerus nodded. "You have more choices."

"Just so," Arminius said. "But I think I know what I'm going to try. . . ."

Soldiers gossiped. They didn't only gossip about who was screwing whom or who was feuding with whom—although, being human, they did waste a lot of time gossiping about those eternal favorites. And, being human, they also wasted a lot of time gossiping about the officials set over them.

Legions XVII, XVIII, and XIX had served together for a long time. Octavian raised them during the civil war against Antony and Cleopatra. A handful of senior centurions had been green kids scooped into the legions more than forty years before. The rest of the men had joined since. There were older legions, and legions that had seen more fighting, but XVII, XVIII, and XIX had nothing to be ashamed of.

"This Varus . . . well, he'll never make a proper general," Lucius Eggius said. He knew all the men in the tavern with him, and knew—or was as sure as you could be about such things—none of them would go telling tales to the new governor of Germany.

"His cavalry commander's not so bad," said Marcus Calvisius, a centurion from Legion XVIII. He was in his early fifties, a little too young to have been part of XVIII's original complement. "Doesn't go around making too much of himself, anyway."

"Numonius? Mm, maybe not." Lucius Eggius weighed whether to give the other newcomer the benefit of the doubt. After draining his winecup, he shook his head. "He won't tell his boss he's wrong. Varus says, 'We'll whip the Germans into shape in an hour and a half.' And Vala Numonius says, 'We sure will. An hour and a half—tops.' He's like a lap dog wagging his tail."

Marcus Calvisius ran a hand through his hair. It was silver, but his hairline hadn't retreated by even a digit's breadth. Add that to a chin like a boulder, and he made an impressive-looking man. "An hour and a half won't finish the job. You're right about that, gods know."

"A year and a half isn't likely to finish the job, either," Eggius said. "I tried to tell 'em so, but did they want to listen?" He laughed bitterly. "I mean, what the demon do I know? All I am is the bastard on the spot. That counts for nothing. They've got orders from Augustus. That counts for everything."

"How come Augustus can't see it's not as easy as he thinks?" Calvisius grumbled. "He's a smart guy, right?"

"He *is* a smart guy," Lucius Eggius said. "But even a smart guy can be dumb about places he's never seen. Augustus never came up here. All he knows is, Germany's not a proper province yet. He's mad about it, too. How can you blame him, if you look at things from down in Rome?"

"Yeah, well . . ." Marcus Calvisius ran a hand through his hair again. "If you look at things from down in Rome, you don't know anything about the Germans."

All the Roman officers nodded. Somebody said, "We're up here, and I don't think *we* know anything much about the Germans." The veterans nodded again.

"They don't *want* to turn into a province. It's about that simple," Eggius said. He shoved his cup over to the tapman, who poured it full. Fancy aristocrats watered their wine like Greeks or children. He drank his neat. So did his friends. What point to drinking if you didn't feel it?

"Gauls didn't want to turn into a province, either. Caesar walloped the snot out of them," Calvisius said. "Now we're here, and they don't mind. Not like that on the other side of the Rhine."

Nobody told him he was wrong. Lucius Eggius knew too well that he was right. Cross the Rhine, and you crossed into a different world. Even the trees and the rivers on the east side seemed to hate Romans. As for the people . . . "Well," Eggius said dryly, "it's not like they don't give us plenty of practice over there."

He got a laugh. How many battles had Legions XVII, XVIII, and XIX fought on the wrong side of the river? *On the far side of the river*, Eggius corrected himself. If Augustus said they were going to bring it into the Empire, the land over there wasn't on the wrong side at all.

Assuming they could do what Augustus said, of course. *Yeah*, Eggius thought. *Assuming.*

A centurion from Legion XIX said, "Some of the Germans are good guys. Some of them get along with us all right."

"Sure." Eggius nodded. He could feel the wine, all right, but it hadn't made him stupid yet. He didn't think it had, anyhow. He knew he wasn't stumbling over his own tongue. That was good. He took another pull at his cup and went on, "Answer me this, though. How many of those Germans who're good guys, those Germans who get along with us all right, would you trust at your back when you've got other Germans— Germans you know are enemies—trying to do you in from the front?"

A considerable silence followed. Lucius Eggius considered it. None of his considerations made him very happy. The centurion from Legion XIX didn't look very happy, either. He got his mug refilled, tilted his head back, and took a big swig; Eggius watched his prominent larynx bob up and down as he swallowed. At last, he said, "Well, there are a few."

Most of the Romans who heard that nodded. Lucius Eggius did himself. "Yeah, there are," he agreed. "But we've been trying to turn that miserable mess of trees and swamps and fogs and frogs into a province for a demon of a long time now. If we were going anywhere with it, don't you figure there'd be more than a few Germans you could count on when your back was turned?"

The centurion didn't reply to that. Nobody else did, either, not right away. Then Marcus Calvisius said, "Well, Eggius, there is one other way to deal with that."

"Oh, yeah?" Lucius Eggius said. "Like what?"

"Kill all the barbarians we can't trust and make a province with whoever's left. Why do you think XVII, XVIII, and XIX are here?"

Eggius did some more considering. When he was done, he let out a grunt. "You've got something there," he admitted. "I do wish we still had Tiberius in command, though. He's a sour bastard, sure, but nobody ever said he doesn't know what he's doing. This Varus . . . Well, who can tell? Gods rot the stinking Pannonian rebels, anyway." He set about the business of getting seriously drunk.

"*Amo. Amas. Amat,*" Segestes muttered. "*Amamum. Amatis. Amant.*"

He was currying a horse. The beast snorted, perhaps at the unfamiliar sounds. Segestes went right on conjugating the Latin verb *to love*. Then he muttered under his breath in his native tongue. Plenty of Germans would have said—plenty of Germans *did* say—he was currying favor with the Romans, too.

He didn't see it that way. If he had seen it that way, he wouldn't have done it. How many folk had gone up against Rome? Lots. How many had lost? All of them—you could look west across the Rhine or southeast across the Danube to see the latest examples. Oh, the Pannonians were still kicking and bellowing, like a bull before it went all the way into the stall. That wouldn't last much longer, though. The Romans were tough, and they had their whole vast empire to draw upon.

He ran his hand over the horse's flank and nodded to himself. That was better. Like most horses in Germany, his was a small, shaggy, rough-coated beast. If you didn't go over it with a curry comb pretty often, it would be all over tangles.

The horse made a snuffling, expectant noise. He laughed and gave it a carrot. It crunched up the treat. Then it nuzzled his hand, hoping for another one.

He laughed. "You're no horse. You're a pig with a mane and a hairy tail." He patted the horse and fed it another carrot. When it tried for a third, he shook his head and stepped out of the stall.

As soon as he did, he wished he hadn't. Thusnelda was out there playing with a puppy. That would have been bad enough any time. Spoiling a horse was one thing, but Segestes wanted his dogs mean. Why have them, if not to ward the steading? With things between him and Thusnelda as prickly as they were . . .

He was more inclined to spoil his horse than his daughter. He didn't see it that way, of course. Fathers never do.

Thusnelda had been laughing as she tickled the pup's stomach. When she saw Segestes, her face closed like a clenching fist. She straightened up and turned her back on him.

"If a man used me like that, I would kill him," Segestes remarked.

His daughter spun toward him, but not out of respect. "And you don't think you're killing me?" she retorted.

"What are you talking about?" For a moment, Segestes was honestly confused. Then he wasn't, but wished he still were. "There's nothing wrong with Tudrus," he growled. They had this argument at least once a day. He was sick of it, even if Thusnelda didn't seem to be. Why hadn't he set an earlier date for the wedding? Then she'd be out of his hair, and Tudrus would have to worry about her.

Something had changed, though. That wasn't just fury in her gray eyes. It was something very much like triumph. "Arminius is back. He's out of the fight in Pannonia, and he's hale." She spat the words in his face.

He already knew that—he'd heard a couple of days earlier. He hadn't said a word. But bad news always got where you didn't want it to. He might have known it would here. "How did you find out?" he asked wearily.

By the way Thusnelda's eyes sparked, he'd hear about knowing and not telling her. But that would be later. For now, she could score more points off him with the news itself. "One of the slaves brought word," she answered. "He said it was everywhere—except here."

So she wouldn't waste time making him pay for keeping it from her. Not now, anyway. He sighed. "It doesn't matter. It doesn't change a thing."

"You don't think so?" His daughter laughed at him.

If she weren't of his own flesh and blood . . . But she was, so he had to hold his temper down. It wasn't easy; he was a proud man. "I don't," he said, shaking his head. "And I don't want a family connection with Arminius any more. He hates the Romans too much to make it safe."

"You didn't think so when you pledged me to him," Thusnelda jeered. "And how can you say that, anyway? He joined the Roman army. *You* never did."

"The man who best knows how to break a cart is one who makes carts," Segestes said. His daughter stared at him as if he'd suddenly started spouting Greek. He couldn't have even had he wanted to. Knowing Greek existed put him a long jump ahead of most Germans. With another sigh, he went on, "Arminius joined the Romans to learn how to beat them."

"He wants us to be free," Thusnelda said.

"Free to brawl among ourselves. Free to run through the woods— and no farther. Free to be as wild as the Wends and the Finns." Segestes named the most savage peoples the Germans knew.

"The Finns tip their arrows with bone. They live on the ground, or in huts woven like baskets. They sleep on the ground." Thusnelda sounded disgusted.

"To the Romans, we look the way the Finns look to us," Segestes said.

"Then the Romans are stupid!"

Segestes shook his head. "They aren't. You know they aren't. They have all kinds of things we don't, and they don't fight one another the way we do," he said. "I want us to live the way they do. So does Tudrus. Is that so bad?"

"We should be free." Thusnelda might have been listening to Arminius. Before he left, she probably had on the sly.

"What good does that do us? Knowing things, living in peace— those do us some good," Segestes said.

Thusnelda stuck her nose in the air. Segestes wondered if Tudrus could charm—or beat—the nonsense out of her. He hoped so.

III

Back before Publius Quinctilius Varus was born, two German tribes invaded Gaul. If not for Julius Caesar, they might have taken it away from the natives before the Romans could. *If not for my wife's great-uncle's great-uncle*, Varus thought, bemused. That his father had killed himself rather than yielding to his wife's great-uncle's great-uncle he forgot for the moment. He remembered little about Sextus Quinctilius Varus. Augustus he knew very well indeed.

And he knew very well what Julius Caesar had done. With characteristic energy, Caesar bundled the Usipetes and the Tencteri back into the German forests. And then he went after them. In ten days, his engineers bridged the Rhine. The German tribes fled before him. He stayed on the east bank of the Rhine for eighteen days, then went back and finished conquering Gaul.

And he left the problem of conquering Germany for another day— for another generation, as it turned out. *For me, as it turned out*, Varus thought. Marching through Germany was easy enough. Holding the place down, really subjecting it, wasn't. Plenty of Romans had proved that, too.

One of his servants intertwined the fingers of both hands, forming a cup into which Varus could step. With help from the leg-up, he swung over his horse's back and straightened in the saddle. A mounting stone would have served as well, although a leg-up from a man better suited a commander's dignity. If he had to, Varus thought he could vault into the saddle with no help at all, like a proper cavalryman. But only a barbarian, and a stupid barbarian at that, would do things the hard way when he didn't have to.

Once seated on the horse, Varus nodded to Vala Numonius. "Let's cross," he said.

"Yes, sir." The cavalry commander nodded. They both urged their mounts forward. The rest of the cavalry detachment followed. The horses' hooves drummed on the bridge over the Rhine.

It was built on exactly the same principle as Caesar's. Roman engineers had fixed two sets of piles in the riverbed. The upstream piles leaned with the current, the downstream against it. They were about twenty-five cubits apart. Trestles slanting against the current on the downstream side helped support the structure. Upstream, a timber breakwater protected the bridge from logs or fire rafts or anything else the barbarians might aim at it.

"Once we subdue the Germans, we'll get a proper bridge with stone piers, not this military makeshift," Varus said.

"That would be splendid, sir," Numonius replied. "A sign of civilization, you might say."

"Civilization. Yes." Once again, Varus fondly remembered Syria. He remembered Rome. He remembered Athens, where he'd stopped on the way back from Syria—and where he, like his son, had studied as a young man. He remembered seeing for the first time the Parthenon and all the other wonderful buildings up on the Acropolis. By the gods, that was civilization for you!

This . . . The day was cool. The sky was a grayish, watery blue. The sun seemed half ashamed to shine. He was riding away from a legionary camp—which, in these parts, counted as an outpost of civilization. He was heading for . . . The gloomy forests that stretched on and on east of the Rhine warned him what he was heading for.

Foot soldiers followed the cavalrymen. One thing the Romans had learned from painful experience: wherever they went in Germany, they went in force. Small parties of men were all too likely to disappear. Better not to tempt the barbarians into doing what they weren't supposed to.

Varus' horse stepped off the bridge and onto the muddy ground on the east bank of the Rhine. Its hooves stopped echoing. They made the usual thumping and squelching noises instead.

Vala Numonius had dropped back by half a length to let Varus precede him. Now he caught up again. "Welcome to Germany, sir," he said.

"Germany," Varus echoed. He didn't seen any Germans here on their side of the river. He didn't particularly miss them. He'd seen plenty in Vetera: big, fair, noisy men with an exaggerated sense of their own importance. Some of the soldiers' women were pretty in an exotic way, though. They had plenty to hold on to, that was for sure.

The cavalry commander pointed toward the trees, which had been cut down for several stadia around the bridgehead. A lot of the timber from them probably went into the bridge. "They're watching us from in there," Numonius said.

"Let them watch. It will teach them respect," Varus said.

No sooner were the words out of his mouth than a German stepped into the cleared ground from among the trees. The man turned around, bent over, undid his cloak, and waggled his pale, bare backside at the Romans. Then he straightened, wrapped the cloak around himself again, and loped off into the woods.

Some of the horsemen behind Varus laughed. Others swore. "So much for respect, sir," Vala Numonius said.

Biting his lip in rage, Varus pointed out to where the German had vanished. "Seize him! Crucify him!" he shouted.

"Sir, there's no hope," said a cavalry officer who'd been on the frontier for a while. "In the forests, they're like animals. They have dens to lay up in, or they can climb trees like wall lizards wish they could. And he might be trying to lure a detachment right into an ambush."

He spoke respectfully, as a man had to do when trying to talk a provincial governor out of an order. Varus muttered, still steaming. But he could see that the soldier made good sense. If he fought on this side of the Rhine, he needed to fight on his terms, not the barbarians'.

"Very well," Varus said heavily. "*Very well*. We'll let him get away with that—for now. But the time will come when this whole province learns better. And that time will come soon, by the gods."

Numonius clapped his hands. "Well said, sir!" he exclaimed. From the other cavalry officer came an unmistakable sigh of relief.

A pale moon shone down on Segestes' steading. Arminius stood at the edge of the trees, looking things over. The steading seemed quiet, the way it should at night. If things weren't as they seemed, chances were he would die inside the hour.

He shrugged. If he died, he would die doing what was right, doing what was important. No one would say he'd let Segestes dishonor him. He knew the woman he'd sent here had talked with Thusnelda. She'd told him so herself, after she came away. She wasn't from his father's steading, so Segestes would have had no reason to suspect her.

But Arminius didn't know how Thusnelda felt. The woman who served him—he'd hired her with the fat gold earring he'd taken from the dead Pannonian—hadn't been able to tell what she thought. She'd kept her own counsel. If she liked this Tudrus, or if she obeyed her father without thinking . . . If any of that was true, Arminius would have a thin time of it tonight.

One of Segestes' dogs let out a tentative bark. A couple of others joined in a moment later. They trotted toward him.

He wore a fat leather sack on his belt. He reached for that instead of his sword. "Come on, boys. Come here," he called, as if the beasts belonged to his own father.

They weren't so fierce as they might have been—that was plain. Arminius' hopes soared. Through the woman, he'd told Thusnelda to feed them as much as they would hold. And now he pulled more chunks of raw meat from the sack and tossed them in front of the dogs.

Greedy as swine, they dug in. Arminius gave them more meat. He kept some in the sack, though: he was certain Segestes had more dogs than these. And, sure enough, two big brutes met him halfway to Segestes' house. He bribed them the same way as he had the others. They hadn't made much noise, and quieted down at once. Anybody who gave them meat had to be a friend.

The door. Arminius tapped it, lightly, with a forefinger. That tiny noise shouldn't bother anyone sleeping in there. But if someone was awake and waiting for it . . .

Was someone awake and waiting in there? Arminius tapped again, a tiny bit harder. If Thusnelda had fallen asleep in spite of everything, wouldn't that make the bitterest joke of all?

When the door opened, his hand fell to the hilt of his sword. If she'd betrayed him to her father, if warriors boiled out through the doorway, what could he do but take some of them with him?

"Arminius?" No warriors. Only a tiny ghost of a voice from the darkness inside Segestes' house.

"Thusnelda?"

She came out into the moonlight then. It shone off her fair hair and glittered from the jewels—Roman jewels, probably—set into the brooch that closed her cloak. He touched her hand. He hadn't done that since they were both children. Her fingers were chilly. Not the night, which was mild, but fear.

"Let's get away," he said, whispering himself.

She nodded. Slowly and carefully, she closed the door behind her. "You got past the dogs."

"No. They ate me," Arminius answered. Thusnelda stared at him in blank incomprehension. It was, he realized, a Roman kind of thing to say. He could explain it another time, if he decided to bother. For now, he just went on as if he hadn't spoken before: "Yes, I'm here. Yes, I'm fine. Let's get away. You *do* want to come with me, don't you?"

He wished he had the last question back as soon as it came out of his mouth, which was, of course, exactly too late. But Thusnelda said, "Yes," and that made it stop mattering.

They hurried away from Segestes' house. When they went past the two dogs Arminius had met halfway there, one of them yawned while the other thumped its tail against the ground. The dogs had to be full to bursting . . . and Thusnelda was with him now, so they were bound to be sure everything was fine.

The other three, the beasts closer to the edge of the clearing, had also had plenty to eat. Thusnelda paused to pat one of them. "Blackie was always my favorite," she said in a strangely muffled voice.

Arminius realized the muffling was swallowed tears. She wasn't leaving only Blackie behind. She was leaving everything she'd ever known. Chances were she would never see this place or her kinsfolk again. No wonder she had trouble sounding steady.

He slipped an arm around her waist. "Everything will be all right," he promised. "I will make sure everything is all right for you from now on. You are my woman now, Thusnelda. You are my wife."

In the Germans' language, *woman* and *wife* were the same word. Arminius repeated himself for emphasis' sake. Latin had two separate words for the two notions. When he asked a legionary why, the fellow had chuckled and said, "So we can think about women who aren't our wives—why else?" He'd poked Arminius in the ribs, too, a familiarity the German wouldn't have put up with from one of his own countrymen.

Germans took their wives' fidelity seriously. They took few things more seriously. Romans joked about it. When Arminius showed how shocked he was, they laughed at him for a greenhorn. After a bit, he learned to stop showing it, so they stopped laughing. But the shock didn't go away.

They really thought like that. Their men were seducers, their women sluts. They made lewd jokes about what should have been one of the most important things in the world. And they talked about how they were making the Gauls and Pannonians like them—and about how they would do the same for the Germans once they turned the land between Rhine and Elbe into a province.

To Arminius' way of thinking, the Romans would be doing it *to* the Germans. That was when he decided he had to fight them, come what might.

Thusnelda took his hands in hers and brought him back from the campaigns in Pannonia to this quiet, moonlit night. "I *am* your woman," she said. "I will be your woman, and your woman only, as long as we both live."

"That's why I'm taking you away," Arminius said. If he was also doing it to stick a finger in Segestes' eye, and in Tudrus', that was nothing Thusnelda needed to worry about.

She looked up at him. He looked down at her. He bent to kiss her. Her arms came up and went around his neck.

One of the dogs—Blackie?—let out a questioning growl. That didn't surprise Arminius, even if it did annoy him. He'd seen it before. Animals often thought people were fighting when they were doing something very different.

Evidently, Thusnelda had seen it before, too. "It's all right. It really is," she told the dog, and stroked it again. Then she turned back to Arminius. "Come on."

They hurried away, along the track by which Arminius had come. He looked back toward Segestes' steading once or twice. The dogs didn't come after him, and he heard no shouts or cries to make him think anyone but Thusnelda had awakened. Joy glowed in his heart. He'd got away with it!

Thusnelda didn't look back even once. She'd made up her mind, and she was sticking with what she'd decided.

The moon went down. Darkness enfolded the world. "Spirits?" Thusnelda asked nervously.

"Before they take you, they'll have to take me first," Arminius said. He'd never seen—or never been sure he'd seen—a nighttime spirit, which didn't mean he didn't believe they were there. Some of the Romans—not all, but some—even laughed at gods and ghosts. If that didn't prove they were a depraved folk . . . plenty of other things did.

Something hooted. Thusnelda started. "Is that only an owl?" It must have been. No spirits swooped out of the sky to strike. No demons came snarling out of the trees where they commonly hid.

"Nothing to fear," Arminius said, and slid his arm around her waist. With a small sigh, she pressed herself against him. Her body felt so warm, he marveled that she didn't light the way ahead like a torch.

Since she didn't, his eyes had to get used to starlight. Little by little, darkness seemed less absolute. Wotan's wandering star blazed high in the south, shining brighter than any of the fixed stars. The Romans had the arrogance to believe they could figure out why and how the wandering stars moved as they did. What answer did any proper man need but that the gods willed it so?

The dim gray light was, at last, enough to show him the place he remembered passing on the way to Segestes' steading. "Here," he said softly. He led Thusnelda off the path and out onto the little meadow he'd found. "Here you will become my woman in truth."

"Yes," she said, even more quietly than he. No going back from this, not for her. Once she'd lost her maidenhead, she was either a wife or a trull—nothing in between. The Romans might joke about women's appetites, but not Arminius' folk.

He undid the brooch fastening his cloak and spread the warm wool garment on the grass. Then he also unfastened Thusnelda's. He spread it on top of his. "The best bed I can make for you," he said, "and the grass is soft."

"It will do, because you are here with me," she said.

He quickly shed his shoes and tunic and trousers. Under his clothes, he wore tight-fitting linen drawers, which proved he came from a wealthy family. By the time he pulled down the drawers, Thusnelda was naked, too. He wished the moon still shone—he wanted to see her better. Foul-mouthed as the Romans were, they had a point about that: it added something.

Well, touch would have to do. They lay down together. He explored her with hands and lips. Then, when he couldn't stand to wait any longer, he poised himself above her. "Oh," she said in a low voice when he went into her. He met resistance—she *was* a maiden. "Oh!" she said again, louder and less happily this time, as he pushed hard. "You're splitting me in half!"

"No," he said, breaking through. "It's like this the first time for women."

"My mother told me the same thing. I thought she was trying to frighten me so I wouldn't do anything I wasn't supposed to."

Arminius hardly heard her. Intent on his own building delight, he drove home again and again. Soon, he gasped and groaned and spent himself. Stroking her cheek, he said, "You *are* my woman now." *And your carrion crow of a father won't take you back no matter what.*

Varus had thought Vetera was the back of beyond—and it was. To a cosmopolitan man, a man used to Athens, to Syria, to Rome, Vetera had seemed the edge of the world. Now that Varus found himself in Mindenum, he would have given a considerable sum to go back to Vetera once more.

Vetera was on the ragged edge of civilization—no two ways about it. When you went from Vetera to Mindenum, when you traveled from the frontier between Gaul and Germany into the heart of the German wilderness, you fell off the edge.

The soldiers and a handful of sutlers who traded with both them and the Germans were the only men from the Empire for many miles in all directions. But for the encampment on the Visurgis, this was *Germany*, pure and simple. Some other fortified camps—Aliso was the strongest—along the west-flowing Lupia led back toward the Rhine. From Mindenum, one of these days, legionaries could press on toward the Elbe, Augustus' ultimate goal.

For now, Varus thought it no small miracle that this Roman island persisted in the midst of the German sea. The endless woods stretching away to north and south, east and west, the tops of the trees rhythmically stirred by the wind, put him in mind of waves scudding across the Mediterranean.

When he spoke that conceit aloud, the officers from Legions XVII, XVIII, and XIX didn't quite laugh in his face, but they came close. "When you see waves on the North Sea, sir, you forget everything you thought you knew about 'em before," said a bluff prefect named Lucius Caedicius. "The ones on the Mediterranean . . . well, they're nothing but babies alongside of these." Several other men nodded.

Absurdly, Varus felt compelled to defend the honor of the sea that was a Roman lake. "Well, but we don't sail on the Mediterranean half the year, for fear of what it might do."

"That's so, sir," Caedicius agreed, and Varus smugly thought he'd made his point. But the prefect continued, "You can get waves like that the year around in the North Sea, and bigger ones come winter."

"Oh." The Roman governor of Germany felt obscurely punctured.

Varus discovered to his dismay that the Germans around Mindenum paid their taxes in grain and cattle and fruit—when they paid them at all. That made a painful contrast to Syria, where the tax collectors used a system older than the Roman occupation, older than the Greek occupation that preceded it, and probably older than the Persian occupation that preceded the Greek. In Syria, the Empire took every copper it was entitled to. Here . . . ?

"They need to use coins with us," Varus told anyone who would listen to him—and, since he was the governor, everyone had to listen to him. "Coins, by the gods! How do we know what a cow is worth, or a basket of apples, or a local measure of barley? The natives must go home laughing at the way they cheat us."

"Sir, the Germans are only just learning about coins. I think you've heard that before," Lucius Caedicius said. "They mostly swap back and forth, like."

"I don't care what they do amongst themselves. That's not my worry." Varus would gladly have sacrificed an ox in thanksgiving that it wasn't his worry, too. "But this is supposed to be a Roman province now. When the Germans deal with us, they should act like proper provincials."

"You said it, sir: this is supposed to be a Roman province," the prefect replied. "But there's a difference between what it's supposed to be and what it is. A dog is supposed to be your friend, but sometimes he'll bite you anyhow."

A lot of the other Roman officers seemed to feel the same way. Their attitude left Varus fuming. How was he going to do the job Augustus had given him if the men who were tasked with helping him tried to thwart him instead? Whenever he rounded on them, they denied with oaths that they intended doing any such thing. But what they intended and what they did—or didn't do—seemed very different to him.

He found he preferred dealing with the Germans to his own folk. With the natives, at least, he knew where he stood. They seemed to lack the refined hypocrisy with which too many Romans armored themselves against the world. When a German said he would do something, he would. When a Roman said he would do something, he would . . . if he felt like it, or if he decided it was to his advantage.

And when a German had a problem, it was commonly a simple kind of problem, one a man could easily deal with. A chieftain paid a call at Mindenum. The German didn't come alone, of course; one measure of a man's status here was the size of his retinue. One of the fierce-looking men in his retinue, a certain Tudrus, was also an aggrieved party.

Varus received the two of them in the fancy tent that did duty for a governor's palace here. He served them wine, as if conferring with equals. In a way, he was: Segestes had been granted Roman citizenship. On advice from his officers, Varus didn't water the Germans' wine. To the barbarians, such moderation was only Roman foolishness.

Segestes did handle the thick neat vintage well enough. Tudrus drank a good deal but said little, content to let his chieftain speak for him. Which Segestes did, in slow, accented, but perfectly comprehensible Latin: "I come to you, leader of the Romans, because my sworn man and I have been wronged by another man who is a Roman citizen."

"Go on, please," Varus said. If he remembered rightly, he'd learned about this quarrel back in Vetera.

"I will do that." Segestes had impressive natural dignity. He was tall and lean, his fair hair graying and his bushy mustache also streaked with snow. "You may have heard that my daughter, Thusnelda, was betrothed to Tudrus here."

The other German stirred. "Yes. It is so." He spoke much less Latin than Segestes did.

"I have heard something of this." Varus sipped from his cup. He'd had his wine mixed half-and-half with water. To his way of thinking, even that was strong.

"Thusnelda was betrothed before, to a man named Arminius," Segestes went on. "As I say, I bring this matter before you not least because he is also a Roman citizen."

"I see." Varus wasn't sure he did. But he asked what seemed the next reasonable question: "What did this, uh, Arminius do to make you break off the connection?"

"He aims to rebel against Rome. Because of this, I want nothing to do with him." Segestes spoke with care. He had to pause now and then to remember an ending for a noun or verb. He went on, "I have been a friend to the Romans ever since you began to bring your power into Germany. That is more than twenty years ago now. I think our folk will gain by coming under the Empire. Ask any of your long-serving officers. They will tell you I speak truth."

"I believe you." Varus did. Not even a German would be silly enough to spout a lie so easily checked. Varus took another sip from his winecup. It bought him a few heartbeats in which to ponder. "Why do you say Arminius is a rebel? That is a serious charge. What will he say when I ask him about it?"

"He will give you whatever lies he thinks he needs," the chieftain replied. "He will say he joined the auxiliaries because he wanted to help Rome. But he is like a snake. He colors himself like grass, so you do not see him before he strikes." He spoke in his native tongue to Tudrus, who nodded vehemently.

"How old is he? How old is your daughter?" Varus asked. "Is she past the age of consent?"

Segestes looked unhappy. "Thusnelda has twenty years," he said reluctantly. "Arminius has four or five more. But I am the father here. You Romans know what it means to be the father."

In theory, a Roman *paterfamilias* had all but absolute power over his descendants. In theory, yes. In practice, the law whittled away at that power year by year. Varus had no idea whether a German father was also, in essence, a *paterfamilias*. His interest in what passed for law among the barbarians was greater than his interest in falling on his sword, but not a lot greater.

"Meaning no disrespect to you or your friend," he said, "but sometimes a woman will do what she will do whether her father wants her to or not. Sometimes she'll do it *because* her father doesn't want her to. Did this Arminius kidnap her, or did she go with him willingly?"

Tudrus asked a question in the Germans' language—probably

wondering what Varus had said. Segestes answered in the same speech before returning to Latin. "She went of her own will," he admitted, even more reluctantly.

"Well, then, my dear fellow . . ." Varus spread his hands. "What do you expect me to do? I am only a governor. I am not a god, to make her undo what she has already done."

"You are the governor, yes," Segestes said. "You can order Arminius to give her up. You can punish him for sneaking on to my land and stealing her."

"Yes, I supposed I could do those things," Varus said. "But then what? Would her match with your friend here go forward as if, uh, Thusnelda never left your home?" He'd heard the Germans valued their women's chastity far more than Romans did. That struck him as something which would have been admirable if it weren't so futile.

Segestes and Tudrus went back and forth in their language. In his bad Latin, Tudrus said, "It to go forward anyhow."

"I . . . see." Varus wondered if he did. Was Tudrus so loyal to his chieftain that he would accept damaged goods from him? Or was he so eager to lie in a young girl's arms that he didn't care if he wasn't the first? With a Roman, Varus would have judged the second more likely. With one of these savages, who could say?

"Tudrus is of my tribe. He is of my clan. He is of my band," Segestes said, as if that explained everything. Maybe, to him, it did.

"And this Arminius?" Varus inquired.

"He is of my tribe," Segestes said. "I would not have sent Thusnelda away from the Cherusci." The choking guttural with which he began the tribe's name sounded badly out of place in a sentence intended to be Latin. He went on, "But past that, no. Tudrus is far closer to me: another reason I like this match better."

"Well, I will summon Arminius. I will hear what he has to say," Varus said. "But if he does not want to give up your daughter, and if she does not want to leave him . . ." The Roman spread his hands again. "There are such things as accomplished facts. You may not like them. I can't blame you if you don't. Sometimes, though, you have to accept them and go on from there. Life is like that."

Segestes looked unhappy. When he translated for Tudrus, his companion looked unhappier yet. "I think you are making a mistake, sir," he said. "If you Romans are going to rule in Germany, you cannot be so mild. You must be strong." He and Tudrus got to their feet. They bowed, and then left the tent without waiting for Varus' permission.

"Strong," Varus murmured. He led three legions. Of course he was strong. Of course Rome was strong. Segestes didn't understand the difference between strength and restraint—or, more likely, the barbarian simply didn't care.

Arminius had never imagined he could be so happy. He'd taken Thusnelda from her father for his honor's sake. What he'd felt about her didn't have much to do with it. He hadn't had any strong feelings about her for her own sake. How could he, when he hadn't known her well?

But he knew her now. He'd lain with her once to seal the bargain of her giving herself to him rather than to her father or to Tudrus. And he'd lain with her every chance he got after that, just for the sake of lying with her. He'd never dreamt anyone could be so beautiful or give him so much pleasure.

He'd never realized that anyone who gave him so much pleasure would naturally seem beautiful to him. He was still very young.

And Thusnelda was as delighted with him as he was with her. He knew he'd hurt her the first time—a man couldn't help it. After that, though . . . After that, she was as eager as he was, which said a great deal.

The two of them amused his father. "I ought to throw a bucket of cold water over you, the way I would with dogs coupling in front of the door," Sigimerus said.

"Why?" Arminius protested. "We don't do it in public. We always put our cloaks up around the bed. No one can see us." Nobody in any German household had more privacy than that.

His father chuckled. "No one can see you, maybe, but that doesn't mean no one can hear you. Your woman yowls like a wildcat."

"Well, what if she does?" Arminius had noticed that, too. He took pride in it, as reflecting well on his own manhood.

Before Sigimerus could tell him anything different, one of the house slaves dashed in from outside, calling, "Lord! Lord's son! Half a dozen Romans are riding up the path toward the steading!"

"Romans!" Arminius exclaimed. Half a dozen Romans might ride some distance through Germany. In a time without overt war, the locals might not want to try to ambush them. Too great a chance one or more would get away—and Roman retribution was something the Germans had learned to be wary of.

Sigimerus cursed Segestes as foully as he knew how. "What will you bet he's complained of you to their chief?" he said.

Arminius hadn't expected that. But he was a Roman citizen, and so was Segestes. If Thusnelda's father had found a way to use that against him . . . If so, Segestes really was a devious Roman, where Arminius wore *his* citizenship as a disguise.

"What do you want to do, son?" Sigimerus asked. "We can kill them if we have to."

"We aren't ready to stand against Rome if we do," Arminius replied, and his father didn't try to tell him he was wrong. He grimaced. "Let me go talk with them and see how serious this is."

He stepped outside. The day was cool and gray: a usual enough German day. The Romans had almost reached the steading. They were not big men, but the horses they rode were large by German standards. They could look down on him, as few Romans on foot could do. Their faces were all planes and angles and imperious noses; their dark eyes showed him no more than polished jet might have.

"I am Arminius, Sigimerus' son," he said in Latin. "I am a Roman citizen. What do you want of me?" His father and the slave stood behind him. Sigimerus' hand rested near his swordhilt, but not on it.

"Hail, Arminius," one of the Romans said, shooting out his clenched fist in the salute his folk used. "Publius Quinctilius Varus, the governor of Germany, summons you to his lodging at Mindenum, so that you may explain your conduct in the matter of the abduction of the daughter of another Roman citizen."

All those genitives thrown in his face one after another . . . The horseman was trying to make things difficult for him. But Arminius followed, though he wasn't sure his father did. "Am I under arrest?" he asked. If the Roman told him yes, he might have to fight. By German standards, Roman notions of justice were harsh and arbitrary.

But the fellow shook his head. "No. I am to inform you that this is an inquiry only."

"Do you take oath by your gods that you tell me the truth? Do you take oath by the eagle of your legion that you tell me the truth?"

"By my gods and by the eagle of Legion XVIII, Arminius son of Sigimerus, I tell you the truth," the Roman horseman replied without the least hesitation.

Romans were born deceitful. Not many of them, though, were depraved enough to swear falsely an oath like that. Arminius had seen that Roman soldiers put their legion's eagle, the symbol of their comradeship, even above their gods. Warriors who could be skulkers and villains in other ways would lay down their lives without a murmur to keep their eagle safe.

"Do you swear I will go free afterwards?" he asked.

"I cannot do that. It is for the governor to judge. But he has a name for fair dealing," the cavalryman replied.

Arminius considered. He knew how badly Segestes had wronged him. Any fool could see as much. If this Varus even half deserved the reputation the Roman said he had . . . Arminius noted that the fellow had not tried to cozen him with a lying promise. That argued that he did take his oath seriously.

It also helped Arminius make up his mind. "I will go with you," he said. "Your governor will use me justly." *I hope.*

"He is not only my governor. He is the governor of all of Germany," the Roman said.

No one did or could govern all of Germany. The very idea made Arminius want to laugh. But he didn't. All he said was, "Let us go."

IV

When Lucius Eggius was in Mindenum, he drank more beer than wine. The locals brewed beer, so it was cheap. Every amphora of wine came cross-country from Vetera. Sutlers made you pay through the nose. Varus could afford fancy vintages whenever he pleased, maybe. As a prefect, Eggius was a long way from poor. But he wasn't made of money like a provincial governor, either.

"You know what else?" he said after a blond German barmaid brought him a fresh mug. "Once you get used to it, this horse piss isn't so bad."

"It isn't so good, either," another Roman said. "And here's the proof—even the cursed Germans buy wine when they can afford to."

"Wine's in fashion, that's why," Eggius said. "Same way as every Roman who thinks he's anybody has to learn Greek so everybody else can see how clever he is, that's how the Germans drink wine. It lets 'em think they're as good as we are, so they do it."

"It must get 'em mighty drunk, too, if they're dumb enough to think like that," the other officer came back, and got a laugh from the soldiers who filled the drink shop.

"Oh, come on. Give me a break. They do like to ape us. Everybody knows that," Lucius Eggius said. "Sometimes it even comes in handy, like when they go to Varus on account of their woman-stealing instead of starting their own private war. We'd just get sucked in if they did."

"We're liable to get sucked in any which way," said a young soldier named Caldus Caelius. "Her father's a big shot, and so is the guy she was promised to, and the guy who ran off with her, too."

"It's like something out of Homer," Vala Numonius said. Had Eggius seen him in the tavern, he might not have made his crack about upper-crust Romans learning Greek. The cavalry commander *was* a Roman like that. He showed he knew the *Iliad*, continuing, "What turned the Greeks against Troy? Paris running off with Helen, that's what. And what made Achilles angry? Agamemnon keeping Briseïs when he had no right to her."

"And they all fought a bloody big war on account of it." Eggius knew that much, anyhow. Who didn't? "We don't want 'em doing that here."

"Me, I wouldn't mind if they did. The more they kill each other off, the better, far as I'm concerned," Caldus Caelius said. "I wished they'd all do each other in." He eyed the statuesque barmaid and appeared to have second thoughts. "Well, the men, anyway."

"There you go, son," Eggius said. "Think with your crotch and you'll always know where you stand." Everybody groaned. Someone threw a barley roll at him. Showing a soldier's quick reflexes, he caught it out of the air and ate it. He would have liked to dip it in olive oil, but not much of that made it to Mindenum, either. The Germans used butter instead. Eggius might have acquired a taste for beer, but he drew the line at butter.

"The father is a Roman citizen. So is the fellow who ran away with the girl," Vala Numonius said.

"An upstanding Roman citizen," another officer put in, and drew more groans.

Numonius ignored him, proceeding down his own track: "So it must be proper for Quinctilius Varus to sort out the rights and wrongs, whatever they happen to be."

He'd come to Germany with Varus. He was going to assume the man from whom he'd got the command was right no matter what. That was how the world worked. Eggius understood such things perfectly well. Who didn't, who hadn't been born yesterday?

Eggius could still get in a jab or two: "So what will he do, then? Tell them to cut the wench in half, so they both get a share?"

"That's what the Jews did once upon a time, only with a baby," Vala Numonius said. "Lots of those crazy Jews in Syria."

He'd been with Varus before, then. Lucius Eggius had figured as much. "Jews and Germans. Two sets of crazy barbarians. They deserve each other," he said.

"No doubt," Numonius said. "They aren't just crazy, either. They're two of the *stubbornest* sets of barbarians anybody ever saw, too." He sighed. "Furies take me if I know how we'll ever turn either lot into proper Romans, but I suppose we've got to try."

"Sure." Eggius finished his latest mug of beer. He looked around for the barmaid. There she was, trying to talk to Caldus Caelius. Except for what had to do with her trade, she knew next to no Latin. Caelius spoke none of her tongue, either. Eggius didn't know whether the barmaid would ever make a proper Roman, but Caldus Caelius, with or without the Germans' language, was doing his best to turn her into an improper one.

When he reached under her shift, she poured a mug of beer over his head. He swore, spluttering like a seal. He started to get angry, but the rest of the Romans laughed at him. If they all thought it was funny, he couldn't very well slap the barmaid around.

Trying might not have been such a good idea anyhow. She was an inch taller than Caelius, and almost as wide through the shoulders. If she had a knife, she'd be deadly dangerous. And, as Eggius knew all too well, Germans always had knives, or a way to get hold of them.

Sighing, he waved to the barmaid himself. She came over and re-filled his mug. He didn't try to feel her up. She nodded, acknowledging that he didn't. In Germany, winning a nod like that came close to a triumph. Lucius Eggius sighed again, and proceeded to get very drunk.

Arminius ground his teeth when he got a good look at Mindenum. It wasn't that the legionary camp didn't look familiar. It did; he'd seen plenty just like it when he campaigned in Pannonia. This one was bigger, because it held more men. Otherwise, it was as much like any of the others as two grains of barley.

No: what infuriated him was that this enormous encampment sat on German soil. The Romans had built it as if they had every right to do so. They'd thought the same thing in Pannonia. The locals there were trying to throw them out, but Arminius didn't think they'd be able to do it. The Romans had already got too well established.

And if they got well established here, the Germans would have a demon of a time throwing them out, too. Arminius scowled. He was cursed if he'd let some slab-faced Roman seal-stamper tell him and his folk what to do. He was cursed if he'd let the Romans crucify his kinsmen who presumed to disobey, too.

Careful, he told himself. *You can't show what you think. If you do, you won't get free of this place.* Dissembling didn't come naturally to Germans. His folk were more likely to trumpet what they aimed to do than to hide it. But the Romans themselves had taught him that lying had its uses. He needed to show this Quinctilius Varus what a good student he made.

He urged his mount forward. It let out a manlike sigh. It was a small horse, and he was a large man. Carrying his weight couldn't have been easy. Well, carrying Rome's oppressive weight wouldn't be easy for Germany, either.

He rode down toward the *porta praetoria*, the encampment's northern gate. Varus' tent would lie closer to that one than to any of the others. Supply wagons came in from the west. The Romans would have brought their goods as far up the Lupia as they could: easier and cheaper to move anything massive by water than by land. But Mindenum lay east of the Lupia's headwaters, right in the heart of Germany.

If I were at war with the Romans now, I could cut off their supplies as easily as I snap my fingers, Arminius thought. How much good would that do him, though? The legionaries would fight their way back toward the Rhine, plundering as they went. The forts along the Lupia and the ships that sailed it could help them, too. They had a formidable force here—people said three legions, and the camp looked big enough to hold them. Cutting their supply line would infuriate them, but probably wouldn't destroy them: the worst of both worlds.

"Halt! Who comes?" a sentry called, first in Latin and then, with a horrible accent, in the Germans' speech. The Romans were alert. Well, in this country they had to be, or they'd start talking out of new mouths cut in their throats. They made good soldiers. They wouldn't have been so dangerous if they didn't.

Arminius reined in. "I am Arminius, Sigimerus' son," he answered in army Latin. "Not only am I a Roman citizen—I am also a member of the Equestrian Order. I have come in answer to a summons from Publius Quinctilius Varus, the governor of Germany." *The chief thief among all you thieves*, was how he translated that in his own mind.

A minute's worth of muffled talk followed. Whatever the sentries had expected, that wasn't it. Arminius advanced no farther. Roman citizen or not, he would have been asking for trouble if he had. He knew how sentries' minds worked. They were like dogs who carried spears. They had to decide for themselves whether he'd thrown them meat.

When one of them showed himself, Arminius knew he'd won. "You are expected, son of Sigimerus," the man said. *Somebody* might have expected him, but these fellows hadn't—not right away, anyhow. The sentry went on, "One of us will escort you to the governor's quarters. Come ahead."

"I thank you." Arminius urged the horse toward the entranceway.

Inside the fortified encampment, Roman soldiers went about their business. They seemed as much at home as they would have inside the Empire. As far as they were concerned, they *were* inside the Empire— they brought it with them wherever they went. Arminius' hands gripped the reins till his knuckles whitened. The gall they had! The arrogance!

A few Germans fetched and carried for the soldiers. Slaves? Servants? Hired men? It hardly mattered. They were traitors to their folk.

A pretty woman stepped out of an officer's tent. Her fair hair blew in the breeze. When she saw Arminius, she squeaked and drew back in a hurry. She wasn't quite dead to shame, then. She didn't want a fellow German to know she was giving herself to an invader.

The legionary leading Arminius was blind to the byplay. "Here y'are," he said. "You can tie your nag up in front of his tent." The Roman also used army Latin. *Equus* was the formal word for *horse*. He said *cabal-*

lus instead. Arminius would have, too. And a German pony *was* a nag by Roman standards.

Going into the tent didn't mean Arminius got to see Quinctilius Varus right away. He hadn't thought it would. The Roman governor might be busy with someone else. Even if he wasn't, he would make Arminius wait anyhow, to impress on the German his own importance. The tent was big enough to be divided into several rooms by cloth partitions. The man perched scribbling on a stool near the entry flap had to be a secretary, not Varus himself.

Because he was a prominent man's secretary, he reflected his master's glory. "And you are——?" he asked, though he had to know. By his tone, he seemed to expect the answer, *Nothing but a sheep turd.*

Arminius might have tried to kill a German who sneered like that. But he knew how to play Roman games, too. "Arminius son of Sigimerus, a Roman citizen and a member of the Equestrian Order," he replied, as he had to the sentries. "Who are you?"

"Aristocles, *pedisequus* to the governor." The secretary sounded prouder of being a slave than Arminius did of being his father's son. No German, no matter how debased, would have done that. Arminius wouldn't have known what to make of it if he hadn't seen it before among Roman slaves. The *pedisequus* added, "The governor will see you soon."

"Good. Thank you." Arminius swallowed his anger. You had to when you dealt with these folk. If you didn't, you threw the game away before you even started playing.

Aristocles went back to his scribbles. Arminius knew what writing was for, though he didn't have his letters. He also knew Aristocles was subtly insulting him by working while he was there. And he had to keep standing while the slave sat. That was an insult, too.

But then, as if by magic, another slave appeared with wine and bread and a bowl of olive oil for dipping. Arminius liked butter better. He didn't say so—to the Romans, eating butter branded any man a savage. He and plenty of other German auxiliaries had heard the chaffing in Pannonia.

Maybe this Aristocles was waiting for him to complain. The skinny little man would glance at him sidelong every so often. Arminius ate and drank with the best Roman manners he had. Maybe they weren't perfect by the slave's standards, but they proved good enough.

Voices rose and fell in one of those back rooms. One of them had to belong to Varus. Arminius listened while pretending he was doing nothing of the kind. A German who'd never had anything to do with Romans would have cupped a hand behind his ear to hear better. So would a lot of legionaries. But Roman chieftains played the game by different rules. Having claimed the status of a Roman chieftain himself, Arminius had to show he knew those rules.

The Romans were talking about keeping Mindenum supplied. They didn't seem to see any problems. No, that wasn't necessarily so: they didn't want Arminius to hear about any problems they saw. They were bound to know he was waiting out here. They were bound to know he was listening to them, too, whether he showed it or not. He hid his curiosity. They hid the truth. Romans used silence and misdirection far more than Germans did.

After a while, the voice Arminius guessed to be Varus' said, "Well, that should about cover it, eh, Numonius?"

"Yes, sir," the other voice replied. "I'll add to the patrols. Nobody will get away with anything—I promise you that."

"I wasn't worried—I know how you take care of things," the first voice said. "Now I've got to talk with that fellow who ran off with the girl." The voice's owner sighed, as if Arminius wasn't worth bothering with.

"I'm sure you'll set things straight, sir," Numonius said. Arminius fought not to gag. Roman underlings flattered those who ranked above them in ways the Germans found disgusting. So much of what the Romans spewed forth was obvious nonsense. If their superiors believed it, they had to be fools.

But fools couldn't have conquered so much of the world. Fools couldn't have built up the army in which Arminius had served, the army that held this fortified encampment deep inside Germany. Which argued that high-ranking men couldn't truly believe all the flattery they got. Why insist on it, then?

The only answer he could find was that Romans didn't think they were great unless others acclaimed them. A German knew what he was worth all by himself. A Roman needed somebody else to tell him what a splendid fellow he was. Then he would nod and smile—modestly, of course—and say, "Well, yes, so I am. How good of you to notice."

Numonius came out. He was short and skinny and bowlegged: he looked like a cavalry officer, in other words. The nod he gave Arminius was somewhere between matter-of-fact and friendly. "The governor told me he would see you in a little while," he said.

"Thank you," Arminius replied. Admitting he'd overheard the conversation would have been rude, even if the Roman had to know he had. The rule among the Germans was much the same.

Aristocles bustled into the back of the tent. He and Varus went back and forth in Greek. Arminius had learned a couple of curses in that language, but didn't speak it. Then the *pedisequus* returned. "I have the honor of escorting you into the governor's illustrious presence," he told Arminius.

"Good," the German said. *About time*, he thought. Some of his folk would have come right out and said so. He might have himself, before he went off to Pannonia to learn Roman ways. Having learned them, he tried to use them to advantage.

Publius Quinctilius Varus sat in a chair with a back, which proved him a very important personage indeed. He didn't rise when Arminius came before him. Arminius stiffened to attention, as he would have to a senior Roman officer on campaign, and shot out his right arm with his fist clenched.

Varus smiled. He waved Arminius to a stool. "So you're the chap who's too fond of his lady love, are you?" he said. Was he laughing at Arminius or with him? The German couldn't tell. He often had trouble figuring out what Romans meant.

Straight ahead, then. "No, sir. It wasn't that. Segestes hurt my honor when he took her away from me and tried to give her to Tudrus."

"Tried to give . . . Yesss." Varus stretched out the last word. He frowned at Arminius. "This Segestes says some hard things about you."

Arminius weighed the words—and the frown. Varus was about his father's age, but a very different man. Sigimerus was tough and hard, like seasoned timber. Romans could be like that; Arminius had met plenty who were. Varus wasn't. He didn't seem like a fighting man to the German. The Romans had people who did nothing but gather supplies for their armies—quartermasters, they called them. The notion had never occurred to the Germans, but it worked. Maybe Varus was stamped from that mold.

Or maybe he really was a fighting man no matter how he looked. With the Romans, you never could tell. Arminius had met one military tribune who acted more like a woman than a proper man had any business doing. But the fellow was a terror, a demon, on the battlefield.

How to reply? With a smile and a shrug he used like a shield to hide what he was really thinking, Arminius said, "Well, he would, wouldn't he? If he can make me look bad, he doesn't seem like a fool and a liar and an oathbreaker himself."

"This, uh, Thusnelda." Varus pronounced the name badly. He put *this* in front of a lot of Germans' names, as if they were things, not people. "She is happy with you?"

"Yes, sir!" This time, Arminius didn't hesitate at all.

Quinctilius Varus noticed. He might not be a fighting man, but he wasn't stupid. Amusement glinted in his dark eyes. "I see," he said. "And you're happy with her, too, aren't you?"

"Yes, sir, I am." How could Arminius explain it to the Roman? "I did not take her because I thought we would be happy, but I am glad we are."

The glint became a smile—a small smile, but a smile even so. "How old are you, Arminius?"

Before the German answered, he had to count on his fingers. "I am twenty-four, sir. Why?"

"Because you make me jealous," Varus said. "It is so easy to be happy with a woman—almost any woman—when you're twenty-four. When you're thirty-four or forty-four or fifty-four . . ." He sighed.

Arminius' mother and father took each other for granted. They were content with each other, anyhow. Happy? He'd never wondered about it. He knew the Romans' laws let them change wives—and, for that matter, husbands—almost as readily as they changed clothes. His folk did things differently. Maybe that meant German men and women *had* to make the best of each other.

As for fifty-four . . . To twenty-four, fifty-four was a journey greater than the one from Germany to Pannonia and back again. Fifty-four was a journey greater than one from Germany to Rome itself and back again. Arminius could imagine going down to Rome. He'd seen Roman towns in Pannonia, and along the Rhine. He imagined the imperial capital as something like a bigger version of one of those, something like an outsized legionary encampment.

He couldn't imagine fifty-four at all. An old man, aching, with bad teeth and short wind? Varus didn't seem as ancient as all that, but he was graying and balding. He'd seen better days, all right. At the height of his own strength, Arminius felt a sudden, startling sympathy—almost pity—for the Roman.

He also knew what Varus had to be thinking. Varus wouldn't want trouble from the Germans. A governor who wasn't a soldier wouldn't want anything but peace and quiet. If Arminius gave them to him . . .

"I do not seek a blood feud with Segestes," Arminius said. "This I swear, by my gods and yours. I have Thusnelda. She is enough. She satisfies my honor. I do not need to spike her father's head to a tree."

Quinctilius Varus' mouth twisted. Too late, Arminius realized he might have left off that last sentence. The Romans worshiped effete gods who drank blood, but not man's blood. How strong could they be if they turned their backs on strong food?

Then Varus chuckled, and then he smiled a broad smile. "You may be a Roman citizen, but some of your ways are still German," he observed.

"It is so," Arminius said simply.

"But you do pledge that this matter is over now, as far as you are concerned?" the Roman official persisted.

"I said it. I meant it," Arminius answered.

Varus smiled again—wistfully. "No, you are not altogether a Roman. What we say and what we mean too often have little to do with each other. A pity, but the truth. When you say something, I believe I can rely on it."

"I am glad of that, sir," Arminius said. And so he was. When he spoke to his own folk, he was indeed the soul of truth. When he spoke to Romans . . . He'd learned enough from the invaders to know how to turn their own arts against them. He could dissemble and never let on. He could, not to put too fine a point on it, lie. He could, and he did.

"All right, then. Go home. Stay there quietly. Enjoy your woman, this, uh, Thusnelda." No, Varus couldn't come close to pronouncing the German name. He went on, "I will tell this Segestes that there is to be no feud. He will hearken to me."

He is your dog, Arminius thought. Again, what went through his mind didn't show on his face. "It is good," he said. "I thank you."

Varus waved that aside. "It's all right, son," he said, and paused thoughtfully. "Do you know, you remind me a little of my own son. You're bigger, you're fairer, but something about the way you hold your head. . . ." He laughed. "Something about the way you hold back, too, so you don't tell me off."

Arminius was alarmed, but only for a moment. This Roman hadn't looked into his heart and seen his hatred for the Empire. No, Varus, an older man, had looked at a young man and seen one eager to be free from the restraints older men put on him. Varus didn't need to be a wizard to do that. He only needed to be a man who remembered what being young was like.

Sure enough, he went on, "Gaius is in Athens now, finishing up his education." He paused again. "Come to think of it, you've had a bit of an education in Roman ways yourself, haven't you? Not the same kind of education, but an education even so."

What kind of education was Gaius Quinctilius Varus getting in Athens? Arminius had no real notion. Carefully, he said, "I learned much in the Roman army." *I learned how dangerous you people really are.*

"I'll bet you did," Varus said, but he was still smiling, so he couldn't suspect what lessons Arminius had drawn from his service. "Nothing like Roman discipline here in Germany now, is there?"

"No, sir." Arminius spoke nothing but the truth there. It worried him. Unless he caught the Romans by surprise, that discipline made them formidable foes. And how could he surprise them when they sent out scouts in all directions?

"When you Germans gain discipline, I wouldn't be surprised if you show the world a thing or two," Varus said. "You need us to teach you what you should know."

"Your folk taught me a lot when I served." Again, Arminius didn't specify what he'd learned.

The Roman governor of his homeland nodded to him. "Good. That's good. Little by little, Germans *will* pick up Roman ways. That kind of thing has been happening for a while now on the other side of the Rhine. Some of the Gauls use Latin more than their own language, they really do. Some of them—may the gods strike me dead if I lie—some of them, I say, are even starting to write Latin poetry."

Arminius tried to imagine Germans writing Latin poetry. If ever anyone from his own folk undertook such a thing, Germany would be a very different place. It would also be a place he had no desire to see.

Nodding again, Quinctilius Varus went on, "Well, I didn't call you here to have you listen to me going on about how things will be a lifetime from now. As long as your woman is with you willingly, this complaint from Segestes can go by the board. But he is a citizen, and you are a citizen, and so it was up to me to get to the bottom of things. I trust you understand?"

"Yes, sir," Arminius said.

"All right, then. You may go." After another hesitation, Varus added, "I hope I see you again sometime."

"May it be so." *May I see you on your knees, begging for the mercy you'll never find.* But none of *that* showed on Arminius' face. He rose from the stool, bowed, and left the closed-off space that served as Varus' office. He also left the enormous tent as fast as he could. *Never give somebody the chance to change his mind* was another thing he'd learned from the Romans.

He jumped onto his horse without needing a leg-up. He would rather have died than asked a favor from a passing legionary. He swung the animal's head around and left the encampment at Mindenum by the gate through which he'd come in.

"He's just a boy," Varus said in slightly surprised tones.

"Rather a large and muscular boy, sir," Aristocles replied.

"Just a boy," Varus repeated, as if the *pedisequus* hadn't spoken. "A boy, besotted with one of those blond German girls." He leered; he couldn't help himself. German women always reminded him of Roman whores. In a mostly dark-haired land, those wigs made the whores stand out. And every time he saw or even thought about the naturally fair German wenches, he couldn't keep lewd imaginings out of his mind.

"So you are going to let him keep her?" his slave inquired.

"Yes, of course I am. I'd have to start a war to take her away. I'm sure she's no Helen, and I'm just as sure I'm no Agamemnon," Varus said. "Unpleasant place to be in, you know—either I make this Arminius angry, or I do the same to that Segestes. Arminius has the girl, and she seems happy enough to be had. As long as she does, her father will just have to find something else to worry about."

"They're all barbarians up here," Aristocles said with a discreet shudder. "Will, uh, Segestes, be so offended you ruled against him that he'll try to kill you without worrying about what will happen to him the next heartbeat?"

"Pleasant thought." Varus sent the *pedisequus* a sour stare. The worst of it was, he couldn't even rebuke the Greekling, because it was a legitimate question. "I don't think so," Varus said after a moment. "For a German, Segestes seemed fairly civilized. Arminius struck me as more likely to imitate Achilles if I took the woman away—except he'd fight instead of sulking in his tent."

"Not an Achilles when it comes to looks." Aristocles said that about every German he set eyes on. The northerners' blunt features didn't appeal to him. That was why he surprised Varus when he added, "I've seen worse, though—I will say that."

"Don't tell me he's gone and turned your head!" the Roman exclaimed with a laugh.

Aristocles tossed his head in an emphatic negative. "Oh, no. Too big and hairy to be really interesting. But . . . not bad. Better than I expected to find in this gods-forsaken wilderness."

"The Germans frown on such sports, same as the Gauls do. Better not to let Arminius know," Varus said.

"Savages," Aristocles said, sniffing. He smiled crookedly. "I'll get by, sir. I'm not one who can't make do with women."

Like a lot of Roman aristocrats, Varus had a boy now and then for variety's sake. He strongly preferred the other side of the coin, though. "I rather fancy Arminius myself," he said. One of Aristocles' eyebrows leaped toward his hairline; like any sensible slave, he knew his master's states. Chuckling, Varus went on, "Not that way. But I like him. He puts me in mind of Gaius."

"You're joking!" Aristocles blurted. Even a slave could occasionally be guilty of saying the first thing that popped into his head.

A slave who did say the first thing that popped into his head could regret it for a long time afterwards, too. But Quinctilius Varus was not a vicious or vindictive man. He had his vices, but that wasn't one of them. "I don't aim to adopt him, for heaven's sake," the Roman governor said. "He does remind me of my boy, though, the way one puppy will remind you of another. He's all big paws and curiosity, trying to see how the world works. He happened to study with centurions, not philosophers, but you could do worse."

This time, the *pedisequus* had his wits about him again, and said nothing at all. The slightest twitch at the left corner of his mouth, the tiniest flare of his nostrils, gave some hint of what he thought of the men who were the backbone of the Roman army. Varus missed those. While a slave had to—or had better—pay close attention to his master's expressions, the converse did not apply.

Varus changed the subject: "Pretty soon, we'll start sending soldiers out to collect taxes. About time the Germans find out what they need to do to make proper provincials."

"Oh, they'll love that, they will." Irony soured Aristocles' voice.

His master only shrugged. "If you climb onto a half-broken horse, he'll do his best to throw you off on your head. But if you don't break him, you'll never be able to get up on his back. If we don't show the Germans that this province belongs to us now and has to follow our rules, then we might as well have stayed on the other side of the Rhine."

"I wish we would have, sir," Aristocles said. "Vetera was bad enough, but Mindenum is . . . worse than bad enough, meaning no offense to our gallant troops and their stalwart officers." By his tone, Aristocles aimed to affront every military man in the entire Roman Empire.

"Well, we'll be back in Vetera come fall," Varus said. "By then, I want the natives to get it through their thick heads that this is our land now, and things will go the way they would anywhere else Rome rules."

"The sooner you set this place in order, the sooner we can get back to Rome or any other civilized place, the happier I'll be." No sarcasm now: the *pedisequus* spoke with deep and obvious sincerity.

"There are other places I'd rather be, too," Quinctilius Varus said. "When Augustus summoned me, I thought he'd send me somewhere else. You know that, Aristocles. This was a surprise, and not a nice one. But being here is also a compliment of sorts."

"One I could do without," Aristocles muttered.

"I understand that," Varus told him. "Believe me, I do. If Augustus needs me here, though, how can I refuse him? This is an important assignment, more important than governing Syria was. Syria is a broken horse. As I said, we still have to break Germany. *I* still have to break Germany." He thrust out his chin.

"Breaking this country is the best thing anyone could do to it," the *pedisequus* said. "If Augustus wanted a horse trainer here, he should have sent a general, not an administrator."

"Tiberius is stuck in Pannonia. I'm sure he'd be here if not for the uprising," Varus replied. "His ties to Augustus are tighter than mine, and he's proved himself a soldier, which I haven't done yet."

"Plenty of other sprats in the sea. Plenty of other officers in the army," Aristocles observed.

"But not plenty Augustus trusts in command of three legions," Varus said. "Remember all the civil wars when we were young? We've had thirty years with none of that. A general who rebelled with three legions at his back could set the Empire aflame again. Augustus gave me this command not least because he knows I'm loyal to him."

He pulled a denarius from his belt pouch and stared at the profile of his wife's great-uncle gleaming in silver. What would it be like to have his own face on money so the whole world knew what he looked like? He'd had VARUS stamped on some of the coins he'd issued to the legionaries here, but that wasn't the same.

He shook his head. If he challenged Augustus, he would lose. Everyone who challenged Augustus lost. Varus had no stomach for war against his benefactor, anyway. He had little stomach for war against the Germans, either. But he would do what he had to do. He wondered if Arminius would help him. He hoped so. Nothing made subduing a province easier than willing native stooges.

 V

Caldus Caelius led a column of Romans through the German woods. People spoke of the woods as trackless, but they weren't really. All kinds of narrow tracks ran through them. Deer had made some, aurochs others, men still others. Deciding which kind was which wasn't always easy—not if you were a Roman.

Orders from Mindenum were to be careful, whatever that meant. Caelius knew what it would have meant in more open country: vanguard, rear guard, and flanking parties out to both sides to make sure nobody could sneak up on the main body of troops. Only one trouble: that kind of due diligence was impossible in this terrain.

Traveling along a path was pretty simple—as long as you marched in single file, or, on what was unquestionably a man-made track, perhaps two abreast. A vanguard too far ahead or a rear guard too far behind could be ambushed and slaughtered before the main force came to its rescue. In this thick forest, flank guards were simply impossible; they hadn't a prayer of keeping up.

And so Caelius had a vanguard and rear guard of sorts, but not the sorts he would have wanted. Instead of flank guards, he had extra *buccinatores*. He had to hope blaring trumpets would make up for lack of protection. The hope wasn't altogether forlorn: other Roman columns were pushing through these woods, too.

"One of these days, we'll have proper roads here," Caelius said. His sword was sheathed, but he could grab it in a hurry if he had to.

"Fat lot of good that does us now," one of the legionaries said.

Several other men laughed. That meant Caelius couldn't blister the mouthy soldier the way he wanted to. A clown could get away with all kinds of things. Instead of swearing, Caelius imagined a proper Roman road, broad and solid, well paved and well drained, the trees cut back on both sides to make way for it. That would be a demon of a lot better than this narrow, miserable, meandering track.

"If Rome needs money so bad, we've got to squeeze it out of places like this, we're all in big trouble," the wit went on. He'd got away with one joke, so he thought he could get away with two.

"Oh, put a plug in it, Lucius," Caelius said. "These Germans are ours now, see? So they've got to get used to acting like they belong in the Empire. And *that* means paying up when it's time to pay. Simple, right. You're pretty simple yourself, right?"

Lucius said nothing. When a superior got on you, nothing was the smartest thing you could say. Caldus Caelius wished again for a Roman highway. The legions could really move down roads like those. And, better yet, they could see what was moving against them.

A raven croaked, up in a tree. Did that mean the Romans had disturbed it, or had it seen some Germans sneaking through the woods? How could you know before you found out the hard way?

You couldn't. When you boiled everything down, that was what you had left. Caelius made sure the sword was loose in its scabbard. If a big enough mob of barbarians jumped his troop, he and all the men he led would die. He knew that. But they'd take a bunch of Germans with them. The natives knew that. It had to be about the only thing that kept them from rising up.

Somebody—*not* Lucius, Caelius was glad to note—asked, "Where's this lousy village we're heading for?"

"Not far now," Caelius said. *I hope it's not far now. If it's where people say it is and we are where I think we are, it shouldn't be far.* In Germany, you couldn't take either of those for granted. You couldn't take anything for granted, not if you wanted to go on breathing. Caldus Caelius was in favor of breathing. He aimed to go on doing it for a long time.

Less than a quarter of an hour later, the track came out into a clearing. Behind Caelius, the legionaries muttered in glad surprise. The sunshine was cool and watery, nothing like the savage sun of southern Italy that had baked Caelius when he was a naked little boy. Even so, he had to blink several times against the unexpected glare.

Pigs with a tall ridge of hair on their backs ran for the woods. Pigs weren't so dumb: they knew trouble when they smelled it. A couple of small, rough-coated ponies and several shaggy cows and scrawny sheep grazed on the meadow. Men and women worked in the fields with scythes and sickles—harvest time was here. They planted in the spring and reaped in the fall. That seemed unnatural to Caelius, who'd grown up in a country where summer rain was a prodigy.

One by one, the Germans stopped working. They stared at the Roman soldiers. "Deploy," Caelius said quietly. Maybe he could forestall trouble by showing he was ready for it.

He had orders—which he didn't much like—not to antagonize the natives. But he was here in the field, and Varus' Greek slave, who'd relayed those orders, bloody well wasn't. Caelius figured he could interpret them as he thought best. If the Germans decided he'd kill them for getting uppity, they'd stay quiet. As far as he was concerned, that was the same as not antagonizing them.

He did advance toward the people working in the fields without a weapon in his right hand. That made him feel naked, but not nearly so naked as he would have felt without a bunch of legionaries at his back.

"Hail!" he called in what came fairly close to being the language the Germans used. He knew a handful of other words, but he'd picked them up from joy girls. These large, somber men wouldn't want to hear them. He went on in his own tongue: "Do any of you speak Latin?"

"I do," said a mustachioed barbarian not far from his own age. "Don't good speak, but speak. You what want?"

"Taxes," Caldus Caelius answered.

"What is—are—taxes?" the German asked. He overtopped Caelius by half a head. A great big sword hung from his left hip. Why would you wear a sword to work in the fields? Because some other savages were liable to jump you—that was the only answer the Roman saw.

And this fellow didn't know what taxes were? Well, he'd find out. Oh, sure! Wouldn't he just? "You're a Roman subject now," Caelius explained. He sounded sympathetic—he couldn't help it. What were taxes? Oh, my! Shaking his head, he went on, "You have to pay to keep things going."

"Pay?" Another word that meant little or nothing to the natives. The Germans mostly didn't deal in silver and gold, or even in copper. They made no coins of their own, and were just learning to use the ones from Roman mints. They traded sheep for barley, or beer for boards, or honey for blankets.

This year, Quinctilius Varus had said the legions could collect taxes in kind. Next year, the Germans would have to start forking over silver like everybody else. One thing: that would make payments a demon of a lot easier to carry away.

Caldus Caelius stopped woolgathering—although he'd be doing just that, literally, soon enough. "Pay," he repeated. "You give me some of what you have, and the Empire lives on it."

One of the other men, an older fellow, asked the one who spoke Latin something. The younger man with the mustaches answered in the Germans' incomprehensible, guttural language. The older fellow growled like a mean hound. His hand dropped to the hilt of his sword.

"Tell your kinsman that isn't a good idea," Caelius advised. He turned and waved at the hard-faced Roman soldiers behind him. "We don't want any trouble, but we're ready for it."

The mustachioed man spoke again. The graybeard's hand fell away from the sword. Hate still smoldered in his pale eyes. The younger man, the one who spoke Latin, didn't exactly look thrilled, either. "You say we taxes pay. You mean you us rob."

"No," Caelius said. *Yes,* he thought. "Robbers take whatever they want. We take only a little, only so much from each steading. The law tells us how much we are supposed to get."

"Law? This is not law. This is robbery," the German said. "Could you from my village take without soldiers behind you? No. Of course not. Robbing."

"In the Empire, the tax collector comes without soldiers behind him," Caelius said. "People give him what they owe, and he goes away." Sometimes. Some places. When the harvest was good two or three years in a row. But it could happen.

"Then your men are without penises born," the German said. It was a funny-sounding insult, but Caelius had no trouble understanding what it meant. The barbarian went on, "And what do your penisless men get for these taxes your robbers from them steal?"

"Roads. Baths. Courts. Soldiers who keep the peace so they don't have to worry about getting robbed and murdered. Things they can't do for themselves—things you people here don't have yet."

"But they lose their freedom." That was not a question.

Caldus Caelius shrugged. "Who cares if you're free if you're stuck in the middle of the woods and nobody ten miles away even knows you're there? The Empire reaches from Gaul to Syria. You could go trading to any of those places. You could be a soldier and serve anywhere. Augustus has German bodyguards even now."

"Dogs," the German said, and spat on the ground. "I am no dog. I am wolf."

"Look, friend, I don't care if you're a dog or a wolf or a purple hedgehog. You've got to pay any which way," Caldus Caelius said. "That's what my orders are, and that's what's going to happen."

"And if I want to fight instead?" the German asked.

Caelius glanced behind him. The native's gaze followed his. The legionaries looked tough and ready for anything. Caelius' mailshirt jingled on his shoulders as he shrugged. "Well, you can do that. You won't like what comes of it, but you can."

The German weighed the odds. Unless Caelius missed his guess, the fellow was also weighing his pride. Was getting his whole clan slaughtered worth it to him? He spoke in harsh gutturals to his countrymen. They went back and forth in that grunting, coughing language.

At last, the German asked, "How much you make us pay?"

Now they were at the stage of doing business. Caelius tried to hide his relief; he didn't want the barbarian to think he was gloating—even if he was. Sounding as matter-of-fact as he could, he answered, "For a village of this size, two cows or eight sheep—or eight denarii, if you've got 'em."

"No denarii," the German said, as if the idea was ridiculous. In his mind, it probably was. He went on, "We give you, you take, you away go, you us alone leave?"

"That's the idea," Caldus Caelius agreed. He didn't say the Romans would be back to collect the tax next year, too, and the year after that, and the year after *that*. One thing at a time. And, with any luck at all, *he* wouldn't be the one who came back to this village.

More back-and-forth in the Germans' language. The barbarians didn't like it. Well, who in his right mind did like paying taxes? You did it, and you thanked your gods you didn't have to cough up more.

"We give you eight sheep, then," said the man with the mustache. "You take them and you go. What is your name?"

"I'm Caldus Caelius," Caelius answered. "What's yours, friend, and why do you want to know?"

"Caldus Caelius." The German said it to or three times, tasting it, fixing it in his memory. "Well, Caldus Caelius, I myself call Ingaevonus. Maybe we meet again, the two of us. We see who then remembers."

"Anywhere you please, Ingaevonus." Caelius knew he made a mess of the big man's name, but he didn't care. "Any time you please. With your friends or without them. With mine or without them, too."

Ingaevonus looked at him in surprise. "It could be, after your own fashion, you have the makings of a man." Before Caelius could even get mad at him for doubting it, the German turned away and started yelling in his own language. A couple of pimple-faced brats yelled back at him. He shouted them down. Caelius didn't know what he said, but it sounded like a storm roaring through bare-branched winter trees.

The older fellow behind Ingaevonus put in his copper's worth, too. The young punks stopped arguing. They trotted off, rounded up the sheep, and brought them back to Caldus Caelius. "Here. You take," one of them said in fragmentary Latin.

"Thanks," Caelius answered dryly. The kid, by the look on his face, wanted the Roman's liver the way the vulture wanted Prometheus'. He probably hated all Romans on general principles.

Hate them or not, though, he'd picked up some of their language. Just about all the Gauls spoke some Latin these days, even if they still used their own tongue when they talked among themselves. Old-timers in the legions said a lot fewer people on the west side of the Rhine had known Latin when they were first stationed there. It would probably work the same way in Germany over the next thirty years.

That wasn't Caldus Caelius' worry. "You have paid the tax for this village, Ingaevonus," he said in loud, formal tones. To his own men, he added, "Now we take the tax back to Mindenum."

They would look like a pack of fools doing it, too: all these legionaries escorting eight skinny sheep. But overwhelming force had its advantages. The Germans weren't going to try to take back their miserable beasts.

"You know what'd be funny?" a soldier said as they headed off toward their camp.

"What's that, Septimus?" Caelius asked.

"If another bunch of our guys hit that village by mistake and try to squeeze eight more sheep out of those natives. You think that big fellow with the fur on his lip wouldn't go up like Mount Etna?"

Caldus Caelius thought about it. Then he chuckled. "Crucify me if he wouldn't."

Laughing and joking, the Romans trudged back to Mindenum.

Arminius scowled in black fury as Roman soldiers led a horse and two sheep away from his father's steading. Sigimerus and the other men there were also angry, but there were too many legionaries to fight. Trying would have meant throwing German lives on the dungheap.

"This is why the Pannonians rose up against Rome, Father," Arminius said, even before the last legionary went off into the woods.

"Yes, I understand that," Sigimerus said. "I always understood it here." He tapped the side of his head with his left forefinger, then added, "Now I understand it here, too." He cupped his testicles with his right hand.

"Well, then?" Arminius exclaimed. The looks on the faces of the other men at the steading were bad enough. The expressions his mother and Thusnelda and the other women wore seemed ten times worse. Their scorn burned like the mix of oil and brimstone and pitch Roman armies used to fire forts that held out against them. If men couldn't protect their chattels, could they protect their women? If they couldn't protect their women, did they really have any balls?

But his father asked, "And how are the Pannonians doing in this war of theirs?"

Automatically, Arminius answered with the truth: "They're losing. It will all be over in a year or two."

"And you think we would do better because . . . ?" Sigimerus let the question hang in the air. By the way he asked it, he didn't think his son had any good reply.

"Because the Romans had plenty of time to rope down the land before the people who live there rebelled," Arminius said. "There were already Roman towns in Pannonia, towns full of retired Roman soldiers and their families. Roman traders were everywhere, too. The colonists helped the legions, and the traders heard about the rebels' moves even before they made them. If we give Rome the same chance, she'll rope us down the same way. Then we'll lose when we do try to fight."

He watched Sigimerus gnaw on his lower lip. His father's unhappy gaze traveled to the women again, and grew more unhappy still. "If we rise and we lose, we're worse off than if we hadn't risen at all. It will spoil our strength for years—maybe forever."

"If we don't rise, we become the Romans' slaves," Arminius said. "By the gods, if we don't rise we *deserve* to become the Romans' slaves! We deserve to pay taxes every year."

That made Sigimerus flinch. Arminius had thought it would. "Taxes!" his father spat, using the Latin word as Arminius had. "This is nothing but a fancy Roman name for stealing. They haven't had the nerve to try collecting them before. And what did that fellow mean when he said they wouldn't take animals next year? Was he talking about barley, or did he mean they would grab a slave—or maybe one of our own folk?"

"Neither one, I think," Arminius said. "He meant we would have to pay in denarii—in silver."

"That's even worse!" Sigimerus said. He was a chief—he had silver, and even gold. But the Germans got their coins in trade from the Romans. And now the legionaries would expect people to give them back?

"You see what I mean, then," Arminius said.

"But you've fought for them. Flavus is still fighting for them." Sigimerus' mouth twisted—all of a sudden, he didn't like reminding himself of that at all.

Arminius grimaced, too. "My brother is like Segestes—the Romans have seduced them both." He was careful to keep his voice down so Thusnelda wouldn't hear him. He didn't run down her father when she was in earshot: he saw no point in stirring up trouble when he didn't have to. But when he did . . .

"I wasn't finished," Sigimerus said. "You and your brother have fought for them. I've fought against them. Call them as many names as you please, but they make deadly foes. If we rise—even now, before the land is roped down, as you say—we are too likely to lose. And to lose would be our great misfortune."

That only made Arminius grimace again. He'd seen the legions in action in Germany and in Pannonia. He knew from the inside out how formidable they were. Well-equipped and orderly to a degree no high-hearted German would have tolerated for a moment, the Romans had plenty of practice holding down folk who didn't want to be held. Pannonia was giving them even more, as if they needed it.

"We have to take them on when they aren't at their best," he said, thinking aloud.

"How?" his father asked bluntly.

It was an important question, however much the younger man wished it weren't. It was, in fact, *the* important question. "I don't know yet," Arminius admitted.

"Well, you'd better walk small till you figure it out—if you ever do," Sigimerus said. "Otherwise, the Romans will make you sorry. Not just you, either. They'll make all the Cherusci—all the Germans—sorry."

Arminius tried to imagine a catastrophe that would affect all the German tribes, from the Chamavi and Tencteri pressed hard against the Rhine to his own Cherusci in the German heartland to the Marcomanni under King Maroboduus north of the Danube (Maroboduus quietly encouraged the Pannonian rebels, but only quietly—he didn't want Roman legions marching after him next) to the Gotones far away in the east. The Gotones had kings, too, but they were so far away that Arminius didn't know the names of any of them. What kind of catastrophe would be big enough to make all those tribes feel it?

The question suggested its own answer. A Roman province stretching from the Rhine east to the Elbe would bring most of the German tribes under Augustus' rule—would enslave them, in other words. The Gotones would still lie beyond Rome's reach, but they would need to change their way of doing things, too. And if—no, when—the eagles decided to lunge forward again . . .

"I have to find a way, Father. We all have to," Arminius said. "If we don't, they'll own us. Have you seen that camp of theirs, that Mindenum?"

"I've heard about it," Sigimerus said.

"That's not enough," Arminius said. "I saw plenty of legionary camps in Pannonia. I lived in one, fought in one, while I learned what they did and how they did it. But Mindenum, by all the gods, Mindenum is the biggest one I ever set eyes on. None of the ones in Pannonia comes close. And in Pannonia, at least the Romans can say they already rule the place. We're still free—or we think we are. Mindenum says something different."

"If we rise and we lose, that would be worse than not rising at all, bec—" Sigimerus said.

"Yes, you told me that before," Arminius interrupted impatiently.

His father went on as if he hadn't spoken: "Because it would geld us at the same time as it gave them the excuse to tighten the shackles on our fatherland. We can't afford that. I think we're lucky to have held out against them as long as we have."

"I promise, Father: when I set us in motion against them, we won't fail," Arminius said. "Or if we do, I won't live to see it."

"I gladly accept the first part of that oath. May the second part not come to pass," Sigimerus said.

"Yes. May it not. But we must fight the Romans. Even the Gauls fought the Romans, though they lost." Like most Germans, Arminius looked down his straight nose at the folk who lived in Gaul. Gallic tribes had settled a good part of Germany, till Germans drove them out of it. Germans would have occupied the west bank of the Rhine, had the Romans—not the natives—not driven them back. Against the Roman legions, honors were about even so far. That thought brought Arminius back to his main idea, "The Gauls fought well enough to keep their honor. If we roll over to show our bellies like whipped dogs, we will have none—and deserve none."

"Dead men may have honor, but they cannot eat of it," Sigimerus said.

"True enough. But those who come after them will remember them for aye. Their names will live in song—and deserve to," Arminius said. "Better that than to live a long life and be forgotten like any other slaves—and deserve to be."

His father sighed. "I cannot persuade you to set this aside?"

"I was not the only one who felt his manhood threatened when the Romans robbed us here. They have more ways to make men eunuchs than just by cutting." As Sigimerus had before him, Arminius cupped his right hand over his genitals.

Sigimerus sighed again. "If you will not set this aside, I had better give you all the help I can. By the gods, son, you'll need it, and more besides. I only hope you find everything you need, that's all."

A smile like the sun coming out from behind stormclouds lit Arminius' face. "If we struggle together, how can we lose?"

"There are ways," Sigimerus replied. "There are always ways."

Quinctilius Varus looked at the accounts his secretaries had compiled. He knew how much the Roman provincial administration took from Syria every year. Germany had yielded barely a twentieth part of that. Yes, this land was poor. How could it be anything else when it had scant gold or silver of its own and when neither the olive nor the vine wanted to grow here? Even if the natives weren't so barbarous, those would have been important entries in the ledger's debit columns.

Varus understood as much, anyhow. Varus had seen Germany with his own eyes. Now that he and the legions were abandoning Mindenum for the winter, he could put seeing Germany with his own eyes in the same place all his other memories went. Yes, he'd come back next spring. He didn't have to dwell on that just yet, though. He didn't have to, and he didn't intend to.

Augustus hadn't seen Germany with *his* own eyes, though. Augustus, fortunate soul, had never crossed the Rhine. What would the ruler of the Roman Empire think when he saw the paltry sum Varus had extracted from this province? How angry would he be?

Were Varus but a little bolder, a little nervier, he would have cooked the books before his wife's great-uncle ever set eyes on them. But he didn't have the guts—didn't have the balls—to risk it. His greatest fear (one that, by the nature of things, he had to keep to himself) was that Augustus had a spy, or more than one, secreted somewhere within his own retinue. If he gave Augustus one set of figures himself, while the spy delivered a different and significantly worse set . . .

The mere idea made Quinctilius Varus shudder. All sorts of nasty little desert islands scattered through the Mediterranean. Varus didn't want to spend the rest of his days on one. And he might, if he got caught telling that big a lie.

Being married to Claudia Pulchra wouldn't pull his chestnuts out of the fire, not if Augustus got angry enough. Augustus' grand-niece's husband? So what? Augustus' own daughter had spent five years on the island of Pandataria, forbidden wine and all male company not specifically approved by her father, before winning a slightly milder exile in Rhegium, on the toe of the Italian boot.

Of course, Julia was guilty of gross immorality, where Varus would only have embezzled. After being used like a game piece in Augustus' dynastic plans—none of which worked out the way he wanted—Julia hadn't cared what she did, as long as it scandalized her father. Varus, for better or worse, was far less flamboyant.

He sighed. "Are you all right, sir?" Aristocles asked.

Letting the *pedisequus* hear what was on his mind wouldn't do. "I suppose so," he said. "Gods know I'll be glad to get away from Mindenum. Who that wasn't crazy wouldn't be?"

"You're right about that!" Usually, Varus had to wonder whether a slave was sincere. Not this time. Aristocles couldn't stand Germany or the Germans, and didn't bother trying to hide how he felt.

"Vetera's not exactly a triple six, either," Varus said. Rome would have been the best throw at dice. So would Athens or Alexandria. Antioch, the capital of Roman Syria, came pretty close. Vetera . . . didn't.

"Better than Mindenum." Aristocles' wave encompassed what was left of the legionary encampment. Troops didn't overwinter here, not yet. When they left for land more firmly in Roman hands, they made sure they either took along or destroyed everything the locals could use. They took all the iron in the camp—everything from surgeons' scalpels to horse trappings to hobnails to spoons. Anything left behind, German smiths would pound into spearheads or knives or swords. The soldiers burned all the timber in the camp. They would cut more next spring. When they were on the march, they built a fresh encampment every day. They didn't mind wrecking this semipermanent place.

"One of these days, this will be a Roman city in its own right," Varus said. "Plenty of towns in Africa and Spain and Gaul started out as legionary camps. They're respectable enough now."

"I suppose so." His *pedisequus* didn't sound convinced. "Those weren't stuck out in the middle of nowhere, though."

Instead of arguing, Quinctilius Varus hid a smile. Aristocles was determined to despise Mindenum no matter what. Back when the Empire was younger and smaller, plenty of towns that now seemed comfortable and near the center of things would have been frontier posts fit only for soldiers.

Vala Numonius came up and saluted Varus. "We're ready to head back to the Rhine, sir," the cavalry commander said. "I won't be sorry to see the last of this place for a while, and that's the truth."

Varus glanced over at Aristocles. The slave radiated agreement the way a red-hot piece of iron on an anvil radiated heat. Varus pretended not to notice. But he couldn't help saying, "Well, neither will I."

Before long, the legionaries would slog through the mud and the muck to the headwaters of the Lupia. After that, the going would get easier. Boats would take many of them down the river to the Rhine. Roman forts on the banks would make sure the Germans could only watch. The arrangement worked well enough, but it didn't strike Varus as suitably triumphant.

"We ought to march through Germany," he said. "We ought to show the natives we can go where we want whenever we care to."

"Yes, sir," Aristocles said resignedly.

"What's the matter? You don't like the idea?" Quinctilius Varus was sensitive to his slave's shifts of inflection.

"Sir, I am delighted to march *out of* Germany," the *pedisequus* replied. "As for marching *through* Germany . . . There's nowhere in this miserable country I care to go to. As far as I'm concerned, the barbarians are welcome to every last inch of it."

Since Varus held a similar opinion, he couldn't exactly tell Aristocles he was wrong. "One of these days, this will make a fine province," he said, hoping he sounded as if he meant it. "We just have to finish bringing it into the Empire, that's all."

Aristocles took an incautious step back and squelched in mud that tried to suck the sandal off his foot. Clothes that would have been perfect anywhere around the Mediterranean proved less than ideal here. Tunics and togas were drafty; no wonder the Germans wore trousers under their swaddling cloaks—the ones who could afford to wear anything under those cloaks, anyhow. And boots stayed on and protected the feet better than sandals.

Muttering in disgust, Aristocles cleaned his sandal and his foot as best he could with a tuft of grass he pulled up from the ground. "It would serve the Germans right if we left them to their own barbarous devices," he said. "They don't deserve to be part of the Empire."

Again, Varus felt the same way. His opinion, however, wasn't what mattered here. "Augustus wants this province. He has his reasons. And what Augustus wants, Augustus gets." That had been true for almost as long as Varus was alive, and Varus, as he knew too well, was no longer young. It might as well have been a law of nature.

"Augustus has never seen this country. He's never seen these barbarians." Aristocles pulled up more grass. He swiped it across a muddy spot he'd missed before. "By the gods, sir, if he had seen them he wouldn't want them."

Quinctilius Varus laughed. He imagined Augustus surveying the outpost at Mindenum. It wasn't that Augustus had never taken the field—he'd beaten Rome's finest marshals during the civil war after Julius Caesar's murder. But Augustus was, without a doubt, a creature of the Mediterranean. Imagining him here in these gloomy woods was like imagining a fish in the Egyptian desert. The picture didn't want to form.

Well, I am a creature of the Mediterranean, too, Varus thought, *and I still wish Augustus had sent me to Egypt, or to Greece, or anywhere but here. I don't belong here, and I never will.*

"Vetera," he said aloud. When he'd first set eyes on the military town on the left bank of the Rhine, he'd thought it the most godsforsaken place in the world. Then he'd crossed over into Germany and found out how little he knew about places the gods had forsaken—if, indeed, they'd ever come here at all. Next to Mindenum, Vetera seemed like Antioch. Next to Germany, even the frontier of Gaul seemed like civilization.

"Vetera," Aristocles echoed. Varus heard the longing in the slave's voice, as he'd heard it in his own.

"We'll be back here come spring, you know," Varus said.

"Yes, sir," Aristocles replied with a martyred sigh. He was part of the price of empire himself. Prominent Romans needed clever Greeks to help run their affairs. The *pedisequus* was better off than he would have been as a free man in poor but proud Greece. Well, he was except for the mud on his ankle and between his toes.

"We can leave the savages to their own devices for a while," Varus said. "We made a decent beginning here, anyhow." He clucked like a worried hen. "I do hope Augustus will see it that way." No, Augustus had never set eyes on Germany. But his will would be done here all the same.

❧ VI ❧

Arminius had seen that, inside the Roman Empire, steadings tended to clump together in villages and towns. In Germany, holdings were more evenly spread. Here was a steading by itself in the woods; here were three or four together, perhaps formed by the descendants of someone who had farmed by himself a few generations earlier; here were a pair of brothers and their households side by side; here another lone farm; here six or eight steadings in a large clearing. His folk did have villages, though not large ones by Roman standards. He'd never seen a town till he took service with the auxiliaries.

Towns had their advantages. He understood that. If you brought news to a town, you had to tell it only once. Everybody in town—or in the market square, anyhow—would hear it at the same time. So would farmers who'd come into town to sell whatever they had, and then they would spread the news through the countryside.

Towns were . . . efficient. The word and the idea existed in Latin, but not in the Germans' tongue. Roman armies were efficient, too. Arminius wished his own people grasped the concept, for it was as much a weapon as the edge of the sword.

But the world was as it was, not as he wished it were. If he wanted to spread news, he couldn't do it by traveling to a few towns. He had to go to one steading after another, talk with one farmer or minor chieftain after another, and persuade or cajole or jolly the man and the lesser followers at each place to his own way of thinking.

That way of thinking was simple enough. Very often, so was getting the Germans to his side. All he had to ask was, "Did the Romans collect taxes from you this past fall?"

More often than not, someone would say, or snarl, the word "Yes." More often than not, that same man or someone else would curse the Romans.

Then Arminius would ask, "And do you want to pay taxes again next year?"

That commonly produced gasps of horror or fury or, most often, both commingled. "They were lucky to get it from me once—they caught me by surprise. Demons drag me down if they'll do that again," was an answer he heard again and again, in almost identical words.

"But they intend to," he would say. It was no less than the truth, either. "They intend to, and they will try to kill you if you don't let them rob you. What do you propose to do about that?"

People didn't always say the same thing then. A lot of them didn't believe him, or didn't want to believe him—the notion was as far outside their ken as efficiency was. He had the advantage over them, though. He'd seen how things in Pannonia worked. He knew the Romans collected taxes there every year.

And he knew something else. "The Pannonians have given the Romans as much fight as they ever wanted, and then some," he would say to anyone who wanted to listen. "Are the Pannonians stronger than we are?"

"No!" Anyone he talked to would say that. The Germans were convinced they were the strongest folk in the world.

Arminius would nod and agree: "You're right. I fought them. They're strong enough, but they're no stronger than we are. Are they braver?"

"No!" That question was guaranteed to affront any German ever born. His folk prided themselves on their courage.

And he would nod again. "That's right—they're not. They're plenty brave—no doubt about it. But they aren't any braver than we are, either. So if they're brave enough to take on the Romans, why can't we do the same?"

Hardly any Germans who'd been taxed by the Romans—plundered by the Romans—saw any reason why they shouldn't go to war against the legions. Arminius began to think his biggest problem would be holding the tribesmen back, not leading them forward. They wanted to march on the Rhine and burn every Roman fortification on this side of the river.

Strangely enough, much of the help he got in restraining the Germans came from Segestes and others who were pro-Roman. There weren't that many of them, but they had influence beyond their numbers. One of the things the Romans did to win the land to their side was to get chieftains to go along with them. The chieftains, and the retinues of warriors they supported, helped sway the views of ordinary folk.

Quite a few of them told the Germans what an idiot Arminius was. He didn't mind. Not many Germans who'd been taxed thought Arminius was an idiot. But the ordinary tribesmen did hesitate instead of rebelling too soon. Arminius found that blackly funny. Irony was one more concept he'd learned among his enemies.

And he had weapons against the pro-Roman chieftains, weapons they couldn't match. "The Romans did this in Pannonia, too," he would say. "I saw them do it. By the gods, I helped them do it so I could learn their ways. It is what they do whenever they enslave a new folk. Our old men will tell you they did the same thing in Gaul most of a lifetime ago. And now the people over there are their slaves."

One graybeard said, "Well, those are only Gauls. We used to beat them, too. They aren't so tough."

"Let Quinctilius Varus keep collecting taxes from you, then," Arminius replied. "Fifty years from now, some Roman master will say, 'Well, those are only Germans. They aren't so tough.'"

People nodded, taking the point. The graybeard bit his lip, but he didn't argue any more. Anyone who argued against Arminius soon wished he hadn't.

Varus was drunk when a courier brought a letter from Augustus. In summer, the weather in this northerly part of the world got warm enough for cultured Romans to drink watered wine. During the winter, though, everybody took his neat to stoke the fires inside himself. Varus thought the habit barbarous till he tried it. When he found how well it worked, he became as enthusiastic as a convert to Judaism.

A servant gave the courier a cup of neat wine. "Much obliged," the man said, and drank it down without blinking. How many winters up here had he gone through? Enough to get him used to strong wine, anyhow. The man led him away for something to eat.

"What does Augustus say, sir?" Aristocles asked.

"I don't know." Varus wondered if he wanted to know. But his right thumbnail lived a life of its own. It automatically dug under and flipped off the wax seal that held the sheet of papyrus closed. Varus held the letter out at arm's length; his sight was lengthening. The same thing must have happened to Augustus, of course, but the letter was in his own hand—Varus recognized it at once.

When he didn't go on right away, his *pedisequus* prompted him: "Well?" Aristocles was still sober, or close enough. He went on watering his wine, and wore a long, thick wool tunic and two pairs of socks for warmth.

" 'My dear Varus—I am glad to hear your first summer in Germany went well,' " Varus read, and breathed a sigh of relief that smoked in the air despite a charcoal brazier. He swigged from his goblet before going on: " 'You seem worried when you tell me what your tax collectors brought in.' "

That made him swig again, drain the goblet dry, and fill it once more with the dipper plunged into the wine jar. He'd done his best *not* to sound worried, to treat the Roman soldiers' sorry performance as nothing but routine. His best proved not good enough. Augustus hadn't ruled the Roman world for more than a generation because he was blind to what lay below the surface.

Quinctilius Varus drank once more. His eyes crossed. He knew he would have a thick head come morning, but morning seemed a million miles away. His slave made a wordless, impatient noise. Varus didn't want to find out what Augustus said next, but knew he had no choice: " 'Lose no sleep over it. The idea is to get the barbarians used to paying taxes. Once they see they have to, collecting more and more will grow easier year by year. Keep up the good work.' "

"He really says that, sir?" Aristocles sounded astonished.

"He really does." Varus couldn't get angry at the Greek—he sounded astonished, too. Augustus was a notorious cheese-parer. He always had been. To have him write that he didn't care how much Varus collected in Germany . . . proved he was also a statesman.

"What else does he say?" the *pedisequus* inquired.

"Who cares?" Varus said, and he laughed raucously. Augustus wasn't angry at him! Next to that, everything else shrank to insignificance. But he finished the letter: " 'The weather here is tolerable—better, I daresay, than what you have. The harvest was good, for which I thank Ceres and the other gods. No danger of hunger this year. Tiberius seems to be bringing order to Pannonia at last, and that is also good news. I am as well as a man of my years can be. I hope the same holds true for you. Next year, you will go on breaking the Germans to the saddle.' " Below that was nothing but a scrawled signature.

It sounded like Augustus: straightforward, to the point, with hardly a wasted word. The closing that got back to the business at hand was very much Augustus' style, too. He never left anyone in doubt about what he expected—unless doubt worked to his advantage, of course. Here, it didn't.

"Let it snow!" Aristocles exclaimed. "We are warmed from the south, so let it snow as much as it please!"

"That's right!" Varus said. "As long as Augustus is pleased, the whole world is pleased!" No matter how cold it was, it felt like spring already.

Varus was not a small man, not by Roman standards. All the same, he thought he'd get a crick in his neck from staring up at one enormous visiting German after another. This particular fellow, who gave his name as Masua, was even bigger than most: he stood several digits above six feet. He wore a bearskin cloak. With shaggy hair, unshaven cheeks and chin and upper lip, and blunt features, he looked like a bear himself.

"Sit down, sit down." Varus waved him to a stool, not least so he wouldn't need to keep looking up at him.

"I thank you, sir." Masua spoke slow, deliberate, guttural Latin. The stool creaked under his weight. He was bear-wide through the shoulders, too. A servant brought in wine. Masua took a cup with murmured thanks. So did Varus. He didn't mix in water, but he did sip cautiously. He didn't want to get drunk so early. By the way Masua gulped, he didn't care.

"You are one of Segestes' men, you told my aides," Varus said.

"That is right." Masua's big head bobbed up and down. "I am one of his sworn band. I fight for him and do what he needs. One of the things he needs now is someone to deliver you a message. He chose me." Pride rang in the tremendous German's voice.

"I see," Varus said, though he didn't, not yet. With luck, he would soon. "And this message is . . . ?"

"This is message is, you are not to trust Arminius for any reason, sir," Masua said. "He goes up and down in Germany. Everywhere he goes, he speaks against the Romans. He speaks against Roman rule beyond the Rhine."

"I see," Quinctilius Varus said again. "Have you heard Arminius say these things with your own ears?"

"No," Masua answered. "I would not walk as far as I can spit to listen to that woman-stealing swinehound."

That last had to be some German insult translated literally. Varus rather liked it. All the same, he went on, "Has Segestes heard Arminius say these things with *his* own ears?"

"Segestes would not walk as far as he could piss to listen to Arminius." Masua paused, considering. "Segestes might walk far enough to piss on Arminius' corpse. He might not even do that."

In spite of himself, Varus had to smile. But he also had to ask an important question: "In that case, how do you know what Arminius is supposed to be saying? How does Segestes know?"

"Everyone knows what Arminius is saying," Masua replied, as if to a half-witted child. Varus thought an oafish barbarian had no business taking that tone with him. No matter what he thought, the oafish barbarian went on, "Arminius makes no secret of it. Like I tell you, he goes up and down in Germany. He says what he says to anyone who will hear him. Many men do—too many men."

"I have met Arminius. He did not seem anti-Roman then," Varus said.

Masua snorted. "He would not. He was in your power. You could have killed him. You should have."

"He fought as a Roman auxiliary. He is a Roman citizen. He has been made a member of the Equestrian Order, a rare and important honor for one who was not born to our people." *For a barbarian*, he thought.

"He is a viper. If you clutch him to you like a woman, he will bite you in the balls," Masua said.

"Segestes sent you to me," Quinctilius Varus said. The German nodded. Varus went on, "Segestes is Arminius' enemy."

"Of course he is," Masua broke in. "Would you not be, if Arminius carried off your daughter?"

If Arminius hadn't carry Thusnelda off, Varus was convinced she would have done more to try to get away on her own. A Roman woman certainly would have. No, the truth was that she preferred Arminius to the middle-aged man to whom her father had tried betrothing her instead. Segestes might not—didn't—like that, which made it no less true.

No point explaining any of that to Masua, who naturally saw things his patron's way. Instead, Varus said, "Segestes naturally wants me to believe bad things about Arminius."

"Yes, indeed." Masua didn't even try to deny it. "He wants you to believe them because they are true. And Segestes, remember, is a Roman citizen, too."

"The enmity comes first, I think." Varus liked Arminius and found Segestes tedious: almost a character out of an old comedy. "Without more proof than you have given me, I don't know what you expect me to do."

"Arminius will give you proof," Masua said. "See how you like that."

Varus' face froze. "I have no doubt that you have now conveyed to me everything your principal imparted to you. That being so, you are excused. Please convey my respects to Segestes."

Even a lout like Masua couldn't mistake his meaning there. *Get out of my sight, and don't ever let me see you again*—that was what it came down to. The German got to his feet. That meant he looked down at—looked down on—Varus. "I go. You would have done better to heed me. I will tell Segestes you are too blind to listen, too deaf to see."

He turned his back. The cloak made him seem even more bearish from behind than from before. He should have gone through polite formulas of leavetaking. Arminius would have—Varus was sure of that. Masua didn't bother. Varus didn't demand them of him, either. The Roman governor was still trying to decide whether the German had been foolish or profound or both at once.

Lucius Eggius watched legionaries march and countermarch. If you didn't keep them working through the winter, they wouldn't be worth a moldy grain of barley come spring. "*I can't hear you!*" Eggius bawled, pitching his voice to carry through the bawdy ballad the soldiers were singing.

They made more noise yet. The song bragged about the havoc Varus would make in Germany and among the blond German women. As far as Eggius knew, the general was pretty moderate when it came to wenching. Maybe the legionaries knew that, too. It didn't matter one way or the other. You needed a good, bouncy song to keep you picking them up and laying them down. The tune for this one went back to Julius Caesar's day. Eggius had heard some of the old words when he was new-come to the army. They were raunchy, too.

The men divided in half and went at one another with pointless spears and wooden swords. You couldn't get killed in drills like those, not unless you were mighty unlucky. But you could get knocked around pretty well. A broken arm, a banged knee, a sprained ankle, assorted bruises and cuts . . . about what you'd expect from a good afternoon's workout.

Everyone seemed spirited enough in the mock combat. That wasn't what bothered Eggius about it. As the surgeons tended to men who'd got hurt, he said, "The trouble with this is, the Germans don't fight the way we do."

"Well, you can't expect us to fight like Germans," another officer said. "Then our men who were aping the barbarians would learn all the wrong things."

"I suppose so," Eggius said, "but now our men who are fighting as Romans are learning all the wrong things."

"No, they're not," the other man insisted. "They're fighting the way we're supposed to fight, the way we've always fought."

"Yes, but they're not fighting the enemies we're going to fight, Ceionius," Lucius Eggius said. "A defense that works fine against a Roman with a *scutum* and a *gladius* will leave you shorter by a head if you go up against a German and his whacking great slashing sword."

"As long as we fight the way we're supposed to, the other buggers can do whatever the demon they want," Ceionius said. "We'll beat 'em. We always have—we're *Romans*. I expect we always will."

Eggius started to say something pungent. Then he hesitated. No doubt the other fellow was a fool. But he was a fool who spouted stuff they tried to ram down your throat every day of the month. Best to go at him with care. "All I can tell you is that we've been screwing around here for twenty years, and we aren't much closer to putting them into the yoke than we were when we started."

"Oh, I think you're wrong," Ceionius said. "We're wearing them down a little at a time. They have a lot of savage customs to unlearn—"

"Like killing Roman soldiers by the wagonload," Eggius said dryly.

The other Roman looked pained. "They're holding markets. Those will turn into towns one day," he said. "They're holding assemblies, some of them with men from more than one tribe coming together."

"So they can plot against us better," Eggius said. "Have you heard what that one bastard who used to be an auxiliary is doing? Going all over everywhere and trying to fire up all the barbarians against us at once."

"I've heard it. I don't believe it." Pointedly, Ceionius added, "His Excellency the governor doesn't believe it, either."

So there, Eggius thought. If Varus didn't believe something, it didn't behoove any of his officers to believe it. Which, most of the time, was all very well, but what if something Varus didn't believe turned out to be true? *Well, in that case we've got a problem.*

"*I* hear the fellow who accused this German has a family squabble with him," Ceionius said in lofty tones.

"Yeah, I heard that, too. So what?" Eggius said. "Suppose somebody ran off with *your* daughter. Would you give him a big kiss? Or would you give him one where it'd do the most good?" He cupped his hands over his privates.

"Well, of course I'd pay back an enemy as soon as I saw the chance," the other officer replied. "But that's the point. Because they're enemies, we can't trust anything the one barbarian says about the other."

"Segestes wouldn't lie about something that big. Even in the wintertime, we've got people in Germany," Lucius Eggius said. "We can get a pretty good notion of who's trying to pull a fast one. Did the governor ask any of our people about that?"

"Not so far as I know. He doesn't think it's necessary," Ceionius said.

Eggius' sigh made fog spring forth from his mouth and nose. "Here's hoping he knows what he's thinking about."

Segestes clasped Masua's hand when the younger German came back to his steading. "Welcome! Welcome, by the gods!" Segestes said. "Come in. Rest yourself. I hope your journey went well?"

"I'm here again." Masua's voice was harsh and flat. A slave hurried up with a mug of beer. Masua nodded thanks, took it, and drained half of it at one long pull. After sucking foam out of his mustache, he said, "Varus wouldn't believe me—wouldn't believe you. And Arminius' friends tried to waylay me on the way home, but I gave them the slip." He spoke with somber pride.

"Why wouldn't the Roman believe you?" Segestes scratched his head, trying to fathom that. "Have evil spirits stolen his wits?"

"He wouldn't believe you about Thusnelda, either." His sworn man got to the bottom of the mug (Roman work, bought from a trader coming out of Gaul) in a hurry. The slave looked at Segestes, who nodded. The slave took the mug from Masua and carried it away to refill it.

"No, he wouldn't." The thought of Thusnelda lying in Arminius' arms still filled Segestes with rage. He made himself push that rage aside, even though it was the heaviest burden he'd ever set himself against. "Not believing me there is one thing. If a man steals a woman, it's a family affair. It is important to the people involved and to their friends. But if a man goes through Germany calling for a rising against the Romans . . . How can Varus not believe that?"

"He does not believe Arminius would ever do such a wicked thing." By the expression on Masua's face, he might have been smelling bad meat. The slave came back with the freshened mug. Again, Masua drank eagerly. He might have been trying to get the taste of bad meat out of his mouth, too.

"Ha!" Segestes said, a noise that was anything but the laugh it sounded like. "Arminius will do anything he thinks he can get away with. And we know what he thinks of Rome, and of Roman rule in Germany."

"We do, yes. This Quinctilius Varus, he will not see it." Masua sounded disgusted, for which Segestes could hardly blame him.

"Strange. He does not seem to be a stupid man," Segestes said. "The Roman king, this Augustus whose face is on their coins, would not send a stupid man to do such an important job as this."

"He is stupid enough. Otherwise, he would hearken to you." As a sworn man should be, Masua was loyal.

Segestes scratched his chin. "Have you ever known a man who cannot tell red from green? There they are, plain as can be in your eyes, but they look the same to him."

Masua nodded. "Yes, a man on the next farm over was like that when I was growing up. His belly griped him all the time, because he would eat berries and apples before they got ripe. But for that, he was a fine fellow. He was bold in the fight—I remember that."

"Good for him," Segestes said. A German who wasn't bold in the fight wasn't a man, not in the eyes of his tribesmen. The chieftain came back to the point at hand: "I think this is what's wrong with Varus. When he looks at Arminius, he can't see what is plain to everyone else."

"It could be so," Masua said after some thought. "Arminius will gripe *his* belly if he isn't careful, though—or even if he is."

"Yes. He will." Segestes remembered something else his retainer had said. "His men tried to ambush you?"

"They did." Masua's big head went up and down. "One of them showed himself too soon, though. It was early morning, and foggy— maybe he thought I would not see him. But I did, and I went back to the steading where I'd passed the night. The men there are your friends— they told me of another way east. Next morning, one of those men started up the path I'd taken the day before. He was near my size, about my coloring, and he had on a cloak much like mine. Meanwhile, I used the side way they showed me. The hope was that the ambushers would think the local man was me, and so it proved. I pray the gods let him get back to his steading safe."

"May it be so," Segestes said. "Good to know I do still have friends here and there. With Arminius making such a racket, it's hard to be sure these days."

"That he-witch." Masua scowled. "He has bespelled the Roman governor. I don't know how, but he has."

"Oh, I know how." Segestes sighed. The fire had died down to embers, and his breath smoked. "Arminius is young and handsome and bold. I seem old and grumpy by comparison. He can say he loves Thusnelda. Maybe he even does. But I think his course is a disaster for Germany. That is why I tried to give the girl to Tudrus, who has better sense."

"I would have done the same," Masua said. "None of my girls is old enough to wed yet, though."

"I know. Wait till you see how lucky you will remember yourself as being," Segestes said. "Women cause trouble. They can't help it. It's part of what they are."

"Oh, and men don't? I have learned something," Masua said.

The chieftain laughed, then sighed again and shook his head. "Arminius causes trouble—no doubt about that. Why would he *not* want to become part of Rome? Such foolishness! Without Rome, where would we get our wine? Our fine pottery? Our own potters make junk—good enough to use, but not good enough to look at. Where would we get rich jewelry, or coins, or all kinds of other good things?"

"You don't need to tell me all this," Masua said gently. "I already know."

"Yes, yes. Anyone with sense enough to cover a mustard seed would know," Segestes said. "But that leaves Arminius out. And it leaves a lot of young Germans out. They don't think of anything but fighting and killing."

"Fighting is good. Killing is good," Masua said. "Of course, when you're young you don't think you might get killed instead. That's not so good."

"No, it isn't," Segestes agreed, his voice dry. "If we rise up against the Romans, how many will get killed?"

"Lots, chances are," Masua said. "Wars are like that."

Segestes came over and kissed him first on the right cheek, then on the left. "You can see this. You are not a blockhead. I can see this, too. I hope I am not a blockhead."

"Of course you aren't," Masua said quickly, as a sworn retainer should have done for his chieftain.

"Well, I thank you for that," Segestes said. "But Arminius can't seen this. He's going here and there and everywhere, telling people we can drive out the Romans without breaking a sweat. What kind of blockhead is he? Those runty little dark bastards don't fight the way we do, but that doesn't mean they can't fight."

"I have seen them do it," the younger man replied. "You are right. They know how."

"Why does he think we can beat them so easily, then? Why?" Segestes said. "Even if we win a battle, they will just bring in more soldiers. That is what they are doing in Pannonia. Their king, this fellow Augustus, is as stubborn a man as ever was born. He will not let go because he burns a finger. Isn't it better to ride the way the horse is already going instead of trying to turn the stupid beast around?"

"I think so," Masua said.

"I told you—you are no blockhead. And we have a lot to learn from the Romans, too. This whole business of writing . . ." Segestes regretfully spread his hands. "I wish I would have come to it when I was young enough to learn it. It seems to me a very large idea."

"It could be," said Masua, who had no interest whatever in writing. "But I will tell you something else." Segestes made a questioning noise. His retainer explained: "That Varus, he has a lot to learn from us."

Serving as an officer in the Roman auxiliaries made Arminius a sophisticated man in Germany. Command meant more among the Romans than it did with his own folk. In Germany, a chieftain had to persuade to lead. If his retainers didn't like what he was doing, they wouldn't follow him.

A Roman officer who gave an order expected to be obeyed because of his rank. If the men under him said no, the Romans made them pay. Having authority like that made Arminius more persuasive, even if he couldn't use it all. If you tried to give a German an order he didn't fancy, he would up and tell you no. Either that or he would walk away and ignore you from then on. Arminius the German chieftain didn't have the coercive tools Arminius the officer of auxiliaries had enjoyed.

But he still spoke as if he expected to be obeyed. Because he did, he got more Germans to follow him than he would have if he'd begged for support the way a lot of would-be leaders did.

"You sound like a man who knows what he wants to do," was something he heard again and again.

"I am a man who knows what he wants to do," he would say whenever he heard that. "I want to throw the Romans out of our country. The more men who follow me, the better. But if I have to fight them by myself, I will."

He would do no such thing. Fighting the legions singlehanded was exactly the same as falling on his sword. It sounded bold, though. It sounded better than bold: it sounded heroic. And the more he said it, the more he repeated it, the less likely it became that he would have to follow through on it.

The Romans had been pushing German customs in their direction a little at a time, so slowly that only old men noticed things weren't done now as they had been in the days of their youth. Had the invaders kept on with that slow, steady pressure, they might have turned a lot of Germans into willing—even eager—imitators of their ways without the locals' even noticing.

But paying taxes the way Roman subjects did was not to the Germans' liking. Arminius seized on that. "Who knows what this Varus will want from you next? Who knows what he will take from you next?" he asked, again and again. "You can't trust him. You don't dare trust him. If you give him a finger, he'll take an arm. If you give him an arm, he'll take all of you. Then you'll be one more Roman slave."

He wanted to talk about Roman soldiers stealing German women. He wanted to, but soon found out he couldn't. It would have been lovely if he could; to the Germans, every Roman alive was a natural-born lecher, a threat to their women's virtue. Whenever Arminius tried that tack, though, a pro-Roman German would sing out, "What about Thusnelda?" A man who'd stolen a woman himself couldn't very well accuse others of wanting to do the same thing.

Oh, he could, but he got no profit from it if he did. And so Arminius, a practical man, soon stopped trying. He found plenty of other bad things to say about Varus and the Romans that didn't leave him open to heckling. His own folk were glad enough to listen to him when he steered clear of talk about women.

He'd just finished another harangue when a man he knew came up to him and spoke in a low voice: "Masua got away. We couldn't nab him, and he's been seen at Segestes' steading. We'll never get him there."

"Thunderweather!" Arminius said. "So he went and told lies to Varus and made it back, did he? That's not good."

"Sorry." The other German hung his head and spread his hands. "He's a sneaky bastard—that must be why Segestes chose him to go to the Roman in the first place. He gave our friends the slip some kind of way. We still don't know how. They thought they were going to catch him and give him what he deserved . . . but they didn't."

"Too bad. Oh, too bad!" Arminius said. "Has anyone we know come back from Vetera? Have you heard whether Varus paid any attention to him?"

"No, I haven't," his acquaintance answered. "The only way to find out will be how the Romans behave come spring."

"Yes." Arminius drew out the word till it sounded uncommonly gloomy. He could picture Varus summoning him to Mindenum. He would have to go if the Roman governor called him. Not going would show mistrust, and would make Varus mistrust him if he didn't already. But if Varus *did* already mistrust him . . . chains and the headsman's axe might be waiting for him when he came to the legionary encampment.

I am a Roman citizen, Arminius thought. *If Varus does try to take my head, I can appeal to Augustus, the Romans' king*. That would put off the inevitable. But how likely was Augustus to spare a rebel chieftain's life? If he was as canny as people said, he would want to nail Arminius' head to a tree or do whatever the Romans did with their sacrificial victims.

"You keep telling people Varus likes you," the other German said. "If he does, he wouldn't have listened to Masua."

"Yes." Arminius stretched the word again. "If." A foreigner's fondness was liable to decide his fate, and his country's. A slender twig to have to trust, but the only one he had.

❧ VII ❧

Quinctilius Varus got the feeling that he'd never properly appreciated spring before. That was what came of living his life around the Mediterranean. Winters were mild there, snows uncommon. Winter was the rainy season, the growing season, the season that led toward spring harvest.

Not here. Not on the Rhine. Varus had seen more snow in one winter than in all his previous life. So he told himself, anyhow, though it might not have been strictly true. He was sure he'd never seen more snow, deeper snow, than the drifts that whitened field and forest around Vetera.

And he'd never seen a greater rebirth than the one that came when the sun at last swung north and melted all the snow. The bare-branched trees enrobed themselves in greenery. Fresh new grass surged up through the dead, wispy, yellow stuff the snowdrifts had hidden.

Butterflies, flying jewels, flitted from one magically sprouted flower to the next. Bees began to buzz. Flies and gnats and mosquitoes also came back to life, and were rather less welcome.

With the insects came swarms of birds. Sparrows and carrion crows and a few others had stayed through the winter. But now the woods and fields were full of music. Swallows swooped. Thrushes hopped. Swifts darted. Robins sang. Varus appreciated them the more because he'd done without them for so long.

Aristocles was less impressed. "If things weren't so awful before, they wouldn't seem so much better now," the slave said darkly.

"I'd rather look on the bright side of things," Varus said.

The *pedisequus* sniffed. "The bright side of things would be going back to Rome. Are we going to do that?" His woebegone expression answered the question without words. Then he used a few more: "No. We're going into Germany."

"Don't remind me," Quinctilius Varus said. Even with the broad-leafed trees across the Rhine getting new foliage, the German forests looked dark and forbidding. Varus had never seen them look any other way. The bright side of things was hard to find. He did his best: "Maybe this year's campaigns will bring the province under the yoke once for all."

"Gods grant it be so!" Aristocles exclaimed. "In that case, you can turn it over to somebody else and go back to Rome after all."

"Nothing I'd like better." Varus lowered his voice. "The company of soldiers begins to pall after a while."

"Bloody bores," Aristocles muttered, which was just what his master was thinking. The *pedisequus* went on, "Is there any chance we could send the legions across the river to do what needs doing while we stay here ourselves? Vetera is bad, but I don't suppose it's impossible. Not next to Mindenum, anyhow."

Regretfully, Varus shook his head. "Augustus put me in charge of the three legions here. If I'm going to command them, I have to *command* them, if you know what I mean. And commanding means being seen to command."

"You have a strong sense of duty," Aristocles said. Varus would have liked that better had the slave not contrived to make it sound more like reproach than praise.

However much Varus wished he could, he couldn't avoid the company of soldiers. Practically everyone in Vetera was a soldier or a retired soldier or someone who sold things to soldiers or someone who slept with soldiers. Some of the legionary officers seemed enthusiastic about the prospects for the coming campaigning season. "One more good push and we've got 'em, I think," Ceionius said at a supper of roast boar.

"Here's hoping," Varus said. By now, he'd got used to drinking neat wine—or he thought he had, anyhow.

"It's still Germany. They're still Germans," Lucius Eggius said. "We've been banging heads with them for a long time, like a couple of aurochs in rutting season. How do we pull a miracle out of our helmet now?"

"We have a fine new leader," Ceionius said. "That's how."

"You flatter me," Varus said, which was bound to be true. Augustus's courtiers were smoother at it than these provincial bumpkins. To keep from thinking about that, Varus added, "Aurochs are a disappointment."

"Not if you boil 'em long enough," Eggius said. "After a while, the meat *will* turn tender. You've got to be patient, though."

"That isn't what I meant," Varus said. "In the *Gallic War*, Caesar makes them out to be fearsome monsters. And they aren't—they're nothing but wild oxen with long horns."

"Caesar likes to tell stories," Eggius said with a shrug. "Sometimes they're true. Sometimes they just sound good."

"How do you know which are which?" Varus asked.

"Sometimes you can tell. Sometimes—like with the aurochs—you can really find out. Sometimes . . ." The legionary officer shrugged. "It's the same way with the stories *about* Caesar, I guess. He's—what?—fifty years dead. Who knows which ones are true and which ones are just crap? Any old way, though, they'll be telling tales about him forever."

"Yes, I suppose they will," Quinctilius Varus said in tones more bitter than he would have expected.

Lucius Eggius wasn't wrong. Julius Caesar's fame would last as long as men endured. So would Augustus'—Varus had no doubt of that. *But what about my own?* he wondered, not for the first time.

If he was the man who brought Germany into the Empire, his name would live. Some historian would write an account of Augustus' reign, the way Sallust had written about the war against Jugurtha the Numidian and about Catiline's plot against the Senate or the way Caesar himself wrote about the war against the Gauls. Nobody could talk about Augustus' reign without talking about the conquest of Germany. And so, to some degree, people would remember that there had been such a man as Publius Quinctilius Varus.

But it wouldn't be the same. Everyone would always know who Julius Caesar and Augustus were. People would always tell stories about them. The stories wouldn't shrink in the telling, either. Stories never did. If a man two hundred years from now wanted to learn the name of the man who conquered Germany, though . . .

So many books were written and then forgotten, never recopied after the author put in the labor of composing them in the first place. Still, these were important times, and would surely attract an important historian, one whose works would be reproduced often enough to last . . . somewhere.

The library at Alexandria was supposed to keep at least one copy of every work in Greek and Latin. It had been damaged in the fighting in Caesar's day, but say it did what it was supposed to do. That would give the future scholar a chance to discover the name of Publius Quinctilius Varus—if he could find the scroll he needed among the thousands in the library . . . and if he could afford to go to Alexandria to do his research in the first place.

Immortality, then. But a shadowy immortality, rather like the one Homer gave the spirits of the dead in the *Odyssey*. Better than nothing, less than enough.

"Something wrong, your Excellency?" Eggius asked. "You look a little peaked, like."

"No, no, no." Varus denied it not only to the soldier but also to himself. "Just thinking about what Germany will be like when it's been Roman for a couple of hundred years, that's all." That wasn't exactly what he'd been thinking, but it came close enough to let him bring the lie out smoothly.

Lucius Eggius made a face. "It'll still be the back woods, you ask me. The Gauls, now, the Gauls are picking things up pretty quick. But these gods-cursed Germans? They're stubborn bastards, no two ways about it. I wouldn't be surprised if they were still mumbling to themselves in their own language, even after all that time."

Struck by an odd thought, Varus asked, "Have you learned any of it?"

"Me?" Eggius laughed. "Just a tiny bit, sir, so I can talk a little with the German girls I bed. They like that, you know? You can tell 'em what you want 'em to do, and they can let you know what feels good to them."

"I suppose so." Varus had slept with some German women, too. What else was he going to do, when Claudia Pulchra'd stayed down in Rome? But he'd made sure his bedwarmers understood enough Latin to get by. The other approach hadn't even occurred to him.

Eggius chuckled again. "Hate to talk business instead of pussy, sir, but when do you aim to cross the Rhine again?"

"How soon can the men be ready?" Varus asked.

"An hour from now, if they have to be." Professional pride rang in Eggius' voice. "If you're not in a hurry, though, a few days to get organized won't hurt."

"All right. Do that, then. I don't think there's any great rush," Varus said.

"Right you are, sir." Lucius Eggius nodded. Then he raised a curious eyebrow. "You sure this Arminius fellow isn't as much trouble as people say he is?"

"I'm not losing any sleep over him," Varus answered. "I don't think anybody else needs to, either."

The Romans had cut back the woods on the right bank of the Rhine opposite Vetera far enough to make it impossible to bushwhack them when they crossed their bridge into Germany. That didn't mean Arminius couldn't watch them cross without being seen himself.

This wasn't the first Roman army on the march he'd seen, of course. He'd fought alongside the legions in Pannonia, and, before that, he'd fought against them here in Germany. He didn't think the Romans knew about that. They wouldn't have granted him citizenship if they did. Back in those days, he'd been nothing to them but another shouting *barbarus* with a spear and a sword and a shield.

Barbarus. His mouth twisted. It didn't just mean someone who wasn't a Roman, the way he'd once thought. It meant somebody who couldn't talk like a human being, someone who made *bar-bar-bar* noises instead.

He'd learned Latin. He spoke it pretty well—not perfectly, but pretty well. He'd never yet met a Roman who came close to speaking the Germans' tongue anywhere near so well.

Romans had an almost perfect contempt for anyone from beyond their borders. He often wondered why, feeling the way they did, they wanted to rule other folk at all. He supposed perfect greed outweighed almost perfect contempt.

No denying they made a brave show, though. Cavalrymen crossed the Rhine first. He envied them their big horses. Germans, big men, rode ponies so small they often jumped off them to fight. Mounts from the Roman side of the Rhine were great prizes. There weren't many horsemen here: enough to smoke out an ambush and hold it off till the foot soldiers deployed.

Behind the cavalry came one of the legions the Romans were using to try to hold down Germany. As a fighting man, Arminius had nothing but respect for the soldiers tramping forward into his country. They were tough. They were brave. In a fight in the open field, they could beat more than their number of Germans. Arminius didn't like that, but he'd seen it was true. The Romans worked together so much better than his own folk did. . . .

He muttered something guttural under his breath. If the Germans were ever going to beat the legionaries, they would have to do it on a battlefield where the Romans couldn't deploy to advantage. The Germans would have to spring a trap, in other words.

Still, the Romans weren't stupid. They sent scouts ahead of their force and out to either flank. They were more careful than Germans, too. Arminius did some more muttering.

Camp surveyors and engineers followed the first legions. Then came Varus' baggage and that of the leading Roman officers, with plenty of horsemen to protect it. Arminius chuckled. The Roman governor wasn't about to let anything happen to what belonged to him.

Varus and his slaves and flunkies came next. The warm breeze fluttered the soldiers' scarlet capes. The slaves, in plain white tunics, were easy to distinguish from their masters.

The horsemen who weren't in the vanguard followed the commanders. Even with their fine mounts, the Romans got less from their cavalry than they might have. Their foot soldiers were so good, they hardly seemed to care about their riders.

More wagons rattled and creaked after the cavalry. Seeing them made Arminius scowl. They carried catapults that could hurl immense arrows or stone balls or pots full of burning oil farther than a bowshot. He'd seen what they were worth in Pannonia. The rebels there couldn't match them. Neither could his own folk. Being struck by weapons to which you couldn't hope to reply naturally spread fear. And the catapults could easily flatten the stockade that warded even the strongest German village.

Arminius had talked about casting the Romans out of his land. Talking was easy. Seeing a Roman army on the march reminded him that actually doing it would be anything but.

Behind the engines marched the other two legions. The *aquilifer* who had the honor of carrying each legion's eagle marched in front of it, surrounded by the lesser standard bearers and the *buccinatores* with their gleaming brazen horns. The *aqulifers'* mailshirts were likewise gilded, and blazed under the bright spring sun.

Camp followers—loose women, sutlers, ragtag and bobtail— made up a disorderly train that straggled along behind the legionaries. There, at least, Arminius felt superior and virtuous. Germans did without such folderol. They also probably would have done without a rear guard. Again, though, the Romans didn't believe in taking chances.

The legionaries brayed out a bawdy marching song. Arminius smiled before he quite knew he was doing it. He'd sung that one himself, tramping through Pannonia.

But the smile didn't last long. The Romans aimed to enslave his land and his folk. He wasn't sure how to stop them: only that he had to try.

Lucius Eggius' head went back and forth, back and forth, like a ball in a bathhouse game of catch. All he saw were fields and, beyond them, just out of bowshot, the dark, endless German forests. Fields and forests were all he saw, yes, but that failed to reassure him.

"They're out there," he said. "They're watching us. Can't you feel the eyes?" He scratched at his arm, as if he were complaining of flea bites.

"Well, what if they are?" Vala Numonius said. "Let them watch all they please. By the gods, three legions marching through their heartland will give them something to think about."

"Yes, sir," Eggius said resignedly. Numonius outranked him—he didn't want to argue too hard. But he also didn't want the cavalry commander to think he agreed completely, so he went on, "I'm worried about *what* they're thinking."

To give Numonius his due, he didn't put on airs. He'd always been a quiet, respectable fellow. He said, "If they aren't thinking we could carve them into mincemeat, they're stupid even for barbarians."

"Here's hoping," Eggius answered. "But they'd have another go at us if they ever saw the chance. In Gaul, the natives are licked. They know we walloped their granddads, and they don't want to try their own luck with us. It isn't like that here. You come into Germany, you're in a country where the people don't think they're whipped."

"Well, if they're fools enough to take on three legions at once, that'll change in a hurry," Numonius said. "I almost wish they would—know what I mean? That would settle things, and then we could get on with the business of turning this miserable place into a proper province."

"That'd be good," Eggius said. "Wouldn't need such a big garrison then. Maybe they'd send me somewhere with decent weather instead."

"I wouldn't mind that myself," Numonius agreed with a rueful chuckle. "If I never see another winter like this last one . . . There were a couple of nights when I thought they'd freeze right off and leave me a eunuch."

"I know what you mean, sir," Eggius said in a high, squeaky falsetto. Both soldiers laughed. Letting his voice fall back to his usual gruff baritone, Eggius continued, "We'd be better off if we could chop the balls off some of these gods-despised Germans."

"I won't quarrel with you—not even a little bit," the cavalry commander said. "A gelding's easier to ride than a stallion, and an ox won't gore you or trample you the way a bull will. We could make the Germans peaceable, and—"

"And sell them for a nice price once we take their family jewels," Eggius broke in. "If we have to sell all the Germans into slavery, we can resettle the place with people who wouldn't give us a hard time. It worked in Carthage. Why not here?"

"I wouldn't complain," Numonius replied. "Now if only the Germans wouldn't . . ."

"They always complain, seems like." Lucius Eggius' head swung from left to right and back once more. Nothing was going to take him by surprise, not if he could help it—and he could. "What's-his-name—Segestes—wants us to skin Arminius for him because Arminius is spreading his little girl's legs. And if you believe even half of what you hear, that Arminius spends all the time when he isn't pumping Thusnelda complaining about us."

"His Excellency believes that's all moonshine and vapors," Vala Numonius said. "When Segestes sent that other barbarian to accuse Arminius a couple of months ago, Varus set a flea in his ear and told him to go away. Segestes is full of sour grapes, if you know your Aesop."

"I know that one, anyhow," Eggius said. "Have to tell you, though, I sure hope the governor's right. We're liable to wind up in a peck of trouble if he's wrong." He paused and brushed an early fly away from his horse's mane. Then he went on, "And you can tell him I said so. I don't care. He knows what I think—I've told him so to his face."

"So he's said to me. He respects you for your forthrightness," Numonius answered.

Lucius Eggius didn't believe that for a minute. Nobody—nobody—liked it when someone came right out and told him he was wrong. But Eggius had risen from the ranks. He wouldn't go any higher than camp prefect. Quinctilius Varus might bust him down to centurion's rank, but no further. He could live with that. Since Varus couldn't destroy his career, he was free to speak his mind.

All that flashed through his mind in a couple of heartbeats. Meanwhile, Numonius continued, "I happen to think the governor's right this time. Segestes is acting like an outraged father in one of Plautus' comedies. You can't believe somebody like that—you really can't."

"Why not?" Eggius said. "Seems to me like he's got a pretty good reason to be mad."

"Well, I don't know." Numonius shrugged. He seemed at home on horseback—he might have been the human half of a centaur. Eggius could ride, but he wasn't enthusiastic about it. When somebody gave him a leg-up, he felt much too far off the ground. And he didn't have enough to hold on to, either. Well, that was also true for Numonius, but Numonius didn't seem to care. The cavalry commander continued, "His Excellency has talked to all these people, remember. If anybody can judge who's telling the truth and who's up in arms over nothing, Varus is the one."

Eggius grunted. "That's so—no doubt about it." And it was. He wished it made him feel better. Unfortunately, it didn't. It only made him fear Arminius was pulling the wool over the governor's eyes.

That had something to do with where he was. His head went to the left once more, and then to the right. The army had flank guards out to both sides, of course. No great swarm of howling German barbarians would catch the legions unawares. He kept peering this way and that anyhow. He might have been in a small detachment that needed every working eyeball it had. He'd been in detachments like that often enough to give him habits almost impossible to break.

Numonius also looked now one way, now the other. Eggius nodded to himself when he noticed that. The other officer had also learned caution in enemy country, then. And this *was* enemy country—no two ways about it.

No wonder Caesar had made more of the aurochs than it deserved after first plunging into the German forests. And he talked about the moose as if it were so large it made trees fall over when it leaned against them—and it couldn't get up again afterwards, because its legs had no joints. And Caesar spoke of another weird beast with a single, branching horn growing out of its forehead. Lucius Eggius hadn't the slightest idea what that was supposed to be. He suspected Caesar couldn't have told him, either. Old Julius had listened to a few yarns too many, all right.

The bad news was, the German forests remained as full of Germans as they were in Caesar's day. And Germans remained more dangerous than all the aurochs and moose (mooses?) and one-horned whatsits put together. Lucius Eggius had no trouble seeing that. He wondered why Varus had so much with it.

Into Germany again. Quinctilius Varus could have done without that. Indeed, he would gladly have done without it. Leaving the Empire behind was harder the second time than it had been the first. The year before, he hadn't really realized what he was abandoning. Now he did.

"Do you know what I don't understand?" he said to Aristocles as the legions made camp one night.

"No, sir," the *pedisequus* answered. "But you're about to tell me—aren't you?"

"Too right I am." If Varus recognized the irony lurking in his slave's voice, he didn't show it. Instead, intent on his own thoughts, he went on, "*I* don't understand why the Germans aren't dropping down on their knees and knocking their heads against the ground to thank us for taking them into the Empire. The way they live now . . ." He shuddered.

"Is it so bad?" Aristocles asked. "You didn't take me along this afternoon when you visited that—what do they call it, sir?"

"A steading. They call it a steading." Varus brought out the *terminus technicus* with sour relish. "And no, it's not that bad. It's worse—much worse, if you want to know what I think. The Germans and their farm animals all shared the same miserable room. The Germans—oh, yes, and the chickens—were the ones who walked on two legs. Past that, it was hard to tell them from the beasts of burden."

Aristocles giggled. Then he tried to pretend he hadn't. Then he gave up pretending and giggled some more. "That's wicked, sir. Wicked!"

"What? You think I'm joking? By the gods, I wish I were. Fetch me some wine from the cooks, will you? Maybe it'll wipe the taste of what I saw out of my mouth," Varus said.

"Of course, sir." Aristocles hurried away. When he came back to Varus' tent, he had a cup of wine for the governor—and one for himself.

Varus didn't say anything about that. Naturally, a slave would look out for himself. After pouring a small libation onto the squashy German soil, the governor asked, "Where was I?"

"What you saw at the steading, sir." Aristocles didn't bother with a libation. Whatever he could gather, he kept.

"Oh, yes. That's right. Of course. And this barbarian was one of the rich ones, as they reckon such things here. Poor dog! He and his weren't hungry, I will say. Past that . . ."

"I suppose they insist they would sooner be free." Aristocles' lip curled in a bravura display of scorn. "Freedom is overrated, I assure you."

"It is, eh?" Varus said, thinking a man from the great days of Greece would have said no such silly thing. "So you'd turn it down if I offered it to you?"

"I am confident you *will* offer it to me, sir—in your will," the *pedisequus* replied. "Till then—and the gods grant that time be far in the future—I am content with my lot. A slave not lucky enough to have such a kind and generous master might seen things differently, I confess."

Of course slaves flattered. A slave who didn't flatter might find his master less kind and generous than he would otherwise. But Varus had heard the same thing from other men he owned. No matter how much he discounted each individual flattery, they likely added up to something when taken all together.

He'd even heard the same thing from women he owned, and not all of those women had been too old or too ugly to keep him from bedding them. Slavery was harder on women than on men. Well, what in this life wasn't? If a nice-looking woman happened to be your property, why wouldn't you enjoy her? Your own property couldn't very well refuse you. And if a slave conceived, that was pure profit.

Still, Varus didn't want his slave women hating him afterwards. He was a cautious, moderate man, and didn't want anybody hating him. People who hated sometimes struck out without worrying about what it would cost them afterwards.

Some men Varus knew didn't care. Some of them took extra pleasure from laying a slave girl who would have spit in their face were she free. Some men liked hunting lions and bears and crocodiles, too. And quite a few hunters died younger than they would if they didn't go after dangerous game.

How many men died sooner than they would have if they'd kept their hands off slave girls who couldn't stand them? Horrible things happened to slaves who murdered openly. That was necessary; it kept other slaves from getting nasty ideas. But not all poisonings, for instance, were easy to detect. If someone came down deathly ill or slowly wasted away, maybe it was fate. On the other hand, maybe it was somebody else's revenge.

Quinctilius Varus didn't want to worry about things like that. He also didn't want Aristocles brooding that he might not be manumitted. And so he murmured, "You're quite right—I've provided for you. I'm sure you'll do well."

Aristocles might have dispraised freedom, but he blossomed like these German flowers in springtime when Varus affirmed he would gain it. "Your Excellency is very kind—very kind!" he said in Greek. Falling into his native tongue was often a sign he'd been touched. "I thank you so much!"

"You are welcome," Varus answered, also in Greek. As far as grammar went, Varus spoke it perfectly. But his accent still proclaimed him a foreigner.

Romans reckoned everyone but themselves and Greeks barbarians. As far as Aristocles was concerned, Varus was as much a barbarian as Arminius or Segestes. The *pedisequus* probably wouldn't say that out loud—his sense of self-preservation worked. Varus had talked with plenty of other Greeks—free men—though. He knew what they thought, even if respect for Rome's might made them mind their manners.

"Things are different for you and the Germans," Varus said. "You understand freedom. You know what it really means. The Germans are free like so many wolves in the woods. We have to be good shepherds, and make sure they don't slaughter our flocks and run wild."

"A nice figure, sir," Aristocles said.

That might have been flattery, too. If it was, Quinctilius Varus didn't notice, because he also thought it a nice figure. He would have thought of the Germans as wolves even if they weren't fond of draping themselves in pelts like *aquilifers* and *buccinatores*. Since they were, the comparison sprang even more naturally to his lips.

Except for his visit to the friendly chieftain, he hadn't seen many of them since Legions XVII, XVIII, and XIX plunged into Germany. That didn't surprise him. Even in provinces the Romans had ruled for years, locals made themselves and their livestock scarce when legionaries marched by. No doubt the farmers in Pericles' Greece had done their best to disappear when phalanxes full of hoplites came near their holdings.

Varus laughed. Back when the Pyramids and Sphinx were new, Egyptian peasants must have tried to steer clear of the Pharaoh's soldiers. Some things never changed.

"What's funny, sir?" Aristocles asked. Varus told him. The *pedisequus* dipped his head in agreement. "I expect you're right," he said.

"I suppose Pharaoh's armies went through Syria every now and then," Varus said musingly. "That's old, old country there in the East. Maybe not so old as Egypt, but older than Greece and Rome."

"Yes." Aristocles' mouth tightened as if he'd bitten into an unripe persimmon. Pride in their own antiquity was one of the few edges Greeks had on Romans. Varus' slave couldn't even complain, because the Roman had already admitted that Syria was older than his own homeland, too.

Then Quinctilius Varus's mouth also tightened, but for a different reason. "From a land as old as time to one where time doesn't seem to have started yet . . . A bit of a change, isn't it?"

"Just a bit. Yes, sir." Aristocles looked around at the oaks and elms and beeches and chestnuts coming into leaf, and at the pines and firs and other conifers whose needles darkened the German forests' aspect. "It is a pity Augustus didn't name you Augustal prefect. Then you could have seen the Egyptian antiquities at first hand. As you say, there's nothing old here except the woods."

"Yes. Indeed." Varus' mouth got tighter yet. A clever slave could get back at his master, as the Greek had just proved. Augustal prefect of Egypt was the most important administrative post in the Empire—after the one Augustus held himself, of course. It was also the post Varus had craved after governing Syria. And it was the post his wife's great-uncle had chosen not to give him.

"I have to do the best I can where Augustus decided to send me," Varus said. "The decision was his." Everything in the Empire was Augustus' to give or to withhold as he saw fit. That was what winning all those civil wars meant. Oh, he'd built up a fine Republican façade to operate behind, but it was a façade, as anyone with eyes to see knew.

Aristocles sighed. "If only the Pannonians hadn't rebelled . . ."

"If, if, if," Varus said, not because the *pedisequus* was wrong but because he was right. If Tiberius weren't putting down the rising within the Empire's borders, he would hold this post now. And if stern, unsmiling Tiberius were whipping the Germans into line, Augustus might well have sent Varus to Egypt.

Had Augustus sent Varus there, Aristocles would have gone along. The Greek sighed again, this time on a more resigned note. "Oh, well. What can you do, eh, your Excellency?"

That question looked for the answer, *Not a thing*. But Varus surprised his slave: "If I'm to make this a Roman province, I *will* make it a Roman province. The better the notion the natives have of what's expected of them, the better Roman subjects they'll make."

"Er—yes." Aristocles blinked. No, he hadn't been looking for that or anything like that. "May your efforts be crowned with success."

"I hope they will. I think they will. Centuries from now, I hope this will be as much Roman land as, say, Spain or Cisalpine Gaul. We'll need hard work to make that happen, but I don't believe any Roman here fears hard work," Varus said.

Plenty of legionaries worked no harder than they had to. Varus took that for granted; legionaries were men like any others, but he also took for granted that their superiors would keep them working hard enough to do what needed doing. What else were officers for?

In his mind's eye, Varus saw towns growing out of legionary encampments in Germany, as they'd done so many other places in the Empire. He saw gleaming marble temples to Rome's gods—and to Germany's, for,

Druids and Jews aside, the Romans didn't meddle with religion. He saw bathhouses and colonnaded market squares where citizens in togas talked over the latest news. He saw amphitheaters for chariot races and gladiatorial games and beast shows. He saw theaters where the locals could watch Plautus and Terence and mime shows. He saw schools and shoemakers, millers and scribes.

It could happen. It would happen, once the Germans got used to the idea of being part of something larger than themselves. What would stop it then? Nothing he could see.

True, the Germans still nailed the heads of men they'd slain to trees, as an offering to the spirits inside. But the Gauls had done the same thing till Caesar conquered them. For that matter, the untamed tribes in Britannia and Hibernia still did. The ones within the Empire's borders were surprisingly civilized these days.

The Germans could be, too. All they needed was a firm hand and a little time.

VIII

Arminius had found himself another forest-screened vantage point from which to watch the Romans encroach on Germany. This one didn't lie hard by the Rhine—the border between Germany and Gaul since Caesar checked the Germans' westward wandering. This one was in the heart of his own folk's fatherland. Now that spring had returned, so had the storks, rebuilding their old nests in dead trees. And so had the Romans, rebuilding their old encampment at Mindenum.

This time, Sigimerus had come with Arminius for a firsthand look at the men who aimed to despoil the Germans of their freedom. What Arminius' father saw impressed him—against his will, but it did. Arminius understood that grudging respect; it was a large part of what he felt about the Romans, too.

"They work hard, don't they?" Sigimerus said. "And they work fast."

"So they do, both," Arminius agreed.

His father scowled. "If you go behind a tree to ease yourself and them come back to watch them again, the palisade will have grown some while you were pissing."

"They wouldn't be so dangerous if they didn't have a good notion of what they were doing," Arminius said. "They've conquered many other folk. They know how to go about it. If they don't make any mistakes, I fear they'll win here, too. They're winning in Pannonia, no matter how strong and how stubborn the rebels are there."

"And you helped them." Sigimerus sounded reproachful.

"I did." Arminius nodded. "One man more or less made no difference in how the war would have turned out."

"A hero——" his father began.

"No." Arminius cut him off, even if that was rude. "One of the things I learned is that heroes don't matter much, not the way they fight. Their soldiers might as well be farmers or potters. Everyone has his particular job to do, and he does it, and their armies mostly win."

"Not here, by the gods!" Sigimerus exclaimed. "We've taken plenty of Roman heads."

"I know, Father," Arminius said gently. "But they've won their share of fights, too. If they hadn't, would they be running up this encampment again? It's a long way from the Rhine to here."

"Isn't it, though?" Sigimerus sounded glum. Arminius couldn't blame him. Roman matter-of-factness at work had a daunting quality to it. The Romans went about their business no matter what, as if convinced nothing could withstand them as long as they kept at it. No, not as if: they *were* convinced of that. Arminius' hitch as an auxiliary had taught him as much, along with many other things.

Here, some Romans felled trees. Others trimmed them. Others hoisted them into position on the palisade. Others dug a trench around the ring of sharpened tree trunks. Others took the spoil from the diggers' work and shaped it into a rampart. And still others stood to arms, ready to ward the laboring legionaries against surprise attack.

"How *can* we stop them?" Sigimerus seemed gloomier still. "They're like ants or bees, aren't they? A big hive of Romans . . ." He ruefully shook his head.

"They can sting, all right," Arminius said. "But you put your finger on it yourself—so can we. Somehow, we have to arrange it so we meet them on ground that gives us the edge. Then . . . we strike!"

"That sounds good, son. But a lot of things that sound good aren't so easy to bring off," Sigimerus said. "Just look at the swinehounds. They're ready for anything. You can tell. They'd almost thank us for wading into them. It'd give them the chance to make us sorry we were ever born."

"Too right. I remember an ambush in Pannonia. The Pannonians thought they were ambushing us while we made camp, but it turned out to work the other way around," Arminius said. "Minucius—the military tribune who led us—picked a spot near some woods, so the enemy could gather there and think he was safe. But we figured they were in there, and we were out in the open, so we had plenty of room to deploy when they showed themselves. Oh, we made them pay!" He smiled at the memory—he'd fought well and his side had won, even if it was also the Romans' side.

His father's expression came closer to despair. "If they always take such pains, how will we ever beat them?"

"I said it before—they have to make a mistake," Arminius answered. "They aren't gods, Father. They're men, and little men at that. They make mistakes all the time, just like us. We have to get them to make the kind of mistake that serves our need."

"Yes, you said that before, too." Sigimerus sounded like a man talking to a young, foolish son, trying to get him to see his foolishness. "What you haven't told me is how you propose to do it."

"I haven't told you how because I don't know." Arminius sounded like the young, foolish son, admitting what he would sooner deny. "But there has to be a way."

"Why?" Sigimerus asked relentlessly. "You want the Romans to be stupid, and you've just spent all this time explaining to me how clever they are. Clever people are clever because they mostly don't do stupid things."

"Mostly!" Arminius seized on the word like a drowning man grabbing hold of a log. "That doesn't mean they're perfect. They aren't! No one is smart all the time."

"No one is smart all the time," his father agreed. But he wasn't looking at the Romans as they built their fortress-camp right in the middle of Germany. No—he was looking straight at Arminius.

The younger man's cheeks and ears might have caught fire. "We *can* beat them," Arminius insisted. "We have to beat them. If we let them go on the way they're going, they *will* enslave us." He stuck out his chin in defiance: of Sigimerus, of the Romans, of everything in the world that dared opposed his will. "Go ahead. Tell me I'm wrong."

Sigimerus sighed. But this time he looked at the Roman soldiers chopping and sawing and hauling and digging and building. He sighed again. His face said a great many things, none of them happy. All he said, though, was, "If we try and we fail, Germany wears the chains of slavery forever."

"She wears them if we don't try, too," Arminius answered. "She's bound to wear them then. But if we fight and win, she's free, free forever!"

His father looked at the Romans once more. This time, he said not a word.

Quinctilius Varus didn't like to sit up when he dined, but even a chair with a back was a luxury in Mindenum. A couch—a whole set of couches—would have made these bluff, straightforward soldiers grumble. Varus knew that, no matter how little he cared for it. He also knew he had to get along with the officers. It was not only that they were the men who carried out his orders. If he didn't stay on good terms with them, he had no one but his slaves to talk to. In this straitened place, that wasn't enough.

Under the chief cook's watchful and anxious eyes, two kitchen slaves—hulking Germans—carried a covered silver tray into the tent doing duty for a dining hall and set it on the table. One of them protected his hand with a big of rag as he grabbed the cover's handle and pulled it off. Steam and savory smells filled the tent. Varus and the other diners exclaimed in delight. A couple of the soldiers even clapped their hands. What could you expect from such people?

Relief in his voice, the cook said, "Roast boar, your Excellencies, with forest mushrooms, on a bed of cabbage and turnips."

"I'd never get bored with that," Lucius Eggius called out.

For a moment, Varus heard it as a hungry man's commonplace. Then he caught the pun. He sent Eggius a look half respectful, half reproachful. Was the wordplay just luck, or was there more to the officer than met the eye?

Varus decided he didn't have to worry about it now. He was the highest-ranking man here, so he was entitled to feed himself first and take the choicest gobbet. He did, seizing a smoking chunk of pork generously outlined with dripping fat. His mouth watered.

It tasted as good as it looked and smelled. Varus could imagine no higher praise. Smiling, chewing, he nodded to the cook. That worthy bowed in delight.

Vala Numonius chose next. The cavalry commander's right hand closed on a slice even bigger and fatter than Varus'. "Good," Numonius said with his mouth full. "Wonderful!" The cook beamed.

One by one, in order of rank, the Roman officers fed themselves. "Begging your pardon, friends," one of them said as he took food with his left hand.

"We know you, Sinistrus," Varus said. The nickname told how thoroughly left-handed the legionary was. His right hand was as clumsy and useless as most people's left—good only for wiping himself. Varus had known a few other men like that. They always apologized when they fed themselves with what was usually the wrong hand.

The mushrooms were different from the familiar Italian varieties, and also different from the ones Varus had eaten in Syria. Not better or worse, the governor judged, but different. One of the officers spoke to the cook: "You tried these out on beasts before you tried them on us, right?"

"Oh, yes, sir!" the cook said, so quickly that the legionaries laughed.

"Some good news, anyway." Lucius Eggius' voice was dry. The Roman officers laughed again. So did Quinctilius Varus. He liked mushrooms, but he also knew you could make mistakes with them. And a mistake with a mushroom was much too likely to be the last mistake you ever made.

Another officer raised a winecup. "Here's to putting Germany under our thumb once and for all!"

Varus was glad to drink to that toast. The rest of the diners followed his lead. All the same, he heard somebody mutter, "What I'd really like is to put Germany behind me!"

He looked around, trying to make out who'd spoken. But he

couldn't. He didn't recognize the voice, and no one's face gave him away. Besides, how angry could he get? He would have liked nothing better than going back to Gaul, going back to Italy, going anywhere but here.

No matter what he would have liked, he had to stay. "By the gods, gentlemen, we will whip this province into shape!" he declared. "And if we have to resort to the lash, that's what we'll do. The Germans need to know who their rightful masters are."

"Hear, hear!" Several officers loudly supported him. Others, though, sat quietly, as if trying to pretend they hadn't heard what he said. Most of the ones who made a point of agreeing had come north with him the year before. Most of the ones who stayed quiet had been fighting the Germans longer than that.

Were the newcomers too hopeful? *Am I too hopeful?* Varus wondered. Or were the veterans of this frontier jaded and frustrated because things here hadn't gone better? Quinctilius Varus decided it had to be the latter. The Germans had stayed pretty quiet even though he'd started accustoming them to taxation. Why *wouldn't* they turn into proper Roman subjects if he kept on traveling the road he'd begun?

And he was sure Augustus wouldn't have sent him up here if the job weren't doable. If anyone had ever had an instinct for such things, Augustus was the man. The veterans had made a hash of things, that was all, and so they built the Germans up to be bigger and fiercer and stubborner than they really were.

He'd made progress. He would make more. If Augustus thought he could do it, he did, too.

Sometimes the Germans would attack a Roman army without the slightest hesitation. Sometimes a couple of Roman soldiers could amble through the countryside and get nothing but friendly treatment. You never could tell.

Caldus Caelius and two or three buddies were ambling through the countryside now. The legionaries weren't stupid about it. They'd told their friends back at Mindenum where they were going. If anything happened to them, the legionaries would make the barbarians pay.

And the Germans around Mindenum had figured that out. Knocking off a Roman soldier here was more expensive than it was worth. Caelius and his friends wore helmets, and swords on their belts—you didn't want to beg the Germans to jump you—but he wasn't what you'd call anxious.

Hard to worry about anything with spring burgeoning all around. New bright grass pushed up out of the ground. New shiny leaves were on all the trees that weren't conifers—and in weather like this, mild and mostly sunny, you could ignore the gloomy needles on the pines and spruces. Flowers blazed across the meadows like stars in the night sky. The air smelled sweet and green.

Birds sang in the trees, throwing out music for anyone who walked by. "Germany wouldn't be a bad place," Caelius remarked, listening to a blackbird's clear notes, "if it stayed this way the year around."

He came from a farming village south of Neapolis, down near the toe of the boot. He knew the difference between summer and winter there: winter was the rainy season, and it did get cooler than the blazing summer heat. But it rarely snowed, and far fewer trees lost their leaves than they did here. Life down there had a more even pace. He missed it.

One of his friends peered into the woods. "Germany wouldn't be a bad place," the other legionary said, "if it didn't have Germans in it."

All the other Romans laughed. Caelius wondered why. "You've got that right, Sextus," he said. "Only way to get rid of them is to kill 'em all, though."

"Don't remind me," Sextus said. "And how many of us would they bump off before we finished with 'em?"

The sun ducked behind a cloud. Some of the brightness would have gone out of the day even if it hadn't. "Too stinking many," Caelius said. "They're tough—no two ways about it."

A rabbit bounded across the trail and disappeared into tall grass. Sextus pointed after it. "The barbarians hide just like that, the buggers."

"There's a difference," Caelius said.

"What's that?" His friend liked being contradicted no more than any other mortal.

"When rabbits hide, they don't take along spears and swords and bows," Caldus Caelius said.

Sextus grunted. "Well, so they don't. And all kinds of things eat them. I wish something would eat up the Germans."

A local, wrapped in his cloak, rounded a stand of trees up ahead. "Watch your mouths, boys," Caelius said quietly. "Some of these bastards know Latin. We don't want to be calling them dogs to their faces."

"Why not?" another legionary demanded. "It's what they are."

"But the officers'll have our guts for sandal straps if we start a fight for no reason," Caelius said. The other soldier, a younger man—not that Caelius was very old—muttered under his breath but subsided. Caelius showed the German up ahead a raised, empty right hand.

Slowly, the native returned the gesture. Even more slowly, he came toward the Romans. He was tall and proud and skinny. His cloak had a bronze clasp in the shape of a beast. The creature's eye was of stone, or perhaps glass paste. That said the German was a man of some substance, though probably not a chief. A real leader would have had a gold or silver clasp for his cloak, and would have worn breeks under it, too. This fellow's hairy shanks stuck out below the bottom of his cloak. His spear was made for thrusting; it was longer and stouter than the javelins Caelius and his friends used.

"We have no quarrel with you," Caelius said in Latin. Then he said what he hoped was the same thing, using his scraps of the Germans' language.

"No? Then go back where you came from." The barbarian's Latin wasn't much better than Caelius' command of his language. He looked at his spear. He looked at the Romans. Several of them and one of him. If he started a fight, he'd regret it—but not for long. And he'd never do anything else that stupid afterwards. With a sigh, he nodded. "I have no quarrel with you—now."

Caldus Caelius gave his pal a look that said, *See? He might have understood you after all.* The one the other Roman returned said something like, *Yes, Mother.* They grinned at each other. Caelius gave his attention back to the German. "There's a little village down this path, isn't there?" he said.

"Why you want to know?" From the anger and alarm in the native's voice, he was wondering whether the legionaries aim to burn the place first and then rape the women or the other way round.

"I thought maybe we'd buy some of that, uh, beer you people brew," Caelius answered. He liked wine better—what Roman in his right mind wouldn't? By all the signs, the Germans liked wine better, too, when they could get it. But all the wine that came to Mindenum started from Vetera. There was usually enough to give each legionary his fair share, but not enough to get drunk on. And so . . . Beer would do.

"*Ach*," the German said: a deep, guttural noise. He nodded again, visibly relaxing. "Yes, there is a village. Yes, there is beer."

"Good. That's good." Caldus Caelius turned to the other Romans. "Come on, boys."

They sidled past the German. Both they and he stepped out of the path while they did it, so neither side admitted to giving way to the other. Caelius had done that dance of pride before. If you respected a German's manhood, he wouldn't feel he had to prove it to you.

Most of the time, anyway.

Caelius looked back over his shoulder once, to make sure the barbarian wasn't trying to get cute. The German was looking back at the Romans. Their eyes met—locked. Slowly and deliberately, Caelius nodded. So did the German. They both looked away.

"Trouble?" Sextus asked.

"Nah," Caelius said after a moment's pause for thought. "Not now, anyhow. He was just . . . checking, you know? Same as me."

Sextus nodded. "Sure. My neck's on a swivel every time we leave the encampment."

"You aren't the only one," Caldus Caelius assured him.

The village, such as it was, lay not quite half a mile down the path. Five or six farmhouses stood close together in the middle of the fields the natives worked. Caelius didn't sneer at it that much. He'd seen cities, sure, but he'd grown up in a place not a whole lot bigger than this one.

Watching the Germans hoeing and planting at this season instead of harvesting still startled him. But what could you expect in a land where it rained in the summertime?

Women tended the vegetable plots, the way they would have in Italy. A lot of the vegetables were familiar, too: onions, lettuces, the indispensable turnips and beets. But the Germans had never heard of garlic. Fools that they were, barbarians that they were, they thought it smelled bad. They grew some roots and leaves the Romans didn't use back home. Caldus Caelius had tried a few of them. He supposed he could eat them again if he had to, but hoped he wouldn't have to.

The legionaries didn't try to get fresh with the gardening women. The Germans hated unwelcome advances at least as much as Italians would have. One squeal from a girl and all the barbarians out in the fields would have come running with mattocks and adzes and whatever else they had out there.

A gray-haired man, bent and stiff with age as old men always were, hobbled out of one of the farmhouses leaning on a stick. Caelius eyed it: it was carved from top to bottom with little animals and men hunting. Clever work, if you had the time to sit down and do it.

Like a lizard, the old-timer soaked up sunshine. He stretched and straightened a little. Scars seamed his arms and legs; he'd seen his share of fighting and then some back in the day. A cataract clouded one of his eyes. The other had stayed clear.

"*Pax*," he said to the Romans. Not only his accent but two missing upper front teeth made his voice mushy.

"*Pax*," Caelius answered. The old man cupped his free hand behind his ear. "Peace," the legionary repeated, louder this time.

Still in Latin, the old man went on, "You come for the beer, yes?" He could make himself understood, all right. How much of his fighting had been against the Romans, how much against Germans from other tribes or from this one? Some questions might be better left unasked.

Besides, the barbarian's query needed answering. "That's right," Caldus Caelius said eagerly. The other legionaries seemed happy enough to let him do the talking, but they added smiling nods.

"You have silver?" the graybeard went on.

"Sure do." Caelius dug a denarius out of his belt pouch. His friends could pay their share later. No matter how much he drank, he wouldn't forget that they owed him: a denarius was close to a day's salary for him.

"*Ach.*" The old man made that guttural noise Germans liked. He held the denarius out at arm's length so he could examine it with his good eye. The silver coin shone in the sun. He was looking at the reverse, because Caelius could see Augustus' right-facing profile on the other side. A slow smile spread across the barbarian's face. "It is good."

"Sure," Caelius said. A denarius might be worth a good bit to him, but it was worth a lot more to the native. Since the Germans didn't mint their own money, they made a big deal of the coins they got from the Romans.

The German said something in his own language. Caelius thought it meant something like *Bring it out—I've got the cash*. That was about as far as his knowledge of the Germans' tongue stretched.

Two women close by left off gardening and went into the farmhouse. One of them rolled out a good-sized oaken barrel—the barbarians often preferred barrels where Romans would have used pottery. The other woman carried earthenware cups and a dipper carved from wood. She handed each legionary a cup.

"Thank you," Caelius said in her language. She blinked, then smiled at him. She wasn't pretty, and she was at least fifteen years older than he was, but the smile turned her from a crone to somebody who might be a nice person.

Down into the barrel went the dipper. The woman who'd handed Caelius his cup filled it for him. "Your health," she said.

"Thanks," he said again. The Roman salute was the same, though he thought it sounded better in Latin. A Greek doctor attached to the legion had once told him Greeks said the same thing, too. That was pretty funny, when you got right down to it.

He drank. As soon as he tasted the stuff, he had to remind himself not to screw up his face. However much he wished beer were sweet like wine, it wasn't. You couldn't do anything about that. But if you drank enough, beer would do something to you.

"I've been up on—over, I mean—this miserable frontier too long," Sextus said. "Gods help me, I'm starting to like beer."

"Tell the doctor's helpers next sick call," Caldus Caelius said. "Maybe they can cure you." Then he laughed. "If you like it enough to drink a lot, you *will* need to see the doctor's helpers at sick call."

"So what?" Sextus said. "I'll be happy while I'm drinking, and that's what counts." He dipped his mug full again, then started emptying it.

Caldus Caelius filled his mug again, too. Why not? They were off duty. They might get teased for coming back to the encampment drunk, but they wouldn't get in trouble.

"You know," another Roman said, "when you look at 'em the right way, these German gals aren't so ugly. They've got a lot to hold on to, you know what I mean?" He eyed the girl who'd rolled out the barrel.

Caelius hadn't drunk himself stupid yet—not that stupid, anyhow. "Careful," he said. "You don't want to get too pushy with them, or you'll bring their menfolk down on us. They like maidens here, same as we do."

"I know, I know," the other legionary replied. "For some silver, though, I bet I can get her to go down on her knees for me, or else take it up the rear."

"If she says no, don't pester her." Caelius jerked his chin toward the fields. "We're outnumbered, remember."

"Sure, sure," Sextus said in a way that meant he was paying as little attention as he could. Caldus Caelius and the rest of the legionaries looked at one another. Caelius wondered if they'd have to knock Sextus over the head and drag him back to Mindenum. If he stirred up trouble, that might be the smartest thing the other Romans could do. They'd come for a good time, not to fire the barbarians up against them.

Sextus drew a denarius from his belt pouch. Holding it out in the palm of his hand, he went up to the German girl. She was within a thumb's breadth of being as tall as he was, and almost as wide through the shoulders. She did have good teeth and a swelling bosom.

Sextus knew even less of the Germans' language than Caldus Caelius did. He used such rags as he had, as well as some gestures that left next to nothing to the imagination. The girl said something to her older friend. Caelius couldn't follow it, but they both got the giggles.

"Well, sweetheart?" Sextus asked in Latin.

Instead of slapping him or turning away and walking off in a huff, she led him to one of the farmhouses. When they came out a few minutes later, he wore a sated smirk while she proudly showed the denarius to the other woman.

"Your lucky day," Caelius said. Sextus' smirk got wider.

"Hey, if she'll do him, maybe she'll do me, too," another legionary said. He too produced a coin. This time, the negotiations were swifter—the young woman knew what he wanted from her. She gave it to him, too. He was grinning like a fool when he came out of the wattle-and-daub hut. "She's good," he declared. "By Priapus, she's mighty good!"

Caelius went next himself. As long as it was business, as long as the barbarians weren't getting upset, why not? If he had the chance, he'd grab it. A denarius was more than he would have paid back at Vetera, but so what? He couldn't think of anything else he'd sooner spend his money on, even beer.

"Lots of silver," the girl said happily when she took his coin. By the time the day ended, she might become the richest person in the little village. The inside of the farmhouse was gloomy. Caelius stood there while she dropped down in front of him. He set a hand on the back of her head, urging her on. She didn't need much urging. Neither did he—he spent himself in nothing flat. She spat on the hard dirt floor. He helped her up. They went outside together.

She ended up satisfying all the Romans. They emptied the barrel of beer, too. As Caelius none too steadily made his way back toward the encampment, he couldn't remember a day he'd enjoyed more.

Arminius stared at the handful of silver the village girl showed him. "Did you people butcher a Roman to get this?" he asked her. "If you did, I hope you hid his body so the legionaries never found out how he died. If one of them gets killed, they avenge themselves on many. They—"

He broke off, because she was laughing at him. "We didn't kill anybody," she said. Then she told him exactly how she'd earned the denarii. "They pay so much for so little! Look at all this silver! I never thought I would have so much in my whole life, and it didn't even take an hour."

He knew what prostitutes were. He'd used a couple himself, to slake his lusts while he served among the Roman auxiliaries. Up till now, Germany had known little of such notions, probably because so few coins circulated here. But if the country came under Roman rule, if money spread here till it was as widely used as anywhere else in the Empire . . . how many girls like this one would there be?

Her father wasn't helpful. "She didn't do anything that made her no maiden," the man said. "As long as she bleeds on her wedding night, nothing else matters. And she will. My wife made sure of that." He held up his middle finger to show how.

"But . . ." Arminius wanted to hit him. "She sold herself!"

"Got a good price, too," the other German agreed. "These Romans must have silver falling out of their assholes, the way they throw it around. Plenty of chieftains with less than we've got now." He eyed Arminius. "Do *you* have that much?"

"Yes," Arminius said flatly. If the other man challenged him, it would give him the excuse he wanted to murder the fellow. But the man just stood there outside of his steading, a foolish grin on his face. Arminius tried again: "Don't you see? Before the Romans set up their cursed camp near here, your daughter never would have done anything like this."

"I should say not," the girl's father answered. For a moment, Arminius thought he'd reached him. Then the wretch continued, "Before the Romans came, nobody could've paid anywhere near so well."

"We have to get rid of them," Arminius insisted. "They'll ruin us if we don't."

The older man stared at him in what Arminius hoped was honest incomprehension. "Why do you want to get rid of them when they're making us rich? I can spend some of this silver at their camp for things they have and we don't. My little girl wants some fancy combs for her hair. Hard to tell her no when she was the one who made the money, eh?

I can even buy wine if I want to. Like I said, I might as well be a chieftain myself."

"You might as well be a swine," Arminius said.

"I don't know who you are, but you've got no cause to talk to me that way." The villager didn't reach for a spear or a sword. He was brave enough running his mouth, but not when he had to back up his words.

So it seemed to Arminius, anyhow. He didn't think about what it might be like to confront a large, fierce, well-armed stranger only a little more than half his age. People half Arminius' age were children; he didn't need to fear them.

He didn't need to fear the shameless girl's father, either. He turned his back and strode away. If his scorn made the other man respond, he would do what he had to do—what he wanted to do. But, regretfully, he didn't think it would. And he turned out to be right.

He wondered if he could make it out of the village without being sick. He managed, but it wasn't easy. The Romans purposely changed the way the folk they conquered did things. He'd heard about that in Gaul, and seen it with his own eyes in Pannonia. They were like potters working with soft clay, shaping it into whatever they wanted.

They also changed people—and peoples—without meaning to. If they hadn't set up their encampment so close to this village, that man would have stayed an ordinary fellow. Oh, chances were he never would have been a hero or any kind of leader, but Arminius wouldn't have wanted to wipe him off the sole of his shoe like a dog turd, either. The man never would have been proud of how much his daughter could make going down on her knees.

And he wouldn't have worried about fancy combs or wine. The Romans might not have known that they used such things as weapons, but they did. Too many Germans craved what they lacked and the Romans had. Wine and luxury goods had bought too many chieftains—Arminius' fists clenched as he thought of Thusnelda's father.

Silver—no matter how you got it—could buy lesser men, too. And if the Romans bought enough men and women, if they persuaded them the way of life inside the Empire was better than their own . . . what then? Why, the folk of Germany would turn into Romans. They would be taxpayers, slaves, the way the Romans themselves were slaves.

Arminius shook his head. "By Tuisto and Mannus, it will not happen!" he vowed. Tuisto was a god born of the earth. Mannus, Tuisto's son, was reckoned father of the German folk. Mannus' three sons were said to be the ancestors of the three divisions of German stock. Some people gave Mannus many more sons, men whose names matched those of the various German tribes. Maybe they were right—how could anyone now know for sure? But Arminius preferred the simpler arrangement.

He wanted things simple in his Germany, too. He wanted his folk to stay free, the way it had always been. And he wanted to drive the Romans back over the Rhine. He would have liked to drive them farther still, but he didn't suppose the spineless Gauls would help.

Men like the gleeful pimp back in that village made him wonder if even his own folk would help.

❧ IX ❧

When Quinctilius Varus rode forth from Mindenum, he rode forth with
the idea that he was somebody and needed to be seen as somebody. He
much preferred civilian clothes to a general's muscled corselet and scarlet cloak, but conscientiously donned them anyhow.

"You look . . . magnificent, sir," Aristocles murmured, tightening
the fastenings that held the corselet's breast and back pieces together.

Did that little pause conceal the word *ridiculous*? Varus suspected it
did, but he couldn't prove it, and the slave would only deny everything.
What else did slaves do? Better not to pick a fight you had no hope of
winning. Instead, Varus said, "I aim to overawe the barbarians. Let them
see Roman might, personified in me. Let them see, yes, and let them despair of resisting."

"Of course, sir," Aristocles said. It might have been agreement. Or
it might have been, *You must be joking, sir.*

Again, Varus couldn't prove a thing. Again, he had sense enough not
to try. Instead, cloak swirling around him, he strode out of the tent. A
cavalry officer standing outside gave him a clenched-fist salute.

The officer also gave him a leg-up. He settled himself in the saddle.
He would have preferred a litter, but he could ride tolerably well. The
Germans, for their part, had made it very plain that they despised litters.
They didn't think a man had any business being carried by other men. To
Varus' mind, that was only one more proof they were barbarians. He
hated having to cater to local prejudices. But, since he did want to im-
press, he found himself with little choice.

Vala Numonius rode with him. So did a troop of stolid cavalrymen. The Germans could still overwhelm them if they wanted to badly enough. But he had enough Romans with him to put up a stout fight. And the Germans had to know his murder would lead to vengeance on a scale they could barely imagine. Varus felt safe enough.

Besides, the village where he was going was supposed to be friendly. The locals had begun holding assemblies to talk about what they should do, very much as villagers in Italy might have done. So reports said, anyhow. One thing Varus had learned in his administrative career: if you trusted reports, if you didn't go out and see for yourself, sooner or later something would bite you in the backside.

Probably sooner.

"We'll make Roman subjects out of them yet," he said to Vala Numonius.

"Gods grant it be so," the cavalry commander answered. "But we could build a new Rome in place of our encampment here, and I still wouldn't be sorry to see the last of this miserable country. No olive oil. No wine. Too cursed many Germans."

"I know what you mean," Varus said. "Still, Augustus didn't send me here to fail. We collected taxes from them last fall. We'll take more this time around—see if we don't—and most of it in silver. Half the battle is getting them used to the idea of paying. Once they are, once they don't grab for their spears every time the tax-collector comes around, we'll be on the road to triumph." He hastily chose a different word: "To victory."

"I understand, sir," Numonius assured him.

Since Augustus became the supreme leader in the Roman world, generals couldn't aspire to a proper triumph: a procession through the streets of Roman acclaiming them for what they'd done. Their victories were assumed to come in Augustus' name and at his behest. If you said you wanted a triumph of your own, it was almost the same as saying you wanted Augustus' position.

Varus . . . wouldn't have minded having it. He didn't think he'd get it after Augustus died, though. Of Augustus' surviving kin, all the signs pointed to Tiberius. Not only had he been (disastrously) married to

Augustus' daughter, he was also Augustus' wife's son and a first-rate soldier to boot. Overthrowing him would take a civil war, and Rome had seen too many.

But Tiberius was within a year or two of Varus' age, and childless. If he died fairly soon . . . *In that case, people might look to me*, Varus thought.

A branch hanging down from an oak into the narrow path swatted him in the face and snuffed out his daydreams of imperial glory. "Never mind building a new Rome here, Numonius," he said. "What we need to build in this benighted place are some decent roads."

"You've thrown a triple six with that, sir!" Vala Numonius exclaimed. "It won't be easy or cheap, though. So much of this country is swamp or bog or mud or something else disgusting."

"We can do it," Varus said. "Back a lifetime ago, the Germans never dreamt we could bridge the Rhine and punish them for sticking their noses into Gaul. Caesar showed them how ignorant they were. And proper highways would be worth their weight in gold here. Except along rivers, we have a demon of a time getting troops where they need to go."

"Don't I know it!" Numonius rolled his eyes. "Horsemen have an even worse time pushing down these narrow, twisting tracks or slogging through the mud than foot soldiers do."

"Yes, I can see how that would be so." Varus' decisive nod was patterned after the one Augustus habitually used. "Roads, then. As soon as we decide it's safe enough for the engineers to start working on them. Or maybe even a little before that."

"A little before that would be very good," Vala Numonius said. "If you wait till you're sure you're safe in Germany, you'll wait forever."

"Ha!" Varus' laugh faded to a rueful chuckle. "That's one of those jokes that would be funny if only it were funny, if you know what I mean."

One of the Romans riding ahead of the governor and the cavalry commander said, "Here's their village, sir." Under his breath, he added, "Gods-forsaken little pisspot of a place, isn't it?"

Quinctilius Varus didn't think he was meant to catch that last, so he pretended he didn't. As the path came out of the forest into the cleared land around the village and he got a good look at it, he found he had a hard time disagreeing with the cavalryman.

The cattle and sheep were small and scrubby, the horses mere ponies. The swine seemed only half a step up from wild boars, while the snarling dogs might have come straight from the wolfpacks that roamed the woods. The houses were huts, with walls of mud and sticks and with thatched roofs that hung out on all sides far enough to keep the rain from melting the mud.

And the people . . . were Germans. Varus had got to the point where he didn't mind watching the women. They were tall, strongly made, and most of them fair. Nothing wrong with any of that. The men, though, were as close to wild as the pigs and the dogs. He'd learned that calling another man a swinehound was a favorite German insult. Now he thought he understood why they used it. It suited them.

Ten or twelve big men, all swathed in cloaks and carrying spears, stood around in what passed for the village square arguing with one another. They shouted. They clenched fists and shook them under their neighbors' noses. No one ran anybody through, but Varus wondered if it was only a matter of time.

"This is the assembly they wanted you to see, sir?" Vala Numonius said. "If they're proud enough of this to want to show it off, gods only know what they do when we're not watching."

"Too true," Varus said with a sigh. Still, he could write to Augustus and truthfully—well, almost truthfully—tell him he'd seen the Germans begin to imitate Roman institutions. Augustus would be glad to hear something of that sort. And if it wasn't as true as it might have been just yet, Varus would make it so before too long. He was confident of that.

Then one of the barbarians startled him by waving and calling out in pretty fair Latin: "Hail, your Excellency! Good to see you! How are you today? Would you like me to translate for you?"

"Arminius!" Varus was pleased he remembered the fellow's name. He'd had it shouted in his ear all winter long, of course, to say nothing of the scandal the summer before. But Arminius was only a German, after all. A lot of Romans wouldn't have bothered recalling his barbarous appellation no matter what. So . . . Quinctilius Varus was pleased.

The Germans in the village debated what they ought to do about men from a village a few leagues away who ran off their cattle on moonless nights. They'd already decided what they would do: they planned to set an ambush and slaughter the thieves. But they couldn't say that in front of the Romans, who aimed to reserve killing for themselves—one more usurpation among so many.

Arminius turned what they did say into Latin for Quinctilius Varus. He couldn't shade the translation much. Varus would have someone else along who spoke the German tongue. Arminius didn't want anyone giving him the lie in front of the important Roman. He just hoped the men in this supposedly Roman-style assembly wouldn't come out with something everyone would regret.

To his relief, they didn't. One of them even asked Varus to send soldiers to the other village to order its men to stop thieving. Why not? The order wouldn't make them stop, but it would humiliate them. They deserved that. So these villagers thought, anyhow.

Arminius didn't care one way or the other. They weren't men of his clan, or even of his tribe. Their very dialect sounded odd in his ears. But they were Germans. They shouldn't have had to pretend to follow Roman customs to make this big-bellied Quinctilius Varus happy.

And Arminius himself shouldn't have had to smile and clasp this big-bellied Roman's hand and pretend to be his friend. He'd made Varus like him the summer before; if he hadn't, Segestes would have used the official to get his vengeance for losing Thusnelda.

From what Varus said, Arminius reminded him of his own son, who was growing to manhood down inside the Roman Empire. That was probably lucky for the German. If Varus had no children or only daughters, or if his son were different . . . Better, perhaps not to dwell on such chances.

To Arminius' way of thinking, if the younger Varus were any kind of a man, he would be here in Germany with his father. What better thing could a son do than help his father accomplish something important for their folk? Maybe it wasn't good to remind the Roman of a son like that.

But Varus himself seemed to find nothing amiss in the youngster's absence. The Romans didn't have the family cohesion Arminius' folk took for granted. Husbands and wives in the Empire divorced for any reason or none at all, and no one there thought the worse of them because of it. Roman women were so fickle, so faithless, that their men had got used to it and even made jokes about it. To a strait-laced German, that was truly shocking.

At last, the farce in the village played itself out. Beaming, Quinctilius Varus told Arminius, "Please convey to these distinguished gentlemen how much I admire their thoughtful and mature deliberations. The course they plan seems wise and just. One day, their grandsons may wear the toga and ornament the debates of the Senate in Rome."

As best he could, Arminius did put that into his own language. Again, he dared not shade the translation, lest some Roman who knew his tongue give him away. He hoped the men who'd gathered in the square would remember they weren't supposed to show Varus what they really thought of him. To Arminius' relief, they did remember. The Roman had brought along enough cavalrymen to massacre the so-called assembly here and the rest of the village besides. That no doubt helped the Germans concentrate on what they needed to do.

Arminius particularly admired them for not showing offense when Varus said their descendants might one day become Roman Senators. Varus meant it as a compliment. The Germans received it as if it were one rather than the last thing they wanted.

"That went very well—even better than I would have hoped," Quinctilius Varus said as most of the men returned to their steadings.

Staying there in the square with all these Romans, Arminius felt very much alone. He did his best not to show it. Wasn't he, in Varus' eyes, a Roman citizen? Wouldn't a Roman citizen be at ease with his fellow citizens? Of course he would . . . seem to be.

"They grow used to the idea that their future will be part of the Empire's future," Arminius replied. He didn't say the men of his folk liked that idea, but neither Varus nor any of the other Romans noticed the omission. Like any men, they heard what they wanted to hear, regardless of whether it was really there.

"This is not your home, is it, Arminius? You live north and west of Mindenum, don't you?" Varus said.

"Yes, that's right, your Excellency," Arminius said. "You honor me by remembering it. One day, perhaps, you will honor me more by visiting me among my clansmen."

"Why, perhaps I shall." If Varus sounded surprised that Arminius should suggest such a thing, he covered that surprise with layer upon layer of practiced Roman politesse. "It would be a rare privilege, in fact."

"May the day come soon," Arminius said.

"Indeed." Quinctilius Varus nodded and smiled. "And, since you find yourself away from home now, would you care to come back to Mindenum and sup with me this evening?"

"I would like nothing more," said Arminius, who would have liked anything more. But he couldn't refuse the Roman, not unless he wanted Varus to believe he mistrusted him. Arminius *did* mistrust Varus, but didn't want him believing that. *And so I stick my head into the bear's mouth again*, the German thought.

"Splendid! Splendid!" Varus' jowly smile got wider. He turned to some of the other Romans who'd come with him to watch the farce in the village. "There, my friends! Do you see?"

Some of the small, swarthy men nodded. Even the ones who did, though, eyed Arminius like hounds eyeing a wolf. So what exactly had the Roman governor meant by that? Something like *No matter what you've heard about this barbarian, he's not such a bad fellow after all?* Arminius didn't see how he could mean anything else.

And what would the Romans have heard about him? Unfortunately, he had no trouble figuring that out, either. Word of what he'd gone through Germany saying during the winter would have got back to them. Well, Arminius already knew it had. Segestes and his henchmen had made sure of that. *If only my friends could have killed Masua*, Arminius thought angrily.

But Varus still believed he was friendly to the Empire, and these other Romans would have to be wondering, wouldn't they? A man who hated their folk wouldn't stick his head into the bear's mouth on purpose, would he? (The Romans would have talked about sticking your head into a lion's mouth. Arminius had seen a lion at a beast show in Pannonia. Any god that could create a wildcat the size of a bear was a god to be wary of.)

Varus' cavalry commander was a dour fellow named Vala Numonius. He eyed Arminius the way a snake eyed a toad. "I'm sure you will enjoy the wine at supper, eh?" he said.

The only reason you said yes to Varus was to guzzle our fine vintages. That wasn't what he said, but it was what he meant. Arminius looked back just as coldly; the Romans often scorned someone who let his temper run away with him. "I like beer about as well," he said in a wintry voice, adding, "I'm no water-drinker. You ask for a flux of the bowels if you do that when you don't have to."

"He's got you there!" Quinctilius Varus said with a chuckle. "You can't very well tell him he's wrong, either."

"No, sir," Numonius answered tonelessly. That quiet reply didn't mean he agreed. Oh, no. It meant he despised Arminius all the more, but he didn't feel like showing it. A German would have. But the Roman was a serpent, all right. He tried to make himself invisible in the grass, but he'd poison you if you stepped on him.

Varus either took no notice of Numonius' unhappiness or affected not to see it. "Well, let's go back," he said. "You have a horse, Arminius?"

"Yes, sir," the German said. He vaulted into the saddle without bothering to ask for a leg-up. It was less of a feat than it might have been; he was a big man getting up onto a small horse. Standing next to the Romans, he was taller than any of them. Riding with them, he was the shortest man in the group. They noticed as soon as he did. Their chuckles said they liked it.

Arminius shrugged. Yes, he craved a charger like the one Vala Numonius rode. But he was still himself, the Romans still themselves. Had he been sitting on a short stool while they used high ones, he still would have been taller than they were. And so he was now, whether they liked it or not.

They didn't have much to say to one another or to him as they all rode back to the Roman encampment in the German heartland. Their glances his way told him they would have liked to talk about him, but their silence proclaimed that they remembered he spoke good Latin.

The Roman sentries frankly stared at him when he rode in with Varus and Vala Numonius and the rest of the Romans. Arminius didn't think he could behave haughtily toward the Roman officers in whose company he found himself. Sentries? They were a different story. He affected not to notice them as he went by.

"Miserable scut!" one of the common soldiers growled.

"Who does he think he is?" another said. Maybe they didn't know he could follow their language. More likely, they just didn't care. Unlike their superiors, they weren't hypocrites. When they didn't like somebody, they didn't try to hide it.

Quinctilius Varus' Greek slave looked surprised to see Arminius in the company of his master. The weedy little man—Aristocles was his name, Arminius remembered—somehow contrived to look down on Romans as well as Germans. Varus and the legionaries here knew it, too, but for reasons beyond Arminius' ken they failed to get angry. Come to that, he'd seen the same thing with the few Greeks he'd met in Pannonia. He didn't understand it, but he was sure it was real.

"I'll let the cooks know we have a . . . distinguished guest," Aristocles said.

"By all means. Thank you." Quinctilius Varus didn't notice the slave's discreet pause—or, if he did, he pretended not to. Yes, Romans were master dissemblers.

He noticed Aristocles' hesitation. He knew what it meant, too. Aristocles thought he would have got angry if he heard something like *We have a hairy barbarian eating with us tonight.* Well, the Greekling wasn't wrong.

"Oh, Aristocles!" Varus called when his slave had already taken a couple of steps away.

The man perforce stopped. "Yes, sir?"

"Bring us some wine when you come back. It's been a long day. We can all use some refreshment."

"Of course, sir." This time, Aristocles succeeded in disappearing.

Of course, sir. What else could a slave say? The Germans kept slaves, too—what folk didn't? Theirs, though, were less like to be body servants, more likely to be farmers who owed their masters a share of what they raised. A German master was less likely to beat or whip a slave than a Roman was. But a German was more likely to lose his temper and kill a man he owned. And why not? It wasn't as if he had to pay any penalty for doing it.

If the Romans got their way, they'd turn all the Germans from the Rhine to the Elbe into slaves—maybe even farther, if they thought their legions could bring it off. They'd already enslaved more lands, more peoples, than most Germans had ever imagined. Arminius remained determined he wouldn't let them do that to his folk.

Aristocles returned with a large tray, cups, a jar of wine, and a jar of water. He set the tray down on a light, folding table: a clever and useful piece of furniture. He mixed wine and water for the legionary officers, but paused before serving Arminius. "How would you like your wine, sir?" he inquired.

"The same way the other Roman citizens are having theirs," Arminius replied. Face carefully blank, the Greek handed him a cup of watered wine.

Laughing, Varus said, "He got you there, Aristocles." The slave affected not to hear. Arminius would have boxed the man's ears for such insolence, but Varus put up with it. Some Romans, as Arminius had seen in Pannonia, let slaves get away with more than free subordinates. No German would do that.

"I thought you would sooner drink your wine neat," Vala Numonius said to Arminius.

"I would if you gentlemen were doing the same," the German answered. "But if I get drunk while your heads stay clear, you'll laugh at me. I don't fancy that."

The Roman cavalry commander looked surprised for a moment. Then he raised his cup in salute. "I've heard you were clever. It seems to be so."

"For which I thank you." Arminius also raised his cup. "Your health." They grudgingly drank to each other.

When the cook came out to announce that supper was ready, Arminius was glad to see the man had a double chin and a potbelly. Who would have wanted a meal from a man who didn't like his own cooking?

He had a skinnier slave of his own—or maybe the man who carried out the heavy tray of food was a more junior cook. The greens course was covered with a mixture of wine vinegar, olive oil, and ground spices. No German would have seasoned them that way, but Arminius had met such dressings in Pannonia. This one didn't drive him wild, but he could deal with it.

Boiled turnips in a cheese sauce seemed less exotic. A German cook might have made the same dish, though the Roman cheese was sharper than Arminius was used to. The main course was roasted slices of boar. The meat was fine. The sauce, on the other hand . . .

"I know you Romans like garlic," Arminius said. "But what's that other spice you put on it, the one that bites the tongue?"

"That's pepper," Varus told him. "It comes into the Empire all the way from India."

"Why?" Arminius asked.

"We like it," Varus answered. The other Roman officers nodded so promptly, Arminius didn't think they were agreeing only because their superior had spoken. Varus went on, "Don't you care for the flavor it adds?"

"Maybe I'm just not used to it," Arminius said. "I suppose it would be good to mask the taste of meat that's going off. But what you have here is nice and fresh. It doesn't need to be hidden by all that garlic and, uh, pepper."

"We think bland food is boring," Vala Numonius said. The officers nodded once more.

"What you eat is your business," Arminius said. "But if you try to feed it to me, I may not like it so well. Romans and Germans are not the same."

A considerable silence followed. Arminius decided he might have said too much even if his wine was watered. Varus said, "Do I need to remind you that you are a Roman citizen?"

"No, sir. I am proud to be a Roman citizen. It is a great honor." Arminius knew the Romans reckoned it one. And he *was* proud—it showed he'd successfully deceived his foes. He went on, "My head and my heart are glad to be Roman. My tongue and my belly remember I was born German. I don't know what to do about that."

Varus and several officers smiled. Not all of them did, though. A man Arminius didn't know asked, "Was it your German tongue that made you say your people ought to chase all the Romans out of Germany?"

The pork suddenly sat heavy in Arminius' stomach. He was in his enemies' power here. If they wanted to stretch out a hand and crush him, they could. The trick, then, was making sure they didn't want to—or, at least, making sure the most powerful one didn't.

"I never said anything like that," Arminius answered steadily. "I never would say anything like that. Whoever told you I did—whoever told you I would—is a liar. There are Germans who do not love me. Segestes insulted me, and you know how I answered his insult. So now Segestes spreads lies wherever he can, and uses his friends to spread them, too. I can't do anything about that except to remind you they are lies."

He waited. They didn't have to believe him. Some of them plainly didn't. But Varus said, "Yes, we've been over this ground before. Don't worry, Arminius. Whatever Segestes and his friends say, we know we need to take it *cum grano salis*."

" 'With a grain of salt'?" Arminius echoed. "I know what the words mean, but not the phrase."

"It means we have to doubt whatever they say," Varus explained. "And that is so—we do." He looked down from the head of the table, waiting for anyone to challenge him.

No one did. At a German feast, someone would have. And when someone challenged him, it would have gone from words to spears in the blink of an eye. The Romans accepted Varus' guidance because he held the highest rank among them.

Was that better or worse than the German way? It was simpler, anyhow. If the man of highest rank knew what he was doing, everyone would do well by obeying his commands.

If he didn't . . . Arminius slept at Mindenum that night. He left the encampment the next morning. The Romans could have rid themselves of a great danger. They didn't. Arminius waited till he was more than a bowshot away from the encampment's earthwork and ditch. Then, making sure he kept his back to Mindenum so the sentries wouldn't notice him doing it, he laughed and laughed and laughed some more.

Roman soldiers liked to complain. Vala Numonius knew as much. But what Lucius Eggius was doing went far beyond complaint. "You really should watch your tongue," the cavalry commander said. "If you don't, someone will say you're trying to incite a mutiny."

"By the gods, maybe we need one!" Eggius burst out.

Vala Numonius looked at him. "I am going to do you the biggest favor anyone ever did. I am going to pretend I didn't hear that. You can thank me when you come to your senses."

To Numonius' vast relief, the other officer realized he'd gone too far. "I'll thank you now, and thank you kindly," he said. "But how we could have let that cursed German walk out of here . . . It makes no sense. You can't tell me it does. Nobody can, not if he wants me to believe it."

"You think Arminius is more dangerous than Quinctilius Varus does," Numonius said.

"He's a barbarian. Why take chances with him? If he's done a tenth part of what his woman's father says he has, he's a menace," Eggius said. "Getting hold of Germany is hard enough if we do get rid of the troublemakers. Why let 'em run around loose?"

"Arminius isn't just a barbarian." Vala Numonius pointed out what should have been obvious. "He's a Roman citizen. He's a member of the Equestrian Order—one step below the Senate. He can appeal any sentence to Augustus."

Eggius snorted scornfully. "Let's see him appeal being dead. We'd all sleep better of nights after he was."

"Would we?" Numonius was anything but convinced. "Or would that start the big German uprising when Arminius alive didn't?"

He startled Lucius Eggius; he could see as much. "That'd be a pretty kettle of fish, wouldn't it?" Eggius said.

"It would." Numonius pressed his advantage: "And what do you think Augustus would do to the people who sparked a rebellion here, especially when Tiberius still hasn't cleaned up the mess in Pannonia?"

Eggius winced like a man contemplating a bad hangover. "That wouldn't be pretty, would it?"

"I don't think so." The cavalry commander thought that made a pretty respectable understatement. "So why don't you be a little more careful before you start talking about killing Germans you don't happen to like? And it won't happen anyway, because his Excellency likes Arminius." Vala Numonius didn't, but he, unlike Lucius Eggius, understood subordination.

"I know he does." If the knowledge gave Eggius any pleasure, he hid it very well. "You think I worry about the barbarian too much? I'll tell you something, Numonius—he doesn't worry about him enough, and you can mark my words. He thinks Arminius is a tame dog. He can't seen a wild wolf when one's standing right in front of him."

Vala Numonius didn't try to argue. What was the point? Instead, he answered indirectly: "All these Germans are wolves—now. A lifetime ago, all the Gauls were wolves, too. They've settled down. Fifty years from now, the governor is sure these Germans will have, too. And we'll be wondering what we ought to do about the barbarians on the far side of the Elbe. That's what the Roman Empire does: we move forward."

"Hrmp." Lucius Eggius' grunt was not one of agreement. "The reason the Gauls settled down is, Caesar walloped the piss out of them. They knew they were licked. They knew we were better men. We cursed well showed them we were. The Germans don't believe it. And why should they? We've won some against them, but they've won some against us, too. We haven't convinced 'em we can squash 'em whenever we put our minds to it."

"It's this miserable country," Numonius said. "Bogs and swamps and woods and gods only know what all else. No place where an army can form a proper battle line and show the savages how real soldiers do it."

"You're right," Eggius said. This time, he surprised Vala Numonius. "Yeah, you're right," he repeated. "But so what?"

"What do you mean, so what?" the cavalry commander demanded. "It's the truth. If it weren't for the country, we would have beaten the Germans a long time ago."

"And if it weren't for the ocean, you could walk from Sicily to Carthage, too," Eggius said. Vala Numonius gasped at the unfairness of the comeback. But Eggius couldn't see it. He pressed ahead: "Don't you get it? Why we haven't beaten the stinking barbarians doesn't matter. That we haven't beaten them does. It matters a lot. They still think they can mess with us. And they may even be right, a plague take them."

"It's not that they're such wonderful warriors," Numonius said. "They skulk, and they hide, and they sneak out and bite us like spiders or scorpions. The lay of the land lets them do it."

"The lay of the land's got blond hair down to here and tits out to there." Lucius Eggius gestured lewdly. Vala Numonius winced. Eggius got more serious—a little, anyhow. "But you're not wrong—this country is a big pile of turds," he said. "The fun and games we go through getting back to the Rhine every winter prove that. I wish we had a route where we weren't up to our knees in muck most of the time."

"I'll bet the Germans know a route like that," Numonius said.

"Sure. But will they tell us? Don't hold your breath, friend," Eggius said, which had the unfortunate ring of truth. "We need proper roads here. We need 'em worse than anything else."

Numonius nodded. "The governor knows that. I expect we'll have them before very long."

"But we need 'em now." Lucius Eggius hawked and spat. "By Venus' cunt, we've needed 'em for years."

"Well, you may be right." That was the most polite brushoff Numonius knew. Some people kept pounding with hammers even when there wasn't a nail in sight. And Lucius Eggius, all too plainly, was one of them.

 X

From perhaps half a mile away, Sigimerus eyed the Roman encampment of Mindenum. "You want us to go in there?" he asked, his voice rising in disbelief.

But Arminius nodded. "I do, Father. I've been in and out several times. Varus thinks I can't possibly be dangerous. And why? Because I don't hide from him, that's why. He doesn't believe someone who is an enemy of Rome would dare let the legionaries get their hands on him whenever they please."

"I can see why he doesn't," Sigimerus muttered.

A train of ox-drawn wagons guarded by Roman soldiers brought supplies from the Lupia River to the fortress. By now, after a couple of years, the wagons had worn deep ruts in the German soil. The Romans thought they were wearing their way into Germany in the same fashion. Arminius stubbornly refused to believe it. That the invaders felt they needed so many men to protect their goods showed how far from victory they were. It did to him, anyhow.

"Come on. He will treat you with honor," Arminius said. "Why shouldn't he? Aren't you the father of a Roman citizen, the father of a veteran of the Roman auxiliaries?" Sigimerus was the father of two veterans of the Roman auxiliaries, but Arminius refused to think about Flavus, who was still fighting in Pannonia.

"Gods grant I am not the father of a fool," Sigimerus said.

Despite the gibe, he followed Arminius toward the fort. He studied it with keen interest as they got closer. Arminius understood that. The

Romans were masters of fieldcraft. No German army had ever dreamt of protecting itself in hostile country the way the Romans did. The Germans thought the Romans worked too hard . . . till they had to attack one of those encampments. Then the legionaries' labor proved its worth—again and again and again.

A Roman soldier outside the rampart spied the approaching Germans and trotted over to see who they were and what they might be up to. "Oh, it's you," he said, recognizing Arminius. He sounded polite but businesslike: not a tone a German would have been likely to take. "Who's this, ah, gentleman with you?"

Who's this barbarian with you? That was what he'd been on the point of asking. Arminius was sure of it. But the Roman had swallowed the insult, so Arminius had to pretend he didn't know it was there. "This is my father—his name is Sigimerus. He has come to meet the great Quinctilius Varus, whose praises he has often heard from me."

No German would have swallowed flattery laid on even half so thick. But the legionary did. The Romans were in the habit of extravagantly flattering one another. They might have been so many dogs, licking one another's privates and assholes. But they were dangerous dogs.

This one wasn't dangerous now; the flattery put him at ease. "Well, he can do that. You can do that. Come along with me, and I'll bring you to the gate."

By the way he spoke, he intended to be obeyed. Arminius had to use an effort of will to keep his hand from dropping to the hilt of his sword. How dared this trooper order him around? But Arminius had seen that Romans always thought they could order anyone who wasn't a Roman around, just because they were Romans.

Yet another reason to make sure they lost their hold on Germany.

Arminius glanced over to his father. Sigimerus was less used to Roman arrogance than he was himself. The older man looked ready to murder the legionary who was leading them to the encampment. Ever so slightly, Arminius shook his head.

His father's raised eyebrows asked, *How can you put up with people like this, even for a moment?* And Arminius' tiny shrug answered, *Well, what choice have I got?* He couldn't see any, not yet.

The men at the gate greeted him politely enough. "Hail," one of them called. "Come to call on the governor again?"

"That's right," Arminius answered.

"Is that your father with you?" the Roman asked. "The two of you have a family look."

"Yes, it is," Arminius replied in Latin. In his own language, he added, "Do you understand them, Father?"

"Well enough," Sigimerus said, also in the Germans' tongue. He switched to Latin slower and less fluent than Arminius' to give the sentries his name.

"Hail, Sigimerus," said the one who'd greeted Arminius. "Welcome to Mindenum."

"I thank you," Sigimerus said. Arminius didn't think he'd ever heard anything less sincere in his life.

His father kept looking around the encampment once they got inside. "These Romans are an orderly folk, aren't they?" he said in his own speech. "They enjoy living like animals in cages, eh? All in row after row. Boring!"

"I think so, too, but it works for them." Arminius added, "Be careful with your words, Father—some of the Romans have learned bits of our tongue."

"I thought you told me they stuck to Latin whenever they could," Sigimerus said.

"They do—especially the officers. They think learning our speech—or any other speech except Greek—is beneath their dignity," Arminius answered. "But the common soldiers aren't so fussy. If they're in the field and they get hungry or they want to sport with our women, they learn the words they need to have. So you never can tell when one will know more than he lets on."

"Sneaky devils. How do you trust people like that?" Sigimerus answered his own question: "Simple. You don't." He eyed the tent in front of which Arminius had stopped. "So this is where the Roman governor lives?"

"Yes, Father." Arminius smiled. Sigimerus could watch his tongue if he worked at it.

The older man delivered his judgment: "Well, if you want to live under canvas all the time, you could do worse than this. But I would not care to live under canvas all the time." *Who in his right mind would?* Sigimerus didn't say that out loud, but his eyebrows were eloquent.

"If they have to, the Romans can move out of this encampment tomorrow," Arminius said. "When I was in Pannonia, I saw them do things like that at a moment's notice. And they build a fortified camp every evening of a march—you will have seen that."

"Yes." Sigimerus nodded. "Too much work, I think."

"Maybe, but it makes them hard to assail." Arminius held the tent flap open so Sigimerus could go in ahead of him. He'd seen how curtains did duty for walls in these fancy tents. Where they stood was the equivalent of an entrance hall.

A swarthy slave nodded to Arminius. "You wait," the fellow said in bad Latin. He hurried away.

"He will bring Varus to us?" Sigimerus asked.

"Maybe. More likely, though, he will bring Varus' chief slave to us," Arminius answered. "You have to go through slave after slave before you finally get to talk to an important Roman." Again, his father didn't say what he was thinking. Again, Sigimerus' expression spoke louder than words.

Sure enough, it wasn't Quinctilius Varus but Aristocles, his *pedisequus*, who emerged to greet the Germans. "Hail, Arminius," Aristocles said. "Is this . . . distinguished gentleman your father, by any chance?"

With him as with the fellow who'd met them outside the encampment, that pause showed he was really thinking something like *graying savage*. But Arminius responded only to the words Aristocles actually used. "Yes, he is. Father, I present to you Aristocles, who is the Roman governor's chief slave. Aristocles, here is my father, Sigimerus by name."

Aristocles' bow lacked for nothing in manners. "I am honored to meet you, sir. With his citizenship and the courage he showed fighting Rome's enemies, your son is an ornament among these forests."

"Good to meet you. Thank you for nice words," Sigimerus answered in his deliberate Latin. "I come here with Arminius to meet Roman governor."

Anyone who knew Sigimerus would have understood that to mean, *Why am I wasting my time talking to a worthless slave instead?* Arminius did, and had to hide a grin. If Aristocles also did, he concealed it well. Romans were good at that; their slaves, of necessity, even better. The *pedisequus* said, "Of course the governor will be delighted to make your acquaintance, excellent Sigimerus. Let me inform him of your most auspicious arrival. And of course you will wish refreshments, to put down the dust of your journey here?"

Before Sigimerus could say yes or no, Aristocles vanished behind a curtain. When the curtain stirred again, out from behind it came yet another slave, this one carrying a silver tray with wine and bread and fruit candied in honey. Like all of Varus' slaves Arminius had seen, this fellow was not a German. Arminius knew the Romans did enslave his folk. Varus was shrewd enough not to rub German visitors' noses in that unpleasant fact, though.

"When I was young," Sigimerus said, "wine was a sometime thing, a once-in-a-while thing. Many more Roman traders nowadays, and much more wine in Germany than there used to be."

"Wine is a goodness," Arminius agreed. Anyone listening to them on the far side of a curtain would find no fault in what they said. But their eyes met in perfect mutual understanding. *Wine may be a goodness. Rome is anything but.*

Quinctilius Varus' voice came from farther back in the tent. So did those of a couple of other Romans. Arminius supposed the governor was conferring with his officers. If Arminius knew Romans, Varus would take care of that before he deigned to meet any barbarians. All the high-ranking officials in Pannonia had acted the same way.

Sigimerus didn't recognize Varus' voice. He probably couldn't follow what the Romans were saying, either. Arminius could get bits and pieces of it, though slaves' chatter in the foreground made him keep missing some.

From what Arminius could hear, Varus was finding out what several different columns he'd sent forth were doing. He had to be confident Germany lay open to him like an unchaste woman if he divided his forces like that. Down in Pannonia, Tiberius had been much more cautious.

But Pannonia was a real war. No one could doubt that, even for a moment. Germany seemed peaceful. Varus must have thought he could take chances here that he wouldn't have risked if the countryside were in arms against him.

Well, let him believe us peaceful. Let him think Germans are nothing but the Romans' curs. Let him send legionaries here, there, and everywhere. The less we worry him now, the better.

"When is the fancy Roman coming?" Sigimerus asked. "Doesn't he reckon we're important enough to see?"

"I don't think it will be too much longer, Father," Arminius answered. "He is talking with his retainers now."

"Hrmm." It was not a happy noise. Sigimerus partly muffled it by taking another swig of wine.

The jug soon emptied. The slave fetched another. Did Varus want the Germans drunk before he met with them? Arminius wouldn't have been surprised. Wine was stronger than beer. Taken neat, it got people drunk faster, especially when they weren't used to it.

"You may want to go easy, Father," Arminius whispered.

"Yes, yes," Sigimerus said impatiently, in a way that couldn't have meant anything but *No, no.*

He wasn't drunk when Varus finally came forth. He wasn't too drunk, anyhow. Arminius made the introductions. "So, Sigimerus, you are the father of this young man?" Varus said. He spoke slowly and clearly and kept his grammar simple—he must have realized Sigimerus was not fluent in Latin.

"I am," Sigimerus answered.

Varus reached out to touch the golden fibula that fastened Sigimerus' cloak. That would have been uncouthly familiar, except for what he said next: "Even more than this, he is an ornament to you."

Sigimerus smiled. "He is," he agreed, running through another part of the conjugation of the verb *to be*.

"I miss my own son. He is far away, studying—learning—in Greece," Varus said. He set a hand on Arminius' shoulder. "When I met your son, it was almost as if I had mine with me once more. Not quite—you will understand that. But almost."

He wore a toga, chalky white wool with a purple border. Sigimerus' cloak was of bearskin trimmed with fine sealskin gained in trade from the Chauci, a tribe that lived by the North Sea. Varus' hair was cut short; Sigimerus let his grow long. Varus shaved his face. Sigimerus wore a beard. The Roman was short and heavyset, the German tall and lean. Varus had none of the Germans' language, Sigimerus only a little Latin.

And yet they were both proud fathers. For a moment, Arminius found them more alike than different. But only for a moment. Sigimerus cared nothing for Varus' son. Varus, whether he fully realized it or not, wanted to enslave Sigimerus'. What difference could be greater than that?

"Please excuse me for keeping you waiting," Varus said. "I was discussing, ah, certain matters with my aides. We aim to bring peace to Germany, you understand."

"I understand, yes," Sigimerus said. Arminius feared he would add, *If you want to bring peace, then leave!* But, to his relief, Sigimerus left it there.

Hearing him say he understood made Varus believe he approved. "Good, good," the Roman said. "I am glad that, like your son, you see the advantages of working with Rome."

How would Sigimerus answer that without spilling the chamber pot into the stew? Arminius' father looked at Quinctilius Varus with wide, blue, innocent eyes. "Pardon me?" he said.

"I was talking about the advantages of cooperating with Rome," Varus said. Sigimerus still looked artfully blank. Varus turned to Arminius. "Perhaps you would be kind enough to translate for your father?"

"Of course, sir," Arminius replied, and he did. Though he was sure Sigimerus already understood the Roman's words, he rendered them into the Germans' tongue. He did a proper job of it, too, in case another Roman, one who knew the language, stood listening behind a curtain.

Sigimerus' enlightenment was a small masterpiece of its kind. The Romans put on stage plays to entertain themselves. Arminius had seen a couple in Pannonia. Once he got the idea of playacting, he enjoyed them. Sigimerus had never seen or even imagined one, but he could have gone up on a stage himself.

"Oh," he said. "Work with! Now I follow you, sir!"

Varus smiled. He didn't notice that Sigimerus didn't say he agreed with him or approved of him. Arminius didn't notice, either, not right away. When he did, he realized there was more to his father than first met the eye: not always the most comfortable realization a young man can have.

"Will you both dine with me?" Varus immediately answered his own question before the Germans could: "Of course you will! You are my guests. I am pleased that you are my guests. Your being here shows the world that Germans and Romans can get along."

"We are pleased to show that, sir." Where his father had evaded, Arminius lied without hesitation or compunction. Under other circumstances, Sigimerus would have had every right to beat him for being so shameless.

"Well, so am I," Varus answered. "And your being my guests will go a long way toward laying to rest some of the, ah, unfortunate rumors that have attached themselves to your name, Arminius."

"That would be very good," Arminius said, to himself alone adding, *especially since those rumors are true.*

His being here might lay them to rest among the Romans who suspected him. But it also might make his fellow Germans wonder whether he was turning traitor. That could cause him problems after the Romans went back over the Rhine to winter in Gaul.

But even if it did, he could repair such things later. For now, he was inside the Roman encampment. As long as he stayed here, he would do well to act as much like a Roman as he could.

Sigimerus coughed a couple of times. What that would have

amounted to had he put it into words, Arminius could imagine. Luckily, Quinctilius Varus couldn't.

"Aristocles!" the Roman called.

"Yes, sir?" The *pedisequus* might have appeared out of thin air. One heartbeat, he was nowhere to be seen. The next, he stood at Varus' elbow.

"Tell the cooks Arminius and his distinguished father will be dining with me tonight," Varus said.

"Certainly, sir." Aristocles vanished almost as smoothly as he'd manifested himself. He might have made a good conjurer, amusing people by pretending to pull coins or jewelry out of their ears and noses. Or, Arminius thought uneasily, he might be a real wizard, one who could snap his fingers and appear or disappear. Arminius thought that unlikely— wizards were more often talked about than seen—but you never could tell.

Or could you? Why would a true wizard let an ordinary man enslave him? That struck the German as something only a fool would do. Aristocles was no fool, which had to mean he was no wizard, either: only a man uncommonly light on his feet.

The cooks served mutton without garlic. That had to be a compliment to Arminius and Sigimerus, because the Romans doted on the stuff. Varus noticed, too. He remarked, "It's, ah, interesting flavored with mint, isn't it? Different from what I'm used to."

"Good," Sigimerus said. The amount of meat he'd put away said he approved of what the cooks had done.

"We might seethe the mutton instead of roasting it," Arminius said. "But I think my father is right—it is very good. We thank you for it." He sucked marrow out of a bone.

"My pleasure, believe me," the Roman said. "And I assure you that it is also my pleasure to see Germans who trust me and my people enough to be our guests and accept our hospitality."

"Who would not want to accept it when it is so generous?" Arminius said. He wasn't sure his father had followed all of what Varus said. If Sigimerus had, he was better at keeping his face straight than Arminius had guessed. If he was, good; in Mindenum, he needed to be.

"Will you two spend the night with us?" Varus asked. "We can run up a tent for you. You, Arminius, will be familiar with our arrangements from your time of service with the auxiliaries. You can acquaint your distinguished father with them as well."

Arminius went back and forth with his father in the Germans' tongue to let him know what Varus had offered. After a moment's thought, Sigimerus nodded. "It would be our privilege, sir," Arminius told Varus in Latin.

"Splendid!" Varus exclaimed. Arminius reflected that he was turning into a better liar than he'd ever wanted to be.

Lucius Eggius looked back at the long column of legionaries he led. They slogged through the German forests and marshes, slapping at the mosquitoes and biting flies that plagued them and swearing at the officers who'd sent them forth.

Since Eggius felt like swearing at those officers, too, he didn't even try to restrain the men. *Let them cuss*, he thought. *It'll make them feel better, and it won't hurt the buggers they're cussing out. . . . Too stinking bad.*

"Come on, boys!" he called. "Looks like better ground up ahead."

"If it was any worse ground, it'd swallow us up and we'd never be seen again," one of the soldiers said.

"Oh, cheer up, Gnaeus," Eggius said. "At least the barbarians aren't giving us any grief."

The legionary was not cheered. "Yes, and that's all wrong, too," he answered. "Why aren't they? It's . . . suspicious, like."

"Quinctilius Varus says it's because they're finally coming to see we really are their masters." Eggius, loyal to the idea of Rome if not necessarily to the blue-blooded chuckleheads who represented that idea in Germany, gave forth with the party line.

Gnaeus wasn't the only soldier who jeered at him—and at Varus. Unlike the governor, the men had been going through these woods for years. They knew the Germans weren't subdued. So did Lucius Eggius, but he'd given up on trying to get his superiors to see it. Sometimes you could yell till you went blue in the face, and it didn't do you any good.

He hadn't been lying to the legionaries. Unlike some of his superiors, he didn't think that was a good idea. The ground ahead did improve. It was higher, less muddy, less swampy. It didn't try to suck the *caligae* off the soldiers' feet at every step they took.

Eggius glanced toward the sun. At least he could see it. With the beastly German weather, there was no guarantee of that. It neared the western horizon. "As soon as we find a spring or a stream, we'll camp for the night," Eggius said.

He didn't think that would take long, and he proved right. He'd never seen any place for water like Germany. It bubbled out of the ground here, there, seemingly everywhere. When the legionaries found a spring, they began digging in around it. Fortified camps took a lot of work, but nobody grumbled. They bumped up your chances of lasting long enough to get gray hair and wrinkles, and the men knew it.

Ditch. Earthen rampart made from the spoil thrown out of the ditch. Sharpened stakes atop the earthwork. Gates facing the cardinal directions. Main streets running north and south, east and west between the gates. Tents always placed just so inside the square perimeter. Every soldier had a particular job to do, and everybody, through long familiarity, did it without much waste motion.

Torches flared along the rampart, ensuring that the Germans couldn't sneak up on the camp. Sentries paced the circuit, exchanging passwords and countersigns. Eggius chose Latin words with r's in them for those. The Romans trilled their r's, while the Germans gargled theirs. Not even a barbarian who'd served as an auxiliary and knew Roman military customs would be able to fool a sentry. Eggius hoped not, anyhow.

Thinking of Germans who'd served as Roman auxiliaries naturally made Lucius Eggius think of Arminius. When his column left Mindenum, the young German and his father had been installed there, happy as a couple of sheep in clover. Quinctilius Varus thought Arminius a house snake, not a viper.

Lucius Eggius sighed. He hoped the governor was right. He had trouble believing it, but he had even more trouble believing he could change Varus' mind. Men like that didn't listen to men like him. To Varus, he was nothing but a craftsman who'd chosen a necessary but nasty way to make a living. No, Augustus' grand-niece's husband wouldn't pay attention to a veteran legionary.

And, since he wouldn't, what point to brooding about it? No point at all. Eggius shoved it out of his mind. He had plenty of more immediately urgent things to worry about.

When the Romans got moving again the next morning, scouts came trotting back from the woods ahead. That they came back was a good sign in and of itself. "No Germans in there!" one of them called.

"Good," Eggius answered. He turned to the men he led. "We'll go on through—double time. The sooner we're out the other side, the better."

Before plunging down the path, he made sure his sword was loose in its scabbard. The scouts had done their job, but you could never be sure they'd done enough. Germans were like any other beasts of prey: they were masters at leaping out from hiding.

The trees blotted out the sun. Eggius' eyes needed a few heartbeats to adapt to the gloom. His nostrils twitched, taking in the spicy scents of pine and fir and the greener, more ordinary odors of oak and ash and elm. Were he a beast himself, he might have sniffed out any lurking barbarians. Or he might not have; maybe the strong odors coming off his own men would have masked them.

Along with the dim light came dankness. The narrow path he followed turned muddy almost at once. His hobnailed marching sandals squelched at every step. He was at the head of the column, too. The going would be worse for the men farther back after their friends had chewed up the track.

Bushes and ferns pushed into the path from either side. It was as if the forest resented having any way through it and was doing its best to reclaim that way for itself. Something large and heavy crashed through the undergrowth off to the left. Before Eggius consciously realized it, his *gladius* was halfway out of the bronze scabbard.

No volley of spears. No screaming German warriors. With a shaky chuckle, another Roman said, "Only an animal."

"Right." Lucius Eggius kept his own voice under tight control as he let the shortsword slide down again. "Only an animal."

A bear? An aurochs? An elk? He'd never know. Now that silence had returned, he could tell himself it didn't matter.

He could tell himself, yes. But he couldn't believe it.

The woods didn't just seem to squeeze in on either side. Eggius felt, or imagined he felt, the canopy of leaves and branches pressing down on him. Maybe everything would close in, like a great green hand making a fist. And when the fist opened again, he wouldn't be here any more. Maybe the whole Roman column wouldn't be.

He laughed at himself. He told himself that was nothing but non-sense, moonshine. This time, he did manage to convince himself he was right. Some Romans had far more trouble going through these forests than he did. They really believed the trees were closing in on them—they didn't just have brief vapors about it. Cold sweat dripped off them. They went pale. Their hearts pounded and raced. Only coming out into the open again could cure them.

Eggius wondered how a German would feel out in the Syrian or African desert. Would he think the landscape was too wide? Would he feel tiny and naked under the vast blue dome of the sky? Would he shudder and shake, wishing he could draw forest around him like a cloak? The Roman wouldn't have been surprised.

Double time. It wasn't just to give the natives less of a chance to set a trap among the trees. It was also to get out of this horrible place as fast as the Romans could.

Roads. Roman roads crisscrossing Germany. Roman roads arrogantly cutting through forests and swamps. Wonderful Roman roads, with the trees cut back far enough on either side to make bushwhacking impossible. They couldn't come soon enough, not as far as Lucius Eggius was concerned.

"Bring on the engineers," he muttered. So what if he was an officer? He would gladly have carried a hod. Anything to make sure the men who came after him didn't have to endure . . . this.

"What did you say, sir?" a legionary asked.

"Nothing." Getting overheard embarrassed him.

"I sure am sick of these trees," the soldier said. "What I wish more than anything is that we had some decent roads through the woods."

"Well, now that you mention it, so do I." Eggius shook his head. He might have known his men would be able to see the same thing he did. They weren't fools. Well, except for the fact that they'd got stuck in Germany they weren't.

After what seemed like forever, Eggius saw sunlight ahead. Even though he'd been double-timing it through the forest, he broke into a run. Before long, he stood at the edge of a meadow and some fields. He breathed hard, as if he were coming up from underwater.

Some scrawny German cattle grazed in the meadow. Some scrawny German herdsmen kept an eye on them. As soon as Lucius Eggius came out of the woods, the barbarians let out several raucous halloos to warn the village a couple of furlongs away. Then they trotted purposefully toward him, hefting their spears as they came.

More Romans, moving almost as fast as he was, emerged from the forest behind him. "What do those buggers think they're up to?" one of them asked. He pointed toward the approaching Germans.

"I could be wrong, but I don't expect they're bringing us wine and dancing girls." Eggius' voice was dry.

By then, the Germans were no longer approaching. Seeing themselves outnumbered, they lost their appetite for murdering strangers. They stopped short; one of them jabbed the butt of his spear into the ground to help himself stop even shorter. Quite suddenly, they all went pelting back the way they'd come. They did some more hallooing as they ran. Now they sounded alarmed, not wolflike.

More Germans came from the fields and out of the village: a surprising number of them. *Bastards must breed like flies*, Eggius thought. Had he come with an ordinary tax-collecting party, the savages might have overwhelmed them. But he had a real fighting column behind him, a column designed to show the natives that Roman might could penetrate even the deepest, darkest corners of Germany.

"Deploy into line of battle," he called to the legionaries as they came out of the woods. "Let them see what they're up against. Maybe that'll make 'em think twice before they try anything stupid."

"And if it doesn't, we'll clean this miserable place out." Eggius didn't see who said that. Whoever he was, he sounded as if he looked forward to it.

Over by the village, the Germans had started to form a battle line of their own. Looking at the swarm of Romans deploying as they debouched from the woods, the locals started arguing among themselves, shaking fists and brandishing spears. Not all of them wanted to commit suicide, anyhow.

Other Germans started running for the trees on the far side of the village. Both sexes here wrapped themselves in cloaks most of the time, so Eggius had trouble being sure, but he guessed those were the women trying to get away. Yes, some of the fleeing shapes were smaller, so they had their brats with them.

Eggius told off a couple of dozen legionaries, two of whom could speak the Germans' language after a fashion. "Come forward with me," he ordered. "We'll parley." He raised his voice to address the rest of the Romans: "If the barbarians jump us, kill 'em all. Hunt down the cunts, too." By the noises they made, he thought they would enjoy obeying those orders.

He advanced, his little bodyguard spread out behind him and on both flanks. He kept both hands away from his weapons and displayed them palm out to show they were empty.

A German stabbed the butt of his spear into the ground and came forward. The middle-aged man also showed off his empty hands. He stopped just out of javelin range and asked, "What are you doing here?" in halting but clear Latin.

Won't need the interpreters, Eggius thought. *Good.* "We are passing through our province," he answered. "Will you give us food and beer?" Asking for wine around here was hopeless.

"*Your* province?" the German said bleakly, and then, more bleakly still, "What befalls us if we feed you not?"

"Well, you can always find out," Eggius said with his sweetest smile.

The German muttered something his mustache muffled. One of the Romans who followed the local language stirred. Eggius pretended not to see him. He didn't care whether the locals loved him, only whether they obeyed. "We will give you," the German said, and then some more things Eggius affected not to notice. The Roman smiled again. Why not? He'd won.

※ XI ※

Arminius was used to sleeping in a tent surrounded by other tents full of soldiers loyal to Rome. His father wasn't. Sigimerus wasn't used to eating Roman rations, either. They seemed to agree with him; his breeches were tighter than they had been when he came to Mindenum.

He seemed unhappy even so. He did have the sense not to talk about it inside the encampment. By the nature of things, Mindenum had no privacy. But Arminius could see something was wrong. He and Sigimerus went for a walk outside the fortified perimeter.

"Tell me what it is, Father, before you burst like a sealed stewpot forgotten in the hot coals," Arminius said.

Sigimerus turned a look of pure hatred on Mindenum. Fortunately, they were too far away for any sentries to make out his expression. "We are that gods-cursed Roman's hounds!" he said. "His hounds, I tell you! We eat from his hand, we sleep in his kennel, we lick his face and roll over to show him our bellies. Faugh!" He spat in the grass.

"He thinks we're his hounds," Arminius answered. "That's what he needs to think. If he thinks we're anything else, he'll close his hand on us instead of patting us with it."

"I want honest war," Sigimerus said. "Better—a hundred times better—than this game of pretending and lying."

"Better if we win, worse if we lose," Arminius said. "Right now, I think we would lose. Not enough of us are ready to fight the Romans. Too many would stand aside and wait to see what happened. And too many traitors to our folk follow Segestes' path." Flavus' path, too, but

Arminius didn't name his own brother. "They're the true hounds, the ones who want to see Varus as governor here and Augustus as king."

Kings among the German tribes reigned by virtue of their blood. Their real power, though, depended on their prowess and their wisdom. If they couldn't get people to follow them, they heard boos and catcalls in the tribal assembly. If they did win approval, the tribe's menfolk clashed their spears together—the sweetest sound a German leader could hear.

To Arminius, Augustus was a German king writ large. He had to be fierce and clever, for men did his bidding even when far out of his sight. That showed he enjoyed both fear and respect. Arminius wished he knew Augustus' tricks—he would have liked to use them himself. If all the Germans followed him the way the Romans followed Augustus . . . well, who could say what wonders he might work?

Right now, he had trouble getting even his father to follow him. Sigimerus said, "I think we should just kill Varus, then get away if we can. And if not, we will have given our folk a mark to aim at."

Among the Germans, if a man died all his designs died with him. Arminius had needed a while to realize the Romans were different. That was one more part of what made them such a menace. "If we kill Varus, Vala Numonius steps into his place till Augustus sends some new governor up from Italy," Arminius said. "And everything they do, they will do as if Varus still lived—except they will also strike at our folk to avenge his death."

"That will do," Sigimerus said. "If they come out of their encampment, we have the chance to beat them."

"But can we? In the fights that have gone on as long as I've been alive, they win at least as often as we do," Arminius replied. "And when they lose, what do they do? They fall back and get ready to fight some more. We don't need to beat them, Father. We need to *crush* them." He bent down, picked up a clod of dirt, and closed his fist on it. Only dust fell when he opened his hand again.

"Yes. That is what we need," his father agreed. "How do we get it? You said it yourself—the Romans don't leave themselves open to such disasters."

"We have to trick them. That must be how to beat them. It's the only way I can see," Arminius said. "If they don't know something dreadful is about to befall them until it does, they're ours!"

"If," Sigimerus said heavily.

"Aren't we tricking Varus now? You complain we are his hounds, but we both know that isn't so," Arminius said. "But does Varus know? If he knew, he would have killed us two weeks ago. Since he thinks he has hounds, he feeds us and houses us."

"Tricking one man is easy. Tricking an army's worth of men must be harder, or we would have done it long since," his father said.

Arminius grunted—his father had a point. Even so . . . "If the man we trick commands an army—and Varus does . . ."

"If this Augustus is such a mighty king, he should have found a better war leader than that fellow," Sigimerus said.

Arminius nodded, for the same thought had occurred to him. "Thank the gods the Roman called Tiberius commands the army in Pannonia," he said. "That is a man to beware of. If he were here, we could not play these games with him."

"Let him stay far away, then." Sigimerus hesitated. "Or maybe not. Some of the things Varus does would rouse our folk against him even if the two of us were never born. Not just taxes, but taxes in coin this year, he says. How many of us can pay in silver?"

"Not many. I know that, even if Varus doesn't," Arminius answered.

"I should hope so. And what is this talk about taking our spears away?" His father spat again. "How can a man be a man without a weapon?"

"Many Romans who are not soldiers in the legions don't carry anything more than an eating knife," Arminius said. Sigimerus snorted his disbelief. Arminius set a hand over his heart. "It's true, Father—I swear it."

"Well, what do they do when they quarrel?" Sigimerus demanded. "With no spears or swords, what can they do?"

"They have lawyers instead," Arminius said. His father snorted again, this time in fine contempt. Arminius went on, "I scoffed when I first heard it, too. But a Roman told me a spear can only kill you once, where a lawyer can make you wish you were dead for months at a time."

"Then you kill the lawyer." Sigimerus was relentlessly practical—or thought he was, anyhow.

Arminius shook his head. "If you do that, Augustus and his servants go to law against you. The Romans have fewer blood feuds than we do, but the king's justice reaches further with them."

"Faugh!" Sigimerus repeated contemptuously. "They're a pretty poor sort of man, if they have to have the king do what they should do themselves."

"It could be so." Arminius respected his father too much to quarrel openly with him. "Yes, it could indeed. But I still wish they were a poorer sort of man yet, for then they wouldn't trouble us at all."

Quinctilius Varus read the report Lucius Eggius had submitted after his foray through the German backwoods. He paused to rub at his eyes. Eggius would never make a stylist. His spelling and grammar left something to be desired. And his script was cramped and tight. The letters were too small to be easy to read when Varus held the papyrus far enough from his eyes to make them clear.

All things considered, then, the governor was glad enough to set the papyrus down when Aristocles came up to him and said, "May I speak to you, sir?"

"What is it?" Varus would rather have talked with his *pedisequus* than with most of the soldiers in the encampment at Mindenum. Aristocles was far more clever than they were. And, being a slave, he always gave Varus his full measure of respect—though the Roman governor didn't put it that way to himself.

"How long do you think those . . . Germans will stay here, sir?" Aristocles asked.

He must have swallowed something like *barbarians*, or perhaps *gods-detested, stinking barbarians*. Varus knew Aristocles didn't like Arminius and his father. Finding out how much he didn't like them might be interesting—and entertaining.

The Greek's sallow cheeks went quite pink when Varus asked him about it. "No, sir, I don't fancy them. They look at me the way stray dogs look at tripes in a butcher's stall."

They did, too. Varus had noticed it. He thought of it as wolves eyeing a crippled fawn, but the *pedisequus'* comparison was just as apt. "They can't help it, Aristocles," the Roman governor said. "They don't understand that a peaceable man should be left to live in peace."

"I should say they don't!" Aristocles exclaimed. "That's why I wish they'd leave."

"Well, I find myself with two things to say about that," Varus replied. "The first is that, however they look at you, they've offered you no harm. And the second is that we've come to Germany not least to make it into a place where a peaceable man can be left to live in peace." He chuckled wryly. "We've come with three legions to make it into that kind of place, in fact."

"Yes, sir." But Aristocles only sounded dutiful, not amused. That disappointed Varus, who was pleased with the line he'd got off.

"They are our guests, don't forget," Varus said. "That matters here. If I send them away, I'd affront them."

"But what if they've come here to murder you?" Aristocles blurted.

That made Quinctilius Varus laugh. He wasn't especially brave: one more reason he felt uneasy around soldiers, many of whom took their own courage for granted. But he could tell when his slave was jumping at shadows. "If they wanted to murder me, they could have done it a dozen times by now—and they could have sneaked away before anyone knew I was dead. Since they haven't seized any of those chances, I have to think they don't aim to do me in. What would murdering me get them?"

"They would have killed the man charged with bringing Germany into the Roman Empire." To Aristocles, it must have seemed obvious.

Varus went on laughing. "Yes? And so?"

"And so—that!" the *pedisequus* replied. "Isn't it enough?"

"Not if they aim to stop Rome from conquering Germany," Varus said. "We'd take such revenge that the savages would shriek and wail and hide under their beds for the next hundred years. Vala Numonius would see to that, he and whoever Augustus sent out to replace me. Besides, you're missing something else."

"What's that?" Like anyone else, slave or free, Aristocles didn't care to believe he could be missing anything.

"Arminius is a Roman citizen. He's a member of the Equestrian Order. He risked his life to put down the rebels in Pannonia and bring that province back under Roman rule," Varus answered. "So why would he and his father want to work against Rome at all?"

His Greek slave only sniffed. "Why do all those people say he was doing nothing else but all winter long . . . er, sir? Seems to me he's the biggest fraud in the world."

The biggest fraud who isn't a Greek, you mean, Varus thought, but he didn't care to wound Aristocles' feelings unless he had to. "I think we heard lies put together by Segestes' claque. I've thought so all along."

"Segestes is a Roman citizen, too," Aristocles said. "He's been one longer than Arminius has."

"As if that proves anything! He's older than Arminius. And he's still trying to fix Arminius for running off with his daughter. With Thusnelda . . . The names these Germans have!" Quinctilius Varus was pleased with himself for remembering hers.

"Doesn't that say something about the kind of wolf—uh, man—Arminius is?" Aristocles replied. "He swoops down like a thief in the night and—"

And Varus couldn't stop laughing. "I'll tell you what kind of man Arminius is. He's a young man—that's what kind. He goes around with a stiff prong all the time. Didn't you, when you were that age?" Without waiting for Aristocles to answer, the Roman governor went on, "Besides, it's pikestaff plain he didn't steal Thusnelda away against her will. She went with him because she felt like it."

"He fooled her. He tricked her." The *pedisequus* was nothing if not obstinate. "And he's fooling you, tricking you, too. And you're *letting* him."

"The day a German barbarian can fool a Roman, he's earned the right to do it," Varus said. "But I don't think that day will come any time soon."

Aristocles sighed. "Yes, sir. I understand. Once upon a time, we Greeks said, 'The day a Roman barbarian can fool a Greek, he's earned the right to do it.' We didn't think that day would come, either. But look where we are now. Look where *I* am now, sir."

"We didn't take Greece by trickery. We took Greece because we were stronger," Quinctilius Varus said. Aristocles didn't answer. One of the master's privileges was the last word. But somehow, even though Varus had it, he didn't feel as if he did.

A torrent of guttural gibberish burst from the lips of the German chief or village headman or whatever he was. Caldus Caelius looked to the interpreter, a German about his own age. "What's he saying?"

"He hasn't got any silver," the young German answered in good Latin.

"All that meant 'He hasn't got any silver'?" Caldus Caelius raised an eyebrow. "Come on, friend. Give me the rest of it."

"I'd rather not," the interpreter said. "He's upset. If you knew what he called you, you might think you had to do something about it. He didn't insult you on purpose—I swear to that. He is angry that your governor tries to make him give what he does not have."

"Oh, he is, is he? How do you know he hasn't got it? What happens if we do some digging and find he's sitting on half a talent's worth of denarii?"

"Let me ask him." The interpreter spoke in his own language. The village chieftain looked appalled—he'd never heard of acting. He blurted out something. The interpreter translated: "He says, 'You wouldn't do that!'"

Caldus Caelius laughed in the barbarian's face. "Tell him we dig in every night when we make our camp. Tell him we don't mind digging up this lousetrap he calls a village. Tell him he can't run far enough or fast enough if we find silver after he tells us he hasn't got any."

The interpreter did. The chieftain went from fair to pale—to fish-belly, really. His glass-green eyes kept sliding towards a spot behind the biggest house, then jerking away. If Caelius had to tell his men to dig, he knew where he'd have them start.

More gutturals from the headman. The interpreter listened, then asked him something. The other German shook his head. He laid a hand over his heart, the way his folk did when they took an oath. "He says he just now remembered he might have a little silver," the interpreter reported. "He says he wasn't trying to fool you before or anything. He says it just slipped his mind—Germans don't use coins as often as Romans do."

That last bit, from everything Caldus Caelius had seen, was true. The rest? He started laughing again. So did several other legionaries who stood close enough to hear what the interpreter said. A Roman officer heard every kind of excuse under the sun from soldiers who'd done what they shouldn't have and hadn't done what they should. This chieftain couldn't have been a worse liar if he tried.

But that wasn't the point. Collecting taxes was. "Tell him he'd better come up with those denarii right away. Tell him he'd better have enough to pay what Quinctilius Varus says he owes. And tell him that he'll end up dead if he tries screwing around with a Roman who's got a nastier temper than I do, and his wife and daughters will be slaves—if they're lucky."

That sounded pretty good in Latin. By the time the interpreter got done with it, it sounded even better in the Germans' language. The headman went red, then white again. He bellowed something—not at Caldus Caelius, but at his own people.

Somebody came out of the biggest house. The man was skinny, unhappy-looking, and barefoot. He wore a ratty, threadbare cloak. If that didn't make him a slave, Caelius had never seen one.

The way the chieftain yelled at him was another good marker. The skinny man went into a building next to the house—a barn, Caelius guessed—and came out with a spade. It had a wooden blade, except for an iron strip at the bottom where it bit into the ground. The fellow who was holding it called a question to the headman.

"He wants to know where to dig," the interpreter supplied.

"Right." Caldus Caelius nodded. If he were the village chieftain, he wouldn't have wanted a slave to learn where the coin-hoard was buried, either. The man could dig it up some moonless night and be long gone— and able to buy not only freedom but friends before anybody caught up with him.

Muttering under his breath, the swag-bellied headman lumbered over and stamped his foot like a petulant girl. *Dig here.* He didn't say it, but he might as well have.

Rich, dark German dirt flew. They had fine soil here. Caelius didn't like the weather or the local menfolk, but the soil tempted him to settle in Germany once it turned into a proper province. Marry one of these big blond German girls, raise crops and kids, and pass the farm down to them . . . You could do worse. Plenty of people did.

Thud! Caelius clearly heard the noise, even from where he stood. The spade had hit something that wasn't dirt. The slave dug a little more, then picked up a small, stout wooden box. He carried it over to the headman. By the way he handled it, it wasn't light.

Caldus Caelius looked at—looked through—the heavyset German. "It just slipped your mind that you had this?"

He waited for the interpreter to translate. The chieftain didn't act well enough to hide the hate on his face, either. He said something. "What difference does it make?" the interpreter said. The chieftain tacked on something else. So did the interpreter: "You have it now."

"That's right. I do." Caelius nodded. "So open it up. Let's see what all you forgot about. We'll both be surprised."

When the interpreter sent him a questioning glance, he nodded. The young German translated. The chieftain glowered some more. Caldus Caelius had enough men at his back not to care.

Inside the box was an oiled-leather sack. Caldus Caelius chuckled softly. The German looked daggers at him. Luckily for the barbarian, Caelius affected not to notice. This wasn't the first German who'd coughed up his cash after protesting that he didn't have any. Without a doubt, he wouldn't be the last. The locals still hadn't figured out that the Romans had heard all their lies and excuses before.

He supposed they would before long. That would make the tax collectors who followed on the army's heels have to work harder to pry money out of these people. Caelius wasted no more sympathy on the tax collectors than on the Germans.

"Come on," he said. "Let's see the silver. If you forgot it was there, you won't miss whatever we take, right?"

His men snickered. The interpreter grinned. Once the Latin was rendered into the Germans' language, the headman didn't seem to appreciate Caelius' wit. The Roman wondered why.

The chieftain had more than enough denarii to pay the village's tax assessment. Caldus Caelius took only what he'd been told to. He handed the rest back to the barbarian. "These are yours," he said. "You see? I am not cheating you."

"No, you are not." But the German wasn't agreeing, for he went on, "You are robbing me. Things should have their proper names."

One of the legionaries hefted his javelin. "Shall we give him what he deserves for his lip, sir?"

"Do I translate that?" the interpreter asked.

By the way the chieftain eyed that javelin, Caelius guessed he had a fair notion of what the soldier said. "Yes, go ahead," he said, and the young German did. Caelius continued, "Now translate this, too. No, we don't hurt him, because he paid what he owed and he didn't try to fight us. Roman subjects pay taxes. That's all there is to it, and he'd better get used to the idea. We'll be back to collect next year, too."

One growled sentence at a time, the interpreter passed the word along to the headman. The older German looked at him. He spat out one word, then scornfully turned his back.

"What's that about?" Caelius asked.

"He called me a traitor." The interpreter shrugged. "Nothing I haven't heard before. These people don't understand that the Roman Empire has better ways of doing things than they ever dreamt of."

"Too right they don't," Caelius said. "Well, that's what we're here for: to fix things so they do understand." *And we'll teach 'em the lesson if we have to kill every stinking one of them to do it*, he thought. But he kept that to himself; some of these Germans might follow more Latin than they let on, and even the interpreter might not fancy it. He finished, "Now that we've done the job here, we go on to the next village and do it again."

"Yes, sir." The interpreter smiled. He was a pretty good fellow. Caelius trusted him as far as he would have trusted any barbarian—not quite so far as he would have trusted a Roman, in other words.

Beyond the fields these Germans cultivated, beyond the meadows where their animals grazed, stretched more forests and swamps. Caldus Caelius eyed them without enthusiasm. Germany had far too many of both, or so it seemed to him. He wondered that the place had any room for Germans. But it did, for altogether too many of them. How long would it take to drag them into the Empire one thatch-roofed village and steading at a time?

As long as it took, that was all. He raised his voice to a shout that would reach all the legionaries: "Come on, boys! Time to go find the next place!"

If they were eager, they hid it very well. But they followed him. And their rear guard stayed alert. If the Germans here thought about getting their own back, they thought again right afterwards. Caldus Caelius nodded to himself. One place at a time, all right. He marched on.

Silver clinked in front of the camp prefect as he counted the cash Roman soldiers had squeezed from German villages. When Arminius took service with the Romans, he'd been impressed to see that they had officers in charge of paying their soldiers. That had never crossed his mind till then. German warriors lived on loot and on gifts from the war leaders they followed. A niggardly leader had a hard time getting men to fight for him. Standard wages took care of that.

That the Romans should also have an officer in charge of money coming in only made the German nod. These people were nothing if not disciplined and thorough. They left as little to chance as they could.

Quinctilius Varus came up behind Arminius and his father. "You see?" the Roman said. "My own men wondered whether we would be able to tax Germany, but we manage. Germans use far more silver than they did when I was a boy."

"That is so," Arminius agreed. "Germans use coins far more often than they did when *I* was a boy." He didn't think he was half of Varus' age.

Even Sigimerus nodded. "When I was young," he said in his slow Latin, "you hardly ever saw a denarius. Now we use them often. The world changes."

"The world does change." Varus sounded enthusiastic about it, where Sigimerus, Arminius knew, hated the idea. The Roman governor went on, "You Germans grow ever more civilized, though you may not notice it. You grow ever more ready to become part of the Empire."

"It could be so," Arminius said before his father could tell Varus exactly what his opinion was.

"Oh, I think it is." Varus thought becoming a Roman province would be good for Germany. He needed to think Arminius and Sigimerus agreed with him, or their role in the resistance would end suddenly and unhappily. He continued, "I don't suppose Julius Caesar would recognize Germany if he saw it today."

Arminius knew a couple of old men who'd fought against the first Roman to invade Germany most of a lifetime earlier. By things his father had said, Sigimerus had known many more, though most of them were dead. No one spoke of Caesar without respect. "He hit hard, he hit fast, and he could talk you out of the brooch on your cloak and make you glad you gave it to him," was how one of the graybeards summed things up.

Romans said Augustus was as great a man as Caesar had been. Maybe it was true; Augustus had stayed king longer than Arminius had lived, which argued that he was formidable. None of the men he'd sent to try to bring Germany into the Empire came close to matching his quality, though. Tiberius might, but Tiberius was busy in Pannonia. Varus didn't—he was no warrior, and uneasily aware of it.

But he seemed happy about what the legionaries under his command had been able to squeeze from the Germans. "Before long, we'll be able to spend the whole year in Germany instead of wintering back in Gaul," he said proudly. "That will be one more step toward bringing this province into line with the rest of the Empire."

"So it will," Arminius said, which let him acknowledge Varus' words without showing what he thought of them. "But not yet, your Excellency?"

"No, not yet." Now Varus sounded regretful. "We'll have to slog back through the mud, through the swamps. . . ." He heaved a sigh.

"You could come farther north, through the land where my tribe lives," Arminius said eagerly. "I know a route that stays on higher ground, on dry ground, all the way back to the Rhine. It's longer, but you won't have to worry about mud for even one step."

Whether Varus and the legionaries would have to worry about Germans was a different question, but not the one the Roman governor was worrying about at the moment. If Varus decided to go that way, Arminius knew the kind of place where he wanted to lead the Romans. He thought he could gather enough of his own folk around that kind of place to give them a proper welcome, too.

To his disappointment, Quinctilius Varus shook his head. "I thank you for the suggestion, my friend, but I'll pass this year. We've already made plans to use the same route we did before. Sometimes even the gods can't change plans once they're made."

Arminius didn't dare push too hard. He couldn't show how disappointed he was, either, not unless he wanted to rouse Varus' suspicions. "However you please, sir," he said. "If you enjoy the muck, you're welcome to it. And if you ever decide you don't, speak to me of that. My route won't disappear. It won't flood, either."

"Neither will the one we usually use—I hope." Varus betrayed himself with those last two words. Knowing as much, he went on, "One of these days, Germany will have proper Roman roads. May they come soon."

"Yes, may they." As Arminius had so often, he lied without hesitation. Roman roads would tie Germany to the Empire, all right. He understood why Varus wanted them. Nothing could possibly be better for moving swarms of men on foot. Traders and travelers and farmers might use Roman roads, but they were for the legions. Varus' dream of soldiers marching through Germany along them was Arminius' nightmare.

"One more step in bringing Roman ways here," Varus said. Arminius made himself smile and nod. He glanced toward his father. Sigimerus was nodding, too, but no smile lightened his features. Varus, fortunately, didn't notice.

Lightning flashed. Thunder boomed. Rain poured down out of a dark gray sky. The Romans squashing through the mire between Mindenum and the headwaters of the Lupia cursed the gods who oversaw the weather in Germany.

Unlike most of the legionaries, Quinctilius Varus was mounted. That kept him from getting muddy past the knees, the way they did. But he couldn't have got any wetter in the pools inside a bathhouse. The chilly, drumming, relentless rain stayed in his eyes, his nose, his mouth, his ears.

"A fish could do as well in this as I could!" He had to shout to make himself heard through the downpour.

"That's a fact, sir." Vala Numonius shouted, too. "And a fish would be more comfortable in its scales than I am in my cloak." The wool garment clung to him the way a caul was said to cling to some newborn babes. Varus' did the same thing. Soaked in rainwater, it was not only clinging but heavy.

The Roman governor's eyes slid to Aristocles. The slave rode a donkey, so he too was out of the worst of it. But he looked like a drowned mouse. Some of the legionaries had their hair in their eyes. Varus and Aristocles didn't: the first advantage to balding the governor had discovered. Water dripped off the end of Aristocles' pointed nose. The *pedisequus* didn't say anything, but every line of his body and of his cloak screamed out a reproach.

"One thing, sir," Lucius Eggius said. "We don't have to worry about the Germans jumping us in a storm like this."

"Oh? Why not?" Varus had been worrying about just that.

"Don't be silly, sir," Eggius said. Before Varus could decided whether to be affronted, Eggius went on, "The savages would have as much trouble moving as we do."

"Ah." That hadn't occurred to Varus. "Yes, one man's miseries are every man's miseries, aren't they?" In spite of the deluge, he smiled, pleased with himself. "I've heard aphorisms I liked less."

Vala Numonius also smiled. Eggius' shrug loosed a small freshet from his shoulders. Varus wondered if he knew what an aphorism was. Career soldiers were more cultured than Germans, but sometimes not much more.

That reminded the Roman governor of something. "We might have been able to steer clear of all this." His horse chose that moment to step into a deep puddle—the poor beast couldn't see where to put its feet, af-ter all. Varus had to grab its mane like a tyro and hang on for dear life to keep from getting pitched headlong into the slop.

Neither Vala Numonius nor Lucius Eggius laughed at him. It could have happened to them, too, and they both knew it. After Varus was se-curely seated once more, Numonius asked, "What do you mean, sir?"

"Arminius told me of a route back to the Rhine that never floods," Varus replied. "If it's raining when we leave Mindenum next fall, to the crows with me if I don't think I'll let him show it to us. I don't care if it is longer, if it means we don't have to put up with this again."

"I didn't think there were any places in Germany that *never* flooded," Eggius said. "Are you sure that blond bastard isn't hiding something under his cloak . . . sir?"

He tacked on the title of respect too late to do himself any good. Better, in fact, if he'd left it off altogether. The slit-eyed look Quinctilius Varus sent him had nothing to do with the rain. "Why would you think showing us a better route smacks of treachery?" Varus inquired.

"I didn't say *that*, sir." This time, Eggius used the title without hesi-tation. But it *was* too late to mollify Quinctilius Varus. "I'd sure want to make sure the route was good before I used it, though."

"Do you imagine a Roman citizen—*and* a member of the Equestrian Order—would intentionally mislead his fellows?" Varus asked in tones colder than the rain.

"He may be a Roman citizen, sir, but he's still a German, too." Lu-cius Eggius was stubborn.

So was Varus. "He may still be a German, but he *is* a Roman citizen. Like you, he's risked his life for Augustus and for Rome."

He waited. Eggius didn't say anything. What could the officer say? If Varus had decided to trust Arminius, nothing he heard was likely to persuade him to do anything else. And he had. And every yard his horse fought to gain made him wish he'd done it sooner.

XII

"He almost bit, Father! By the gods, he almost did!" Arminius couldn't hide his own excitement as they made their way north and west, back toward their own country. "He was like a fat trout. He nibbled at the worm, and he never saw the hook."

"Like a trout, or like a water dragon?" Sigimerus asked. "What would you have done if he'd decided to take your route? What could you have done except let him take it—and eat half a dozen tribes out of house and home along the way? No one in Germany would have loved you after that. And you couldn't have gathered an army together fast enough to fight him."

Arminius scowled, not because his father was wrong but because he was right. Rain dripped through the pines. Arminius and Sigimerus both had their cloaks up over their heads. They were both wet even so. The rain also turned the track to mud. They slogged on without complaint—things in Germany had always been like this.

"Next year," Arminius said. "Next year we can be ready—I'm sure of it. All Varus has to do is take the bait."

"And then what?" Sigimerus insisted on looking at all the things that could go wrong. "Varus and the Romans see we have an army. So what? They have an army, too. They don't fight like us, but that doesn't mean they're bad at it. If they were, we would have driven them off years before you were born."

Rain dripping off the end of his nose, Arminius scowled again, for the same reason as before. He knew how good the Romans were. He hadn't just seen them fight or stood against them—he'd used their system. He not only understood that it worked, he understood how it worked.

In his mind's eye, he heard Roman trumpets blaring. He saw the swarthy little men moving from marching order to line of battle without wasted motion. He imagined the blizzard of javelins they'd send up, the wall of their big shields, and the way their sharp swords would bite like vipers.

"We have to ruin them before they can deploy." He'd said that before. His inner picture of the legions getting ready to face a German host only made the words seem more urgent now.

Urgency failed to impress his father. "All very well to talk about it. How do you aim to do it?"

The question was as pointed as a Roman *gladius*. "We have to take them in a place where they can't swing from column into line," Arminius said.

"And where will you find a place like that?" his father asked. "You can wish for one, but it's not the same thing."

"I'll do more than wish. I'll be traveling this winter anyhow. Everywhere I go, I'll look for what we need. Sooner or later, I'm bound to find it. Germany isn't all flatlands and fields. If I keep my eyes open, I'll find something." Arminius made himself sound confident.

"I hope you're right," Sigimerus said. "Me, I'll be glad to get home to your mother for a while. And I expect you won't be sorry to see Thusnelda again, either."

In spite of the rain, Arminius' blood heated. "That's so," he said. He'd bought relief a few times while staying at Mindenum. Seeing German women selling themselves for silver distressed him, but not enough to keep him from taking advantage of them. He thought his father had done the same thing, though neither asked the other about it. If you were a long way from your woman, you took what you could find.

If she did the same while you were away, you had the right to slit her throat and fling her faithless body into a bog. Men didn't need to be chaste, but women did.

"You should get a child on her," Sigimerus said. "That will bind her to you even after passion fades."

"Good advice." Arminius smiled wolfishly. "You'd best believe I aim to try." Both men laughed. Arminius tried to pick up the pace, but the sloppy path wouldn't let him. "Gods curse this mud," he said, and laughed again, this time on a different note. "Now I understand why the Romans want to build their roads in our land."

"So they can get to our women in a hurry," Sigimerus said: one more gibe with too much truth behind it.

A jay screeched, high up in a pine. Most of the birds were gone now, heading off to the south: toward the Roman Empire. Some stubborn ones stayed through the winter, though. Vultures and ravens and carrion crows squabbled over carcasses regardless of the season. Arminius wanted to glut them on Roman meat. He had a plan. He needed a place.

My third winter in Vetera, Quinctilius Varus thought with a kind of be-numbed wonder. When he first came up to the Rhine, he could have imagined no fate more dismal than spending three winters here. Now, though, this Roman military town seemed an outpost of civilization compared to what lay beyond the river.

He wasn't the only one who felt that way. "By the gods, sir, it's good to have real walls around me and a proper roof over my head," Aristocles said. "Meaning no disrespect to you and the job you're doing, but I get tired of living under canvas."

"I don't think you'll fall over dead with surprise if I tell you I feel the same way," Varus said. "One day, Mindenum will make a fine city, I suppose. Plenty of places that started out as legionary encampments are. Even Vetera's on the way, though I wouldn't have believed it when I got here. But Mindenum does have . . . some way to go yet."

The *pedisequus* dipped his head in Greek agreement. "Oh, doesn't it just!" he said fervently. "Why, on this side of the Rhine I can go out beyond the wall by myself without worrying that some savage will murder me and spike my head to a tree."

"That's . . . not too likely around Mindenum." Varus hid a smile, though part of what he hid was wistful. Being a slave, Aristocles didn't have to pretend to courage he didn't own. As Roman governor of Germany, Varus did. He knew he'd been better suited to peaceful Syria. Unfortunately, Augustus didn't, and Augustus' will was the only one that counted. Not only for Aristocles' sake but for his own, Varus went on, "The Germans around there have learned more of our ways than any others, I do believe."

"More, maybe, but not enough." Plainly, nothing would turn Aristocles into a Germanophile. Well, he wasn't the only one who felt that way.

"We need time, that's all." Again, Varus worked to convince himself, too. "When I was born, these Gauls on this side of the river were nothing but trousered barbarians still smarting after Caesar's conquest. You can't tell me they don't make good Roman subjects now."

"Tolerable, I suppose." Truth to tell, Aristocles didn't approve of anything north of the Alps. "At least they mostly use olive oil, not butter." He wrinkled his nose. "More than you can say about the Germans."

"The olive won't grow there," Varus said. "For that matter, it won't grow here, either, though it will farther south in Gaul. But our merchants take the oil all over the province. They can do the same in Germany. They will, once we get the place a little more settled."

"That day can't come soon enough." Aristocles' long nose twitched again. "Butter on bread is bad enough, even when it's fresh. But the unending stink of the stuff in the lamps . . . It sticks to your hair, it sticks to your skin, and you can't get away from it. And every German reeks of it."

"Not every German." Varus shook his head. His *pedisequus* would have tossed his. Varus was long used to that difference between Romans and Greeks. He continued, "Arminius and his father smell the same way we do."

"They do when they're scrounging our food and aping our ways," Aristocles sniffed. "If you called on them in their village now, they'd be as rancid as all the other German savages."

"Enough!" Varus snapped so he wouldn't have to think about that.

"Arminius is a fine young man. We already have Roman Senators from Spain. Before too long, we'll probably have some from Gaul. And, if Arminius lives long enough, he may be the first man of German blood to don the toga edged with purple. If he is, I don't expect any of the other Conscript Fathers to complain about how he smells."

"They're polite. Arminius . . ." It was chilly in Varus' residence despite fires and braziers, but that had nothing to do with Aristocles' shiver. "He looks at me like a fox eyeing a pullet—and his father is even worse."

"Sigimerus is a formidable man," Varus said. Arminius' father reminded him of a tough old wolf, too. "But if we tame the younger man, he will tame the elder for us."

"Yes, sir. If." A slave wasn't supposed to take the last word when he argued with his master. Aristocles walked away anyhow, leaving Varus with his mouth hanging open.

The Roman said something that would have made Aristophanes blush. But he said it quietly, to himself. And then he started to laugh. He'd dealt with slaves his whole life. Every once in a while, you had to remember they were people, not just property with legs.

The governor of Germany summoned his leading officers to plan the next campaigning season's moves inside the province the Romans didn't quite rule. "I want to see more of Germany than Mindenum and the miserable route we use to reach it," he declared.

"It's not *so* miserable, sir," Lucius Eggius said. "We can use boats most of the way. They're faster than marching, and they're safer, too."

"Foot soldiers can use boats," Vala Numonius said. "Not so easy for cavalry, by the gods! There are never enough boats for the horses—"

"Or for the mules and donkeys and oxen," a quartermaster broke in.

"That's right." Numonius nodded. "We slogged back through the mud every cubit of the way. If the savages came screaming out of the woods, we wouldn't have had a smooth time of it, either."

"I see. I understand." Eggius nodded, too. Quinctilius Varus thought everything would go smoothly after that. But Eggius aimed a sarcastic dart at the cavalry commander: "You enjoy marching through mud so much, you want to take the long way back from Mindenum and go through even more of it."

Vala Numonius turned red. "No, curse it! I want a route that *doesn't* go through mud."

"Good luck, friend. It's Germany," Eggius said. "You've got swamps, and you've got woods. Sometimes, just to keep you on your toes, you've got swamps *in* woods. That's what the country is."

That certainly fit what Varus had seen. Even so, he said, "Arminius tells me that if we swing north of the low hills north of the Lupia, the land is drier. He says we can march up around there and keep our feet dry almost the whole way."

If a portrait painter had wanted to sketch insubordination, he could have used Lucius Eggius as a model. "Meaning no disrespect, sir, but I'd sooner not trust a German if I don't have to," Eggius said.

Whenever a man said *Meaning no disrespect*, he meant disrespect. Varus had learned that rule when he hardly needed to scrape down from his cheeks. It had served him well ever since, and he recalled no exceptions to it. "I think Arminius is reliable," he said now. "Never mind his past service to Rome. Would he have spent so much time at Mindenum last summer if he meant us ill? He prefers us to his own savage kind."

"Will you say his father likes us better, too, sir?" Lucius Eggius asked. "The old bastard spent as much time at Mindenum as Arminius did."

Varus opened his mouth, then closed it again. He might want to say that, but no one who'd ever set eyes on Sigimerus would claim he was Romanized, even if his son was. "He came along with Arminius to see what Roman ways are like. He didn't seem to mind sleeping soft or drinking wine." Having said so much, Varus knew he'd gone as far as he could.

Eggius' chuckle had a wry edge. "Your Excellency, I like sleeping soft and drinking wine, too. That doesn't tell me much about what this barbarian'd do to me if he ever got the chance."

"The Germans seem to pay more attention to Arminius than they do to Sigimerus, and Arminius is in our company any way you care to use the phrase," Varus insisted.

Another officer—a junior man, one whose name Varus was always forgetting—said, "What about those things Segestes keeps telling us? If even a quarter of that's true, Arminius isn't such a big friend of Rome's as he makes himself out to be."

Several other soldiers nodded. Varus fought to hide his exasperation: a losing battle. "Oh, by the gods, mm, Caelius!" he said. There—he'd remembered. "You might as well be Jews and Egyptians and Cappadocians back at Rome, caring more for gossip than you do for truth."

Vala Numonius nodded. Most of the other legionaries eyed Varus in stony silence. They didn't like him calling them a bunch of Jews. He groaned silently. Now he'd have to waste Mars only knew how much time jollying them along till they weren't angry at him any more. They were even more foolish than Jews; they reminded him of spoiled children. He was tempted to tell them so, but that would only make things worse.

It began to pour outside. Vetera might have been built of wood rather than canvas, but the place wasn't *well* built of wood. Every other roof leaked, including this one. Water started plinking into two pots set out under the leaks. The sound would have annoyed Varus most of the time: it would have reminded him how far away he was from places where they did things properly. Now, though, it came as a welcome distraction. Pointing towards one of the pots, he said, "Well, gentlemen, it's still winter. We don't have to make up our minds right now."

That seemed to satisfy the soldiers, at least the ones with sense enough not to show too much. Some of them—the more naïve ones—would believe him when he said nothing was decided yet. The rest would see that antagonizing Augustus' kinsman by marriage wasn't the smartest thing they could do.

"For now, let's discuss something else," Quinctilius Varus went on. The officers looked relieved. "We took far more taxes in silver last fall than we did the year before, and correspondingly less in kind," he said. "I want that trend to continue next fall. Before many more years go by, I expect Germany to use as much money and to take money as much for granted as any other Roman province. . . . Yes, Eggius?"

"Only one thing wrong with that, sir," the military prefect said. "There isn't as much money in Germany as there is in an ordinary province. The natives mostly don't buy and sell amongst themselves— they swap back and forth, like. So sometimes we can squeeze silver out of 'em, sure, but sometimes they just don't have any."

Varus' smile showed genuine pleasure. Now he was arguing on his ground, not the legionaries'. "As the province grows more settled and more used to Roman rule, we can expect to see more traders entering from Gaul, and from Rhaetia south of the Danube. They'll bring silver with them—they want to do business in cash whenever they can. The more denarii there are in Germany, the more we can take out in taxes. Doesn't that seem sensible to you?"

He didn't even have to make his tone suggest *That had better seem sensible to you, or you'll be sorry*. The mildly spoken words were plenty by themselves. And Lucius Eggius got the message. He might be a stubborn nitpicker; unlike some of his colleagues, he wasn't a stupid stubborn nitpicker. "Well, yes, sir. As long as everything in Germany stays smooth, that has a fighting chance of working out, anyway."

"Why wouldn't everything stay smooth?" Now Varus let himself sound ominous.

But if he hoped to impress the officers, he failed. At least half a dozen of them chorused, "Because it's fornicating Germany!" Several others nodded. All Varus could do was fume.

Somewhere ahead lay the ocean. Arminius had never seen it, but he could smell the salt tang on the wind blowing down from the north. Serving in Pannonia, he'd heard Romans talking about the sea. To them, it was blue and warm and generally friendly. But he'd also heard men from the Frisii, the Chauci, the Anglii, and other seaside German tribes. They called the ocean green or gray. They said it was cold—freezing in the wintertime. And they thought it was at least as dangerous as a wolf or a bear. Either somebody was lying or the ocean was more fickle than any woman ever born. Arminius still hadn't made up his mind which.

He was up near the marches between his own Cherusci and the

Chauci. He wanted to talk to the men who lived north of his tribe. He knew they were fierce; the wars they'd fought against his own folk proved as much. The Cherusci would long since have conquered any tribe that couldn't match their ferocity. Arminius might not love the Chauci, but he respected them for many of the same reasons he respected the Romans.

And the Chauci would respect him—unless they decided to take his head instead. If they did, they would face another round of war with the Cherusci. They had to know it.

That north wind brought more than sea-scent with it. Rain started dripping down out of a lead-gray sky. Arminius pulled his cloak up over his head. His father was doing the same thing at the same time. Neither of them got upset. It was winter. If it didn't rain, it would likely snow.

"Living close by the sea, the Chauci have wetter winters than we do," Sigimerus said.

Arminius shuddered. "One more reason to be glad we don't belong to their tribe," he said. "Some of the Romans told me it never rains in summer in their country, and hardly ever snows in winter."

"No rain in the summer! How do they raise their crops?" his father asked.

"They plant in the fall and harvest in the spring," Arminius said. "They do get rain in winter. It waters the grain."

"I think those Romans were lying, the way they would if they said their trees grew with branches underground and roots in the air," Sigimerus said. "They just wanted to see what you'd fall for."

"I don't know, Father," Arminius said. "Pannonia plants in spring and reaps in the fall, the same as we do. The Romans kept talking about how funny that was."

"Well, I wasn't there," Sigimerus said—a polite way of skirting an argument. His foot came down in mud. He pulled it out and scraped the muck off on some dying grass. "I wish I weren't here, too."

"If you know a better track that goes north, you should have told me about it," Arminius said. This one snaked north and west along the edge of a bog. The reasonably hard ground was wide enough for three or four men abreast, no more.

Sigimerus pointed. "It does get a little better up ahead—just a couple of bowshots up ahead, as a matter of fact. The ground up there gets higher, and. . . . Are you listening to me, Arminius?" He raised his right hand, as if he were on the point of cuffing his son for not paying attention. But that was only old habit. Arminius was too big to cuff, even if he wasn't listening.

And he wasn't. He was looking at the higher ground Sigimerus had pointed out. By the way he was looking at it, he might have seen the Germans' fierce gods feasting there.

Sigimerus stared. Try as he would, he couldn't see or even imagine the gods there. Because he couldn't, he went on grumbling: "When I was a young man, we respected our elders. We didn't forget they were there."

"I'm sorry, Father." Arminius didn't sound *very* sorry. "It's just that—"

"What?" Sigimerus snapped.

"Now I know what to tell the Chauci," Arminius said. Sigimerus spent the next two days trying to get him to explain what he meant. To the older man's disgust, Arminius wouldn't. His smile, though, was even broader and more self-satisfied than it had been when he brought Thusnelda home from Segestes' house.

Quinctilius Varus had just sent away a German girl when Aristocles tapped on his door. Varus grumbled to himself; the *pedisequus* was pushing things by bothering him so soon. Couldn't a man have some leisure to enjoy the afterglow? Had Varus been as young as the girl, he would have enjoyed another round. In his fifties, he'd have to wait a day or two—or three—no matter how many leeks and eggs and snails he ate. Not even oysters would help much, and they'd likely spoil by the time they got here from the coast.

And so, grouchily, he said, "What is it?"

"Please excuse me, sir," Aristocles said as he came in, "but there's someone here I think you'd better see."

"Oh, really? Who?" Varus asked. The first person he thought of who might fit that bill was a messenger from Augustus. If the rebels in Pannonia had surrendered or been crushed, if Tiberius was on his way to finish the job in Germany . . . Varus wouldn't be affronted. *By the sweet gods!* he thought. *I could go home!*

But a glance at his slave's face told him the news wasn't that good. Voice faintly apologetic, Aristocles answered, "The distinguished German gentleman named Segestes."

Varus knew that, as far as Aristocles was concerned, there was no such thing as a distinguished German gentleman. He also knew Segestes was about the last person he wanted to see. "I don't suppose you could tell him I've gone down to Italy to get the hair in my nose and ears trimmed?" he said.

Aristocles tossed his head. "I don't think he'd be happy to hear something like that, sir. He did come all this way. . . . He talks as if he thinks he has important news."

"The only trouble with that is, he always thinks he has important news, and he's been wrong every time so far." Quinctilius Varus heaved a sigh. "Oh, very well. You can't really tell him to turn around and go on back to Germany. Take him to the small dining room and give him wine and whatever else he fancies. I'll be along soon."

"I'll do that then, sir." The *pedisequus* bobbed his head and hurried out of the bedchamber. With another sigh, Varus draped himself in his toga. Roman fashions weren't made for winters like this. He understood why the Germans wore breeches under their cloaks. He wished he could himself, but what people would say if a Roman governor started aping the barbarians did not bear thinking on.

He did put on thick wool socks that rose almost to his knees. He could wear those without loss of dignity, and his wife's female slaves had knitted him several pairs. Trousers would have covered more of him, but the socks were better than nothing. They did help keep his feet warm, anyhow.

When he walked into the small dining room, Segestes was drinking neat wine and eating figs candied in honey. The German jumped to his feet and clasped Varus' hand. "Your Excellency!" he said in his gutturally accented Latin.

"Good day, Segestes. Always a pleasure to see you." One thing long experience in Roman politics had done for Varus: he could lie with a straight face and a sincere voice. "What brings you to Vetera today?"

A Roman might have used polite evasions for a while. Segestes' words were as blunt as his features: "About what you would expect. I bring you news of Arminius. It is not good news, not for anyone who cares about Rome and the Roman province of Germany."

Quinctilius Varus poured wine for himself; the house slaves had thoughtfully left two cups on the table. "Well, tell me what it is." He went on doing his best to sound friendly. But he felt he was going through the same thing more often than he wanted, as if he kept burping up fish that hadn't been quite right to begin with.

"He has gone up to the north, to talk with the Chauci." Segestes' wintry eyes widened to show what a wicked deed that was.

"And why has he gone there?" Varus asked patiently. He wasn't altogether sure Arminius had; he disliked taking Segestes' word for anything. He kept quiet about that. If the German thought Varus reckoned him a liar, things might take an unpleasant turn.

"They dwell far from Mindenum, sir. The power of the legions is not much felt in their land. And they have been a strong, fierce tribe for many years. Why else would Arminius go to them but to seek their help in his fight against Rome?" By the way Segestes laid things out, he might have been a Greek geometer drawing in the dust with a stick to prove a theorem.

Suddenly and powerfully, Varus missed the warm sun of Athens, missed the bright sky, missed standing in the shade of an olive tree with gray-green leaves as a Greek geometer drew his figures and then erased them with his sandal. He missed everything the sun and the tree and the geometer stood for, too. He missed civilization.

He'd never dreamt his work would involve extending civilization to Germany. Dealing with this wolfish savage told how hard the job was and would be. And, as far as Varus could see, Segestes *hadn't* proved his theorem now, any more than he had any other time he trotted it out.

"Did you hear Arminius speaking to these Chauci? Do you know for a fact what he said to them?" the Roman governor asked.

"Did I hear him? No." Segestes shook his big head. Like so many Germans, he towered over Varus. Varus didn't like it. His unwelcome guest went on, "But I know what he must have said."

"How?" Varus demanded, perhaps more bluntly than he'd intended. The wine he'd poured himself was as neat as Segestes'. Unmixed wine kept you warm in the wintertime. It also mounted straight to your head.

"I will tell you how, sir." Segestes might have drunk more than one cup himself. Bright red spots burned on his cheekbones. His teeth seemed uncommonly long and sharp as he continued, "I know because, if I stood before the Chauci blazing with hatred for Rome, it is what I would say."

"Ah. There we have it." Varus pounced. "Why do you claim Arminius blazes with hatred for Rome? You will have heard, I suppose, that he and his father guested with me at Mindenum this summer? They showed no hatred then."

"Have you ever caught a duck with your hands?" Segestes asked.

"What on earth does that have to do with anything?" Varus asked irritably.

"You haven't, then. I did not think so." The German nodded to himself. "You sit by the riverbank. You sit very still, so you don't scare the duck off right away. After a while, it grows easier at having you around. You toss crumbs of stale bread or whatever other food you have into the water. The duck swims closer and closer. It loves you now. You go on sitting still, but for when you feed it. And then, when it comes close enough, you grab it"—he lunged at Varus, who involuntarily stumbled back—"and you wring its neck!"

He could have wrung Varus' neck had he wanted to. Both men knew it. It made them oddly complicit, there in the chilly little dining hall. With what dignity Varus could muster, he said, "I am no duck, nor is Arminius hunting me."

"So you say," Segestes replied. "If you kill Armenius and I am wrong, though, you do Rome no harm. But if you do not kill him, if you let the worthless swinehound live, and I am right, you do not just hurt yourself. You also hurt Rome. You may hurt Rome badly, for you do not grasp how ambitious Arminius is."

Ambitio was a word to conjure with in Latin. Quinctilius Varus wondered whether Segestes knew. A man ambitious for himself rather than Rome was the greatest danger to the state. Ambitious men had brought down the Republic. Now Augustus, having gained all his ambitions, did his best to keep others from having any.

"Ask any man in any clan in any tribe in all of Germany," Segestes went on. "If he knows my name, he will tell you I am Rome's friend and ally. Ever since my beard began to grow, I have been on the Roman side. I have fought for Rome inside Germany. Arminius never has. He never will. He thinks you are a duck, sir. He throws stale bread on the water to make you swim closer. Will you let him grab you?"

He didn't go for Varus' throat again. From what Varus had seen of Germans, that showed unusual restraint from Segestes. "Well, you may be right," the Roman governor said after silence stretched.

In the Roman Empire, anyone with ears to hear would have understood that as *Quiet down and go away. You're boring my toes off.* Segestes might be a Roman citizen, but he was no Roman sophisticate. "You wait. You look close. You . . . will see I am right." He had to pause to remember how to form the future.

Varus just wanted him to leave. They'd played this scene too many times now. Did actors get sick of roles after performing them over and over? If they didn't, why not?

Segestes poured himself more wine and drank it down. The red patches on his cheeks burned bigger and brighter. He reached for a candied fig, then pulled his hand back. When he looked at Varus again, his eyes were bright with unshed tears. "Ask you something, your Excellency?" he said, his speech slightly slurred.

"Of course," Varus said, more cordially than he felt.

"You had Arminius as your guest for all that time at Mindenum," the German chieftain said, which didn't sound like a question to Varus.

He nodded anyway. "Yes. That's right. He was there, he and his father both." *And if you don't like it, too bad.*

Segestes muttered to himself. Then, slowly, painfully, he brought out what was on his mind: "While Arminius was with you, did he speak of Thusnelda? Did he say she was well? Did he say she was happy?"

He loves her. He cares about her, Varus realized in surprise. He'd assumed Segestes resented Arminius for showing him up, not for stealing away someone who mattered to him. But the middle-aged chieftain wasn't just posturing. He missed his daughter, and he worried about her.

Varus had to think back. Arminius hadn't talked much about Thusnelda one way or the other. But what did that prove? Varus hadn't talked much about Claudia Pulchra, either. He remembered speaking of his own son—of whom Arminius reminded him a little—but not of his wife.

He picked his words with care: "In all the time he was there, I never heard anything to make me doubt it. He is not a man who enjoys hurting someone and then laughing about it."

Varus had hoped that would make Segestes feel better, but it didn't seem to. The German heaved a sigh. "No, I suppose he is not that kind of beast," he allowed. "That does not mean he is no beast. He takes what he wants and then, once he has it, he puts it on a shelf and forgets about it. Not so bad, if you talk about a fancy pot or a silver statuette. But if a girl sits on a shelf and gathers dust, it is cruel, not so?"

Plenty of girls gave their all to men who got bored with them afterwards. Varus didn't think Segestes wanted to hear that. "I hope it will turn out for the best in the end," the Roman said: one more sentiment that sounded good and cost him nothing.

"I always hope for this." Segestes' slow, deliberate Latin seemed strangely impressive. "But what I hope for and what I expect are two different things." He sighed once more. "I can not persuade you. I can not, uh, convince you. All I can do is to say again, Try not to be a duck, your Excellency." He sketched a salute and strode out of the small dining room with no more ceremony than that.

Aristocles appeared a moment later. Varus nodded, unsurprised. "Were you listening?" he asked.

"Of course not, sir!" The *pedisequus* sounded shocked: so shocked, Varus didn't believe him for a heartbeat.

"He does go on, doesn't he?" the Roman governor said.

"And on, and on," Aristocles agreed, not caring that he'd just given himself the lie. "What was that nonsense about ducks? I couldn't follow all of that."

"Don't worry—it's not worth following. But he really is fond of his daughter." Varus shook his head in wonder. "You never can tell."

"With Germans, you never can tell about anything," Aristocles remarked.

"True," Varus said, and then wished he hadn't.

❧ XIII ❧

Caldus Caelius' *caligae* clunked on the timbers of the bridge across the Rhine. "One more time," he said to nobody in particular. "Maybe we'll finish the job this year. Then we can go do something else."

"Or settle down in Germany for garrison duty," said the man marching on his left. "Wouldn't that be fun?"

"Sometimes I think so," Caelius answered. "Sometimes I'm not so sure."

"Silence in the ranks!" a military tribune bawled. Caelius marched on without a word. Sooner or later—probably sooner—the senior officer would find something else to worry about. In the meantime, Caelius didn't feel like getting screamed at.

His hobnailed marching sandals stopped clunking and started thumping: dirt underfoot, not planks. "Germany," the legionary beside him said. "Again."

Both men's eyes darted now left, now right. Neither was foolish enough to turn his head and risk drawing the tribune's notice. Caldus Caelius took an extra-long stride to avoid a horse turd in his path. The governor and the cavalry had gone on ahead of the legionaries . . . and left souvenirs for the unwary.

A couple of ranks behind Caelius, somebody swore sulfurously. The tribune barked at him. "What's that all about?" whispered the man to Caelius' left.

"He must've stepped in the shit," Caelius whispered back. "I saw it coming, so I missed it. He must not have."

"Is that why you hopped? I thought something went and bit you," the other legionary said.

"Not yet. Give it another month," Caelius answered.

The other man grunted. Quinctilius Varus had started them for Mindenum early. The trees that shed their leaves were just beginning to get them back. Germany seemed to have fewer mosquitoes than Italy did. But it had more midges and gnats and biting flies. When spring was a little further along, they would rise from the swamps and marshes in buzzing myriads. Spring brought forth all kinds of life, including the unwelcome.

Thinking about the unwelcome naturally made Caldus Caelius think about Germans. "Wonder if the governor's tame barbarian'll come round again," he murmured.

"Huh!" the other legionary said—a book's worth of commentary packed into what wasn't even a word. All the same, the soldier went and amplified it: "Did you ever see a German who was really tame?"

"There's the one who keeps coming to tell the governor what a rotter the other savage is," Caelius said. "If he's tame, the other fellow isn't. And if he isn't, the other bugger is."

"Or maybe neither one of 'em is," the other Roman replied. "I say they're both stinking barbarians, and I say to the crows with 'em."

"That you running your mouth, Caelius?" The tribune rasped like a saw blade hacking through marble.

"No, sir." Caldus Caelius lied without compunction or hesitation.

"Well, *somebody* cursed well is." The military tribune was half mollified, but only half. "Whoever it is, he'd better shut up if he knows what's good for him."

Caelius didn't respond to that. If he had, the centurion would have suspected he had a guilty conscience. He did, but he also had the sense not to put it on display.

The legionaries plunged into the woods. If you wanted to go anywhere in Germany, you had to go through the forest or through mud or, more likely, through both. Because so many of the trees were pines and spruces and yews, the air took on a faint spicy scent. That odor was almost the only thing about the woods Caelius liked.

He had a javelin in his right hand. He also unobtrusively made sure his *gladius* was loose in its sheath. He didn't think the Germans would try to ambush the legionaries so close to Vetera, but you never knew. They might try an ambush here just because they guessed the Romans wouldn't expect it.

Several soldiers in front of him were checking their weapons, too. After you'd gone into Germany a few times, you realized every tree had eyes and every bush had ears. Legionaries who took stupid chances usually regretted it—but not for long.

A raven high up in a spruce croaked gutturally. "Hear that?" the man next to Caelius said. "It's going, 'Feed me. Feed me.' "

"We aren't supposed to do so much fighting now," Caelius said. "This is supposed to be a working province."

"Now tell me one I'll believe," the other Roman said. "So this is a province like Gaul, say? Then I can walk around wherever I please in a tunic, and maybe a cloak if it's chilly outside? I don't need any armor?" He shrugged to make his chainmail jingle. "I don't need any weapons?" Like Caelius, he carried javelins and thrusting shortsword, as well as a leather-faced wooden shield with an iron boss in the center and bronze edging.

Caldus Caelius had to laugh. "I said it was supposed to be that kind of province. I didn't say it was yet."

"Good thing, too. Only place in Germany where I can walk around in my tunic and not worry about getting scragged is inside the rampart at Mindenum. Oh, yeah, and I guess in Aliso and the other riverside forts, too."

"Silence in the ranks!" the tribune bellowed again. "Caelius, this time I know it was you! Didn't making centurion give you any extra sense?"

The ordinary soldier marching next to Caelius snickered—he hadn't got caught. Caelius contrived to step on his toe, which not only made him bleed but also made him swear. The military tribune pounced like a wildcat jumping a field mouse. Caelius didn't laugh . . . not on the outside, anyhow.

A gray-bearded warrior, his face drawn and grim, approached the funeral pyre torch in hand. The pale corpse on the pyre looked like a thin, wasted version of him, and was in fact his younger brother. The dead man's spear and dagger and a shortsword he'd captured from some legionary lay on his breast.

When the graybeard touched the torch to the pyre, the wood began to blaze at once. Standing in the crowd of mourners with his head bowed, Arminius caught the odor of burning butter. The Romans used olive oil, sometimes perfumed, to make sure their pyres burned strongly. Butter worked just as well, as it also did in cookery.

"Alcus was a worthy fighter. No man of the Chauci could ask for greater praise," his brother said, stepping back from the flames.

A low murmur of agreement ran through the crowd. Arminius hadn't known Alcus alive, but added his respects now that the man was dead. He didn't want an affronted ghost dogging his tracks. A man could fight the Romans. How could anyone hope to fight a ghost?

"He would have gone to war once more against the invaders of our fatherland," Alcus' brother continued. "Now his spirit will watch to make sure we fight as fiercely as he would have."

More murmurs of approval rose. Again, Arminius joined them. Leaping flames engulfed Alcus' body. The stink of charred meat mingled with the odors of butter and wood smoke in the air. Coughing, Arminius sidled away so he was upwind of the pyre. Beside him, his father was do-ing the same thing. So were the Chauci, so the two Cherusci didn't stand out. All the mourners swung to the left.

How long had the Chauci been burning bodies in this meadow? A long time, judging by the number of turf mounds that rose here. Arminius had seen that the Romans raised stone memorials above their dead. Like any German, he thought those oppressively heavy. A ghost might not be able to get out from under one of them. Cut turves were better.

And then, suddenly, he forgot about Alcus, forgot about the sorrow he was supposed to share with his hosts. He nudged his father and loudly whispered, "Turves!"

"Turves?" Sigimerus echoed. "What are you talking about?" His tone suggested he would clout Arminius if he didn't like the answer he got. He'd done that often enough when Arminius was smaller.

But Arminius repeated, "Turves!" When the Romans wanted to re-member something, they could write it down and preserve it as if they were smoking pork. Most Roman officers had their letters. Only a hand-ful of men in Germany did, to write Latin rather than their own tongue; Arminius wasn't one of them. When he needed to hold something in his memory, he spoke to make his ideas stick—and to pass them on to some-one else so they wouldn't stay in his head alone. He went on, "If we pile them up to make a rampart at that spot we found coming here . . ."

"Ah! I see what you're saying!" Sigimerus sounded as excited as he did.

Several of the Chauci sent them scandalized glances. Arminius was embarrassed; he wasn't behaving as a mourner should. "Where are your manners, guest among us?" a big man rumbled. *His* tone suggested there might be bloodshed if he didn't like the answer he got.

"My apologies," Arminius said. "I just had a notion that will help us in our fight against the Romans. In my excitement, maybe I spoke louder than I should have."

"You did." The big man nodded. "But that is a good reason for bad manners. I say no blame sticks to you." He eyed his fellow tribesmen as if daring them to disagree. No one did.

Another man was not so easily pacified. "You say you want to do this and that and something else to the Romans," he told Arminius.

"I do," Arminius replied. "And I say it for the best reason: it is true."

"You say it," the man from the Chauci repeated. "But *is* it true? Or are you a spy for them? You spent last summer in their stinking camp! Are you a proper German, or are you the Romans' lapdog?"

"I am a German. Never doubt it," Arminius said. "If you fish for trout, don't you put a fat worm or a cricket or a bit of meat on your hook? Of course you do. The bait will help you catch your fish. I am the bait that will help Germany catch the Romans."

"So you say," the other man returned.

"Yes. So I say," Arminius agreed. "And if you say I lie, you had bet-ter say it with something more than words."

The other man had a spear in his hand and a knife on his belt.

Germans from all tribes carried their weapons everywhere, even to a funeral. The fellow dipped his head to Arminius. "I am ready. Shall we begin?"

Sigimerus set an urgent hand on Arminius' arm. "What if he kills you?" he whispered. "You can't do this. You risk too much."

"The gods will not let him kill me," Arminius said calmly. "And even if they do, you can lead our folk to victory against the Romans. You know everything I've done and everything I aim to do. You have the name of a brave warrior, no less than I do. Men will follow where you lead."

"If you fall, the first thing I'll do is kill this ass with ears," Sigimerus growled.

"I'm not going to fall," Arminius assured him. Then he bowed to Alcus' brother. He didn't want to anger the Chauci; he wanted them fighting the legions alongside his own Cherusci and as many other Germans as he could gather. "I mean no disrespect to the fine fighter now lying on his pyre. But you surely are a man of honor yourself. Would you let anyone say you did not tell the truth? How could you show your face among men afterwards if you did?"

"You will do what you will do, and the gods will show us all who has the right of it," the older man replied.

"Just so," Arminius said. The Chauci who had been mourning Alcus now buzzed excitedly. Some of them pointed towards Arminius, others in the direction of their fellow tribesman. They argued in low voices. Arminius knew what they were doing: getting their bets down. If he weren't in the fight, he would have done the same thing. Like most Germans, he loved to gamble. Men who'd lost everything else would bet their own freedom. And, if they lost that, too, they'd go into slavery without a word of complaint and with their heads high.

The Chauci formed a circle around Arminius and the man who'd called him a liar. "You know who I am. Tell me your name, please. I would not kill a stranger."

"I am Vannius son of Catualda. I had heard that the Cherusci were a rude lot. I see that is not so," the other man replied.

"We hear those things about the Chauci, too. It must come from living beside each other for so long." Arminius raised his spear in salute. "Shall we begin?"

"Let's." Vannius advanced on him. By the way the fellow held his own spear, Arminius knew him for an experienced warrior. Well, he was a few years older than Arminius: few Germans reached that age without a battle or two under their cloaks. The two men were about the same size. Vannius might have been a little thicker through the shoulders.

Arminius hefted his spear as Vannius stalked closer. If he threw it and hit, he could end the fight before it began. If he threw it and missed, he'd be left with a Roman *gladius* against a spear with four times the reach. He'd die in short order, in other words.

Vannius had to be making the same calculations. Arminius' foe showed no sign of wanting to cast his spear. Of course, nobody with a grain of sense would till the instant before he let fly. Why let your enemy get ready to dodge or duck? But Vannius seemed to want to fight it out at close quarters.

I told Father the gods wouldn't let him kill me, Arminius thought. *Was I right, or was I fooling myself?* Before he could wonder for more than a fraction of a heartbeat, his right arm went back, then forward again.

He watched the spear fly as if it had nothing to do with him. He didn't even reach for his sword. One way or the other, he didn't think it would matter.

Vannius waited till the last moment to start to spring aside. Maybe he was gauging the spear's flight. Or maybe he wanted to show how brave he was. Whatever the reason, he waited too long. As he tried to fling himself to the right, the spear caught him square in the chest.

He stood swaying for a couple of heartbeats, looking astonished. When he opened his mouth to say something, blood came out instead of words. Blood also bubbled from his nose. He slowly crumpled to the ground.

His feet drummed and scuffed at the grass. Cautiously, Arminius approached him. "Do you want me to give you peace?" he asked, ready to jump back in a hurry if Vannius went for his knife.

But the other man only nodded. He was biting his lip to hold in a shriek now. Wounds often didn't hurt for a little while. Then, as Arminius knew too well, they did.

He drew his *gladius* and drove it into Vannius' throat. The other man twisted and jerked. His life rivered out of him as Arminius pulled out the shortsword and plunged it into the ground again and again to clean off the blood. After a few moments, Vannius lay still, his gaze set and staring. Arminius felt for his pulse and found none. Setting his foot on the corpse's chest, he jerked out the spear.

He bowed to the wide-eyed Chauci. "He was as brave as any of you," he said. "I don't think I ever saw a man die so well. May the gods give his spirit peace."

"May it be so." Alcus' brother spoke for his fellow tribesmen. "You downed him in a fair fight, where he had a like chance to slay you." He eyed the other Chauci. "Let no one here claim otherwise."

A few of the man's tribesmen stirred, but no one challenged him. No one challenged Arminius, either. That relieved him. He didn't want a blood feud with the Chauci. The Germans could fight among themselves later. They needed to join together now to drive the Romans beyond the Rhine.

And then what? Arminius wondered. Gaul was supposed to be a rich country, richer than Germany. The Romans hadn't ruled there for even a lifetime yet. Old men remembered when the Gauls were still their own masters. Several German tribes had tried to take new lands west of the Rhine. The Gauls weren't strong enough to stop them. Unfortunately, the Romans always had been.

If the Romans were cast out of Germany, though, wouldn't they also be thrown into disarray in Gaul? Then the Germans could burst forth in a vast wandering of peoples. They could lay hold of all the living space they craved and deserved.

And, with the Romans all topsy-turvy, who could stop the German tribes? *No one*, Arminius thought exultantly. *No one at all!*

Shoveling. Chopping. Hammering. Sawing. Endless profanity and obscenity. By now, Quinctilius Varus was far more familiar with the sounds that went into making a legionary encampment than he'd ever dreamt he would be. Like the phoenix, Mindenum was rising from its own ashes once more. Varus remembered thinking it would make a fine provincial town one day.

The only trouble was, he didn't want even the finest provincial town. He wanted Rome as a lover longed for his beloved. He wasn't perfectly faithful to Rome. Alexandria would have done. So would Antioch, from which he'd ruled Syria. And if Athens was good enough for his son, it was good enough for him as well.

Mindenum wouldn't make an Athens, an Antioch, or an Alexandria for the next two thousand years. And Mindenum wouldn't make a Rome for . . . well, forever.

But it would make a place from which to administer Germany for another summer. One of these years, Varus supposed it would make a place from which to administer Germany the year around. He devoutly hoped somebody else would govern Germany by then. If a man wasn't allowed to return to even the dubious civilization of Vetera . . . he would be a mighty unhappy man after a while.

He would if he was anything like Varus, anyhow. Some stolid soldier might enjoy the kind of town Mindenum would be by then. Plenty of officers seemed to like Vetera well enough. No accounting for taste—or lack of taste.

"Would you care for a cup of wine, sir?" By the slight slur in Aristocles' voice, he'd already had a cup of wine, or several cups, himself. He went on to explain why: "If you drink a bit, you don't notice the racket so much. Or at least *I* don't."

"That's not a bad idea," Varus said. "Why don't you make it a cup of neat wine, as a matter of fact?"

"I'll do that, sir." The *pedisequus* winked. "Turning into a German, are you?"

"By the gods, I hope not!" Varus exclaimed. "I've been called a lot of things in my time, Aristocles, but what did I do to deserve that?"

"Well, sir, the next German I see who likes his wine watered will be the first. Be right back for you." Aristocles hurried away.

Rome. Alexandria, Varus thought longingly. *Antioch. Athens.* His nearest approach to Athens was a Greek slave here in Mindenum. That wasn't close enough. And the slave was bringing him neat wine at his own request: not only un-Greek but un-Roman as well.

The trouble was, in Mindenum neat wine was medicinal. Anything that helped you forget you were in Mindenum for a little while was medicinal. He would have used poppy juice if the physicians could have spared it. It was expensive, but he had no better uses for his silver. Still, the reason it was expensive was that it was the only remedy for real, physical pain. He could understand why the doctors didn't care to use it for anything less.

Aristocles came back with the wine. "Your health, sir," he said, handing Varus the cup.

"Wine will help my health." The Roman governor poured a small libation on the rammed-earth floor. He drank, and smiled at the warmth sliding smooth down his throat. "Going back to Italy would help it even more."

"Going back to Italy would help my health, too. Can we do that?" Aristocles practically quivered with eagerness.

Quinctilius Varus shook his head. "Not until my wife's great-uncle gives us leave." What would Augustus do if he threw up this governorship and went back to Rome on his own? Maybe nothing. Maybe he would understand Varus simply wasn't the right man for the job.

Or maybe he would make an example of his grand-niece's husband. Closer relatives were spending the rest of their lives on small, hot, barren Mediterranean islands. While the weather at a place like that was bound to be an improvement over Mindenum's, the rest of the arrangements wouldn't be.

And the humiliation! If he went home, anyone who remembered him after he was dead would remember him for a sentence in some as yet unwritten history that read something like, "In the thirty-sixth year of Augustus' reign, Publius Quinctilius Varus was exiled to Belbina for neglecting his duties." And anyone who cared (if anyone at all cared) would have to consult some geographer's work to find out where the demon Belbina was.

To keep from thinking about Belbina (Varus knew too well where the arid rock was, and knew it wasn't much more than a good piss long, and maybe half that wide), he poured down the wine. The legionaries had fortified Mindenum. The wine fortified Quinctilius Varus. He thrust the cup at Aristocles. "Fill this up again." When you were talking to a slave, you didn't even have to say *please*.

Aristocles gauged him the way a sailor gauged clouds boiling up to windward. Like a prudent sailor, the *pedisequus* shortened sail. "Yes, sir," he said, and not another word.

He came back with the refilled cup faster than he'd brought it before. Varus poured a *very* small libation this time. The rest of the wine went straight into him.

After two of those good-sized cups of potent vintage, he felt like finding a nice, quiet spot somewhere, wrapping his cloak around him, and going to sleep like a dormouse. In Germany, nobody could tell him he couldn't do something like that if he wanted to. The only person in the whole Roman Empire who could tell him any such thing was Augustus— and Augustus was a long way from Germany.

But not even Augustus' designated governor could keep some kind of commotion from starting in front of his tent. "What's going on now?" Varus asked irately.

"I'll go see, sir." Aristocles went off to find out. He came back sooner than Varus had expected. His expression was altogether unreadable.

Voice as carefully blank as his face, Aristocles said, "The German named Arminius has returned, your Excellency. His father is with him, as he was last year."

"Oh, good!" Varus said. Aristocles' face took on an expression then. Had Varus tried to name it, he probably would have called it unwatered horror.

Arminius had wondered whether he would get back to the site of Mindenum before the Romans finished rebuilding it. But no: the camp or town or whatever you called it was a going concern by the time he and

Sigimerus came southeast from the country of the Chauci to central Germany.

The Roman sentries bristled like angry dogs when they spotted Arminius. Varus might enjoy having him around, but they didn't. Only the governor's rank kept them from showing how little they enjoyed his company. Even that wouldn't have sufficed if they were Germans.

"In the name of your eagle, greetings," he called to them. He didn't want the Romans angry at him now. That might ruin everything. Maybe reminding them that he knew and respected their customs would make them happier. He didn't want somebody knifing him in the back while he was walking through the encampment. If somebody did, he would bet gold against copper that Varus never caught the murderer.

He didn't soften up the Romans as much as he'd hoped. "Our eagle has its eye on you," one sentry snarled. The others nodded. A couple of them let their hands fall to the hilts of their *gladii*.

"Careful, now," Sigimerus said out of the side of his mouth, his lips barely moving.

"I know," Arminius answered the same way. When he addressed the Romans again, he raised his voice: "Would you please be kind enough to let his Excellency the governor know I'm here?" If Varus knew, the legionaries couldn't kill him right here and then claim they hadn't realized who he was. And the looks on their faces said they wanted to.

Most reluctantly, one of the sentries went back into the encampment. "May we enter?" Sigimerus asked in his slow, halting Latin. "I am not a young man any more. I get tired standing out here in the sun."

He and Arminius had practiced at swords not long after sunup. If he'd been tired then, Arminius hadn't noticed. Sigimerus might not be quite so fast or quite so strong as he had been when he was Arminius' age. But he was still fast and strong enough to be dangerous—and he knew every trick all his years of fighting had taught him.

Shouts rang out inside Mindenum. Arminius hid a smile. His father was probably doing the same thing as he murmured, "See how much they love you?"

"Nothing we didn't already know," Arminius said. He raised his voice again: "May we come in? I don't want to harm my father's health." The Romans were like Germans in respecting their elders. And, once he and Sigimerus got into Mindenum, the legionaries would have a harder time throwing them out than they would excluding them in the first place.

But one of the sentries answered, "Let's see what the governor's got to say. If it were up to me . . ." He didn't say what would happen then. Arminius drew his own conclusions.

Another sentry looked over his shoulder. "Here comes his Excellency now!" The legionaries stiffened to attention. They expected their auxiliaries to do the same thing. Arminius had never seen anything so ridiculous in his life, but he'd learned the silly pose. Going along was easier than arguing, especially for one lone man facing a ponderous military machine.

The Romans thought all of Germany would take the easy road, go along, and submit to their yoke. But the Germans were not one lone man. They outnumbered the invaders. They were more determined than the Romans, too. *I'm more determined than the Romans are*, Arminius thought. *And I can kindle Germany. I can, and I will.*

A stocky figure mounted to the top of the earthen rampart. The sun gleamed from the Roman's bald scalp. Arminius smiled and waved. "Hail, your Excellency!" he called. If the smile never reached his eyes, Quinctilius Varus couldn't hope to notice from that distance.

Sigimerus waved, too. If he didn't smile so broadly, he *was* an older man, and carried himself with more dignity. Arminius hoped Varus would think so, anyhow.

And evidently Varus did. He was at least as old as Sigimerus, but he wore a smile wider than Arminius'. "Hail! Welcome!" he said. "I didn't know if we'd be lucky enough to see the two of you back here this year."

"Here we are, sir," Arminius said. "May we come into Mindenum? Your men didn't seem to want us to."

"You know how soldiers are," Varus said. And Arminius did: he was one himself. If the Roman governor wasn't, or didn't think of himself as one, why did he hold this position? Smiling still, he went on, "You certainly have my permission to come in. I'm sure I will want your advice again and again on how best to civilize this province."

Sigimerus growled down deep in his throat. Arminius' gaze flicked over to his father, but the older man's expression didn't change. And the Romans wouldn't have heard him. Arminius wore his smile like a mask, hiding his fury. What Varus meant by civilizing Germany was taking away its character and its freedom.

"Always a pleasure to help," Arminius lied.

"Spoken like a Roman citizen—like the member of the Equestrian Order you are," Varus boomed. After a moment, Arminius realized the Roman governor wasn't really speaking to him, or wasn't speaking to him alone. Varus was reminding the legionaries that the man outside was a tame German, a good German. He didn't say anything to or about Sigimerus. But if the soldiers accepted Arminius, they wouldn't mind his father.

Arminius drew himself up straight and delivered a clenched-fist Roman salute. *Yes, let the legionaries see I can ape their customs. Let them see that I'm a tame German, a good German. And, when the time comes, I'll show them just how tame and good I am.*

None of that showed on his face. He probably had more practice dissembling than any other German since the gods first created his folk. Among themselves, Germans were always altogether honest (unless, of course, they saw some pressing reason not to be, as Segestes had when he broke his pledge to Arminius and tried to give Thusnelda to Tudrus). What they thought of as their innate honesty put most of them at a disadvantage when they tried to deal with deceitful foreigners.

Arminius had been shocked to discover that the Romans reckoned his folk a pack of lying, thieving savages. How could they be so blind? He finally decided that, since the Romans were liars and thieves themselves, they thought other peoples shared their vices.

"Pass in, Arminius. Pass in, Sigimerus," Quinctilius Varus said loudly. If the sentries tried to go against that now, they would be mutinying against the provincial governor—indirectly, against Augustus himself. The Romans had some fearsome penalties for anyone who dared such a thing.

Any folk that had such penalties was bound to need them——one more argument against Rome and all its ways.

Legionaries mostly held their faces straight as Arminius and Sigimerus walked into Mindenum. They probably wouldn't have done that if they weren't under Varus' eye. Then again, they probably wouldn't have let the two Cherusci into Mindenum if not for Varus' orders.

"That one soldier is smiling at us," Arminius' father whispered. "What's wrong with him?"

Arminius got a corner-of-the-eye glimpse of the Roman his father had to mean. Sure enough, the fellow had a broad, welcoming smile plastered across his face. Arminius didn't think the man was putting it on for Varus' benefit, either.

"Some of the legionaries must see that the governor is right and that we aren't dangerous to Rome." Arminius also spoke quietly, but you never could tell whether somebody with a big nose and sharp eyes was eavesdropping. He could say what he meant even if he used words that said the exact opposite if you took them the wrong way.

"Ah. Of course." Sigimerus understood him just fine. If a snoopy Roman thought he meant something different . . . well, that was the chance you took when you listened in on conversations not meant for you.

Several legionaries paced the Germans as they walked through the encampment. *Our hounds*, Arminius thought, *or maybe our keepers.* He called out to one of them: "Will we stay in the same place we did last summer?"

The Roman seemed embarrassed at being noticed. Arminius wondered why. The only way he could have made himself more obvious was to paint himself blue. After a moment, the man recovered enough to answer, "Yes, I think so."

"All right. Thanks." Arminius hadn't really expected anything else. As he'd seen in Pannonia and here, Roman camps varied little from one place to another or from one time to another. If the legionaries had put them there last year, chances were they'd do the same thing again.

It was boring. It gave ordinary men no room to deviate from the pattern. But it worked. The Romans wouldn't have conquered so much of the world if it hadn't. They always camped the same way. They always fought the same way, too. If you offered them battle on ground where they could do what they usually did, chances were they'd make you regret it. No one could doubt that the Germans were the fiercest fighters the gods ever made, but the Roman legions had given them all they wanted and then some for a generation now.

We need to fight them on our own terms, then . . . if we can, Arminius thought. That same notion had spun round and round inside his head ever since he came back from Pannonia. Like so many things, it was easier to imagine than to bring off—as his father hadn't tired of reminding him. But Quinctilius Varus really did think he was a tame German. That was bound to help. Would it help enough?

❧ XIV ❧

Quinctilius Varus paused halfway through his latest report to Augustus. He knew he sounded as hopeful as things in Germany could possibly allow, and then a little more besides. When you were writing to the ruler of the Roman world, you didn't want to have to tell him things weren't going well. Even a man married to Augustus' grand-niece could spill his career in the chamber pot if he forgot that.

And if, after Varus returned to civilization, anyone asked him why he'd seemed so optimistic, he could point to the reports he'd got from subordinates all over Germany. He'd kept every single one of them, dating back to the day he'd first crossed the Rhine. And he'd based his optimism squarely on theirs.

He started to write again, then paused with the reed pen only a digit above the papyrus. "Damnation!" he muttered. Of course he made everything in Germany seem good to Augustus, whether it really was good or . . . not quite so good. Wouldn't his own underlings do the same thing with him?

They would if they thought they could get away with it. He was sure of that. They wouldn't want him breathing down their necks, any more than he wanted Augustus breathing down his. But he had to accept their reports. How else was he supposed to know what was going on?

You could travel all over the province and see for yourself, he thought. But he was shaking his head as soon as the idea formed in his mind. If he spent all his time on horseback and in the sorry camps legionary detachments built for themselves while patrolling the German wilderness, how was he supposed to administer the land between the Rhine and the Elbe? He saw no way.

But he didn't like having to depend on reports he couldn't check. "Aristocles!" he called.

"Yes, sir?" As usual, the *pedisequus* appeared with commendable haste.

"I'd like to speak with Ceionius for a bit. Fetch him, if you'd be so kind." Some Romans would have said Varus wasted politeness on a slave. But a little honey made the gruel more appetizing. It wasn't as if politeness cost anything.

"I'll bring him directly." Aristocles hurried away.

While Varus waited, he wrote a little more of the report. Some inspiration seemed to have oozed out of him, but he persisted even so. Augustus expected to be informed on how Germany was doing. And what Augustus expected, Augustus got. More than a generation of his rule had proved that.

If Aristocles couldn't find Ceionius, if he brought Lucius Eggius back instead . . . Varus wouldn't be very happy about that. The two camp prefects were as different as chalk and cheese. You could reason with Ceionius, while Eggius, curse him, was as stubborn, as cross-grained, as any man ever born. He didn't have nearly enough respect for his betters.

To the governor's relief, his slave returned with Ceionius. "Hail, your Excellency!" the prefect said, saluting. "What do you need today?"

"I expect you'll know, ah, reliable centurions in most of the detachments we've got wandering through Germany," Varus said.

Lucius Eggius might not have caught his drift. Ceionius did. Leaning forward and lowering his voice, he asked, "Reliable in what way, sir?"

"If some of their superiors are trying to gild lead in their reports, that's something I should hear about, don't you think?" Varus said.

By the camp prefect's vulpine expression, he did think so. "It's something I ought to hear about, too," Ceionius murmured. He nodded thoughtfully. "Yes, sir, I'm sure I can find centurions like that. Quietly letting them know what you need will take a bit of doing, but I can manage it."

"I thought you might be able to," Varus said. "The more ways we have to learn what's really going on, the better. And, as you say, best to do it under the rose."

"I'll get right on it, sir. Off the top of my head, I can think of three or four men who'd be perfect." Sketching another salute, Ceionius hurried away.

Aristocles had listened, as discreetly as if he were part of the tent canvas. "Not bad, sir. Not bad at all," he said.

"Who knows whether these field commanders truly are doing all the wonderful things they claim?" Varus said. "If some of them are lying and I can show they are, that will make all of them tighten up."

"Just so." Aristocles dipped his head in agreement. "Do you need anything else from me right now, sir?"

"No. You may go," Varus said. The *pedisequus* vanished as smoothly and quickly as he'd manifested himself. Varus attacked his report for Augustus with renewed vigor. He might not tell Claudia Pulchra's great-uncle things weren't perfect here, but at least he could come closer to the truth himself.

Varus paused once more, muttering to himself. He was setting spies on his subordinates now, to make sure they did what they told him they were doing. He was a good enough administrator. Realistically, though, the Empire had plenty of others just as capable, even if they didn't enjoy his connections.

Augustus, now, had long since proved he was one of a kind. No one else could run things the way he did. That being so, wouldn't he have had men quietly keeping an eye on Varus and Germany all along?

What were they saying? How well did they think Rome was doing here? If they thought Varus was botching things, would he suddenly get a letter recalling him to Italy?

Would I be sorry if I did? Varus wondered. He would be sorry Augustus judged he'd failed—he would be especially sorry if Augustus shipped him to an island in the middle of the sea—but would he be sorry to get out of Germany?

"No," he said firmly. With a sigh, he re-inked the pen and started writing again.

Lucius Eggius watched the old German come out of his village and approach the legionary detachment. Eggius kept his hand on his swordhilt. Even if this fellow was graying and balding, you never could tell with Germans.

But the native held up his right hand with the palm out to show it was empty. "Hail, Romans," he called in fair Latin. "Come ahead, if you like. We have no quarrel with you."

"Thanks," Eggius answered. "Can you feed us?"

"Some," the German said. "We are not rich. This is not a large village, either. But we will give you what we can."

They would try to hold out on the legionaries. Lucius Eggius had heard that song often enough to know all the verses. Well, his men had got plenty of practice at squeezing out more than the barbarians felt like giving. And if the Germans didn't like it, too bad.

"We will take what you can give," Eggius said aloud. Several of his men grinned. A few of them chuckled. They'd take anything else they thought they needed, too. Again, what could the locals do about it?

"Come. Be welcome," the old man said. He wasn't going out of his way to make trouble, anyhow. Eggius wished the locals were this reasonable more often.

As soon as he got into the village, he figured out why nobody here felt like getting uppity. The place held plenty of women and girls of all ages, but only a handful of men between fifteen and fifty. Youths with downy cheeks, yes. Fogeys like this fellow who spoke Latin, yes. In between? No.

"Where are your warriors?" Eggius asked bluntly. If they thought they could ambush his detachment, they'd be sorry—but not for long. And he had plenty of hostages, if it came to that.

But the old German pointed northwest. "There is trouble with the Chauci, may the gods cover their backsides with boils." Eggius had to hide a grin; sure as sure, the native had learned his Latin from legionaries. "And so they go off to fight."

"Good luck to them," Eggius said. He'd fought the Chauci himself, and hadn't enjoyed the experience. Even for Germans, they were rough, tough, and nasty. "I hope they help cut those buggers down to size." He meant every word of that. If the Germans fought among themselves, they did the legions' work for them. Every German some other German killed was a German the Romans didn't have to worry about.

"It will be as the gods decide." But after a moment, the barbarian added, "Any gods who would favor the Chauci over our tribe don't deserve the sacrifices we give them."

"There you go," Eggius said as the German ambled off.

"Quinctilius Varus won't be sorry to hear the savages are squabbling," one of his aides said in a low voice.

"I was thinking the same thing," the camp prefect answered. "For once, I won't have to make up pretty stories when I write to him."

"You don't do much of that," the junior officer said loyally.

"No more than I can help," Eggius agreed. "If I told him what things were really like in this gods-forsaken province, he'd sack me. Not that I'd mind getting back to the real world—who would, by Venus' pretty pink nipples?—but I hate to walk away from a job before it's finished."

Women—mostly women too old to be interesting—and youths brought out barley mush and beer. Eggius politely suggested that they kill some pigs, too. He would have got less polite had they said no, but they didn't. The savory smell of roasting pork made spit flood into his mouth. Some soldiers said meat made them slow. He'd never felt that way himself.

He eyed the graybeard who'd come out to greet the Romans. "You fed us pretty well, I will say," he allowed.

"We don't want trouble right now," the German said.

Right now? Eggius wondered. But probing what was likely just a slip of the tongue would only stir up trouble. He didn't think it would tell him anything he didn't already know. He teased the barbarian instead: "So you're finally getting used to the notion of living inside the Empire, eh?"

The German looked back at him with eyes suddenly as cold and pale and flat as a sheet of ice. "Of course," he said.

You lying bastard, Lucius Eggius thought. But the natives here didn't have to like anything about submitting to Rome. They just had to do it. If they kept doing it long enough, their grandchildren would like it fine. And Eggius' full belly told him they were getting used to doing it.

Rain drummed down on Mindenum. The Romans squelching along the encampment's muddy, puddled streets swore at the miserable weather. Arminius had to work hard not to laugh at them.

They were used to winter rains. He'd seen that in Pannonia, which had weather like Germany's. Spring and summer could be wet there, as they so often were here. The Romans, arrogant as usual, thought the pattern they were used to was the only natural one. Thinking that way only made them hate northern weather even more than they would have otherwise.

One of the legionaries twisted his fingers into the horned gesture they used against the evil eye. If he'd aimed it at Arminius, the German would have had to start a fight to salve his own honor. But the soldier shot his hand up at the sky. He might have been telling the gods they had no business letting it rain at this time of year.

They wouldn't listen to him. No matter what he thought, rain in spring and summer was no prodigy, not in Germany. It happened all the time. The gods wouldn't stop it on one Roman's account; he reminded Arminius of a yappy little dog barking at his betters. No, the gods wouldn't heed him. But they might—they just might—remember he'd been rude.

A wagon train came into the encampment: supplies fetched from the headwaters of the Lupia. If men had trouble getting through the mud, heavy wheeled wagons had far more. The wheels only tore up the ground worse. The oxen hauling the wains struggled forward one slow stride at a time. The soldiers guarding the wagon train had to shoulder wagons forward whenever they bogged down. By the mud soaking the men, they'd already done a lot of shouldering.

"Most excellent Arminius!"

That precise, fussy voice belonged to Aristocles. Sure enough, here came Varus' chief slave. He was fussy about his person, too, and looked even more unhappy at going out in the rain than most of the Romans did.

"What can I do for you today?" Arminius asked. He treated the skinny Greek as politely as if Aristocles were free. You had to do that with prominent Romans' prominent slaves. Your life wouldn't be worth living if you didn't. Some of them ran their masters rather than the other way around. That would never have happened among Germans. Slaves here knew their place. If they forgot it, a clout in the teeth reminded them what was what.

"The governor wishes to confer with you," Aristocles said.

He could be polite, too. Arminius had no trouble imagining what Varus had told Aristocles. *Go fetch the German*, he would have said, or, perhaps more likely, *Go fetch the barbarian*. He wouldn't have cared whether his slave honey-coated the message or not. But Aristocles did.

"I am always pleased to confer with the governor," Arminius replied. *He can give me orders as long as I'm stuck in this terrible encampment.* So many things the German and the Greek weren't saying. Arminius wondered if Aristocles heard them nonetheless.

He watched the *pedisequus* flinch delicately as rain poured down on him. That almost made him laugh. A German who minded getting wet would soon go mad. Besides, Arminius could always pull his cloak up over his head. He didn't bother here. Impressing Aristocles counted for more.

"This weather leaves much to be desired," the Greek said.

Arminius only shrugged. "It's often like this here," he said, which was nothing but the truth.

"But you say it's better north of the hills?" Aristocles asked.

"Is that what the governor wants to talk about?" Trying to hide his sudden excitement, Arminius parried question with question.

"He doesn't tell *me* such things," the slave sniffed. " 'Aristocles, go find Arminius and bring him to me'—that's what he said." Arminius smiled— that was close to what he'd imagined, all right. Striking a pose even in the rain, Aristocles continued, "I found you, so now I'll bring you."

"So you will," Arminius agreed. He followed the Greek back to Varus' tent. If he was going to be seen as a proper Roman friend and ally, he had to act like one, no matter how it made his stomach churn.

Once under thick canvas, he shook himself like a dog. Water sprayed every which way. Aristocles squawked: some of it got him in the eye. "What did you go and do that for?" he said.

"To dry off before I see the governor," Arminius answered. As he'd guessed, mentioning Varus calmed Aristocles down. All the same, Arminius added, "Sorry." If you were going to act like a friend and ally, you *did* have to act like one, curse it.

Aristocles hurried off, no doubt to tell Varus he'd done his duty. Arminius could hear his voice, but couldn't make out what he was saying; the folds of cloth muffled words. Then the slave came back. "This way," he said.

As Quinctilius Varus so often was, he was writing something when Aristocles ushered Arminius into his presence. "Your Excellency," Arminius said, and waited for the governor's pleasure.

Varus set down the pen with every sign of relief. He got up from behind the folding table he was using for a desk. High Roman officers in Pannonia had almost identical tables. The Empire expected its commanders to read and write, which had always struck Arminius as strange.

But he didn't need to dwell on it now. Varus advanced on him with every sign of pleasure and clasped his hand in a grip firm enough to remind him the Romans were no weaklings even if they did care too much about their precious letters. "Welcome, welcome, three times welcome!" Varus said, and then, to Aristocles, "Why don't you bring us some wine?"

"We haven't got any, sir, not till they unload this convoy just coming in," Aristocles answered.

Arminius learned a couple of Latin phrases he hadn't heard before. Then Varus heaved a sigh. With the air of a man sacrificing on the altar of friendship, he said, "Well, bring us some beer, then."

"Yes, sir," Aristocles said, and, sensibly, not another word.

Arminius minded beer not at all. Why should he, when he'd drunk it since he was weaned? Before he could say as much, Varus spoke first: "This *ghastly* weather! We're lucky the wagons got here at all!"

"Yes, sir." Arminius said it, too. He suddenly wished he hadn't shaken off some of the rain. He wanted—he needed—to remind Varus how wet it was here. He swallowed his sigh. Too late to fret about it now.

And Varus went on, "You must love it, too—you're soaked."

"Rain happens at this season in these parts," Arminius said. Evidently he still looked soggy. "We go on as best we can. It is better on the far side of the hills. Not perfect, maybe, but better." He didn't want the Roman to expect too much, especially since there was no real difference in the weather up there.

"It couldn't be much worse," Varus muttered. Arminius didn't think that was true. Near the sea, it was definitely cloudier and rainier, with fogs that sometimes lasted all day even in summer. But Varus didn't need to hear such things.

Aristocles returned. He served the beer with as much ceremony as if it were finest Falernian. Arminius raised his mug in salute to Varus. "Health, your Excellency."

"Your health," Varus echoed. They drank. It was, Arminius thought, plenty good beer. The Roman governor sipped gamely. He didn't screw up his face the way his folk often did after tasting beer. "I've certainly had worse," he said.

"Nothing wrong with beer," Arminius said. "Not so sweet as wine, maybe, but nothing wrong with it."

Barbarian. Quinctilius Varus didn't silently mouth the word. Aristocles did. Arminius was more amused than affronted. Aristocles looked down his nose at Romans, too. To him, anyone who wasn't a Greek was a barbarian. The Romans had conquered his folk and ruled them for lifetimes? He himself was a Roman's slave, as much his chattel as the writing table? Details. Only details. They dented his conceit not at all.

Quinctilius Varus drank again, and again managed not to wince. "You must tell me more about the route we would take if we went north of your hills. A bad rain just as we were on our way to the river on the old route could ruin us. We'd bog down in the mire, and the wild Germans might swoop down and cause us no end of trouble."

"They do not understand that they and their children and their children's children will be better off under Roman rule," Arminius said. He didn't understand any such thing, either, but Varus didn't need to know that . . . yet.

The Roman governor beamed at him. "That's just it! They don't. Well, they'll come to see as time passes. Gaul needed a while to get used to things, but the people there are happy enough now."

"I believe it, sir." Arminius wasn't lying. Germans had a low opinion of Gauls. His folk had thumped them time after time till the Romans reached the Rhine—and, worse, crossed it.

If he could do what he wanted to do to Varus' legions, he didn't intend to stop there. How many troops would the Romans have left along the Rhine after a disaster in the heart of Germany? Enough to stop a triumphant army blazing with righteous rage—and hungry for all the good things Romans and Gauls enjoyed? Arminius didn't think so.

"Speak to my military secretaries," Varus told him. "Describe the route you have in mind in as much detail as you can. Tell them of the distances involved and of ways to keep the legions supplied on the march. If what you've been talking about seems at all feasible to the secretaries, to the crows with me if we won't try it on the way home this year."

"Your Excellency, I will obey you as if I were your own son," Arminius said. Varus' eyes went soft and misty. Arminius realized he'd come out with just the right thing. The Roman had talked about his son before, and how Arminius reminded him of the young man. Under most circumstances, Arminius would have taken that for an insult, not praise. As a matter of fact, he still did, but it was an insult he could use. Anything—anything at all—to make Varus trust him.

There stood Mindenum, an island of Roman order and discipline in the middle of Germany. Segestes eyed the encampment's ramparts from perhaps a mile away. "By the gods, I don't know why I'm bothering to do this," he said mournfully. "That fat, bald fool won't listen to me."

Masua gave him a sidelong glance. "*I* know why you're bothering," his retainer said. "You're a Roman citizen. You're a friend and ally of the Romans. If you walk away from a promise you made, what kind of friend and ally are you? Not the kind you'd want to be."

Segestes grunted. "Well, you're right. But it seems to me that this stupid Roman is walking away from me. Why he'd want to listen to gods-cursed Arminius . . ."

"Maybe he wants to stick it up his ass," Masua said. "Everybody knows the Romans enjoy those games."

But Segestes shook his head. "Varus likes women. He likes German women, in fact—all the gossip from Mindenum and Vetera says so. I suppose the ones he got used to in Rome seem little and skinny next to ours. No, he doesn't want to bugger Arminius. But he doesn't see that he's being played for a fool, either. I don't know why not, but he doesn't."

"He'd better wake up pretty soon, or he'll land in more trouble than he knows what to do with," Masua said.

"That's why I'm here—why we're here: to wake him up. We've got to try." Segestes sighed again. "Come on. We can't very well turn around after we've come this far."

High summer hung over the land, warm and muggy. The birds that had sung so sweetly in springtime were silent now. They'd found their mates and were raising families, so they didn't need to sing any more. Thinking of mates and families made Segestes think of Thusnelda. His right hand tightened on the spear he carried everywhere. His left folded into a fist. He would have warned Varus against Arminius even if Arminius hadn't stolen his daughter. *Of course I would*, he told himself.

And Varus might have been—probably would have been—more ready to listen to him if Arminius hadn't sneaked off with Thusnelda. Latin had a word for that: irony. Segestes hadn't understood the notion till this happened to him. He would gladly have gone without the language lesson.

"They see us," Masua said.

"Well, they'd better," Segestes replied with a snort. "If they fall asleep on the ramparts, they won't need Arminius to make them sorry they were ever born."

A legionary cupped his hands and shouted, "Who comes?"

"I am Segestes, a citizen of Rome," Segestes shouted back. "With me comes my friend Masua, also a Roman citizen."

The soldiers put their heads together. Segestes realized he was as welcome as a hornet. He'd known he wasn't in good odor among the Romans, but hadn't realized things were this bad. After a bit, a legionary seemed to remember he was there. "Wait," the fellow called, and then went back to the colloquy.

Segestes perforce waited. Time stretched. Time, in fact, dragged. What were they doing? Sending to Varus to find out if he'd deign to let in a couple of Germans? Standing there in the warm sunshine, Segestes decided they were doing just that.

At last, another legionary waved to him. "Well, come on, then," the Roman said grudgingly.

"Thank you for your gracious kindness." Segestes had learned enough from the Romans to appreciate irony. His own stab at it slid off the soldier like rain off the oily feathers of a goose.

"If they try and search us, by the gods, I'm going to break some heads," Masua said. Like Segestes, he carried a sword and a dagger along with his spear.

"They won't." Segestes sounded more confident than he felt. "An insult like that would turn even me against them, and they have to know it." The legionaries had to know, yes, but did they have to care? By all the signs, Quinctilius Varus cared very little for Segestes' feelings these days.

The sentries huddled again. Segestes would have bet they were wondering whether to frisk him and Masua. But, when the huddle broke, one of them said, "Pass on through."

"Thank you," Segestes repeated, this time more sincerely. He didn't want a row at the gate, but he too had his pride. He had more than Masua did, truth to tell. His comrade was a man of his sworn band, but he was a chief. If he let the Romans rob him of his pride, what did he have left? Nothing, and he knew it all too well. Fortunately, the issue didn't arise.

How many Roman encampments had he visited in his time? A great plenty of them—he knew that. Even Vetera, across the Rhine, still plainly showed it had grown from a camp. And Mindenum was one more. They varied in size, depending on how many men they had to hold, but they were all made to the same pattern. Once you'd learned your way around one, you could find what you wanted in any of them.

Here, Segestes found something he didn't want. Coming up the straight street toward him and Masua was Sigimerus. Arminius' father and Segestes were about of an age: a little old to fight at the front of a battle line, but both seasoned warriors. They stiffened. Segestes lowered his spear a little, but only a little. Inside the camp, Sigimerus wasn't carrying a spear. His sword came halfway out of its sheath, but no more than halfway.

Sigimerus greeted him: "You swinehound! You son of a swinehound!"

"Better a swinehound's son than a swinehound's father," Segestes retorted. "If I thought you were worth killing, I'd kill you now."

"Men better than you have tried," Sigimerus said. "Ravens and badgers tore them once they were dead, while I still live."

"I have killed, too," Segestes said. "After so many, one more—especially a nithing like you—is easy."

"You can't do, so you talk," Arminius' father jeered.

"You know more about idle talk than I ever will," Segestes retorted.

Romans gathered to watch the confrontation. They grinned and nudged one another. Segestes knew what they were doing: betting on who would come out alive, or on whether anyone would. Germans would have done the same thing. Also seeing that, Masua said, "You make a spectacle for them."

"I know," Segestes answered. He raised his voice to Sigimerus: "Let us go by. I didn't come here to kill you, no matter how much you deserve it."

"No—only to spit poison into the Roman governor's ear." But Sigimerus let his sword slide back down till the blade was out of sight. "Well, come ahead. Why not? No matter how many lies you tell, Varus won't listen to you."

Segestes feared that was true. It had been true every other time he tried to open Varus' eyes. But what kind of friend to Rome was he if he didn't make the effort? "Either you know nothing of lies or you know too much," he said. "Any man with his wits about him can guess which, too."

He started forward, Masua a pace behind him and a pace to the left, ready to guard his flank. Slowly and deliberately, as if to show himself no coward, Sigimerus stepped out of their path. "Watch yourself," Masua said loudly. "He may stab you in the back."

"I don't waste treachery on weasels like you two," Sigimerus said.

"No? You must save it for the Romans, then," Segestes said. Sigimerus haughtily turned his back.

Anywhere but here, Segestes would have attacked him for that offensive arrogance. He made himself walk by instead. Varus *wouldn't* hearken to him if he killed Arminius' father. He knew that too well.

The governor occupied what would have been the general's tent in any other encampment. Segestes had expected nothing different: that was where the highest-ranking officer posted himself. For better and for worse, the Romans were a predictable folk.

"Hail, Segestes. Hail, Masua," said Varus' Greek slave. Segestes took it as a good sign that the man remembered his comrade's name. He took it as another when Aristocles continued, "The governor will see you without delay."

"We thank you." Segestes had wondered whether Varus would try ignoring him without seeming to, keep putting him off with excuses, each plausible by itself but all together adding up to *I want nothing to do with you*. No German would play that kind of game; a German who didn't care to see him would come straight out and say so. But Segestes had enough experience of Romans to know they could be sneakily rude.

Not today, though. As promised, Aristocles led Segestes and Masua straight to Quinctilius Varus. The slave managed to disappear the moment Segestes took his eye off him. Segestes wished he hadn't, for one look at Varus' face told the German he'd done no good coming to Mindenum.

"What can you possibly tell me now that you have not told me time and time again?" the Roman governor demanded, his voice as cold and cutting as sleet.

"I could tell you you would have done better to listen to me before," Segestes said. "Your Excellency."

Varus flushed. He understood that what should have been a title of respect became one of reproach. "I do not believe that to be the case," he snapped.

"If no, the more fool you," Masua said in his halting Latin.

Varus did pretend he wasn't there. Speaking only to Segestes, the Roman said, "I am afraid you have wasted your time and are wasting mine."

"Will you say the same, sir, after I tell you warriors are gathering on the route Arminius wants you to use?" Segestes returned.

"I have had no report of this, not from friendly Germans and not from Romans, either," Varus said.

"I am not surprised," Segestes said. "It would be worth most Germans' lives to inform on your precious Arminius now. I know for a fact it has already been worth some honest Germans' lives. And as for your legions . . . Your Excellency, this is not their fatherland. They see what people want them to see. They hear what people want them to hear. Past that . . ." He shook his head.

"We are not so blind, nor so deaf, as you seem to think." Varus sounded as haughty as Sigimerus.

"You are not so wise as you seem to think, either," Segestes said.

"I shall have to be the judge of that," Varus said. "I do not believe you wish me ill, Segestes. I would not leave you at liberty if I did. But I do believe you have become altogether unreasonable about anything that has to do with Arminius. I believe you will blacken his name on any pretext or none. And so, as much as I regret to say it, I do not believe . . . you."

Segestes stood. Half a heartbeat later, so did Masua. "You may think you regret to say it now," Segestes told Varus. "The day will come—and I fear it will come soon—when you regret it in good earnest."

"Soothsaying?" the Roman governor asked sardonically.

"If you please," Segestes answered. "But a man does not need to read entrails to know a hanging stone will smash whatever lies below it when it falls at last. Good day, your Excellency. May your days be long.

They will be longer if you see you cannot trust Arminius, but I cannot make you do that. Only you can lift the veil from your eyes."

"I do not believe there is any such veil," Varus said.

"Yes. I know." Segestes nodded sadly. "A fool never believes he is a fool. A cuckold never believes his wife opens her legs for another man. But whether you believe or not, others do, by the gods."

"Farewell, Segestes," Quinctilius Varus said, his tone even more frigid than before.

"Farewell, sir," Segestes replied. "If we meet again in a year's time, you may laugh in my face. I will bow my head and suffer it as best I may."

"I look forward to it," Varus said.

"Believe it or not, your Excellency, so do I." Segestes left with the last word. He could have done without it.

XV

Heat came to Germany but seldom. When it did, as on this stifling late-summer day, it came with a thick blanket of humidity such as Mediterranean lands never knew. Sweating, itching, scratching, swearing legionaries tore Mindenum to pieces.

"Gods, I hope we never have to do this shitty job again," one of them said.

"Sure—and then you wake up," another Roman said with a scornful laugh. "We build 'em. We take 'em down. Then we build 'em one more time."

Quinctilius Varus nodded as he watched the legionaries work. That was what they were for, all right. They were beasts of burden, more clever and versatile than mules or oxen, but beasts of burden all the same.

"Well, I hope the stupid fucking governor makes up his stupid fucking mind one of these years," the first soldier said.

"Sure—and then you wake up," the other man repeated. This time they both laughed, the way men will when there's really nothing to laugh about but the only other choice is to go on swearing.

Somebody behind Varus laughed, too. The governor whirled angrily. Aristocles' face was as innocent as if he'd never heard anything funny in his life. Arminius and Sigimerus also might have been carved from mirthless marble. Varus fumed, his ears burning. Sometimes even a man of exalted rank could look ridiculous in front of his inferiors.

He pulled himself together. "We'll be ready to march soon," he told Arminius.

"Yes, sir. So I see," the German said. "Your men always do every-thing very smoothly."

"Roman efficiency," Varus said, not without pride. "I expect we'll show you more of it on the march."

"Oh, so do I," Arminius replied. "And I thank you for finally taking me up on the route I offered you."

Tall, wet-looking, anvil-headed clouds drifted across the sky. The sun played hide-and-seek behind them, but the day got no cooler, no less muggy, when it disappeared for a few minutes. Two days earlier, some of those clouds had let loose in a thunderstorm the likes of which Varus had seldom seen. For all he knew, they might do it again any time—when the legions were on the move, for instance.

"If the weather is better—drier—farther north, that's the way we want to go," he said.

Arminius nodded. "Oh, yes. It almost always is." He nudged his fa-ther and spoke to him in their guttural tongue.

Thus prompted, Sigimerus also nodded. "Weather better. *Ja*," he said in his dreadful Latin. The last word wasn't really, but it was one of the handful Varus had learned from the Germans' language.

"You will see the country I spring from." Arminius was far more fluent—far more civilized, when you got right down to it.

"Oh, joy. One more bloody flea-bitten pesthole in a land packed full of them," Aristocles said.

For a moment, Varus wondered why Arminius didn't draw his sword and try to cut the insolent slave in half. Then he realized the *pedi-sequus* had spoken with a straight face and mild tones—and, much more to the point, had spoken in Greek. To Varus, with his fancy education and years of service in the East, it was as natural as Latin. To a rude German, though, it would only be noises.

"Now, now," Varus said, also in Greek. "It's his, such as it is. Only natural for him to be proud of it."

"A swallow must be proud of a nest of sticks and mud," Aristocles retorted. "That doesn't mean I want to go out of my way to visit."

Arminius looked from one of them to the other. When neither offered to translate, the German shrugged his broad shoulders. Maybe he wondered if they were talking about him behind his back, so to speak. If he did, he didn't look angry about it, the way Varus thought a barbarian would be bound to do.

Clang! A legionary threw an iron tripod into a wagon. The Romans would bury more iron, but not where Arminius or any other German could watch them do it. They didn't want the savages digging up the metal and hammering it into spearheads and sword blades.

Things did go smoothly. And why not? The soldiers tore Mindenum down every year at this time. They'd had plenty of practice by now. Would they still wreck it at the end of summer twenty years from now? Or would they stay here around the year by then, to garrison a peaceful province? *If they don't,* Varus thought, *I haven't done my job.*

That led to another thought. *If I don't do my job, what will Augustus do to me?* Varus had already brooded about some of those possibilities. Disgrace. Exile. A desert island miles and miles from anything but another desert island. Even if he escaped all those, failure would bring Augustus' disapproval down on him, and Augustus' disapproval was colder than any blizzard on the Rhine.

I'd better not fail, then, he told himself.

"Did you ever hear it rains less up on the other side of the hills than it does down here?" Lucius Eggius asked Ceionius.

The other camp prefect shook his head. "No. But I never heard it rains more there than it does here, either. So that should be a wash. These Germans are like so many Syrian fig-sellers: they'll tell any kind of lie to get you to go their way. But I think it'll work out all right."

"Hope so," Eggius said. "This stinking trail sure isn't everything it ought to be. We had what was almost a proper path—not a real road, on account of it wasn't paved, but a path, anyhow—going straight west from Mindenum. This scrawny little thing isn't anything like it."

"It's all right as long as we're in the meadows. I just don't like it when it twists through the woods." Ceionius returned to his previous theme: "Don't worry about it, Lucius. Like I say, Germans lie all the time.

Do you know what that old fox of a Segestes said to blacken Arminius' name while you were out on patrol?"

"Tell me," Eggius urged.

"He said warriors were heading off to jump us somewhere." Ceionius laughed. "I'd like to see 'em try."

"I wouldn't." Eggius wasn't laughing. "I passed through a bunch of half-empty villages and steadings this summer. The old men who'd stayed behind claimed their fighters were off getting ready to go to war against the Chauci. If they were getting ready to go to war against us instead . . ."

"You always were more jittery than you need to be," Ceionius said.

"I've got more experience with the Germans than you do," Lucius Eggius replied. "No such thing as being too jittery around them. They always try to come up with sneaky new ways to screw us over. I'd better talk to Varus."

"He won't listen," Ceionius predicted.

That struck Eggius as much too likely. Even so, he said, "I'd better try."

"Don't say I didn't warn you," Ceionius warned him as he booted his horse forward. A stubborn man, Eggius nodded and pressed on.

He had a demon of a time catching up to Varus. The trail did dive into a forest. Tree trunks pressed close on either side. Marching legionaries could hardly squeeze in close to make way for him, no matter how he shouted and swore. Regardless of his rank, they swore back at him.

There was the governor's Greek slave, up on his donkey. And there was Quinctilius Varus himself, laughing and joking with Arminius. Eggius was no courtier, but even he could see this wasn't the time to beard Varus. As well tell a man his dog killed ducks while the beast was licking its master's hand.

Eggius sat his horse between two massive oaks till Ceionius finally came up. Ceionius eyed him. "You didn't say anything."

"That's right," Eggius admitted. "How could I? He had Arminius right there with him. You think he would have paid any attention to me?"

"No." Ceionius couldn't help adding, "Told you so."

"Ahhh—" But Eggius didn't say anything about the other officer's mother. You could do that with a close friend, but Ceionius wasn't one. He might think Eggius meant it, and things could end in blood if he did. "Maybe I'll try again later," Eggius said.

"Sure." Ceionius didn't believe a word of it. Since Eggius didn't, either, he couldn't even call him on it.

Arminius wanted to caper like a colt. He wanted to dance for joy. The Romans were doing exactly what he wanted them to do. If not for the training in duplicity they'd given him, he might have betrayed himself. He couldn't believe things were going this well.

The only person he could talk to was his father, and then only in tiny whispers at night in their tent. "Just don't get too excited, that's all," Sigimerus said. "It may not work as well as you hope."

"I know," Arminius answered. "Believe me, I know. But it may, too. And if it does, by the gods——!"

"Worry about it then." In his own way, Sigimerus was as practical as a Roman. "In the meantime, get some sleep."

Most of the time, Arminius would have had no trouble sleeping. What else could you do after the sun set, especially without a warm, friendly woman to keep you awake for a while? He could hear legionaries snoring in the encampment. He could hear mosquitoes buzzing, crickets chirping . . . and sentries exchanging password and countersign as they patrolled the rampart they'd built a few hours earlier. Yes, Romans were hard to surprise, curse them.

A couple of days later, Chariomerus rode up as the legionaries were readying the night's camp. Arminius' clansmate clasped hands with him and with Sigimerus. "What are you doing here?" Arminius asked the other German. He was ever so conscious of the listening legionaries, and hoped Chariomerus was, too. The wrong words, even in their own language, could mean disaster.

"When you left for Mindenum, you left Thusnelda with child," Chariomerus said.

Sigimerus allowed himself a rare smile. "I shall be a grandfather!" he exclaimed.

"If the gods grant it," Chariomerus said. "The confinement has been rough. The midwife is worried about Thusnelda—she fears her hips may be too narrow for an easy delivery. And Thusnelda wants nothing more than to see you again, Arminius."

"I would be there soon enough anyhow," Arminius said, frowning. "The governor counts on me to show him the way north and west."

"Go to your woman, son," Sigimerus said. "I am here. I can bring the Romans along as well as you can—I've known the way longer than you've been alive." He used his own tongue, as he almost always did. The legionaries would have wondered why he suddenly started spouting Latin with his son and the other German. Some of them would follow what he was saying now regardless of the language he used.

"I promised his Excellency that I'd do it," Arminius said.

"Go talk with him. Take Chariomerus with you. Let him tell the governor what he just told you. Varus will give you leave to go home. He is a fine man, an understanding man." Sigimerus spoke with a perfectly straight face. Arminius admired his father. He hadn't thought the older man could act so well.

He had to hide his own admiration. The Romans shouldn't see it. Dipping his head, he said, "I will do as you say. Come on, Chariomerus."

Arminius wasn't surprised when Aristocles greeted him with "This must be your fellow tribesman" outside of Varus' tent. News flashed through a legionary encampment quick as lightning, as it did through a German village.

"Just so." Arminius introduced Chariomerus to him, then went on, "He brings news from my home. We need to speak of it with his Excellency."

"Let me find out if he can see the two of you," the Greek slave said. Chariomerus looked worried. Arminius reassured him with his eyes. Aristocles always said things like that—they made him seem important. But Arminius was confident Varus would meet with him and Chariomerus.

Sure enough, when the *pedisequus* came back he beckoned them on without another word. Maybe someone could have made something of

Chariomerus' relieved grin, but Arminius didn't think so. Anybody would take it to mean that Chariomerus was glad he wouldn't have to waste his time standing around outside. If Arminius hadn't known the circumstances, he would have taken it that way himself.

"So your woman's got a bulging belly, eh?" Quinctilius Varus said after Arminius presented Chariomerus to him and told him the news.

"Yes, sir," Arminius replied. The Roman had a bulging belly, too, but only because he made a glutton of himself. Arminius went on, "My clansmate tells me she worries about her health. So does the midwife. And so Thusnelda wants to see me. I'd like to see her, too."

"There is the matter of guiding us along your much-praised route to the Rhine," Varus said.

"My father will stay behind with you and the legions, sir," Arminius said. "He told me himself that he knows the way better than I do." He smiled. "You know what fathers are like."

That proved a mistake. Mouth twisting, Varus shook his head. "Not of my own experience. My father . . . passed away when I was quite young." More to himself than to Arminius, he added, "He always clung to his ideals, even in the midst of civil war—and he paid for it."

"I am sorry, your Excellency. I did not know," Arminius said. Chariomerus murmured sympathetically.

"Thank you both. You are kind," Varus said. "You may go, Arminius. If your, uh, Thusnelda has a boy-child, I hope father and son will know each other for many years."

"You leave me in your debt, sir." Arminius knew how he intended to repay Varus, too. He eagerly looked forward to it. And yet, in an odd way, he meant what he said. He didn't hate Varus for anything the Roman had done, but because Varus *was* a Roman. For a German who wanted to see his land free, that was reason enough and more.

Varus wrote something on a scrap of papyrus. "Here. Give this to the sentries. They will pass you out with no fuss."

"Thanks again." Whatever shame Arminius might have felt, he made a point of stifling it. He and Chariomerus bowed their way out of the governor's presence. Chariomerus started to say something in their own language. Arminius sharply shook his head. To his relief, his comrade took the point and kept quiet. To have some sneaky Roman understand inopportune words now, when things were coming together . . . Arminius shook his head again. If the plans he'd spent so long laying fell apart because of something like that, it would be too much to bear.

Well, it wouldn't happen. The pass did help him and Chariomerus leave the camp easily. As Varus had promised, the sentries didn't fuss at all. The two Germans rode away. "Out in the free land again!" Chariomerus exulted.

Arminius didn't reprove him, not when they were out of earshot—and bowshot—of the legionary encampment. "Soon the whole land will be free again," Arminius said. "Very soon."

The middle of Germany. Three legions. No one dared approach the Romans or challenge them. Anyone foolish enough to dare would have died, either quickly and unpleasantly or slowly and unpleasantly, depending on the soldiers' mood. But having all the legionaries gathered together in one long, sinewy column reminded Lucius Eggius that everything around them was enemy country.

Whenever they passed by a steading or through a village, it seemed almost empty of warriors. Of course, most German steadings and villages seemed almost empty of everybody. The barbarians didn't want to meet the legionaries and make friends with them. Had an army of Germans come tramping through Italy, Italian peasants wouldn't have hung around to greet them, either. Peasants and soldiers were oil and water.

Eggius and Quinctilius Varus were oil and water, too. The camp prefect knew it. All the same, he caught up to Varus the morning after Arminius rode out of camp and said, "Talk with you for a little while, your Excellency?"

"You seem to be doing it," Varus answered coolly.

"Er—right." Eggius had guessed this wouldn't go well. Now he saw how right he was. Even so, he plunged on: "I sure hope that Segestes fellow didn't know what he was talking about when he said the Germans were getting ready to jump us."

"Oh, of course he didn't." Quinctilius Varus went from cool to irritable in less time than it took to tell.

Eggius sighed. "Yes, sir." You couldn't come out and tell a governor he had his head up his . . . But, oh, by the gods, how you wished you could! Since Eggius couldn't, he continued, "We still shouldn't take any chances we don't have to. Better to worry too much and not need to than to need to and not worry."

"I have nothing against the customary precautions. Do we neglect our encampments? Do we forget to post sentries?" Varus said.

"No, sir. But I was just thinking . . . maybe we shouldn't have come this way at all." There. Eggius got it out.

And it did no good. The governor stared at him. "Do you want to turn around and go back? For what amounts to no reason at all?"

"Might be safer if we did," Eggius said.

Varus stared at him as if he were something sticky and stinky on a sandal sole. "Yes, I suppose it might—if you believe Arminius to be a traitor and Segestes an honest man. *Do* you believe that, Eggius?"

To the crows with you if you do, Eggius. The camp prefect could hear what Varus wasn't saying as well as what he was. Picking his own words with care, Lucius Eggius replied, "Sir, I don't like taking chances any which way. If we don't have to, I don't think we ought to."

"Well, I don't think we are," Varus said. "And that settles it."

How right he was. When the governor of a Roman province decided something, the only man who could overrule him was Augustus. And Augustus was in no position to overrule Varus about this, even on the unlikely assumption that he would. Legions XVII, XVIII, and XIX were stuck with Varus' decision. Eggius just had to hope the governor was right.

Vala Numonius was waiting to see the governor when Lucius Eggius left Varus' presence. "Everything seems to be going well enough," the cavalry commander remarked.

Eggius eyed him with something close to loathing. "Easy for you to say," he growled. "If things get buggered up, you and your boys can gallop off. The rest of us, we're just in for it."

"Do you think we'd do that? Do you?" Vala Numonius sounded deeply affronted. "We're all in this together, and there's no reason to worry about any fighting. The Germans are as peaceful as they've ever been."

"Too peaceful," Eggius said. "His Excellency isn't worrying enough, if you ask me."

"I didn't. I'm sure the governor didn't, either," Numonius said pointedly. "Have you been dropping your own worries in his lap?"

If you haven't, I will. That was what he had to mean. Eggius glared at him, then shrugged. "Say whatever you cursed well please," he answered. "He won't hear anything from you that he hasn't heard from me. Maybe he'll even listen to you. I can sure hope so."

Numonius edged past him as if afraid he had something catching. Lucius Eggius knew too well he didn't. If the truth were contagious, it would have spread more. The cavalry commander was more likely to spread good, old-fashioned slander.

"I hope everything is all right, sir," Aristocles said as Eggius stormed out of Varus' tent.

"So do I," Eggius answered. "I wouldn't bet more than a copper on it, though."

Clouds piled up in the northwest, tall and thick and dark. The wind blew them toward the marching Romans. Quinctilius Varus' nostrils flared. If that wasn't the wet-dust odor of rain on the way, he'd never smelled it.

Curse it, Arminius had told him rain *wasn't* so likely in these parts. Varus looked around before remembering the German was off seeing to Thusnelda. Then Varus looked for Sigimerus. He didn't see Arminius' father, either.

He did see Aristocles, who, as usual, rode his donkey instead of a horse. And the Greek slave saw him, too. "Ah, your Excellency—?" he said, as insolently as a man could use an honorific.

"What is it?" Varus snapped—he could hear the testiness in his own voice.

As he'd known Aristocles would, the *pedisequus* pointed out the obvious: "I hate to say it, your Excellency, but it looks like rain."

"If you hate to say it, then keep your miserable mouth shut," Varus growled.

"I'm sorry, sir." Aristocles didn't seem to know whether to sound scared or hurt.

Quinctilius Varus sighed. Owning a man, holding his life in your hands, could make you feel pretty big. It could also make you feel pretty small if you struck at him for something that wasn't remotely his fault. Sighing again, Varus said, "Nothing you can do about the weather. Nothing anybody can do about it, worse luck."

"*That's* true, sir." Aristocles was nothing if not relieved. If Varus felt like striking out at him, what could he do about it? Nothing, as he had to know too well.

After looking around again, the Roman governor felt his frown deepen. "Have you seen Sigimerus lately?"

The slave's neck twisted as he too looked this way and that. "No, sir, I haven't. He's got to be somewhere, though."

"Everybody's got to be somewhere." This time, Varus looked up to the heavens. The clouds were darker and closer, the smell of rain more distinct. Unhappily, he clicked his tongue between his teeth. "But where the demon is Sigimerus right now?"

Aristocles made as if to peer inside his belt pouch, which drew a snort from Varus. "*I* haven't got him," the Greek said.

"Well, neither have I." Varus looked around one more time. No, still no sign of Sigimerus. He called to one of the Roman cavalrymen riding nearby: "Find me Arminius' father. I need to talk to him."

"Yes, sir." The rider sketched a salute. He told off two or three other horsemen of lower rank. They worked their way forward and back through the long column, calling Sigimerus' name.

"That'll flush him out." Aristocles might have been talking about a partridge hiding in the brush—or, given how carnivorous Sigimerus seemed, a sharp-clawed wildcat rather than a helpless, harmless, hapless bird.

Varus heard legionaries shouting "Sigimerus!" louder and louder and more and more insistently. What he didn't hear was Arminius' father answering. "Where could he have got to?" Varus said.

"He doesn't seem to be anywhere close by," Aristocles replied, which wasn't what the Roman governor wanted to hear.

A little later, the horseman Varus had first asked to find Sigimerus came back and said the same thing in different words: "Sorry to have to tell you, sir, but curse me if it doesn't look like the miserable bugger's gone and given us the slip."

"But how could he?" Quinctilius Varus' wave took in the thousands of marching legionaries. "So many of us, only the one of him."

The cavalryman shrugged stolidly. "Wouldn't have been that hard—begging your pardon, sir, but it wouldn't. Suppose he goes off into the woods a couple of hours ago. If anybody asks him, he says he's easing himself or something like that. But chances are nobody even cares. He doesn't mean anything to ordinary soldiers except for being one more nuisance they've got to keep an eye on."

"Well, why didn't they keep enough of an eye on him to notice that he didn't come out of the woods?" Varus demanded. The cavalryman's guess struck him as alarmingly probable.

He got another shrug from the fellow. He could figure out what that meant even if the horseman didn't feel like putting it into words. He himself might care about Sigimerus, if for no other reason than that the German was Arminius' father. Ordinary Romans, though, wouldn't be sorry if the barbarian disappeared.

"It wouldn't look so bad if he'd told you he was going off to keep Arminius company," Aristocles observed: one more thing Quinctilius Varus didn't care to hear.

"Shall we beat the bushes for him, sir?" the cavalryman inquired. "The boys'd like that—you bet they would. More fun than hunting a wild boar or an aurochs, even if we couldn't butcher him or roast him over hot coals once we caught him." He smiled thinly. "Or maybe we could, though we wouldn't eat him after he cooked."

Reluctantly—reluctantly enough to surprise himself—Varus shook his head. "No, better not," he said. "He may still have left for some innocent reason."

"Huh," the horseman said: a syllable redolent of skepticism.

"He may," Varus insisted. "And Arminius is a true friend. He wouldn't stay one if we hunted his father with hounds."

This time, the cavalryman's shrug suggested that he couldn't care less. Varus was surprised again—surprised and dismayed—when Aristocles shrugged exactly the same way.

Before the Roman governor could say anything, a drop of water splashed down onto the back of his left hand. He stared at it in amazement. Where could it have come from? *Well, you idiot, where else but . . . ?* Varus looked up at the dark and gloomy heavens. Another raindrop hit him in the right eye.

"So much for Arminius as weather prophet," Aristocles said, brushing at his cheek.

"He did warn me that he couldn't promise." Varus' voice sounded hollow, even to himself. Before long, it started to rain in earnest.

"Come on!" Arminius called. "You can do it! *We* can do it! And we have to do it fast, too!"

German warriors built slabs of turf they'd cut into a concealing protective rampart on a hillside. Arminius also cut and carried and stacked. When he said *we*, he meant it. He wasn't asking the men he'd called together to do anything he wouldn't do himself.

He made a point of being very visible as he labored. The warriors weren't from his small sworn band, or his father's larger one. Most of them weren't even Cherusci. They would have been battling amongst themselves if he hadn't persuaded them to try to deal with the Romans first. They might yet, and he knew it. He had to keep them loyal to him till the legions arrived. After that . . .

After that, he would either be the biggest hero Germany had ever known—or he'd be dead. Whichever way things turned out, he wouldn't have to worry about fractious followers after the fight.

"Arminius!" somebody called.

He threw his chunk of turf into place and waved a grimy hand. "Here I am!"

"They're coming!" the German said. "They're not far! And—"

Arminius didn't let him go on. He yelled, "They're coming!" himself. His voice reached all the working warriors. Some chieftains had that knack. Most Roman officers did. The Romans could teach a man how to make his voice bigger. Arminius had learned the trick from them.

How the Germans cheered! Suddenly, this seemed real to them. They could do it. They *would* do it. They were less steady than Roman legionaries, less steady even than Roman auxiliaries. But they had more fire. With the goal plainly there in front of them, they would work like men possessed. *For how long?* Arminius wondered. For once, the question answered itself. *For long enough.*

The messenger came up to him. "There's something more," the man said, in tones not meant for the rest of the men.

"What is it?" Arminius asked, also quietly.

"Your father is free of them," the other German said. He looked back over his shoulder. It had started to rain; he couldn't see very far. But he smiled as he turned towards Arminius. "In fact, here he is now."

"Father!" Arminius shouted.

He ran toward Sigimerus. The two big men embraced. Sigimerus peered through the raindrops at the growing rampart. He pounded Arminius on the back. "I did not think you could bring this off. By the gods, son, I did not. And, by the gods, I own I was wrong."

"We aren't finished yet," Arminius warned. "You know what they say about pricing the colt before he's born."

Sigimerus went on as if he hadn't spoken: "They'll come right past here. They have to—they've got no other choice. None. The track leads straight here. And if they go off it, they go into the swamp, into the mud. They don't know the secret ways through it—and those ways won't let them move that many men, either."

"Won't let them *deploy*." Arminius used the precise Latin word. "This is what we've been looking for all along."

"You found it," Sigimerus told him. "You said you had when we went up to talk to the Chauci, and you were right. And this mound——"

"*Rampart*." Again, Arminius used a Latin word in place of a less accurate one from his own language.

"*Rampart*," Sigimerus agreed indulgently. "You'll stick on leaves and branches and such, so they don't know what it is till too late?"

"Oh, yes." Arminius grinned. "You're thinking along with me, all right."

"You can talk about *deploying* and *ramparts* and all that fancy stuff as much as you want," his father said. "Just the same, you'd better remember I was ambushing Romans before you were born."

"Some people do need a head start." Arminius sounded as innocent as a child.

"Why, you miserable puppy!" But Sigimerus started to laugh instead of walloping him. "I'm among my own kind again! Gods, it feels good. And pretty soon——"

"No more Romans among us," Arminius finished for him. "If everything goes the way it should, I mean." No, he didn't want to price the unborn foal.

"Where are your warriors cutting those turves?" Sigimerus asked.

Your warriors. Arminius didn't answer for a moment, savoring that. It was as if his father had passed him the jeweled pin that closed a highborn man's cloak. Pride made his heart swell—and almost choked him. He had to try twice before he could say, "Over behind the hillock there." He pointed. "We don't want the Romans to notice anything wrong."

"You thought of everything." Sigimerus' eyes glowed. "Well, I'll go back there and cut some myself. I want to be part of all of this, even if it means fetching and carrying like an ox or an ass."

"I've cut them and carried them, too," Arminius said. "I feel the same way you do—and seeing me work hard makes the rest of the men work harder."

"That's one of the tricks, all right," his father agreed. "I hate to say it, but I was some older than you are before I figured it out."

"One more thing I picked up from the Romans," Arminius said. "Anybody knows fighters will follow a strong fighter. But in the legions and auxiliaries, any officer who works himself, no matter at what, can get his men to do the same."

"The Romans have taught us plenty of lessons," Sigimerus said. "Now we teach them one: they don't belong in our country. We've been trying to get it across since I was a little boy. This time, maybe . . ."

"Just one more thing we've got to do," Arminius said.

"What's that?"

"We've got to win."

# XVI

From behind Caldus Caelius came the usual racket of a Roman army on the march, somewhat muffled by the rain's dank plashing. Legionaries squelched through puddles on the track they were following. The ground to either side was worse—much worse. Chainmail clinked faintly. Like most of the other soldiers, Caelius had rubbed his mailshirt and helmet with greasy wool. That would help hold rust at bay, but only so much. He'd have a lot of scrubbing and polishing to do once the legions got back to Vetera.

Ahead? Through the rain, he could see a couple of horses' rumps, and also the glum-looking cavalrymen atop the animals. The way the riders' shoulders slumped said they wished they were anywhere but here.

As a matter of fact, Caldus Caelius felt the same way. That German who'd served with the auxiliaries over in Pannonia had told the governor this part of Germany had better weather than Mindenum did—so scuttlebutt insisted. As far as Caelius could see, the barbarian had sold Quinctilius Varus a bill of goods. It was coming down like a mad bastard.

Caelius stepped into a puddle—and went in deeper than he'd expected. He swore wearily. His voice was only one note in a massive grumbling chorus. The legionaries would complain marching on a paved road in perfect weather. Since this was neither, they groused and groused.

Water dripped from the visor of his helmet. Most of the time, it didn't drip onto his face. Every so often, though, the wind would swing and blow the drips—and the rest of the rain—into his eyes . . . and into his mouth, and onto his nose, so he had new drips from the end of it. With his feet soaked, too, chances were he'd come down with catarrh. *Just my luck*, he thought.

He shook his head, as much to look to right and left as to try to get rid of some of the water. Not much to see in either direction: only swamp that was starting to fill up with nasty little puddles. He didn't spot any Germans. He hadn't for some time now. Part of him was unsurprised—they wouldn't have wanted to live in this gods-forsaken country, either. But Germany was full—much too full—of savages. He'd seen worse terrain packed with big blonds trying to scratch out a living. Why weren't more of them doing the same thing here?

Maybe Varus could ask his pet German. As soon as that thought crossed Caelius' mind, he shook his head again, this time annoyed at himself. The accursed German was off dealing with his woman. His father had buggered off, too; nobody quite knew why. But it was unsettling. The neck-guard on Caelius' helm kept water from dripping down his back. He had that chilly, unsettling feeling all the same.

Something a little more substantial than usual in this marshy landscape loomed up ahead and to the left: a low, grassy hillock. Not just grassy, Caelius saw as the path brought him closer to it. Branches and bushes sprouted from it. Caelius wished he could get a better look, but the rain wouldn't let him. His mailshirt clattered about him as he shrugged. You could find anything in Germany. Why get all hot and bothered about one poorly manicured little hill?

It looks funny, a voice inside him said. He told the voice to shut up and go away. It wouldn't. *That hill doesn't look right*.

Caldus Caelius shrugged again, this time in exasperation. If anything were wrong, the horsemen up ahead would be catching it right now, as they rode past. And they weren't. They were riding along wishing they were somewhere else, the same way he was marching. At least their feet weren't soaked.

Something's wrong, the small voice shrilled. Ignoring it, Caelius pulled his left foot out of the mud and stuck his right foot into it.

Arminius peered out between two lovingly transplanted bushes. Roman cavalrymen rode by on their big horses, almost near enough for him to reach out and touch them. One looked his way. He froze. The Roman looked straight ahead again—he hadn't noticed a thing.

The gods are with us, Arminius thought jubilantly. To make sure they stayed on the Germans' side, he hissed, "I'll kill the man who casts now—d'you hear me? I'll gut him like a swine. Remember—you've got to wait."

Behind the rampart they'd built, the German warriors seethed like boiling soup. They jumped up and down, nerving themselves for the fight ahead. They brandished their spears. They brandished them, yes, but nobody threw one. They all understood what the plan was. And if that wasn't a gods-given miracle, Arminius didn't know what would be.

His own right hand clutched a spearshaft tight enough to whiten his knuckles. He was ready himself, ready and then some. But he too needed to wait. This was the one chance he'd have. He had to remember that. If he moved too soon, if the Romans got a chance to recoil and to fight on ground that gave them any kind of chance . . . In that case, who could say when his folk would be able to try again with the odds on their side? Who could say if they ever would?

More horsemen rode past, and more still. The Romans were going through the motions of protecting their van, but their leaders didn't really believe trouble was anywhere close. That attitude rubbed off on the men. They were laughing and joking and grumbling about the weather and bragging of what they'd do to the whores once they got back to Vetera. They weren't paying so much attention to what lay around them as they might have.

The rain did make it harder for them. On Arminius' side of the barricade rose a growing hum and murmur of excitement. He'd charged every leader here and in the woods off to the right—which held even more warriors—with keeping his men quiet. The chieftains were doing what they could, but it wasn't enough. Arminius fidgeted like a man with the shits. Killing wasn't near enough for the loudmouthed fool who betrayed his comrades because he couldn't shut up.

But the Romans never twigged. The drumming rainfall muffled the noise from the German host. *Truly the gods favor us*, Arminius thought. *When we conquer, we have to give them rich offerings indeed.*

He peered out again. The last Roman cavalrymen were going by. There would be a little gap, and then. . . . Oh, and then!

"When?" someone beside him asked. For a wonder, the other German didn't look out to see for himself. It wasn't Roman discipline—it wasn't anything close to Roman discipline—but it was more than Arminius could reliably expect from a man of his own blood.

"Soon," he answered. "Very soon." Here came the foot sloggers. Arminius waved. The chieftains were supposed to be waiting for that signal. They were supposed to ready the fighters who'd accompanied them and to pass it on to the men in the woods. Had Arminius been leading legionaries or auxiliaries, he would have been confident that what was supposed to happen really would. With his own folk, he could only hope.

Very soon indeed. He could see the Roman foot soldiers' faces through the rain. They looked less lighthearted than the riders. And well they might—they were doing the work themselves, not letting their mounts carry them along.

As soon as the first rank passed that bush . . . Arminius had promised himself that as soon as he came back from his long stretch lulling the Roman, lulling Quinctilius Varus in particular.

Idly, he wondered how things would have gone had Varus not had a son about his age. He shrugged. *I would have found some other way to do what wanted doing*, he told himself. Was it true? He thought it was, which was all that really mattered.

On came the legionaries. Closer . . . Closer . . . The nearest man in the lead rank had a long chin and a broken nose. Arminius' right arm went back on its own, as if freed at last from some unjust imprisonment.

"Cast!" he roared. His arm shot forward. Like an eagle, like a god's thunderbolt, his spear flew free.

Caldus Caelius kept staring at the little rise off to the left of the track. It just didn't look the way it should have. He'd tried getting some of the Romans near him to pay more attention to him. He hadn't had much luck. They didn't want to think about funny-looking landscape. All they wanted to do was get through this gods-despised muddy stretch of ground and make tracks for the Rhine. Since that was all he really wanted, too, how could he blame them?

When you got right down to it, he couldn't.

Somebody shouted something. It didn't sound like Latin. Caelius' head snapped to the left, toward that hillock. But the cry sounded closer than the reverse slope should have been.

He wasn't the only one who heard it. "What the demon?" another Roman said, his hand dropping to the hilt of his *gladius*.

Something sliced through the air. No—several somethings. No again—a swarm of somethings. For an instant, Caelius thought the cry had flushed a flock of birds, or perhaps even came from the throat of one of them. Only for an instant. Then, suddenly, horribly, he knew exactly what those somethings were, and he knew he and all the Romans with him had been betrayed.

The spears reached the top of their arcs. Some of them clattered together in the air. A few, knocked spinning, fell short. But most of them crashed down on the head of the Roman column.

Like his comrades, Caldus Caelius marched with his *scutum* slung over his back. The big, heavy shield would have been impossibly awkward on his arm. It was for battle, not travel. And so the shields did no good as the spears struck home.

One of the spears came down not half a cubit in front of Caldus Caelius' foot and stood thrilling in the mud. Another pierced the thigh of the legionary marching to his left. The man stared at the shaft and the spurting blood for a couple of heartbeats, more astonished than in pain. Then reality caught up with amazement. He shrieked, clutched at the spear and at his leg, and crumpled.

A soldier two men to Caldus Caelius' right took a spear through the throat. He made horrible gobbling noises, gore pouring from his mouth in place of words. Then his eyes rolled up in his head and he too slumped to the muck of the track the Romans were following. In a sense, he was lucky: he didn't suffer long before oblivion seized him. There were plenty of worse ways to go.

Caelius wished he hadn't had that thought. How many worse ways would he see before this day died? *And what sort of end will I find for myself?* he wondered fearfully.

He turned to find out how the rest of the soldiers were faring. The answer was simple: worse than he could have imagined in his most dreadful nightmare. That enormous volley of spears had wrecked the head of the column. Dozens—no, more likely hundreds; maybe even thousands—of legionaries were down, some mercifully dead, more wounded and thrashing and screaming their torment and terror up to the wet, uncaring sky. The agonized din made him want to stuff his fingers in his ears.

More cries came from the Romans' left. Those weren't wails of pain but fierce, triumphant bellows. The Germans realized what they'd done with their shattering volley. Well, they could hardly *not* realize it, could they? They might be barbarians, but they weren't stupid barbarians. They'd just proved that, by the gods!

They proved it again a moment later. They'd built ways to get up and over the curving rampart that concealed them. They dropped down on the near side and loped toward the legionaries. And they rushed out of the dark woods next to the rampart. Jove's thunderbolt could not have struck the Romans a harder blow than those deadly spears.

"Fight!" Caldus Caelius yelled, shrugging out of his pack and drawing his sword. "We've got to fight them, or they'll slaughter us like sheep! Deploy! Form line of battle!"

He wasn't the only legionary shouting orders like that through the wounded soldiers' howls and screams. Here and there, Romans did their best to obey. But the presence of their injured comrades not only demoralized them but also hampered their efforts to form up.

And, as Caldus Caelius rapidly discovered, even if that hadn't been so, there was almost nowhere for the Romans *to* deploy. When they stepped off the track to the right, they sank to their knees in muck. The ground to the left was a little better, but sloped swiftly upward toward the hillock from which the spears had flown—and down which the baying German horde now swarmed.

Along with a few unwounded comrades, Caelius set himself. The legions were ruined. Even a blind man could see that. The barbarians were going to slaughter every Roman they could catch. A few legionaries floundered out into the swamp, desperate to get away. Caelius might have done the same thing if it didn't seem so obviously hopeless. Since it did . . .

"Come on!" he shouted. "We'll make the whoresons pay for our hides, anyhow!" And if he made them kill him in battle, it would all be over pretty fast. Then they wouldn't have the chance to amuse themselves with him at their leisure afterwards.

Something hard caught him in the side of the head. A stone? A spearshaft? The flat of a sword? He never knew. Inside a heartbeat, his vision went from a red flare to blackness. He crumpled into the mud, his hands scrabbling feebly.

Quinctilius Varus and Aristocles were arguing in Greek about Plato's *Symposium*. It made time go by and helped Varus forget about the wet, gloomy German landscape all around.

"What *I'd* like to see is the *Symposium* on the stage," Varus said.

"It's not a play. It's a dialogue!" Aristocles sounded shocked. He was fussy and precise. To him, everything had one proper place—and one proper place only.

"It could be a play," the Roman insisted. "Aristophanes and Alcibiades are both wonderful roles, to say nothing of Socrates himself. You might—" He broke off and fell back into Latin: "By the gods! What's that?"

The color drained from Aristocles' face. "Nothing good," he answered. Numbly, Varus nodded. The two of them rode just in front of the baggage train, near the center of the long, straggling Roman column. That sudden eruption of shrieks and screams and wails from up ahead . . . It sounded like the noises from a slaughterhouse, but monstrously magnified.

No. Varus made himself shake his head. *Thinking such thoughts is a bad omen. I won't believe it. I won't let myself believe it.*

He kept on not letting himself believe it for five more minutes, maybe even ten. Then a bloodied legionary came running back toward him, crying, "We're buggered!"

"What do you mean?" Varus demanded. He feared he knew, but clung to ignorance as long as he could. Sometimes, as with a spouse's infidelities, not knowing—indeed, deliberately looking the other way—was better.

But the wounded Roman cried, "The Germans! There's a million Germans up there, your Excellency, and they're slaughtering us."

"No," Quinctilius Varus whispered. "It can't be."

It could. He knew that only too well. And if the barbarians had attacked the legionaries . . . If that had happened, then Arminius' infidelities were likely to prove far more lethal than any mere spouse's.

"What do we do, sir?" his *pedisequus* asked.

For a moment, Varus had no answer. Everyone from Segestes to Aristocles to Lucius Eggius had tried to tell him Arminius was not to be trusted. He hadn't believed any of them. He'd been sure he knew better than all of them put together. And they were right. And he was wrong. And, because he was wrong, because he'd trusted where he shouldn't, three Roman legions were in deadly peril.

No treachery since Helen of Troy's had caused this kind of slaughter. Being remembered with Menelaus was a distinction Varus could have done without. He hadn't even got to lay Arminius—or wanted to, no matter what some people thought.

"What do we do, sir?" This time, Aristocles and the wounded Roman soldier asked it together. They sounded more urgent that way—

more frantic, really. *A tragic chorus*, Varus thought, and wished he hadn't. He paused to listen to the racket from up ahead. It sounded worse than ever. Sure enough, the wounded man had told the truth. Varus couldn't imagine why the fellow wouldn't have; he could feel himself grasping for straws.

No time for that now. "We have to fight," Varus said. He pointed to the man who'd brought the news. "Tell the troops ahead to form line of battle and give the barbarians worse than they get. And tell them to remember they're Romans. We'll win this yet."

The wounded man set his hands on his hips, exactly as Claudia Pulchra might have done after Varus said something truly stupid. "Sir, they *can't* form line of battle," the fellow said, as if speaking to an idiot. "There's nothing but swamp on one side of the track, and nothing but howling savages on the other. That's got to be why the Germans picked this place to begin with."

Hearing that, Varus knew at once that it must be true. He also knew the depth of his own folly. How long had Arminius been cozening him, stringing him along, while at the same time drawing Germans from all over the province to this . . . this ambuscade? From the very beginning, probably. From before the beginning, even: why would he have taken service with the auxiliaries if not to learn how the Romans fought and how to turn what he learned against them?

"Your Excellency—!" If that wasn't desperation in Aristocles' voice now, Quinctilius Varus had never heard it. The wounded Roman shifted from foot to foot, too, as if about to piss himself.

Varus wondered why *he* wasn't more afraid. Maybe because, understanding that the worst had happened, he saw he couldn't do much about it now. If your only real choice was making the best end you could . . . that was what you had to do.

He drew his own sword. "Well, my dears, we shall have to fight," he said. "If we can't deploy, we'll take them on one by one, that's all." Something else occurred to him. "Oh—Aristocles."

"Yes, sir?"

"Don't get too far from me, please. If worse comes to worst"—even now, Varus wouldn't say *when worse comes to worst*—"I don't aim to let the savages take me alive. I'd appreciate a friendly hand on the other end of the sword, if you'd be so kind."

The Greek gulped. He couldn't very well misunderstand that, even if his expression said he wanted to. Licking his lips, he said, "If I have to, sir, I'll tend to it. I hope somebody will do the same for me, that's all."

"I think you may be able to find someone," Varus said dryly. That might prove his last understatement, but it surely wasn't his smallest.

Vala Numonius' head whipped around. Only a dead man could have ignored that sudden, dreadful racket. "By the gods!" a mounted officer near him exclaimed. "What the demon is that!"

Although the cavalry commander feared he knew, he didn't want to say the words out loud. Sometimes naming something could make it real where it hadn't been before. Maybe that was only superstition. On the other hand, maybe it wasn't. Why take chances?

And Numonius didn't have to. A man galloped up from behind him, crying, "The Germans! The Germans!"

"What about them?" Numonius knew the question was idiotic as soon as it passed his lips, which was just too late.

The man coming forward, fortunately, didn't take it amiss. But that was the only good news the cavalry commander had, for the fellow went on, "They're killing the foot soldiers, sir! Slaughtering them with spears!"

"We have to save them!" cried the officer who'd exclaimed about the awful noise.

"If we can," Vala Numonius said. The officer looked at him as if he couldn't believe his ears. Face hot with shame, Numonius realized the cavalrymen would have to make the effort. If he didn't order it, they'd mutiny and go back without him. Easier to lead them in the direction they wanted to go . . . if that didn't get them all killed. Vala Numonius licked his lips before he shouted, "Back! We'll do all we can for our comrades!"

Cheering, the horsemen turned and rode south and east, in the direction from which they'd come. Numonius drew his sword. Maybe the charge would frighten the Germans away. He hoped so. If it didn't, the Roman cavalrymen would have their hands full. Vala Numonius knew *he* would. With the sword in one hand, he would have only the other to use to hang on to his saddle grip. If his left hand slipped, he might go right off his horse's back.

Mounted spearmen were in the same predicament. They couldn't charge home with the full weight of their horses behind them. A rider would go over his mount's tail if he tried anything so harebrained. If only a man's foot could grip the saddle as well as his hands could! Numonius laughed at himself. Talk about harebrained! If there were a way to do something like that, someone would surely have thought of it by now.

Then the laughter died. Vala Numonius had imagined the Germans attacking the Romans, yes. But he'd never imagined such horrible swarms of them, all thrusting and ululating and having a grand old time. And he'd never imagined that the Roman cavalry wouldn't be able to stand off and ply the savages with arrows. In this rain, that was hopeless; a wet bow-string was as useless as no bowstring at all.

They would have to close with the Germans, then, if they were going to rescue their friends . . . if they *could* rescue them. How many thousands of barbarians were battening on the legionaries? Numonius led a few hundred horsemen; Roman armies were always stronger in infantry than in cavalry. Riders were fine for scouting and pursuits. For real fighting, you needed men on foot.

So the Romans had always believed, and centuries of experience had taught them they were right. Crassus' disaster against the Parthian cavalry a lifetime earlier was the exception that tested the rule. But what the Parthians had done meant little to Vala Numonius. They'd had an army of horsemen then. He had a detachment. He somehow had to beat an army with it.

Hoarse yells said the Germans saw the oncoming Romans. So did a shower of spears flying toward the Roman riders. A wounded horse screamed terribly. A wounded cavalryman added his shrieks to the din. The horse with a spear in its barrel staggered and fell, pitching off its rider. The animal just behind tripped over the wounded beast. The man atop it also flew off with a wail of dismay.

Numonius swung his sword at a German. Laughing, the barbarian sprang back out of range. In his excitement, the cavalry commander almost cut off his horse's right ear. The German picked up a fist-sized rock and flung it at him.

The fellow was too eager. Had he let Numonius ride past and then struck him from behind, he might well have brought him down. As things were, Numonius saw the stone hurtling toward him. He flattened himself against his horse's neck. The stone brushed his left shoulder as it flew by. He yelped, but it was an involuntary noise. A heartbeat later, he realized he wasn't hurt.

He also realized his cavalrymen wouldn't be able to drive the savages away from the Roman infantry. As the fight came to closer quarters, he saw how many legionaries in the front ranks were already down. *What* had the Germans done? Whatever it was, it meant that a whole great slavering pack of them had interposed themselves between his detachment and the surviving foot soldiers farther back. The riders hadn't the slightest chance of hacking through so many.

From behind, he slashed a barbarian who was about to spear another Roman horseman. The German leaped in the air in surprise, blood pouring from his right shoulder. He howled like a wolf. A Roman who saved a comrade's life in battle earned a decoration. Vala Numonius feared he wouldn't survive to claim it.

Sure as demons, the decoration was the least of his worries. A savage with a sense of tactics was shouting and gesticulating, trying to move his men to surround the Roman riders. Was that Arminius, who'd learned too many lessons from Rome? Numonius couldn't be sure, not through the rain. It seemed all too likely, though. So Varus was wrong straight down the line. He didn't do things by halves when he went wrong, did he?

Another German threw a spear that pierced Numonius' greave and bit into his calf. The wound wasn't nearly so bad as it would have been were he unarmored. He pulled out the spear and awkwardly threw it back.

Then the pain hit. The warm trickle of blood running down his leg joined the cold trickle of rainwater. Numonius couldn't even look down to see just how nasty the wound was, not unless he wanted to unstrap the punctured greave. He wanted nothing less. Suppose he got hit again!

That thought fanned the rising flames of panic inside him—and they already blazed high enough. High enough? No, too high. The torment of his wound and the sight of savages loping along to cut off his men made him shout orders that left the riders staring at him.

"Away!" he screamed. "Save yourselves! The legionaries are lost! Get away if you can!"

He wheeled his own horse and roweled it with his spurs. The animal squealed. It bounded off so powerfully, it almost threw him. But he clung to the handgrips like a burr. After a bit, the horse slowed some and steadied its pace.

Many cavalrymen fled with him. Some shot past him as if launched from a ballista. Maybe they'd get away. *Maybe I'll get away*, Numonius thought. The selfishness of fear made him forget everything else.

Other cavalrymen went on doing what they could for their comrades on foot. They had to know they were throwing away their own lives. Vala Numonius looked back over his shoulder. He saw the Germans pull a rider off his horse and, slowly and deliberately, shove spears into the man. He imagined he heard their hoarse, baying laughter. But it was only his imagination—he'd got too far away by then.

Maybe I will get away, he thought again as his horse bucketed north and west. *Maybe I will. Maybe. Please, gods. Just let me get away.*

Under his cloak, Arminius had an erection. The most beautiful, most sensual woman in all of Germany couldn't have roused him like this, not if she danced naked in front of him. To plan for years, to see all your plans not only come to fruition but turn out better than you ever dreamt they could . . . If that wasn't enough to put some fire in your balls, you probably didn't have any.

The Romans did things like that. One of the Latin words Arminius had learned in Pannonia was *eunuch*. The idea was enough to sicken him. To treat a man as if he were a stallion or a bull or a ram . . . The idea almost made his yard shrink. And one of the Roman officers down there had had such a creature for a slave. Seeing a eunuch, *hearing* a eunuch—that had put Arminius off his stride for days.

But he'd cut the ballocks off the Romans in Germany! *Curse me if I haven't*, he thought. He'd had a bad moment when the cavalry came back to try to rescue the legionaries. Too late for that, though! The Roman horsemen had figured that out themselves. Now they were running. Some of them might even make it back to the Rhine. But his folk would hunt most of them down before they could.

And if a few did escape . . . well, so what? Arminius nodded to himself. That could even turn out for the best. If the refugee Roman cavalrymen spread panic ahead of them, the Rhine garrisons might flee instead of fighting the Germans. In that case, Arminius would have an easier time taking Gaul away from the Empire.

He intended to do just that. He had a victorious army behind him. What else could you do with an army but use it? As long as he led it from one triumph to another, it would stay his. And as long as it stayed his, he could use it for whatever he wanted.

Germany needed a king. Germany might not know that yet, but he did. The Romans had done very well with one man telling them what to do. As long as the Germans followed scores of tribal chieftains and war leaders and petty kings, they'd waste most of their strength fighting one another. Led by somebody like Arminius, they could turn all that strength against foreign foes.

Led by somebody just like me, Arminius thought, nodding. He could do it. He was sure he could. After a victory like this, who would dare stand against him? But for himself, the strongest German king was Maroboduus of the Marcomanni, far off to the southeast. Everyone knew Maroboduus had stirred up the Pannonian rebellion to keep the Romans from invading his lands. That was canny, no doubt. But Maroboduus hadn't had the nerve to attack the Romans before they came after him.

I did! Arminius exulted. "I did!" he shouted, thrusting his sword up into the air.

A dying legionary groaned. Several Germans stared at Arminius.

"You did what?" one of them asked. He wore a shabby cloak held closed by a bronze fibula tarnished green. He was a nobody, in other words, and had probably never got close enough to Arminius before to have any notion of what he looked like.

"I brought the Romans here," Arminius answered. "I lured them to destruction!"

"Who do you think you are? One of the big shots?" The other German eyed his cloak of fine wool trimmed with fur, eyed the garnet-studded gold pin that closed it, and eyed the sword. Only rich men carried swords. The spear was the common German weapon. Grudgingly, the fellow went on, "Well, maybe you are."

"I am Arminius." Arminius wanted everyone to know who he was and how wonderful he was. Like the Romans, his folk reckoned a proud reputation one of the most important things a prominent man could have. What made you prominent, if not fame among your neighbors?

He impressed the unknown German less than he'd hoped. "Well, maybe you are," the man repeated. "But two other fellows already told me the same thing."

"Point them out to me, so I can kill them," Arminius snarled. No one would rob him of his glory. No one would cling to his good name and suck the blood from it like a leech in a swamp, either.

"Don't seem 'em now," the other German answered. Maybe he didn't. Or maybe he didn't care to watch a fight among his own folk. That might be wise. Arminius realized as much even before the poor man continued, "We ought to be killing these gods-hated Romans instead."

"Well, you're right. So we should," Arminius agreed. "Let's go do it."

A legionary down with a leg wound stretched out an imploring hand and called, "Mercy, comrade!" in Latin.

Most of Arminius' comrades wouldn't have understood the words, though they probably would have figured out the gesture. Also in Latin, Arminius said, "Here's all the mercy you deserve." He drove his sword into the Roman's neck. The man gasped and choked as life gushed from him, then slumped over to lie still.

Arminius knew he *had* been merciful. Already Germans were leading or dragging chained Roman prisoners away from the field. After the uneven fight finally sputtered out, they would offer the captives to the gods. How many interesting and unusual ways to kill legionaries would they find? All of them, Arminius was sure, would make harder deaths than a cut throat.

Here and there, individual Romans and a few stubborn knots of them still showed fight. Maybe they knew what would happen to captives and aimed to make the Germans kill them. Maybe, like brave soldiers anywhere, they were simply too stubborn to give up. Arminius admired their courage. But it would do them no good. They'd had no chance to form up, the head of their column was destroyed, and their foes had got in amongst them. If they wanted to die fighting, die they would.

Other Romans wanted to live. They stumbled out into the swampy mire that lined the track to the right. Quite a few of them got stuck in it. The Germans had a high old time throwing spears and stones at them. Men made bets with one another—who could hit the most Romans, or the ones farthest away, or who could hit a particular soldier with a particular cast.

A few legionaries managed more progress than the rest. Some were liable to get out of the swamp and have to be hunted on better ground. A few might even escape. Others staggered up onto higher, drier patches of ground within the swamp. A couple of those groups, perhaps led by hard-bitten underofficers, tried to ready themselves for defense. They would die in due course, too, but finishing them off might prove costly.

First things first. The Romans at the rear of their column hadn't even been attacked yet. Arminius shouted and sent more of his men after them. "Their baggage train will be back in that direction, too," he added. That got the Germans moving, all right. They did everything but slaver at the prospect of three legions' worth of booty.

"You don't fight fair," a wounded Roman moaned as Arminius trotted past. The German chieftain almost stopped and bowed. He couldn't imagine finer praise, even if the legionary hadn't meant it that way.

Something else struck Arminius. "Take Varus alive if you can!" he bawled. "We'll give him to the gods. They deserve to feed well for what they've done for us today. What would make them happier—what would make them fatter—than a fat Roman with the gall to call himself governor of Germany?"

How the warriors all around shouted and cheered! That acclaim tasted even sweeter than a woman gasping and quivering under Arminius. Most men could pleasure a woman. How many, though, ever won fame like this? As long as the German folk endured, men would remember Arminius. What greater immortality could a man claim?

"Come on!" Arminius said. "We won't just beat them. We'll slaughter them. They'll never dare set their toes on this side of the Rhine from now till the end of the world. In fact, we'll go take away their land on the far side!" The Germans cheered him again.

❦ XVII ❦

Lucius Eggius lurched through the mud. He had a nasty wound on the outside of his right thigh. Blood soaked the strip of cloth he'd tied around it and ran down his leg. It hurt like a bastard. So did several lesser gashes. It wasn't often given to a man to know the date of his own death. Though not dead yet, Eggius knew when he would die.

Today.

Soon, in fact. The only reason he wasn't already dead was that no German had decided to come after him instead of some other Roman and finish him off. At first, that had been nothing but luck. (Eggius was no longer convinced it had been good luck.) Later, after so many men fell in the first dreadful barrage of spears, Eggius not only stayed alive but fought back. He'd used his javelins. His *gladius* had blood on it, though the rain was washing that off. He'd made the barbarians pay for his tanned and scarred hide. And much good it had done him or anybody else.

Shrieks from the southeast said the Germans were still working their way through the Roman column. Under normal circumstances, a Roman army had a considerable advantage over a German army of the same size. Legionaries fought together, deployed together, and enjoyed all the benefits of superior discipline.

"Under normal circumstances," Lucius Eggius muttered bitterly. Amazing how three words changed everything!

The Romans couldn't deploy here. There was nowhere to deploy; except for the road, everything was muck and trees. The legionaries couldn't form a shield wall to ward themselves against enemy spears while they hurled their own javelins. A horrific number of them had died or been put out of action before they ever got their shields off their backs.

Off to Eggius' left—deeper in the swamp—whooping Germans slaughtered a small knot of Romans who'd managed to put up a bit of a fight before they died. That was about as much as the legionaries could manage.

It wasn't just the terrain. This battle was lost, and catastrophically lost, the instant the barbarians' first spears flew. Three legions were getting massacred not least because they couldn't believe what was happening to them. Too many men were too dumbfounded even to try to fight back. And their fall only made their fellows' predicament worse, which dumbfounded *them*, which led to. . . .

It led to Lucius Eggius calf-deep in clinging ooze. It was liable to lead to three legions wiped out almost to the last man. It was liable to lead to three legionary eagles being lost. Eggius' jaw dropped. Even after everything that had happened and was happening, that thought only now crossed his mind for the first time. Legionaries guarded the eagles with their lives. They would rather die than let an enemy seize the sacred symbols of their trade.

They were dying, all right, whether they wanted to or not. And once they finished dying, Arminius would have the prizes he must have craved all along.

Even thinking of Arminius made Lucius Eggius spit in the mud in disgust. Thinking of Arminius also made him think of Publius Quinctilius Varus. He spat again, harder this time. "As soon as the vulture gets done with Prometheus' liver, it can start gnawing on Varus'," Eggius growled.

He'd tried to warn the governor of Germany—now *there* was a title that had just turned into a monstrous joke!—about Arminius. So had gods only knew how many other Roman officers. Varus didn't want to listen. His rank meant he didn't have to.

So he didn't. And now he was paying for not listening. And so was everybody else.

Eggius limped toward some trees. If he could hide among them till the fighting stopped and the Germans went away, maybe he'd be able to sneak back toward the Rhine later and. . . .

He laughed. In spite of everything, the idea was funny. He didn't think he could make it to the trees. If he did, he didn't think he'd be able to hide for long. And even if he concealed himself, he didn't think he'd ever see the Rhine again.

A guttural shout. A tall blond man pointing at him. Four more barbarians coming along the edge of the track toward him. Two of them carried spears, one a captured Roman *gladius*, and one a *gladius* and a spear. One of them had a cut on his left arm. The other three seemed unwounded.

They would, Eggius thought as he turned and tried to find the best footing he could. Sure as Hades' house, he wasn't going to reach those trees. But at least he could—he hoped he could—make the Germans kill him. You didn't want them to take you alive. Their gods were thirsty for blood, and captives fed them.

"Surrender!" one of the barbarians yelled in Latin. Eggius shook his head.

"You don't surrender, you die," the German warned, shaking his spear.

"Now tell me something I didn't know," Eggius answered. The barbarian only scratched his head. That must have been more Latin, or harder Latin, than he could deal with. But he didn't have to deal with it. He had the brute simplicity of sharp iron on his side.

He flung the spear at Eggius. The Roman ducked. The spear grazed his left shoulder as it flew past. The German jumped up and down, shouting something hot and guttural. Plenty of spears lay on the ground, though. He picked up another one and jumped into the muck, heading purposefully after Eggius. Two more savages followed him. They grinned and laughed in anticipation.

Grimly, Eggius set himself and waited. He couldn't outrun them, not with his leg wound. He had to make the best fight he could. In other words, he was about to die.

He didn't want to. But soldiering had long since shown him you had to do all kinds of things you didn't want to. One certainty: once he did this, he wouldn't have to worry about anything else.

That lead German thrust at him. Eggius twisted to one side and stepped forward—he still had one quick stride in him, anyhow. His *gladius* pierced the barbarian's belly. The man looked absurdly surprised as he crumpled. Eggius twisted his wrist to make sure the stroke cut guts and killed.

Even before he could clear the sword, the other two Germans speared him. He'd known they would. Nothing to be done about it. He screamed—no dignity when you died, none at all. He fell on top of the barbarian he'd taken with him. After a while—not nearly soon enough—the pain faded and the torch of his life went out.

The baggage train! For many of Arminius' Germans, the chance to loot three legions' worth of booty was the only reason they'd joined his force. So many things here, all in one place! Traders from inside the Empire would have charged more for them than any ordinary man could hope to pay. But now anyone with a spear could take away as much as he could carry. Ordinary men could get their hands on things chieftains would envy.

By the time Arminius got to the baggage train, a lot of ordinary men were drunk. One of the things the Romans carried with them was their wine supply. In a close-run fight, that might have meant disaster. As things were, it only served to make them fiercer and, at the same time, more foolish.

Laughing like a loon, a shaggy-haired warrior capered in a transparent silk tunic some high-ranking Roman must have bought in Mindenum and been bringing back to Vetera for his ladylove. The change must have been easy for him, because he'd worn nothing underneath his stout wool cloak. He'd had nothing else to wear. He shook his hips at Arminius. "Aren't I gorgeous?" he bawled.

"Don't tear that cloth," Arminius told him—the big man seemed about to burst from the tunic in several different places. "Have you got any idea how much it's worth?"

"Why should it be worth anything? It's hardly here at all." The warrior put a hand under the fabric to show what he meant. "You can see right through it."

Patiently, as if to an idiot child, Arminius said, "That's why. Imagine it on a woman. Imagine it on *your* woman."

"Ohhh," the other German said in a low voice. Because the silk was so transparent, Arminius could see exactly what he thought of that. He liked the idea. Arminius had thought he might. No doubt much more carefully than the fellow had put on the tunic, he took it off again.

Several dozen Romans from the rear of their column—the part that hadn't been so irretrievably shattered—counterattacked then. They had it all their own way for a moment, because the plundering Germans weren't expecting anything like that. The legionaries fought with the desperation of men who had nothing to lose. They had to know they wouldn't get away. They were just trying to sell their lives as dearly as they could, and doing a good job of it.

In their *caligae*, Arminius would have done the same thing. As it was, he pushed his own men into the fight, and went into it himself. He didn't want to be seen—he couldn't afford to be seen—hanging back. He thrust with his spear and then, after some Roman's sword stroke shattered the shaft, he slashed with his sword. Red drops flew from the blade every time he swung it.

One of the legionaries recognized him. "You traitor dog!" the man shouted. "If I can drag you down to Pluto's house in the underworld, I will!"

His *gladius* flicked out, quick and deadly as a striking viper, but Arminius wasn't there to take the stroke. Quick and deadly himself, he danced away, then returned to the fight. His sword thudded off the legionary's shield. The man was good; if he hadn't been good, he would have died a while ago, on this field or on some earlier one.

No matter how good you were, though, nothing saved you from one German when another one tackled you from behind. The legionary let out a despairing wail as he went down. The wail cut off abruptly when Arminius' sword descended on the back of the Roman's neck. The stroke hewed halfway through; the legionary's whole body convulsed. Arminius hacked again, then picked up the man's head and waved it about.

"That was well struck!" the other German said, nodding to him. "Want to share the bugger's stuff?"

"You can take it," Arminius answered. "I have plenty."

"Obliged," the other man said. "I think his mailshirt will just about fit me. Sandals, too. The Romans make good stuff. Why can't we do more things like that?"

"I don't know," Arminius said. "But they didn't know how to win this battle—we did. That counts for more, because now all the good stuff they made is ours."

"Sure is," the other warrior agreed. "Get right down to it, and that's what counts most."

"That's what counts for everything," Arminius said. He looked around. Things seemed to be under control. The counterattacking Romans had done as much as flesh and blood could do—and now almost all of them had met the universal fate of flesh and blood. The last few still on their feet kept fighting hard. They wanted to make the Germans kill them outright, and it looked as if they would get their wish.

Which reminded Arminius . . . "Where is Varus?" he asked. But the question answered itself. Anybody who'd seen one Roman marching column had seen them all. The commander always placed himself in the same position: not far ahead of the baggage train.

Arminius' grin was gleefully feral. How he wanted to take the Roman general alive! How the gods would love to drink Varus' blood, to savor his screams as he died a digit's width at a time. How Arminius himself wanted to gloat in Varus' face. The Roman, fool that he was, had trusted him. How you could trust anyone who wasn't your closest kin . . . Well, Varus had done it. And he'd paid, and Rome had paid with him. Rome would go right on paying for generations to come. Varus wouldn't last that long.

The last legionary from that counterattacking band went down, a spear through his throat. He'd got himself a quick end. On this field, that made him one of the lucky ones. Arminius didn't want Varus to share his luck.

"Come on!" he called to the Germans around him. He pointed forward. "Let's go grab the Roman general!"

That drew less eagerness than he'd hoped. "Why bother?" one of them said. "He'll get killed pretty soon any which way. And the plunder's bound to be better here. The plunder here is better than anything!" Several other warrior solemnly nodded.

"We have to make sure," Arminius insisted. "Besides, I want him alive. The gods in the sacred grove deserve their fair share of his suffering."

A few of the men nodded, but only a few. The fellow who preferred looting said, "If the gods want him taken alive, they'll fix it so he is. They don't need us to do it right now."

"I've got another reason for you to come with me," Arminius told him.

"Oh? What's that?" the other German asked.

"I'll cut your lazy, cowardly heart out if you don't," Arminius said.

He braced himself, wondering if he'd have a fight on his hands in the next instant. The other German said, "I've killed enough Romans so no man can call me a coward. Lazy? Why not? Only a fool or a slave works harder than he must."

Since Arminius felt the same way, he had trouble arguing with that. The Romans wouldn't have agreed; they'd done great things with hard work. But what had it got them in Germany, here at the end? Only death, three legions' worth of death.

"Come with me, then," Arminius said. "Kill some more Romans. That still needs doing. And if you do it well, I'll reward you from my own share of the booty."

"Now you're talking like a man!" the warrior exclaimed. "Let's go!"

Others came with them, too. Even so, Arminius noticed fighters sidling off so they wouldn't have to quit stealing. He swore at them, but sometimes there was no help for a situation. And the men he did have would probably be enough.

They had to shove their way through more plundering Germans. A couple of times, they almost had to fight their way through their countrymen. Yes, the baggage train drew his folk the way nectar drew bees. And, here and there, small groups of legionaries kept on fighting. A few of them, as mad for *things* as the Germans, seemed to be defending their personal property. Much good it would do them when they were dead! And dead they were, in short order.

But the sun was sinking in the west. Days were shorter than they had been in high summer. Some Romans might escape in the coming darkness. If Varus turned out to be one of them, Arminius promised himself he would kill the warrior who'd delayed him by talking back. That bonehead might not know what was important, but Arminius did.

Another determined group of Romans: determined enough to die on their terms rather than those of the Germans, anyhow. If that was what they wanted, Arminius and his comrades would oblige them. He struck and slashed like a man possessed. He split a *scutum* clean in half with a sword stroke, which was supposed to be impossible. The Roman holding what was left of the shield reeled away, terror and awe on his face. Arminius sprang after the fellow and cut him down.

"A god has hold of him," one of the other Germans said to another. The second warrior nodded. That was what possession meant, wasn't it?

Arminius didn't think he was in a god's clutches. He just wanted Varus. Anything that stood between him and the Roman had better watch out. And, since the legionaries standing in the way couldn't watch out, they fell, one after another. How much time had they bought their commander? Too much? It had better not be too much!

"Onward!" Arminius roared, hoping he wasn't too late.

Night was falling, literally and figuratively. When the end came, the best you could do was face it with style. Publius Quinctilius Varus looked around. The end was coming, all right. The end, in fact, was just about here.

An officer with wild eyes and with gore from a missing right ear splashed all over that side of his mailshirt staggered out of the ruination ahead. Varus was shocked to recognize Ceionius. The military tribune had always been so neat, so spick-and-span. No more, no more.

"Let's surrender, your Excellency!" Ceionius cried. "If we give up now, maybe the Germans will let us live!"

Even at the end of all things, some people could still cling to illusions. Varus had clung to his much too long, but he was free of them at last. As gently as he could, he shook his head. "It's no use any more," he said. "We might as well fight as long as we can."

"But——" Ceionius said.

"No." Quinctilius Varus cut him off. "Do as you please for yourself, and good luck to you. But the legions will not surrender."

"You cursed stupid old fool!" Ceionius shouted. Varus bowed his head, accepting that. With a howl of despair, Ceionius dashed off toward the swamp. Maybe he'd get away. Maybe he'd find a German who would take his surrender and let him live as a slave. Maybe——but Varus didn't believe it for a moment.

An embattled centurion not far away shouted for men to go forward and hold off the barbarians a little longer. Quinctilius Varus took him by the arm. The man jumped. His sword twitched, then stopped. Varus realized he'd almost died a little sooner than he'd intended. Well, what difference would it have made? Not much, not now.

He said what he needed to say to the centurion: "I'm sorry. I made a mistake, and we're all paying for it. My fault—no one else's. I *am* sorry."

"Too late for that, don't you think?" the other Roman growled.

"Too late for everything," Varus agreed.

"Ah, bugger it," the centurion said. "Too late for everything is right. What do you aim to do now?"

"Die," Varus said simply.

"Want me to do the honors?"

"My slave will attend to it," Varus replied. "But if you'd be kind enough to take him off quickly after I'm gone, I'd be grateful, and so would he."

"I'll tend to it," the centurion promised. "And then I'll look for somebody to do the same for me."

"Thanks," Varus said, and then, raising his voice till he sounded almost gay, "Aristocles! I've found someone to kill you!"

"Oh, thank you, your Excellency!" Relief filled the little Greek's voice. "Better one of our own than . . . this."

His wave took in the madness all around them. The Germans would have assailed them sooner, but a whole great swarm of the barbarians were plundering the baggage train, which wasn't far behind. Some of the Germans guzzled wine. Others stuffed themselves with barley bread. Still others led off pack horses and murdered the slaves who'd tended them. All the barbarians seemed to be having a rare good time.

Here and there, small groups of Romans fought on. But there was no room for the legionaries to make war as they usually did, and the Germans, who were used to fighting as individuals, had all the better of it.

"I'll be glad when I'm dead," the centurion said. "Then I won't see the savages steal our eagles."

"I'm sorry," Varus said again. He knew what the eagles meant to the men who served under them. Three legions were going down here. Was it any wonder their eagles would be lost?

A spear flew through the air. It pierced the soft ground and stood quivering only a few cubits from Varus' feet. Aristocles said, "Not meaning to rush, sir, but I don't think we should wait much longer."

"No, no. Neither do I. If anyone here ever sees Augustus, tell him I'm sorry, too," Varus said. He drew his sword. He'd never used it in war here—the first blood it would drink in Germany would be his own. He handed it to his *pedisequus*. "Here you go, Aristocles. I daresay you've dreamt of doing this for years. Strike hard!"

If Varus had little experience with the sword, Aristocles had none. A slave—a slave who wasn't a gladiator, anyhow—caught with a blade commonly died a cruel death. Rome had seen too many slave uprisings and plots for anything else to seem safe. And so the skinny Greek held the blade as if it were a kitchen knife—and as if he didn't know what to do with kitchen knives.

Sighing, Varus pulled up his tunic and ran his forefinger between two ribs on the left side of his chest. "Put it here and stick it in," he said, as if he were a girl helping an eager boy lose his cherry. But you only did this once.

Aristocles set the sword in place. He gulped. He closed his eyes. With a horrible grimace, he shoved it forward.

It hurt. It hurt like nothing Varus had ever known before. He knew a certain pride that he didn't pull away from the blade. He couldn't help shrieking, though. When the sword came out, he fell to the ground and waited for the end.

It took longer than he'd hoped it would. From what he'd seen, dying always took longer than you hoped it would, and hurt worse. Blood filled his nose and mouth. He felt as if he were suffocating, but he was really drowning, drowning from the inside out.

Aristocles screeched. The centurion had struck him down from behind, by surprise. That wasn't so bad. But, as Varus' vision faded, he saw that the soldier needed a second stroke to finish the job. *That* wasn't so good. But Aristocles was in no position to complain. And, after a bit, neither was Varus.

Arminius hadn't slept for a day and a half, maybe longer. Excitement kept him going. He wondered if he'd ever sleep again.

It was all over now. Well, close enough. The Germans still hunted Roman stragglers through swamps and woods and fields. Sooner or later, they'd track down most of them and kill them. A few might get away. Arminius had stopped worrying about it. They would spread fear ahead of them, spread it all the way into Gaul. And behind the fear would come . . . Arminius.

Three legionary eagles lay at his feet. He knew what the eagles meant to Roman soldiers—knew as well as any German could, anyhow. They defended those eagles to the death. They had defended these eagles so, and now they were dead.

Varus' head lay at his feet, too. Varus was also dead by the time the Germans found him and took it. His scrawny slave had lain dead beside him. That disappointed Arminius. He'd wanted to offer them to his gods after they watched him offering plenty of other Romans. He shrugged. You couldn't get *everything* you wanted. He had more than enough.

A German carrying a wine jar from the Roman baggage train staggered past. He gave Arminius a sozzled grin. "Good!" he said, his broad, extravagant wave taking in—well, everything.

"Good," Arminius agreed. And so it was.

More Germans led lines of captured legionaries, their hands chained, off toward the oak groves where they would be sacrificed. Even now the dying cries of men being offered to the gods rose in the distance. His folk often worried about whether the gods got enough to eat. They wouldn't have to worry for a long time, not after the bounty the gods were enjoying now.

Here and there, two or sometimes four Romans carried an unconscious comrade toward the sacrificial groves. Nobody wanted to waste any of this enormous feast for the gods. If a man still breathed, his spirit was nourishment.

Sigimerus came up to Arminius and bowed before him. "You did it," he said. "You truly did."

"Germany is free," Arminius said. "The Romans will never dare stick their noses across the Rhine again. We'll visit them on their side before too long."

"I do believe we will." His father sounded almost dazed at the size of their triumph. "And after that . . ." He shook his head. Plainly, he couldn't imagine what might happen after that.

Well, neither could Arminius. But he was sure he would think of something when the time came.

When Caldus Caelius came back to himself, he thought he was dead and being punished in Tartarus. His head ached as if it had been smashed to pieces—and so it nearly had. He needed a little while to realize he might have been better off if he were already dead.

He tried to raise a hand to his throbbing brow. Both hands came up—they'd been chained together. The links between the manacles clanked as they moved. Why would anyone have . . . ? Slowly, realization returned. "Oh," he muttered. "The battle. We must have lost."

If you lost a battle to the Germans, what happened next? No sooner had that thought crossed his mind than he got an answer of sorts. A shriek rang out that made him wonder if he hadn't been right when he first regained consciousness. Maybe he really had landed in a realm of eternal punishment.

No matter how much his battered head hurt, he made himself turn it so he could see where that shriek came from. A moment later, he wished he hadn't. Several Germans were holding down a legionary—the luckless Roman was also chained, just like Caelius—while another barbarian slowly and clumsily decapitated him. The screams subsided into a gurgling wheeze. Blood poured out onto the damp ground and spattered all over the Germans.

At last, the sword—it was a Roman *gladius*—found its way between two neck vertebrae. With a grunt of satisfaction, the German held up the dripping head. To Caldus Caelius' horror, the head wasn't just dripping. Even after it was severed from its thrashing body, it blinked several times before its eyes finally sagged shut. Its mouth might have tried to shape a word. Caelius hoped that was his imagination, but feared it wasn't.

The other Germans congratulated the one who'd done the beheading. He grinned and shuffled his feet as if he'd never deserved such praise before. Then he carried the Roman soldier's head over to one of the nearby oaks. He used a leather thong to tie it to a low-hanging branch. Other legionaries' sightlessly staring heads already hung there. Still others were spiked to the trunk. Nor was that the only tree sprouting such fruit. The whole grove was full of butchered Romans. The iron stink of blood clogged Caelius' nostrils.

And things only got worse. Along with heads and other pieces of legionaries hung the eagles of Legions XVII, XVIII, and XIX, as well as the lesser emblems from the cohorts that made up the beaten legions. Seeing them there, offerings to the grim German gods, wounded Caldus Caelius almost as much as the rest of the atrocities put together. He wished he could die of shame. He wished he could die any way at all, so long as it happened fast.

A big German came over and looked down at him. The man wore a legionary's helmet at a jaunty angle and carried a legionary's shortsword in his right hand. And he proved to speak Latin, too, for he said, "You are the one called Caldus Caelius, eh?"

"That's right," Caelius answered automatically. "Who the demon are you?"

"My name is Ingaevonus," the barbarian answered. "Do you remember me?"

Caelius started to shake his head. Then he stopped, not only because it hurt but because he did remember. "That village," he croaked.

Ingaevonus nodded. "Yes. That village. *My* village. Taxes." He spat the word out through his mustache. "We do meet again, eh?" He thoughtfully hefted the *gladius*.

"Yes." Caldus Caelius forced the word out through dry lips. He didn't want to show fear, though the barbarian had to know he felt it.

"I kill you," Ingaevonus said. "I kill you slow, Roman. I kill you nice and slow, Caldus Caelius. I go think how to do it, then I come back, eh?" He ambled off, testing the sword's edge with his thumb. Over his shoulder, he added, "Won't be long."

Not nearly far enough away, another legionary started screaming for his mother. The Germans were gutting him, the way they might gut a slaughtered boar. But they hadn't slaughtered him first. They drew out his bowels a few digits at a time, laughing as they worked. The legionary kept on screaming. One of the barbarians had a new idea. He cut again, lower. The Roman wailed again, higher. The German stuffed what he'd cut off into the man's mouth to muffle the noise.

Caldus Caelius shuddered. His chains clanked again. If Ingaevonus needed ideas . . . "Not me," Caelius muttered hoarsely. "He wouldn't do that to me." But how could he possibly stop the barbarian?

If the Germans wanted to, they could have done it to him already. They seemed to be picking most of the men they tormented at random.

A savage would point at a Roman, a couple of others would seize him, and then they would set to work to see how much horror they could pack into the end of his life.

No one had pointed to Caelius yet. But Ingaevonus would, and soon. Maybe they'd waited for him to come to. They did prefer their victims aware and suffering till the end.

"Not me," Caelius whispered again. If he'd had a sword, he would have fallen on it. If he'd had a dagger, he would have hoped it could reach his heart, or else slashed it across his throat. If . . . But what he had was a head already half shattered and a stout set of manacles and chains.

And then, amidst the stench of blood and the worse stench of terror, sudden mad hope flowered in him. If he could use the manacles to finish the job of crushing his skull . . . But what if he couldn't? His laugh sounded more than a little mad, too. If he couldn't, how was he worse off?

He pulled himself to a sitting position. That drew the Germans' notice, as he'd feared it would. One of them shouted for Ingaevonus. Three more strode toward him, anticipatory grins on their faces. *Now or never* flashed through his mind. He smashed at himself with all his fear-fueled strength. The last thought he ever remembered having was *I hope I spoil their fun.*

Vala Numonius' horse stumbled south and west. The poor beast was on its last legs. The Roman cavalry commander—the Roman fugitive in a land all traps and snares for Romans—urged it on even so. If it foundered, when it foundered, he'd have to use his own legs, and its were swifter.

He was, he hoped, still ahead of the news of Quinctilius Varus' army. He'd seen a few Germans working in their farm plots. They hadn't paid him much special attention. They still thought of him as a Roman soldier, not as a fugitive from black disaster.

As long as they thought of him so—as a man who was dangerous to approach, as a man who would be avenged if he fell—he was fairly safe. But he knew better, or worse. Even if they didn't, he knew he was nothing but a runaway. He also knew that scores, hundreds, maybe even thousands of Roman fugitives cluttered the German landscape. The barbarians might not have to hear the news. Just seeing so many Romans wandering at random over the countryside could be plenty to tell them the legions had met catastrophe.

And that wasn't Vala Numonius' only worry. Oh, no—far from it. Sooner or later, the cavalry commander knew he'd have to sleep. A German could come up to cut his throat or knock him over the head, and he'd never know it till too late. The legionaries joked about waking up dead if they got stuck in the middle of enemy country. Numonius didn't think those jokes were funny, not any more he didn't.

Maybe worse yet was that news and rumor would go right on spreading while he slept. They were liable to get ahead of him, even if he still had a lead on them for the moment. If they did . . . If they did, the Germans would know he didn't have the Empire's might behind him now. They would know he'd suddenly become fair game. And they would hunt him.

He rode past a farm. Women and boys and one graybeard with a crooked back worked in the fields. No warriors. The Romans had wondered about that on their way north. Vala Numonius' mouth quirked in a bitter grin. By the gods, he didn't wonder any more! Sometimes, though, knowledge came at too high a cost. People talked about that all the time. Now Numonius understood it in his belly, in his balls.

The barbarians all stared at him as he went by. They would know where their menfolk had gone, and why. But they wouldn't—he prayed they wouldn't—know what had happened. Maybe Numonius was only a scout, with a victorious Roman army not far behind him.

Maybe I am—but I'm not. The nonsense formed of itself inside his mind. It was one more measure of how worn he was. He wondered whether his horse's head was full of moonshine, too. More nonsense. He was starting to have trouble even recognizing it.

He still had half a loaf of barley bread left. When it was gone, he'd need to buy food from the Germans, or steal it from them. The commander of the Roman cavalry, reduced to chicken thievery! Well, better that than being reduced to what had happened to the poor, sorry foot soldiers.

Numonius was glad when the track went into the woods and he couldn't feel the Germans' pale eyes on him any more. The barbarians watched him like wolves watching a sick, staggering doe. If it fell over, they would feed. If it didn't, they could catch something else before long.

He hated the German woods. Everything seemed to close in on you. You couldn't see any farther than you could spit. Anything might lurk in there and lunge out at you. Anything. Wolves. A bear. A wide-horned aurochs, as fearsome as any meat-eating brute. Germans, the most fearsome brutes of all. You'd never know danger drew near till too late.

But when every breath was danger, the woods didn't seem to matter so much. And, if the hunted couldn't see far, neither could the hunters. Vala Numonius slid off his horse and led it away from the track. Then he tied it to a sapling and went back and covered its tracks, and his, as best he could. He didn't know if his best would prove good enough, but you had to try.

Half a bowshot away from the path, he gnawed on the barley bread. It was dense and chewy. Bread made from wheat flour would have risen better. It would have tasted better, too. But it wouldn't have packed so much nourishment into such a small space. For soldiers who had to carry their own rations, that mattered more.

He gave the horse a couple of bites of bread, too. That was all he had for the animal. A few ferns and weeds grew in the gloom under the forest canopy. The horse nibbled at those. It raised its head and gave Numonius a reproachful look, as if to say, *You work me to death, and then all I get is this?*

"Sorry," he told it, his own voice a weary whisper. "Carry me back across the Rhine and I'll fill you full of oats and barley. By Epona, I will." Maybe the Gallic horse-goddess would hearken to his prayer here in the German woods. Plainly, the gods of his own folk held no power here.

He lay down beside the horse. No matter what the risks, he simply had to sleep. He'd soon be a babbling idiot if he didn't, liable to tell the Germans he was on the run even if they hadn't already figured it out. That most of them knew no Latin while he had only a handful of words in their tongue bothered him not at all. Once he lay down, nothing bothered him. Bare ground might have been Jupiter's divinely soft bed up on Mount Olympus.

He didn't wake up with his throat cut. Maybe Epona was listening. Maybe it was just luck. Whatever it was, he had to make the most of it. He found a few mushrooms growing not far from where he'd lain. He didn't know German mushrooms well, but stuffed them into his mouth anyhow. If they poisoned him . . . well, so what?

His horse wanted nothing to do with mushrooms. All it wanted was rest. He couldn't have cared less. A convenient stump made mounting easier than it would have been otherwise, but he knew he would have managed one way or another. A cavalryman had to be able to vault into the saddle from flat ground. So did a cavalry commander who expected his men to follow him. Vala Numonius met the requirements.

How many of his men had followed him away from the trapped foot soldiers? How many of them still lived? How many Roman infantrymen still did? Not many, he feared. Three legions, thrown onto the sacrificial altar and butchered.

What would Augustus say when he learned? *Maybe I can be the one who brings the news to Rome*, Numonius thought. That dignified his flight with purpose.

Of course, it had had purpose all along. If survival wasn't a purpose, he couldn't imagine what would be. But the Germans had a purpose, too: slaughtering Romans. Theirs seemed more likely to be fulfilled than his, curse them.

He managed to find the track again. Without it, he might have wandered in circles till he starved . . . or till the barbarians found him. But he still had a chance to get away.

The track came out into open country as abruptly as the trees had swallowed it. Vala Numonius could ride faster—could flee faster—now. But who were those horsemen out there ahead of him? More Romans, he feared. If they'd got ahead of him in the night, word of the Germans' victory would have, too.

And so it proved. Now the barbarians who spotted him didn't stare and wonder what he was up to. They knew he was on the run. They pointed and shouted and came after him. He booted the horse up into a shambling, drunken trot, so the spears some of them flung fell short.

Dogs ran howling after the horse. Vala Numonius supposed they were dogs, anyhow; they obeyed better than wolves would have, no matter what they looked like. They terrified a brief gallop out of the horse. Then, no matter how Numonius screamed at it and beat it, it decided it could run no more, and stood still.

That was the last thing he wanted. Barbarians loped toward him behind the dogs. Few of them were in the prime of life, which didn't mean their spears couldn't kill him. Knowing he was in trouble deeper than the sea, he slid down from the horse's back and started to run.

Some of the dogs gave chase. He slashed one in the snout with his cavalry sword, which was longer than the *gladii* foot soldiers carried. The horrible beast yelped in surprise and pain and fell back, bleeding. He hoped the others would turn on it, but no such luck. Another gray, sharp-eared beast darted forward to snap at his leg. He killed it.

But while he fought the dogs, he couldn't flee their masters. Here came the Germans: youths and even one rugged blond woman who must have fancied herself a warrior. A sword was a perfectly good weapon against a pack of dogs. Against spears with three or four times the reach? That was a different story.

"No," Vala Numonius whispered. "Please, no." The Germans' eyes were paler than their dogs'. That was the only difference between them, for both sets held death. The barbarians moved to surround the cavalry officer. He turned this way and that, about as helpless and hopeless as his horse.

The Germans surged forward. Before too long, it was over—but not nearly soon enough to suit Numonius.

Before Arminius could lead his swarms of Germans into Gaul, he had to finish driving the Romans out of his own country. Destroying three legions wasn't quite enough—almost, but not quite. Several Roman fortresses persisted east of the Rhine. The men those forts sheltered might prove dangerous if he just forgot about them, and so he set out to reduce the forts one by one.

Having served in the Roman auxiliaries, he knew a little something about siegecraft. What he failed to take into account was that the average German knew nothing, or perhaps a bit less. And the legionaries shut up inside the wooden palisades knew they would die horribly if his men broke in. Not many Romans had escaped the massacre of Legions XVII, XVIII, and XIX, but some few had, and spread word of what had happened there to the garrison troops. To his surprise, it made the men in the forts determined, not afraid.

Aliso caused the most trouble. It stood on the south bank of the Lupia, not far east of where the smaller river joined the Rhine near Vetera. The Roman garrison inside Aliso was large and very stubborn.

Speaking soldiers' Latin, Arminius shouted to the legionaries: "If you surrender and come out, I swear I will let you keep your arms and march back to Gaul with no more attacks. I will give hostages to prove it."

A centurion came up to the edge of the palisade to answer him. Arminius recognized the Roman officer for what he was as much by his ingrained arrogance as by the transverse crest on his helmet. "No!" the man shouted. "You wouldn't be howling out there if you hadn't cozened Quinctilius Varus and murdered his men. The promises you make aren't worth piss."

Every word of that was true, which only infuriated Arminius the more. He shook his fist at the Roman. "You'll pay," he said. "When we break in, we'll give you all to our gods, a fingernail at a time."

"Come ahead and try." The centurion spat in his general direction. "I don't think you can do it, you bald-bottomed son of a whore. I bet your asshole's as wide as a tunnel, from all the times you had Varus' cock up you." To make sure Arminius—and his followers—understood him, the Roman said that again, pretty fluently, in the Germans' language.

"You turd with legs! I'll see how far your lying guts can stretch when I lay hold of you!" Arminius bellowed in blind fury.

"Come ahead and try," the centurion repeated calmly, and stepped away.

Arminius bellowed orders. The Germans shot flight after flight of arrows at Aliso. Then, roaring like angry bears to fire their spirits, they rushed toward the fort with scores of scaling ladders. If rage and ferocity could overcome skill and a strong position, Arminius' followers would do it.

But they couldn't. The Romans dropped stones on the Germans who threw bundles of brush into the ditch around the palisade. They shot at them through holes drilled into the floor of their walkway. With hardly any risk to themselves, they used forked branches to reach out and over-turn scaling ladders that did get placed against the walls. They poured boiling water and sizzling oil on the Germans swarming up the ladders.

In spite of everything, a few Germans did make it to the top of the palisade—but only a few. They didn't last long up there. In a fight like that, the armored, disciplined, and desperate Romans had every advantage.

Cradling a horribly burned arm, a German who'd fallen off a ladder groaned, "They fight dirty."

And so they did. Arminius acutely felt his folk's ignorance of siege-craft. When he served with the legions in Pannonia, he'd seen the variety of engines and stratagems the Romans could roll out against a strongpoint that presumed to resist them. But having seen such things didn't mean he could duplicate them. He didn't know how to make the catapults that flung darts or thirty-pound stones farther than a man could shoot an ar-row. Nor were Germans miners. He couldn't order them to tunnel un-der Aliso and make the palisade fall over.

Even if he could have given that order, he wouldn't have. He knew too well he couldn't hold his army together long enough to let mining work. They would run out of food from the surrounding countryside pretty soon. One more trick of Roman siegecraft, he realized now when it was too late, was the stream of wagons that kept besiegers fed. Roman armies didn't come down sick as often as those of the Germans, either. He couldn't make his own men keep their camp clean and orderly, and he couldn't stop them from dumping waste upstream from where they drew drinking water. They would have laughed at him had he tried.

Knowing he wouldn't be able to stay outside of Aliso long, he kept trying to break in, hurling his warriors at the palisade again and again. Maybe luck would be with them, as it had been before. Maybe the Romans would despair. If they didn't fight back with all their might, the German tide would surely lap over them and wash them away.

No matter how Arminius hoped either or both of those things would happen, neither did. The legionaries inside Aliso might have been some of the last Romans left alive on this side of the Rhine, but they fought as if they still thought they would turn Germany into a peaceful province any day now.

After a week of fruitless assaults, Sigimerus took Arminius aside and said, "This isn't working, son. If we're going to take Gaul away from the Empire, we can't waste any more time hanging around here."

"We can't leave these legionaries in our rear, either," Arminius answered. "One more try. They can't hold us out forever."

Maybe the Romans couldn't. But they could hold the Germans out during that last assault. And, as Arminius had feared, a flux of the bowels and a coughing sickness broke out among his men. They started getting hungry, too. And word came that the Romans were rushing soldiers to the Rhine from all over Gaul.

Men began streaming away from Aliso and heading for their homes. Arminius cursed and wept and pleaded, all to no avail. The Germans had one great deed in them, but not two. Watching his army break up, he gloomily wondered if the same held true for him.

❧ XVIII ❧

Late summer in Rome was the hottest, most unpleasant time of the year. Romans with even the faintest pretensions of importance got out of town. Some of them had seaside villas. Others went up into the mountains; on higher ground, the weather wasn't nearly so oppressive. The truly rich enjoyed estates on one or another of the little islands that dotted the Tyrrhenian Sea.

Augustus had seaside villas. He had mountain hideaways. He had island estates. He had no pretensions of importance. He had no need for pretensions, and they would have seemed wantonly ostentatious on him. He *was* important, and he knew it. And so did everyone else in the Roman Empire.

Without pretensions, he stayed in Rome for the summer. If he went to one of his retreats, couriers would have to find out which one he'd chosen and then go there themselves. Things might get delayed for days. The Roman Empire ran slowly enough as it was. Making it run slower than it had to might turn indignation to rebellion, or might cost the chance to nip and invasion or a famine in the bud. Going out to a summer place might slow down good news: just a few days before, word came in that Tiberius had finally quelled the Pannonian uprising.

"The Palatine Hill is not so bad," the ruler of the Roman world said to whoever would listen—and, when you were ruler of the Roman world, everyone listened to you. "We're up almost as high as we would be in the Apennines."

His countless servants and slaves listened, yes. And, behind his back, they rolled their eyes and spiraled their forefingers next to their ears. They knew bloody well it was hotter and nastier in Rome than it would have been at any of the many summer refuges Augustus could have chosen. If he wanted to put up with sweat and with city stinks wafted on the breeze, that was his business. If he wanted *them* to put up with those things, too . . . that was also his business, and all they could do about it was grouse and fume when he wasn't watching or listening.

He liked to nap in the afternoon—no wonder, not when he was as old as he was. It gave his servants and his bodyguards (some Romans, others wandering Germans chosen for their size and ferocity) more of a chance to complain. And, as luck would have it, he was asleep when the courier from the north rode up on a horse he'd come as close to killing as made no difference.

Seeing the sorry state of the animal, one of Augustus' grooms clucked reproachfully. Another said, "You could have come slower, friend, for he's sound asleep right now. He'll be up and about in a couple of hours."

"Wake him," the courier said in a flat, hard voice.

"Wha-at?" both grooms chorused, as if not believing their ears. One of them added, "He'd skin us if we did."

"He'll skin you if you don't," the courier said. "The news I bring is that important."

"What is it, then?" asked the groom who'd talked of skinning.

The courier looked through him. "It is for Augustus—that's what it is. He'll skin you if anyone hears it before him, too."

"Well, go on in," that same groom said. "Not for us to say who sees Augustus and who doesn't," *It's not* my *job*: the underling's escape hatch since the beginning of time.

In went the courier. He had several brief but heated exchanges with Augustus' slaves. He finally unbent enough to tell the senior servitors he brought news from Germany. When they asked him what the news was, he looked through them, too. They muttered among themselves, in Greek and Aramaic and perhaps other languages that weren't Latin. By the way they eyed the courier, they loved him not at all. He was making them decide things in the absence of their master. If Augustus didn't think they should have let him be disturbed . . .

But, in the end, the courier's stubbornness carried the day. "Stay here," one of the senior servitors told the fellow, sending him a baleful stare that he ignored. "We will rouse Augustus and tell him you are here with your important news. What he does after that is up to him, of course."

"Of course," the courier said, and visibly composed himself to wait.

He didn't need to wait long. Augustus, a little stooped, hurried into the anteroom a few minutes later. His gray hair was tousled, his tunic wrinkled and rumpled; he rubbed at his eyes to get sleep out of them. "You have news from Germany?" he said without preamble. "Give it to me at once."

"Yes, sir." The courier bowed. He respected the master of the Roman world, if not the lesser men surrounding him. "I am sorry, sir, but the news is as bad as it can be. Quinctilius Varus' three legions are destroyed in the Teutoburg Forest, only a handful of men escaping. Their eagles are lost, captured by the Germans. Varus trusted the chieftain named Arminius, and the barbarian betrayed him to his doom. When Varus saw the fight was hopeless, he had a slave slay him. He died as well as a man could, but thousands more died with him and because of him."

As the courier spoke, color drained from Augustus' face, leaving him pale as bleached linen. "You are sure of this?" he asked in a hoarse whisper. "No possible doubt?"

"None, sir. I'm sorry. The man who gave me the written message"—the courier took it off his belt and handed it to Augustus—"had it from one of the horsemen who somehow escaped the massacre inside Germany. The rider filled his ears with worse things than ever got written down, and I had some of them from him. To say it was a bad business beggars the power of words."

"It can't be," Augustus muttered. "It can't." Moving like a man in the grip of nightmare, he broke the seal on the written message, unrolled it, and held it out at arm's length to read it. The scribe who first composed the message must have remembered it was bound for an old man, for he'd written it large to make sure the intended recipient could make it out. By the look of anguish on Augustus' face, the power of written words to describe what had happened in Germany wasn't beggared after all.

"Are you all right, sir?" one of his underlings asked in Greek-flavored Latin, real anxiety filling his voice. The ruler of the Roman world was the very image of a man overwhelmed, a man unmanned, by disaster unlooked-for. Oedipus could have seemed no more appalled, no more horrified, on discovering he'd lain with his mother.

Were any pins or brooches handy, Augustus might well have sought to blind himself as Oedipus had done. As things were, he reeled away from the courier and the slaves and servitors who helped make him the most powerful man in the world. He might as well have been blind as he fetched up against the frame of the doorway through which he'd entered the antechamber.

He pounded his head on the sturdy timbers of the frame. While his servants exclaimed in alarm, he cried out as if he were indeed the protagonist of a tragedy on the stage: "Quinctilius Varus! Give me back my legions!"

In a tragedy, everyone knew—though the actors' skill might almost disguise the fact—that the events portrayed came from the realms of myth and legend and history, and were not happening to those portraying them. Here . . . It was real. No one would muster the men of Legions XVII, XVIII, and XIX again. They were dead—all too often, horribly dead.

"Give me back my legions, Quinctilius Varus!" Augustus wailed again, his forehead bruised and swelling. "Give them back, I tell you!"

Neither the courier nor any of the servitors seemed to know what to say. None dared say anything, for fear it would be wrong. When Augustus cried out once more and yet again battered his head against the doorframe, one of the men who served him—the men who helped him rule the Roman Empire—gestured to the courier.

By then, the man who'd brought the bad news was glad to get away, lest he be blamed for it. Augustus' servitor took him off to the kitchen and told the lesser slaves there to bring him bread and wine and olives. "Obliged, sir," the courier said, and then, "I'm sorry. I knew it would be bad. I didn't think it would be this bad."

"He never imagined failure," the servitor said. "Why should he, when he's known so much success?"

"Beats me." The courier gulped wine. He would never be able to drink enough to forget the look on Augustus' face when the Roman ruler realized all his plans for Germany had just collapsed in ruin. "What will he do now?"

"I don't know." From one of Augustus' aides, that was no small admission. "I fear we shall have to change our policy, which is not something we usually do. Gods curse those barbarians for being difficult!"

As the courier nodded, Augustus' voice echoed down the halls from the chamber where he still stood: "Quinctilius Varus, give me back my legions!"

Scowling, Arminius stared across the Rhine. He wouldn't be able to invade Gaul now, and he knew it. As soon as he'd stopped encircling Aliso, the Romans trapped inside the fortress broke out and fought their way west to the Rhine. Most of them had made it across. So had the garrisons from forts on the Lupia closer to the greater river.

And two full legions had rushed up from the south when the Romans in Gaul got word of what happened to their countrymen in Germany. Over on the west bank of the Rhine, a detachment from one of those legions paced Arminius' army. He hadn't been able to shake loose of the Romans, even with night marches. He wouldn't be able to fight on ground of his choosing if he did force a crossing. On ground of *their* choosing, the legions had the edge. He wouldn't have had to work so hard to draw Varus into his ambush otherwise.

Someone called his name. "I'm here!" he answered, waving, glad for any excuse not to think about the west bank of the Rhine.

A man from his own clan came up to him. "Good news!" the fellow said. "Your woman has given you a son. She and the baby are both doing well."

"Gods be praised! That *is* good news!" Arminius took off a golden ring—spoil from the vanquished legions—and gave it to the other German. "This for bringing it to me."

"I thank you." The other man found a finger on which the ring fit well. "What will you call the baby?"

"Sigifredus," Arminius said without the least hesitation, "in memory of the victory I won against the Romans." That victory, however great it was, was also turning out to be less than he'd hoped it would. With an old man's sour wisdom, his father insisted things were often thus. Arminius had hoped Sigimerus was only carping. When he looked across the Rhine and saw the Roman soldiers there, he knew his father had a point.

"I also visited the grove of the sacrifice," his clansman said. "Never have the gods feasted like that before, not in all the days since the world was made. So many heads spiked to the holy oaks and hung from them!" The man's eyes glowed. "And three eagles! Three! Have the Romans lost three since their realm began?"

"That I don't know," Arminius admitted. He'd served with the legions long enough to know the Romans had suffered military disasters before. But they were tight-lipped about them. Well, what warriors in their right minds boasted of battles lost?

"Ah." The other German didn't much care about the answer. He was only making conversation. He went on, "In among all of them, though, I didn't see Varus' head, and I wanted to."

"You wouldn't have. I brought it with me as we moved toward the Rhine. I wanted to use it as a talisman to frighten the Romans, but that didn't work out so well as I hoped it would." Arminius sighed. "Can't have everything, I suppose." For a little while, he'd thought he could. He'd thought he had. Almost, but not quite—the price he paid for aiming so high.

"What will you do with the head now? Pitch it in the river?" the other German asked.

"Well, it was partly burned before I got my hands on it. I salted it down, but it's getting high anyway." Arminius wrinkled his nose. "Still, I don't aim to throw it away. I'll send it southeast, to Maroboduus and the

Marcomanni. It will show him what we Germans can do when we set our minds to it."

"Won't it just!" his clansmate exclaimed, eyes glowing. "Oh, won't it just!"

Till Arminius' meteoric rise, King Maroboduus had unquestionably been the most powerful German of all. He'd drawn Augustus' watchful attention, too. Had the revolt in Pannonia not broken out, he likely would have drawn Augustus' legions as well. Maroboduus loudly denied he'd had anything to do with stirring up that revolt. Arminius believed not a word of it. He was sure Augustus didn't, either. But the Roman ruler hadn't found the chance to attack Maroboduus, and odds were he never would now.

Thanks to me, Arminius thought proudly. Maroboduus might have stirred up others to fight against Rome. Arminius had done his own fighting, against foes who invaded his land. If the folk of Germany couldn't see which of those was the greater accomplishment . . . Arminius couldn't imagine that his countrymen would be so blind.

"A Roman who dreamt of ruling us," his clansmate said. "And what is he now? Nothing but a stinking souvenir!"

"A stinking souvenir," Arminius echoed. A slow smile spread over his face. He nodded, half to the other German and half to himself. Yes, he liked that. And it was true of more than Quinctilius Varus alone. Roman hopes for Germany had also fallen into decay. And they were no more likely to rise from the dead.

Segestes lived quietly on his steading. A good many of his sworn retainers stayed there with him. A few of them—younger men, mostly—had gone off to fight the Romans with Arminius despite what Segestes thought of the man who'd stolen his daughter. Enough remained to fight a war if Arminius decided to try punishing Segestes for staying loyal to the Empire.

So far, there'd been no signs such trouble was coming, nor even threats. Segestes gave Arminius reluctant credit for that—or maybe Arminius was so enmeshed in great affairs that his woman's father had fallen beneath his notice. Segestes sighed, out in front of the thatch-roofed farmhouse. He'd always thought of himself as a man of consequence, but he could hardly deny that events had outrun him these past few months.

"They wouldn't have if he'd listened to me," Segestes murmured.

"What's that?" one of his warriors asked.

"Varus," Segestes said. "If only he'd listened to me. Are there any words sadder than *I told you so*? The only time anyone ever gets to say them is when it's already too late for them to do any good."

"I never thought of it like that." By the puzzled expression on the retainer's face, he didn't waste a lot of time thinking. He was a good man with a spear in his hands, though. Everyone had his strengths and his failings. Segestes sighed again. *His* failing was that he'd been born into a German body, not a Roman one.

He knew what the Romans thought of his folk. He knew that, in Varus' eyes, he'd been as much a barbarian as Arminius. He sighed once more. Time would have solved that. Had the Romans brought Germany into the Empire, his grandchildren's grandchildren would have been unquestioned Romans, as babies born in Gaul now were.

That wasn't going to happen, not now. Whether Arminius had done something good or bad, men could argue one way or the other. That he'd done something great . . . nobody could doubt.

Germany would not be Roman. Three legions gone? Taken all in all, the Roman Empire had no more than thirty or so. One soldier in ten from all the Empire had perished in the swamps and woods not too far north of where he stood. Augustus was a canny man. He wouldn't risk such a disaster twice. He wouldn't have wanted to risk it once. But Varus thought he could trust Arminius, and. . . .

Three or four Roman fugitives had made it here after the battle. Segestes hid them for a little while, fed them, gave them barley cakes and sausage to carry when they left, and sent them away by night. He wished he could do more, but more would have cost him his life if word got out . . . and word of such things always got out. You did everything you could do, not everything you wanted to do.

Unless you were Arminius. Segestes' scarred hands folded into fists.

Arminius had done everything anyone could have wanted to do.

Or had he? Men said he'd intended to cross the Rhine and plunder Gaul—maybe even try to take it away from the Romans. His army got to the river, but it didn't cross over. What would he do with all those warriors now? How long could he keep feeding them? How long before the galloping shits or chest fever broke out among them?

Segestes laughed harshly. Arminius had served with the Romans, learning their ways so he could fight them better. Segestes had served with them, too, years earlier. Arminius would have seen how the legions kept themselves supplied. He would have seen how they kept their camps clean.

And how much good would it have done him? He was dealing with Germans here, not Romans. Supply wagons? Rafts carrying grain along rivers? Segestes laughed again. He knew his own folk hadn't a prayer of organizing anything like that. German encampments were always filthy, too. The Romans said dirt led straight to disease. From everything Segestes had seen, they knew what they were talking about, as they commonly did.

"What's funny, lord?" his retainer asked.

"Funny? Everything in the world, or maybe nothing at all," Segestes said.

The warrior scratched his head. A moment later, he squashed something between his thumbnails. That made Segestes want to scratch, too. "I don't think I understand," the younger man said.

"Well, don't worry your head about it," Segestes said. "I don't think I understand, either."

His retainer scratched some more. He didn't come up with any new vermin—or, if he did, Segestes didn't see him do it, which was good enough.

A few days later, a solitary warrior approached the steading. The chieftain's followers led the fellow to Segestes himself. Three of them stood between the man and Segestes. If the fellow had come with murder on his mind, he'd have to go through them to get at his target.

"This is poor guesting," he observed.

"It is, and I am sorry," Segestes said. "But times are hard, and I have a strong foe. Can you blame my retainers for staying wary?"

"When you put it so, I suppose not," the other man replied. "My news comes from his steading, in fact. You will have heard your daughter gave birth to a boy?"

"Yes, I know that." Segestes nodded. One of these days, that grandson might lead him to reconcile with Arminius. One of these days . . . but not yet. "What of it, stranger?"

"My name is Alcus," the newcomer said. "I am sorry to have to tell you the baby is dead. A flux of the bowels, I hear—it was quick, and seemed painless."

"Woe!" the retainers cried. They covered their faces with their cloaks.

"Woe!" Segestes said with them. He too covered his face. Tears ran down his cheeks, so he could uncover himself without shame—no one would think him coldhearted or mean of spirit. In truth, though, he didn't know what he felt. "You are sure of this?" he asked.

"I am. There is no doubt," Alcus said. "My fields lie next to Arminius'—I have the word straight from his retainers."

"Yes, it is so, then," Segestes said. "Woe! Woe, indeed! Always hard when a babe dies untimely."

"Harder when the babe is your grandson. I beg you, Segestes— don't hate me for being the one who brought you the news," Alcus said. "I know you and Arminius . . . are at odds. If I had not come, you might not have heard for some time."

"True. I might not have." Segestes wondered if that wouldn't have been for the best. Reluctantly, he shook his head. The news would have come sooner or later. And, sooner or later, grief would have speared him. Sooner wasn't better, but it also wasn't really worse. "I do not hate you, Alcus. You did what you thought best, and who is to say you did not have the right of it?"

"Thank you, lord. That is well said."

"And I will show you good guesting." Segestes realized he had to do that if he were not to be reckoned liar and niggard. "Eat as you will of my bread and meat. Drink as you will of my beer, and of my wine from beyond the Rhine. Sleep soft tonight before you fare forth to your farm."

Alcus bowed. "You are gracious. You are kind."

"Yes. I am," Segestes said bleakly. "And much good any of that has done me."

Rain pattered down on Rome. It was winter: the proper season for rain, as any man who lived round the Mediterranean would have agreed. Augustus was one of those men, and faced a problem common to a lot of them—his roof leaked. A drip near the entrance to his great house plinked into a bowl.

He gave the bowl a jaundiced stare. New leaks started every winter. The men who laid roof tiles always promised that everything would be perfect this time. They always lied, too. Augustus shook his head. In the scale of human calamities, there were plenty worse. His mouth tightened. He knew too much about that.

He opened the door and looked out. The guards standing outside stiffened to attention. "As you were, boys," Augustus said, and they relaxed.

"What can we do for you, sir?" one of them asked.

"Not a thing. I'm only looking at the weather."

"All right, sir. However you please." The guardsman grinned at Augustus. He had a strong-nosed face with cheekbones that made sharp planes below his eyes. He spoke Latin like the native of Italy he was. All his comrades came from Italy, too.

In the frightening, frightened days after news of Varus' disaster came to Rome, Augustus had eased all the Germans—and, for good measure, all the Gauls—out of his personal guard. Most of them, maybe all of them, remained loyal to him, but he dared not take the chance that they would do something to help Arminius. He didn't cashier them. He did send them out of Rome. Quite a few of them were garrisoning Mediterranean islands these days.

Against whom were they garrisoning those islands? Pirates?

Drunken fishermen? Skrawking sea gulls? Augustus had no idea. But doing things that way had preserved the honor of the Germans and Gauls. If he ever needed them again, he could use them.

He'd begun repairing the mutilated Roman army, too. The legions he'd raised in the aftermath of the disaster were no match for the ones Arminius had destroyed. He knew that. They held far too many older men, far too many squinting craftsmen and chubby shopkeepers. He'd had to draft men to fill out their ranks at all, which caused no end of grumbling.

But he'd done it, and he wasn't about to look back and tell himself he shouldn't have. Yes, those raw new legions would get hacked to bloody bits if they ever faced rampaging Germans in the field. Augustus knew that. So did the officers under whom the reluctant soldiers served.

All the same, the new men could fill up forts. They could protect backwaters that needed only a show of force to stay quiet. And, in doing things like that, they could free up better troops to deal with real trouble.

Augustus sighed. "Cheer up, sir," one of the guards, said. "The rain'll make the grain grow." He was a stubby little fellow, and seemed all the more so when Augustus remembered the hulking blonds who'd protected him before. If you couldn't trust your bodyguards, though, what were they worth to you? Not even a lead slug.

"I know, Sextus. I know," Augustus answered. If Sextus wanted to think the weather was what was wrong, he could. Augustus only wished he could think the same thing himself.

Quinctilius Varus, give me back my legions! How many times had he howled that in his torment? More than he cared to remember. He had no guarantee he wouldn't start howling it again, either, if the black mood seized him again.

He'd gone on so long and done so well, maybe he'd started believing he couldn't make mistakes any more. If so, he'd got a reminder of his own humanity, his own fallibility, far blunter and more brutal than the stinking turds in his chamber pot.

Forty years. That was how long he'd ruled the Roman world, the Mediterranean world. In all that time, he hadn't had to pull back his horns very often. Oh, death had forced him to change his mind more than once about his successor. Irony there: he'd been sickly in his younger years—he was often sickly even now—but he'd outlived almost everyone to whom he'd thought to entrust the Empire after he was gone. Still, no mortal could outwit or outreach death.

Since he'd never had a son of his own body, he supposed Tiberius, his wife's son from an earlier marriage, would have to do. Tiberius made a fine soldier. He'd proved that in Pannonia. If he hadn't been busy settling that revolt, he might have proved it in Germany instead.

Quinctilius Varus, give me back my legions! Again, the howl of torment rose unbidden in Augustus' mind, though he managed not to cry out loud. Those legions were gone, gone forever.

Tiberius made a good soldier, yes. But did he have what it took to continue the delicate charade Augustus had carried on with the Roman Senate all these years? Augustus held all the power in the Empire worth holding, but he'd artfully pretended to be no more than a magistrate of the Republic. That was likely one reason, and not the smallest one, he'd escaped assassination for so long. People had feared his great-uncle would make himself into a king—and so Julius Caesar died under the knives of men who'd been his friends. Augustus cared little for the show of power. The reality sufficed.

He wasn't so sure about Tiberius. Tiberius didn't suffer fools gladly. If the Conscript Fathers got pushy . . . Tiberius would do whatever he had to do to remind them where power really lay. They wouldn't like that. Tiberius wouldn't care. Different parts of the Roman government shouldn't squabble with one another.

Augustus had to hope they wouldn't. He saw no one but Tiberius to whom he could hand over the reins. Death had cut down his other choices. When he was gone, all this would be his stepson's worry.

And so would Germany. Bringing it into the Empire as Julius Caesar had brought in Gaul would have been Augustus' greatest legacy to his successor. It would have been, but it wouldn't be now. Augustus knew he would never—could never—mount another campaign to annex Germany. The Rhine and the Danube would remain the Empire's frontiers.

Maybe, after enough time had passed, Tiberius would be able to avenge this defeat. Even as the thought formed, Augustus shook his head. Some wounds were just too large, too deep. *Quinctilius Varus*, *give me back my legions!*

Again, Augustus kept the shriek inside him. The first few weeks after the catastrophe, he couldn't even manage that. All his servants flinched whenever he cried out. Varus would have flinched, too, were he not beyond any reproaches but the gods'.

Arminius, curse him, had managed what only death had done before: he'd made Augustus withdraw from a policy he'd set his mind to. If Germany was not to be Roman, it would stay . . . German. It would stay squalid, it would stay barbarous, it would stay independent. It would stay troublesome. Augustus could see that. He had to hope it wouldn't become too troublesome too soon.

Three days later, a courier down from the Danube reached the great house on the Palatine Hill. He spoke to the grooms. One of the guards spoke to one of Augustus' senior servants. The freedman approached Augustus himself. "Sir, I think you would do well to see this man, to hear him, to see the burden he bears."

"Send him to the anteroom, then. I'll see him there." Only after the words were out of his mouth did Augustus remember that was where he'd seen the messenger who brought word of the battle in the Teuto-burg Forest. *Quinctilius Varus* . . . Augustus spat into the bosom of his toga to turn aside the evil omen.

The courier looked nervous when Augustus strode into the small antechamber. Augustus knew that meant nothing. Couriers coming before him mostly looked nervous. At the man's feet lay a large leather sack. Augustus' nostrils twitched—a faint foul odor rose from it.

"Well?" Augustus pointed toward the sack. "What's that in aid of?"

"Sir, let me give you this first. It will explain better than I can." The man handed him a letter festooned with the usual wax seals and ribbons.

"Very well." Augustus broke the seals and unrolled the letter. The script was small and none too neat. After struggling with it for a moment, Augustus passed it to his servitor. "Read this to me."

"Of course, sir," the freedman said. "I begin: 'I am Gaius Libo, a wine merchant and a Roman citizen. I am at the court of King Maroboduus of the Marcomanni, north of the Danube. King Maroboduus has no letters himself. He asks me to write to you to explain the gift this letter comes with.'"

Augustus pointed to the sack again. "Whatever's in there?"

"That's right, sir," the courier said.

"All right." Augustus turned back to his servitor. "Go on."

"Yes, sir. 'Not long ago, Maroboduus received from Arminius, another German princeling, the head of the Roman general Publius Quinctilius Varus. Maroboduus says he has no quarrel with you and no quarrel with Varus. To show this, he sends you the head for burial.'"

"Ah," Augustus said, to give himself a moment to gather his thoughts. Then he asked the courier, "Do you know if this is truly Varus' head? Or is it the head of some nobody Maroboduus is using to curry favor with me?"

"Sir, I don't know. I never met the gentleman alive, and I would not recognize him," the courier said. "I also have to tell you the head is not in the best of shape. But I have heard that Arminius did send Varus' head to Maroboduus."

"Yes. I have heard the same thing," Augustus said unhappily. Even more unhappily, he went on, "Take the head out of the sack. If anyone is likely to recognize poor Varus, I am the man."

He could have summoned Julia Pulchra or her son—no, the younger Quinctilius Varus was studying in Athens. But he would not have done that to his grand-niece, and he couldn't do it to the peaceable youth. He'd seen battlefields and their aftermath, even if not for many years.

He braced himself. The courier didn't reach into the sack—he didn't want to touch what it held, and who could blame him for that? Instead, he turned it inside out, spilling the head onto the mosaic floor. The stench the sack had contained filled the audience chamber. Gagging, Augustus' freedman beat a hasty retreat. He knew no more of battlefields than Claudia Pulchra or the younger Varus did. His ignorance—the ignorance of so many in the Empire—was Augustus' doing, and something for Augustus to be proud of.

But battlefields hadn't disappeared altogether, even if Augustus wished they—and one in particular—would have. He stalked around the severed head, examining it from every angle, weighing the wreckage here against what he remembered of his grand-niece's husband. His gorge didn't rise—yes, he remembered what death and its aftermath could do to flesh.

"Well, sir?" asked the courier, who'd stood his ground—and won credit with Augustus for doing it. "Is it him?"

"Yes," Augustus said in a voice like iron. "That is Publius Quinctilius Varus, or what remains of him. The bald crown, curly hair at the temples and nape, the nose, the chin . . . There can be no doubt. That is Varus."

"He died well, sir, from what people say." The courier offered such solace as he could.

"So he did. But too many died with him—too many died because he let Arminius trick him." *Quinctilius Varus, give me back my legions!* Quinctilius Varus never would. The disaster in Germany was no nightmare to wake up from. It was real, and would stay real forever. With a sigh, Augustus nodded toward Varus' remains. "Would you be kind enough to put—that—back in the sack?" he said to the courier. "I will give it decent burial, but not right now."

"Yes, sir," the other man answered resignedly. Getting the head back into the sack wasn't so neat as taking it out had been. When the nasty job was done, the courier said, "May I wash my hands?"

"Of course." Augustus called for some slaves, for a basin of warm water, for scented oil—"The sweetest and strongest we have, by the gods"—and for a bronze strigil so the courier could scrape his fingers clean.

"Thank you kindly, sir," the man said as the slaves brought what Augustus required.

"No. I have to thank you: for your help there, and for the word you brought me," Augustus said. "Now we know what became of . . . this much of Quinctilius Varus, anyhow. And now we can lay this much to rest."

After the courier had scraped off as much of the corpse-reek as he could, Augustus dismissed him with a gift of five goldpieces for all he had done. The ruler of the Roman world wished he could have dismissed the whole German problem as easily. But the foul odor from Varus' head lingered in the audience chamber even after a slave gingerly carried away the sack. The larger problem that foul smell symbolized lingered, too.

And he couldn't do anything about it. He'd tried, and he'd failed, as he'd failed against death. The death reek here brought back memories of those earlier failures. Wild German tribes would go on prowling the Roman Empire's northern borders.

Because they were separate tribes, a canny ruler might be able to play them off against one another. Maroboduus and Arminius had no love for each other now. Chieftains in years to come would also surely be rivals. Augustus knew he could exploit a situation like that.

But he also knew his day was passing. If he lived five years more, he would be surprised; if he lived ten more, he would be astonished. How many of those who came after him would share his peculiar combination of talents?

He grimaced. He couldn't do anything about that. He'd done everything he could about Germany, and it hadn't been enough. If only he'd had two Tiberiuses. If only Pannonia hadn't rebelled when he was about to lay hold of Germany once and for all. If only . . .

"Quinctilius Varus, give me back my legions!" he cried once more. The empty, useless words echoed back at him from the antechamber's walls.

HISTORICAL NOTE

What happened in the middle of Germany two thousand years ago has had a profound effect on the history of Europe ever since. The battle of the Teutoburg Forest (Teutoburger Wald in German), in A.D./C.E. 9, made sure that Germany would *not* become part of the Roman Empire, and that the Germans would not become Romanized as the Gauls had before them. To this day, the division between Romanized and non-Romanized peoples in Europe is easily visible in the languages and cultures of the nations that grew up on the wreckage of the Roman Empire in the West: a collapse accomplished in military terms primarily by Germanic tribes whose histories would have been altogether different had Germany been annexed to Rome (if, indeed, they would have had separate histories for long after that point).

Our written sources for the battle are less good than we might wish they were. Closest in time is the account of Velleius Paterculus, a retired military officer who wrote his epitome of Roman history around A.D./C.E. 30. His work does not get much respect from modern historians; he was no great stylist, and he was an admirer of Augustus' successor, Tiberius, whose character had a good many features less than admirable. Imagine a modern U.S. colonel who served in Vietnam and some years later wrote a memoir full of extravagant praise for Richard Nixon. That will give you some notion of why historians raise an eyebrow at Velleius Paterculus.

On the other hand, the man actually served in Germany. He knew at least some of the people involved in these campaigns. And he has information about them that we simply can't get from anyone else. So his account is certainly worth reading.

Other historians in the Roman Empire who touched on the fight in the Teutoburg Forest wrote at least a lifetime after the events occurred. They include Florus, Suetonius, and Cassius Dio (also known, at least as often, as Dio Cassius), the last of whom wrote in Greek rather than Latin. In addition, Tacitus mentions the battle in passing as he treats in more detail the retaliatory campaigns the Romans waged in Germany in the early years of Tiberius' reign. Augustus' anguished cry of "Quinctilius Varus, give me back my legions!" comes from Suetonius.

For many years, the actual site of the Battle of the Teutoburg Forest was unknown. There is a large, heroic statue of Arminius holding an upraised sword near Detmold, Germany, which was believed to be close by the battlefield. In fact, it is farther north and east, near the village of Kalkriese. This was proved beyond a reasonable doubt through the excavations conducted by Tony Clunn, one of the gifted amateurs who have contributed so much to archaeology. In the 1980s, Clunn was a British Army officer serving in Germany; the coins and other artifacts he uncovered—including the remains of the rampart Arminius' men built up—demonstrate where the fight took place.

Clunn has written a fascinating book detailing his discoveries: *The Quest for the Lost Roman Legions: Discovering the Varus Battlefield* (Savas Beattie: New York, and Spellmount, Limited: Staplehurst, UK, 2005). Also extremely valuable, in addition to the primary sources, was Peter S. Wells, *The Battle That Stopped Rome* (W. W. Norton & Company: New York and London, 2003). I have not always agreed with their conclusions, but console myself by remembering that I am writing a novel, not history. (Clunn also includes his own fictional version of the Battle of Teutoburg Forest, its installments separated by italics from the rest of the book. I carefully did not read those installments, not wanting his take on things to influence my own.)

Arminius, Augustus, Caldus Caelius, Ceionius, Lucius Eggius, Publius Quinctilius (sometimes spelled Quintilius) Varus, Segestes, Sigimerus,

Thusnelda, and Vala Numonius are real historical figures. So are Claudia Pulchra, Flavus, Julia, Maroboduus, Tiberius, and Varus' son (to whom I have given the praenomen Gaius; his actual praenomen is unknown), who are mentioned but stay offstage, as it were. Accounts of Caesar's deeds in Gaul and Germany a couple of generations earlier than the time in which *Give Me Back My Legions!* is set are as accurate as I could make them; so are those of Crassus' less fortunate deeds farther east. Varus' father did commit suicide as described.

Two key questions underlie the events leading up to the Battle of the Teutoburg Forest. First, why was Segestes so strongly opposed to Arminius? Second, why did Quinctilius Varus prefer to believe Arminius rather than Segestes?

Arminius *did* elope with Thusnelda, Segestes' daughter, after Segestes betrothed her to another man. When this happened is uncertain; it may well have been later than I've put it, perhaps even after the battle. I've chosen to move it forward in time to give Segestes a strong motive for disliking Arminius—and to give Varus a reason for discounting Segestes' claims about Arminius, as he reckons them fueled by personal animosity. I've also made Varus especially susceptible to Arminius' deceit by having the German remind the Roman of his own son. I can't prove either of those speculations. Then again, I don't have to: I'm writing fiction. I can, and do, hope my readers will find them plausible.

In the novel, I've mixed modern and ancient place names. Where modern names are likely to be more familiar to the English-speaking reader, I've used them: e.g., Rome, Athens, Rhine, Danube. Less widely known places go by the names the Romans gave them: e.g., Vetera rather than Xanten, the Lupia River rather than the Lippe. Gaul is a special case; to call it France after the Franks, the Germanic tribe that later affixed a new name to it, would be anachronistic. The Romans' large encampment in central Germany was built where the modern town of Minden lies. No one knows what the Romans called it, so I've given it a classical-sounding name based on the modern one.

Thusnelda's giving birth to Sigifredus is fictitious, as is, of course, that baby's death. A few years later, she did bear Arminius a son. To this day, no one has discovered just where the Roman fortress of Aliso lay. Roman forts east of the Rhine were abandoned in great haste after the Battle of Teutoburg Forest.

Arminius and the pro-Roman Flavus faced each other in war when Flavus served with the punitive expedition in the time of Tiberius. Arminius was killed by men of his own tribe, the Cherusci, in A.D./C.E. 21. Maroboduus, the king of the Marcomanni, ended his days in exile inside the Roman Empire. While the Germanic tribes did eventually help overthrow the Empire's western half, this did not happen till centuries after the Battle of the Teutoburg Forest. The battle marked a crucial turning-point in history, but no one should make the mistake of thinking it marked an immediate one.